FIVE FLOWERS

by Franki deMerle

Katmoran Publications

ISBN: 978-0-9840051-7-8
www.katmoranpublications.com
www.reincarnationbooks.com

Cover Katmoran Productions

This book is fiction.

Acknowledgements

Special thanks to Marta Moran Bishop, Dr. Adrian Finkelstein, Karen Hall, Dr. Ian Stephenson, Dr. Jim B. Tucker, Dr. Paul Von Ward, and especially Karen VunKannon.

Sources

Jess Bravin
Vincent Bugliosi
Karlene Faith
Philippa Gregory
Ed Norris
Bob Slosser
Alison Weir
ABC
BBC
CBS
CNN
Google
NBC
Wikipedia

PART I

Discarnate souls
Disturbed by emotions
They cannot control

Unconscious patterns
Recurring devotions
To coveted matters

Lack of discipline
Mental illness
Total stimulation

Catharine of Aragón
16 December 1485—1511

One morning in April 1499, when I was thirteen years old, I sat in front of the vanity as one of my ladies brushed my long golden auburn hair. I enjoyed her company and the peaceful moment before a busy day. My wide blue eyes, round face, and fair complexion stared back at me from the mirror.

Although I was now awake, the dream I had still lingered over me like a mist not yet burned off by the sun. In the dream, I lived in a far away and very cold land in some olden, primitive time. My father in the dream, who was not my father now, was a tall, handsome king with red hair. My clothes were plain, simple, and practical. Then right before my eyes, I saw my red-haired father turn into a small boy. He took my hand, and as he did, a golden crown studded with jewels appeared on his small head. As he led me into a chapel, I was aware of being in my present time. He led me to the altar, where we stood before a coffin, and he placed a ring on my finger. The red stone in the ring was shaped like a pomegranate. Then I awoke. It was so very strange—I dared not mention it to anyone.

"King Henry VII of the House of Tudor of England," my lady explained to me as she brushed my hair, "was first to recognize the unification of our country. And yet there are still many in Europe who do not recognize Henry VII as the rightful King of England."

I was born Catalina de Aragón 16 December 1485 in Archbishop's Palace, Alcalá de Henares, near Madrid on the Iberian Peninsula. My most noble father was King Ferdinand II of Aragón, and

my most noble mother was Queen Isabella I of
Castile. Their marriage united our country, Spain,
now the strongest Christian country in the world. I
was their youngest surviving child.

I was a child when my parents sent Señor
Christopher Columbus on his first great expedition
across the ocean to find the Orient. There was much
controversy about his discoveries when he returned,
but he did return. And more voyages and
explorations followed.

Spain had the greatest navy in the world. I
was blessed to be part of its ruling family. Even
though I was their youngest, my parents found a
husband of great position for me. He was Arthur,
the elder son of King Henry VII of England.

"Why is the King of England not
recognized?" I asked my lady, who was an old
friend of my mother.

"Because of his illegitimate lineage," she
explained. "You, by contrast, are legitimately
descended from English royalty. Your great-great-
grandmother, Philippa of Lancaster, was the eldest
daughter of John of Gaunt, the first Duke of
Lancaster and the son of King Edward III, by
Edward's first wife, Blanche. Blanche, the first
Duchess of Lancaster, was the mother of King
Henry IV of England and also the mother of Queen
Philippa of Portugal, elder sister of King Henry IV."

I had been taught all of this already, but still
it was difficult to remember. And so she reminded
me. I nodded appropriately and smiled, while
stifling a yawn.

"Your great-grandmother was Catalina
Plantagenet, or Katharine of Lancaster to the
English, after whom you were named," my lady
continued. "Katharine was the younger half-sister of

King Henry IV. Katharine of Lancaster was also a legitimate daughter of John of Gaunt, but her mother was Princess Constance of Castile, the second Duchess of Lancaster and John of Gaunt's second wife. Henry VII is also descended from John of Gaunt, but illegitimately."

I stood so she could dress me in my favorite emerald green gown. "So King Henry VII is my third cousin."

"Yes." She tucked my hair up into my starched headdress as was the custom. An attached veil of matching green covered my hair. She towered above me, as I was very short. "And his wife, Queen Elizabeth of York, is your fourth cousin. She is the daughter of King Edward IV of England and the older sister of King Edward V, who succeeded their father as a child. Their Uncle Richard, the Duke of Gloucester and brother of King Edward IV, was named protector and regent of Edward V. Duke Richard had himself crowned King Richard III, and Elizabeth's two younger brothers, King Edward V and little Richard, disappeared in the Tower of London. And so, Elizabeth is not only the daughter and sister of English kings, but also the niece of King Richard III, and now wife of King Henry VII, who won the crown from Richard III on the battlefield."

"She is true royalty. Her marriage justifies King Henry's crown. And Prince Arthur, whom I am to wed, is also true royalty." I chose a strand of pearls to wear around my neck.

"That is correct," she continued as we walked toward the chapel. "John of Gaunt was the brother of King Edward III."

"So many names," I sighed.

She smiled. "The important thing for you to remember is that Henry VII ended the bloody English civil war known as the War of the Roses. Now the English people are united again by the marriage of their king and queen."

"And I am to be the wife of Prince Arthur Tudor, who is next in line for the English throne."

"And your marriage to him will bestow legitimacy on the English crown again in the eyes of Europe and Christendom."

I turned to face her as we reached the door to the chapel. "Arthur and I exchange letters in Latin, our only common language. He does not write in Spanish, nor do I yet read or speak English, but I will learn. Let us pray that he will be pleased with me, and that I will be a good wife and Princess of Wales."

We entered the chapel. I dipped my right hand into the holy water and made the sign of the cross, genuflected in front of the crucifix on the altar, crossed myself again, entered my pew, and knelt. I fought to brush aside the memory of the coffin at the altar in my dream and the crowned child, who had been my father in another time and place, putting a ring on my finger. I prayed to understand this dream or be spared more of them in future. I prayed to avoid the sin of vanity when being told how pretty I was. I also prayed to maintain my modesty while wearing the beautiful gowns and jewels appropriate for a princess of Spain and England.

After mass and a small breakfast, I began my classes. I was studying religion, Latin histories, canon and civil law, heraldry, genealogy, and, of course, the classics. I already spoke, read, and wrote Spanish and Latin and spoke French and Greek.

Religion was my strongest subject. After my classes, I practiced needlepoint, embroidery, and lace-making. I studied music and dancing as well, and now I would learn to speak, read, and write English.

Prince Arthur and I were married by proxy 19 May 1499—he was in far away England, and I was in my parents' chapel in Spain. My husband and I continued to write each other in Latin, and I continued to study English—a most difficult and confusing language—until Arthur was fifteen years of age.

Finally, I made the long, much-anticipated journey to England. This new country of mine was so different from Spain. England was a green, fertile land, but cold and humid. At last, when I was fifteen, I met my husband in Hampshire at a place called Dogmersfield. The date was 4 November 1501. After such hope and anticipation throughout my journey, I was very surprised to find that, although Arthur and I could write to each other and read each other's letters, we could not understand each other when we spoke. We had each learned a different pronunciation for Latin. But still, we were husband and wife, and we were eager to learn each other's ways—as eager as I was to make sense of the English language. I had spent my entire life learning and preparing to assume my duties as a royal princess, but now it was all so real—and so very different than anything I could possibly have imagined. I might have been frightened had I not been so well educated to trust in God's will.

We traveled together to London. London was nothing like Madrid, but at least the mass and the sacraments were the same. Without my faith and royal upbringing, I might have lost my bearings.

Madrid was bright and sunny, but London was dark, wet, and gloomy. In London, we were officially married in St. Paul's Cathedral on 14 November 1501. It was a beautiful church. As Arthur's wife, I was crowned Princess of Wales.

There was no time after our wedding for us to spend together in private. As we were both raised, duty came first. My husband's duties required his presence at Ludlow Castle, in Shropshire on the border of Wales, immediately after our official wedding ceremony. It was the duty of the Prince of Wales to preside over the Council of Wales, and so we went together to Ludlow Castle.

Ludlow Castle was built in the eleventh century to defend the English border with Wales. It was well built and on high ground just south of where the River Corve joined the River Teme. The only windows were narrow slits for defense. I was so very cold there. While it was not the same as my parents' wealthy court, I could not complain. I did not wish to burden my new husband with an unnecessary letter, our only means of communication. And I was not raised to complain of such trifles, but to maintain my dignity as a royal princess. My husband and my ladies-in-waiting did their best to make me comfortable. I was more concerned with learning to communicate with Arthur and with learning how I could best be of assistance to him. It was also my duty to manage the household.

We spent several months at Ludlow Castle. My husband was pale and tired when we arrived, and I was also exhausted after my long journey from Spain. I thought the rainy weather extremely unpleasant, but Arthur took it in stride. We both needed our rest. Still, he had neither the energy nor the stamina to attempt to perform his manly duty in our bed, and I, being modest and also tired, did not encourage him. I respected and admired his modesty and piety. We were young, and there would be time enough to consummate our marriage eventually.

The sweating sickness was spreading throughout the area around Ludlow Castle. I prayed for God's protection, not for me, but for my dear, new husband. God's will was not as I'd hoped. We were both taken sick. I was weak, feverish, and confined to my bed. I nearly died. I felt the close presence of Our Lord, and it was a mighty comfort. The sickness lasted for weeks, but gradually my ladies nursed me back to health. I recovered only to learn my sweet, young husband had left us to join Our Lord on the second day of April. At sixteen, I was the widowed Princess of Wales.

I had been prepared for death in a spiritual way, but the reality of it was so much more personal. The very man I expected to be with me throughout my life was already dead. I recalled the dream I had shortly before our proxy marriage so long ago, where a child wearing a large crown had led to me the altar, and in front of a coffin, had placed a red ring on my finger. I shuddered to realize that this dream had been a message that I still did not understand.

I might have died as well, but that would have been easier to handle. I was only just beginning to know dear Arthur. I was afraid I would forget his face in my mind—I had known him for such a short time. If it wasn't for my ladies-in-waiting, I would feel all alone in a foreign land. But it was my duty to manage my ladies and somehow give them strength.

I found myself, by God's will and that of King Henry VII, sent with my ladies to London. We were housed in Durham House. It was pleasant enough for us, but I had no income to maintain it. My father-in-law was not anxious to return my dowry, and so I was unable to return home to Aragón. By this time I had surmised that the War of the Roses took a financial toll on the throne of England, and the king was mindful of his pennies. At least we had a decent place to live. I was a widow who had never been taken as a wife. I was left with a household of servants to somehow manage and support. I prayed for patience and courage to endure what Our Lord in His infinite wisdom had given me. And my father in Spain was aware of my plight.

An agreement was made between my father and my father-in-law. They decided I was to marry my husband's younger brother, Henry, Duke of York. He was now heir to the English throne, and so once again, I was to marry the next King of England to establish the validity of the House of Tudor. Henry was five and a half years younger than me, but I was greatly relieved that my future was again secured, and it was basically the same mission upon which I had originally embarked. But I was still haunted by the dream I'd kept secret.

During the dreadful year of 1502, Henry VII and King James IV of Scotland signed the Treaty of Perpetual Peace. The following year, my late husband's sister, Margaret, was married to King James of Scotland. My sister-in-law, Margaret, was in age between my late husband and my promised Henry. Her new husband was sixteen years older than her and desperate for an heir for the throne of Scotland. My father-in-law was doing his best to secure the borders of England and prevent another war. He knew well how costly war had been, and his people desired peace. I didn't envy my sister-in-law her journey north to a strange land. I could not imagine being so young and wed to someone so much older. My husband Arthur had been only one year older than me. I wondered if Scotland could possibly be colder or wetter than England.

Margaret's brother, young Henry, wasn't pleased she was now a queen, while he was still just a prince. I was inwardly appalled, but Henry was young and had only recently lost his elder brother. I prayed he would grow in selflessness and humility as he matured. I prayed I, as his wife, would be able to guide him to be happy for others, and I prayed for his understanding of his elder sister's difficult duty. I was well aware by now Henry was the red-haired child in my dream so long ago. In temperament he was so very different from Arthur. I hoped this was due to the difference in age, as Arthur and I had gotten along relatively well in spite of our communication problem. But at least I'd learned to converse in English.

Margaret and Henry also had a younger sister, Mary. My youngest sister-in-law was only six years old when Arthur died of the sweating sickness. I never had younger siblings of my own, and so Margaret, Henry, and Mary were more new experiences for me. I had no chance to become close to Margaret, and Mary didn't respond to the letter I sent to befriend her. I decided perhaps it wasn't considered my place to reach out to Arthur's younger sisters, and they didn't reach out to me.

So I looked after my household and vowed to do my duty as Henry's wife, to not wait to be bedded by him, and to prepare for my future role as Queen of England. While Arthur was alive and Prince of Wales, Henry had been educated in preparation for a position with the Church, even though his temperament didn't seem to me well-suited for the clergy. It wasn't my place to judge, but apparently God agreed with me. But I was pleased to know my second husband had been well-schooled in religious matters.

I was also pleased that, as he grew into his manhood, Henry became very attractive. He grew to be tall and well-muscled with golden red hair. He would be quite a handsome king. God would reward my patience and endurance with beautiful children.

My conscience was clear; my marriage with Arthur was never physically consummated. I would marry Henry as both a virgin and a widow. God had truly worked in a mysterious way. Henry was too young for marriage just yet, so my second marriage was delayed.

Meanwhile, I found it difficult to support myself and my lady servants at Durham House without income. I frequently fasted to allow my attendants to eat, but I was grateful we had adequate shelter.

When I was nineteen years old, my dear mother, Queen Isabella, was taken by Our Lord 26 November 1504. I could not imagine my home, country, family, or my father without her. I was still struggling to come to terms with losing Arthur, whom I barely knew. I knew she would watch over me, and we would see each other again in Heaven.

Castile was inherited by my older sister, Joanna, who was not mentally stable. Joanna complicated my uncomfortable situation in England. She was unlikeable, and her erratic behavior was viewed unfavorably by the other royals of Europe. Henry was certainly old enough to marry by June of 1505, having reached the age of fifteen—the same age as Arthur when we married. But I could not marry while I was in mourning for my mother. And thanks to Joanna, King Henry VII was now hesitant to allow the marriage.

I wrote to my father in his grief, "I choose what I believe and say nothing, for I am not as simple as I may seem." I hoped to comfort him with the knowledge I would manage to maintain my dignity and composure in spite of my sister and my father-in-law. I told my father, "I'm grateful for the excellent education I received as your daughter. I will continue with my mission to unite Spain and England through marriage."

I trusted God's reasons for this temporary burden. Then we received good news from Scotland that took my mind off my troubles. Henry's sister Margaret gave birth to a son, James, on 21 February 1507. King James IV now had an heir for his throne. At least she was more successful in her duty to her new country than I'd been to mine. I was truly happy for her.

Meanwhile, my father, a true and generous Christian king, understood my situation as well as King Henry's cautious and frugal nature. While King Henry showed no interest in my affairs, my father knew I had a household to feed and clothe. In 1507, my father found himself without a Spanish Ambassador to England, and so I was appointed to the task. I served my father and Spain well and demonstrated to King Henry I was worthy of his son and the future title of Queen of England. The payment I received from my gracious father enabled me to take proper care of my household. Though I served as ambassador for only six months, I was the first woman ambassador in all of Europe and the Christian world.

To marry the younger brother of my late husband required a papal dispensation. I knew this would be no problem, as I'd always been faithful to the Church of Rome and an obedient servant of the Spanish Order of Observant Franciscans. So I truthfully testified in writing that my marriage to Arthur was never consummated. The Holy Father in Rome granted the necessary dispensation.

Just when it seemed all would be well again, there was tragic news from Scotland. Only one week after his first birthday, young Prince James died. He had been christened, but I prayed for Margaret in her grief. How fragile was our mortal existence. I had lost my young husband and beloved mother, but I could not imagine what Margaret experienced. My ladies were also stunned. Our prayers seemed to have been answered when we learned Margaret was expecting again soon after the tragedy. But as if my poor sister-in-law had too few trials to bear, on 15 July 1508 she gave birth to a daughter, who died shortly after.

My father-in-law, King Henry VII, died 21 April 1509. For his few faults, he was a good Christian king who brought stability, peace, and prosperity to his country, once so war-torn, embittered, and divided. He was succeeded, of course, by his son, Henry, Duke of York, who was eager to solidify England's relationship with Spain. King Henry VIII, partly due to his youth, was not as cautious as his recently departed father. The new King sent for me soon after his father was laid to rest. "We are most anxious to secure our inheritance and demonstrate to the rest of Christendom that our place on the throne of England is legitimate," he told me. "You are a beautiful, gracious, and noble lady, and we would have you as our wife and queen without further delay."

I blushed and smiled at his flattery, as I curtseyed deeply and responded, "Your will is my own, Your Majesty. May our marriage be blessed by Almighty God."

Henry appreciated my own English ancestry, as well as my physical beauty and experience from being older and having performed well as Spanish Ambassador to his own country. I would have thought it more prudent for him to mourn his father, but I understood the duty of a monarch must come before all else. We were married 11 June 1509 in a private ceremony in Greenwich Church. Henry had been born at Greenwich Palace, and he was quite fond of Greenwich. Located on the River Thames, it was only about fifty years old and served as the primary royal residence in England. After Ludlow Castle and Durham House, Greenwich was a refreshing and luxuriant change for me. The windows were plentiful and let in much light and fresh air. I found the furnishings to be comfortable and in good repair. I had an extra mass offered in thanksgiving.

I was twenty-three years old at the time of my second marriage and had been a widow for seven years. Henry turned eighteen just over two weeks later on 28 June. He was possibly the most handsome king in Europe. We were crowned King and Queen of England together on 24 June 1509 by the Archbishop of Canterbury at Westminster Abbey. Our coronation was followed by a banquet in Westminster Hall. My husband was not as frugal as his late father, and it was a grand banquet.

Henry's heraldic badge was the Tudor Rose, while mine was the Pomegranate of Granada. We symbolized the flower and fruit of European royalty, and we believed God had blessed us with a great match. It did not take long for love to follow, nor was there any delay in consummating this marriage. Henry was strong and passionate in bed. I found the experience quite enjoyable and always welcomed his advances. I trusted the symbolism of the pomegranate would express itself through the many sweet children we would have.

The Tudor Rose was a combination of white and red roses, which symbolized the union of England after the bloody War of the Roses. The pomegranate flower was an orange trumpet with no thorns. I found it very pleasing to the eye, especially knowing it brought forth a fruit prolific with sweet juice and seeds as red as the blood of life.

I admit I had disturbing thoughts about my new husband occasionally. Mostly they came to me in my dreams. I dreamt that he was angry with his elder brother, Arthur, and his father, Henry VII, because Arthur was crowned Prince of Wales and married me, whom young Henry considered so beautiful. Upon waking, I remembered how he'd been so upset with his elder sister, Margaret, when she became Queen of Scotland. He was just a child at the time, but so headstrong and adamant that none should be higher in rank than he. Whenever I had these disturbing dreams, I prayed to the Blessed Virgin Mary, Mother of Our Lord, to remove these thoughts, so I might be a better wife, queen, and Christian woman.

Meanwhile in Scotland, our-sister-in-law gave birth to another son 20 October. He was named Arthur after my first husband. Henry and I both prayed for the new Prince Arthur's good health and gave thanks for Margaret's good fortune. But after our prayers of gratitude, I heard Henry grumble under his breath, "England is far more important than Scotland, and therefore more in need of a son than Scotland."

We didn't know at the time, but I was also pregnant. Henry's grumbling turned to joy when I told him of my condition. Later, I confessed to my priest, "I fear God might punish Henry for begrudging the birth of his nephew in Scotland. I cannot shake this sense of foreboding."

But my confessor reassured me, "You have suffered many losses in such a short time. It's only natural to fear more loss. Mortal life is often short, but it is just as often long. You must trust in God's will."

I did my best to follow his advice. I prayed only for God's will to be done. Then on 31 January 1510, I prematurely delivered a stillborn daughter.

I never before knew such grief. Neither the loss of my mother nor the death of my first husband stabbed at my heart like the lifelessness of my own little daughter. She was taken away from me as soon as she was born, and I did not look upon her precious face, but that only made my grief greater. I knew my attendants only meant to spare me more suffering, but that wasn't possible.

I grieved and prayed. My husband never spoke of her or his own grief and disappointment, but I could sense it—even through my own. I prayed this great loss would bring us closer together. I was twenty-four years old, and Henry was nineteen.

My only solace was my faith. My personal devotions included mass, prayer, confession, and penance, but I did not outwardly celebrate saints and holy relics. I was well-educated for a woman and well aware of the human failings of men. The saints were mortal men, and I found the relics disturbing. Church officials were also mere men. This was not something of which a woman would speak, but it was important in my position to see the true nature of men. I acknowledged and accepted our Pope in Rome was the Vicar of Christ on earth, but he was also a man and capable of mistakes. A good Christian should not dwell on the shortcomings of others, but instead pray for their divine guidance, as I hoped my beloved subjects of England prayed for mine and Henry's.

My prayers were soon answered. Henry and I became closer after I realized I was again pregnant. We were happy and confident the baby would be a boy. Henry so wanted a male heir. I would have been happy with a healthy child of either gender, but I understood he was anxious for me to give birth to his heir.

In the midst of our joy, tragedy struck once again in Scotland. Young Prince Arthur was taken ill and didn't recover. He died 14 July 1510. How much grief was poor Margaret to endure? I understood this time, having lost a child of my own, how devastated she must have been.

Soon Henry and I experienced our own personal triumph. We were right—ours was a male child. He was born 1 January 1511, christened Henry, and given the title Duke of Cornwall. The country celebrated with us. But our happiness did not last. After only fifty-two days of life, our little babe died. We were heartbroken. God had given my proud husband his heir only to take him away so quickly. I struggled to deal with my grief. I sought solace in my faith, but I felt Henry's was shaken. I hoped this experience would humble him before Our Lord.

Later that year, the Holy Father in Rome, Pope Julius II, made an alliance with Spain, England, and the Holy Roman Empire against France. France remained an ally of Scotland. I trusted the Treaty of Perpetual Peace would hold strong through the presence of Henry's sister on the Scottish throne.

Anne Boleyn
26 April 1507—1514

My first memory was of arguing with my sister, Mary. I felt the need to tease her since the day I was born, 26 April 1507. She was eight years older, but I was the demanding one. We were complete opposites. Mary was reserved, submissive, blonde, fair, and lovely, while I was bold, confident, dark-haired, and dark-eyed with a swarthy complexion. We were the daughters of Thomas Boleyn and Elizabeth Howard. Our maternal grandfather was Thomas Howard, second Duke of Norfolk.

 We also had a brother, George, three years older than me, who like Mary, was born in Norfolk. The three of us grew up together at Hever Castle in Kent. Our family was one of the most prominent families in Tudor England. Our father, a wealthy courtier, worked in the diplomatic service of King Henry VII and continued service under Henry VIII, who succeeded his father five days before my second birthday.

 Our home, Hever Castle, had been the Boleyn family home since 1462. My father inherited it, and it became our home in 1505. As a result, I was born at Hever. It was a grand castle, and we lived in our own dwelling inside. Our home included a large dining hall, many rooms, and many servants.

 My father travelled in his service to the King. Though I already lived in a castle, I dreamed of the grand courts of Europe that Father visited. I wished to see them myself and to live in grander places than Hever.

 My height was average. I had black hair and beautiful black eyes, my best feature other than my slim, long neck. I often fancied my dark coloring would be quite striking contrasted with a bouquet of white lilies. I was the perfect complement to such fair and heavenly flowers. My mouth, though a bit wide, was quite pretty in my oval face. My worst flaw was an upper front tooth that protruded slightly, but I practiced in the mirror which expressions best covered it. Indeed, I learned to use those expressions to punctuate my conversations and accent my quick wit. What I lacked of Mary's fairness, I more than made up for in cleverness. I had an innate ability to read people that Mary never understood. I used that ability to tease, amuse, and get what I desired. Of the two of us, I was the true flower.

Because of Father's diplomatic service to King Henry and Queen Catharine, he had the opportunity to impress the regent of the Netherlands, Princess Margareta of Austria, Duchess of Savoy and daughter of Maximilian I, Holy Roman Emperor. Father served in the Netherlands from the spring of 1513 until October 1514. Princess Margareta was so pleased with him, she offered a position in her court for one of his daughters. He chose me. I was only seven years old, but I would be eight the following spring. I was so excited.

Catharine of Aragón
1512—1514

More good news came from Scotland. Another prince was born to James and Margaret 15 April 1512. While I prayed for the child's good health and long life, Henry seemed agitated that the good fortune was theirs and not ours. I reminded him, "God will provide according to His Will."

Henry responded with a scowl, a dismissive wave of his hand, and then ignored me. I could not calm my husband's jealousy. Unfortunately, at the end of the year, poor Margaret gave birth to another stillborn daughter, but Henry showed no empathy for her.

The next year, I again became pregnant, and Henry's mood improved greatly. That summer, as we dined in our private chambers, Henry set his goblet on the table and announced, "I will wage war on France."

I was stunned. "France?" I questioned.

"Yes," he answered decisively, "We will take more land in France."

"But France is an ally of Scotland, and our own sister is Queen of Scotland."

"Women are not expected to understand such matters," he said dismissively.

"Your own father invested great effort in making peace with Scotland to secure the northern border. I understand that, and so should you."

"This war is sanctioned by the Pope's own alliance against France," he answered coolly. "Not a matter for women."

"But you would leave me in a most vulnerable position, sir," I humbly protested, lowering my head. "I would much prefer to have you with me during my pregnancy."

He smiled. "We shall first appoint our dear wife as Queen Regent of England."

I returned his smile. "I am truly honored by your confidence in me. I will do my best for you and England as Queen Regent. I will pray for the success of your campaign."

We were a good team, Henry and I, and by this time I loved him dearly. But I worried for his safe return and for the safety of our northern border.

After some time, I received word he had been victorious over the French in the Battle of the Spurs. I prayed he would return unharmed before the birth of our child. I feared my worry would bring harm to the child I carried.

By the end of the summer, the Treaty of Perpetual Peace crumbled as King James led his Scots in an invasion of England. As Queen Regent, the responsibility for England's protection was mine and mine alone. I gathered an army of good and loyal Englishmen. Together we rode north to defend our border. While carrying the heir to the throne, I donned full armor and led the troops. It was my duty.

The campaign against Scotland climaxed when we arrived at Flodden Field in early September. I addressed the English Army before the battle. They fought well for me and for England. When the terrible loss of life had ended, England had won, and poor Queen Margaret was a widow. I knelt on the field and prayed for the soul of King James, for the souls of all the brave Scottish and English men who had died, and for Margaret. The stench of spilled blood and dead bodies was almost more than I could bear. Only by focusing deeply on my prayers was I able to quell my nausea. I was determined that I would not dishonor the dead with the weakness of my pregnant stomach.

After I returned to London, I sent a letter to Henry in France with the bloodied coat of King James IV, our own brother-in-law. I had saved England, but the stress took its toll. Before Henry returned home, I delivered a stillborn son.

I was Queen Regent for six months. Henry was pleased with the victory at Flodden Field over the Scots, but he was more displeased with the loss of his son. He had no sympathy for his widowed sister, and made no offer of assistance to her.

"Margaret's duty was to dissuade her foolish husband from invading her own country," he proclaimed, "and yours was to protect our son and heir. Your duty was to the future King of England. Instead, you, a woman, took it on yourself to lead an army."

"I had a duty to protect England," I explained. "You, sir, appointed me Queen Regent. You left the country in my hands, attacked Scotland's ally, and now you blame me for doing my duty."

"I left our son in your hands. Your duty was to protect him and leave the army in the hands of our noblemen. God has punished you for acting in a man's place by taking away our child."

I could not believe my ears. Henry was actually blaming me for the death of our son. He showed no gratitude to me for our victory at Flodden Field. He expressed no kindness toward his own sister or the widows of the many men who had died on both sides of the battle. He was not concerned for Margaret's fate as the widowed queen of a defeated country. He showed no remorse for leaving me in my condition to start the war that caused such tragedy. He took no responsibility.

I knew I had done my duty as Queen Regent. I put the country first above my own safety. Only God knows which choice was right, but Henry made me Regent and left the country in my hands. May God forgive me if Henry was right and I was wrong, but I did the best I could. If Henry hadn't invaded France, he would have been here to lead the army himself, but then Scotland would not have invaded England. War is man's foolishness. Henry VII understood the sense of peace and prosperity, but he had already lived through the ravages of war. I could only pray this disaster would teach Henry to be more prudent.

The following year in April, the widow Margaret gave birth to another son. She named him Alexander. She was now regent for her child, James V. James was only two years old. He and his little brother would never remember their father, the king Henry blamed for his own demise. My husband was more jealous of his sister's sons than concerned for her protection. It wasn't my place to judge, but I understood how little my husband valued women— even the women of his own blood.

Shortly after the news of Alexander's birth, I learned I was yet again with child. This helped to calm Henry for several months, as he anticipated the arrival of his own male heir. I prayed for patience in dealing with my husband's fickle moods.

Henry secured peace with France by sending his younger sister, Mary, to wed King Louis XII. It was no secret that Mary had fallen in love with a nobleman, Charles Brandon, but Henry, as king, decreed Mary would be Louis' wife. It was Mary's duty as her brother's subject to obey. Mary was eighteen years old. King Louis was forty-eight. He was known as the father of his people, but he was also old enough to be Mary's father. While I had felt that the fate of her older sister was harsh, Mary's fate was horribly cruel. She would be Queen of France to restore the peace Henry destroyed. Mary was married in October and crowned 5 November.

        Later that month, our child was born. It was a son, but he was lifeless.

Anne Boleyn
1515—1516

Mary said, "Good-bye, Anne. You're being sent away, because I asked Father to give me some peace from your relentless teasing."

"You're jealous of me," I laughed.

"Mother and Father love me too much to send me away."

I didn't care what Mary said. I was on my way to serve in a foreign court. It was most unusual at my young age, but Princess Margareta took good care of me and my education. She told me many times how bright and clever I was, and of course, I knew this was true.

While I was in the Netherlands serving Princess Margareta, my father arranged for me to attend Princess Mary Tudor, sister of King Henry VIII, during her wedding to King Louis XII of France. This was an exceptional honor. I was in the Netherlands only a short time before I went to France. I became Queen Mary's youngest lady-in-waiting. I loved France, but unfortunately, my sister, Mary, also arrived to serve Queen Mary. When the other maids went home to England a few weeks after the wedding, Mary and I stayed in France. Father had become the English Ambassador to France.

King Louis died on New Year's Day, Queen Mary was widowed, and I still had not yet had my eighth birthday. My sister and I stayed with Father in the French court, but now Mary and I served the new Queen of France, Claude. Queen Claude was fifteen years old, the same age as my sister.

I became interested in fashion and religious philosophy. I learned French culture and etiquette. I was known as an excellent dancer, and I was happy. The fleur de lis was the symbol of France, and in the summer, the court was filled with beautiful, enchantingly fragrant lilies. I loved the lilies. The French court had become my home.

I made friends with Queen Marguerite, wife of King Henry II of Navarre. She was a patron of humanists and reformers, the sister of King François I, and often visited the French court. I was impressed with her intelligence, and she was kind to me. She told me I was charming and encouraged me to study literature and poetry. Marguerite was an author and promoted reform. She influenced me greatly.

Catharine of Aragón
1515—1520

King Louis XII of France died 1 January 1515.
Henry chose Charles Brandon, the Dowager Queen
Mary's true love, to escort her back to England. But
before sending Charles to France, Henry made
Charles promise there would be no talk of betrothal
to Mary. I thought it cruel, but by now I knew not to
interfere with Henry's commands.

Charles Brandon's love for Mary was
stronger than his promise. Mary and Charles
married in secret in France. Henry was enraged
when he found out. He ranted, "They have
committed treason."

I spoke to Lord Chancellor Thomas
Wolsey, Archbishop of York, who then reasoned
with Henry on the couple's behalf. Henry forgave
them after Charles paid a fine, and the two
newlyweds returned safely to England. They were
publicly married at Greenwich Palace in May. At
Greenwich, Henry was pleased to have his sister
safely home, and I openly expressed my happiness
for them. How quickly Henry's moods turned.

I became pregnant again the same year. By
this time, I knew to take every precaution not to tax
my mortal body. I withdrew to my rooms during the
day and went to bed early each evening. Henry
understood and approved of my caution. We prayed
together each day for our child. I began to suspect
my husband approved of me keeping to my rooms,
because he had taken one of my ladies to his bed.
Her name was Bessie Blount, and she was only
thirteen years old. I was no fool when it came to the
behavior of men, and a king could do as he pleased.
I graciously feigned ignorance.

In December, I reached my thirtieth birthday. Henry and I knew my years of childbearing were passing quickly. Then we heard from Scotland that Margaret's younger son, Alexander, had died. We prayed this was not an omen.

On 18 February 1516, I gave birth to a healthy daughter. We named her Mary, after the mother of our dear savior. She was christened three days later at the Church of Observant Friars, while I remained at rest in my bed. It was important that she be christened quickly—infants were at high risk of illness and death. But the Blessed Mother watched over our little Mary, and she lived. Henry was pleased to at last have a live child of his own. He beamed with pride when my ladies told him how much she resembled him. He loved to hear that she was a truly robust Tudor child, but he made no secret to me that he still needed a son. I prayed Our Lord would grant us one, but I quietly feared Henry's lack of humility before God would prevent it. I was grateful for Mary's good health. Henry should have shown more appreciation for such a blessing.

In 1517, a man named Martin Luther in Wittenberg, Germany, made terrible allegations of corruption against the Roman Catholic Church. I was no fool. I knew his allegations were truthful, but to challenge the Church in such a way was extremely dangerous. While I knew this good man, Martin Luther, told the truth, my duty was to defend the Holy Father. I publicly denounced Martin Luther's arguments. For this, my confessor, Fray Alfonso de Villa Sancta, friar of the Observant Franciscans, nominated me as a "Defender of the Faith," a title that was granted to my husband instead. Henry's receipt of the title didn't concern me, for in my heart, I knew I did not deserve it. I lied to defend the Church. But Henry was proud to receive the honor.

That May, terrible events took place in London. People objected to the presence of foreigners. Once a foreigner myself, I was appalled. The trouble started on Easter Tuesday with a speech that called for Englishmen to defend and protect their own against outsiders. The same speech also demanded harm to foreigners. This was not the Christian way, and I didn't understand Christian people with such thoughts. But two weeks later, a riot of protest took place. Homes of foreigners were looted, and countless crimes were committed. The streets of London erupted in mass panic and anger. Thomas More tried to calm the situation, but once he had successfully reasoned with the crowd in the street, others indoors began to throw bricks, stones, and boiling water out of their windows.

Henry and I were at Richmond Palace on the south bank of River Thames, when the riot broke out. Henry was awakened by his guards in the middle of the night. The Duke of Norfolk rode into London and restored order. No one was killed, but many were hurt, and much damage was done to property. Hundreds were arrested. I begged Henry for mercy for the sake of the criminals' families. "Perhaps an example of mercy would best teach them kindness, where violent punishment would only reinforce their violent ways."

Henry looked at me thoughtfully for a moment, and then turned away with a loud, "Humph!" But most were pardoned, and for that I was thankful. Still, someone had to be punished, and more than a dozen men were convicted of treason and executed.

In 1518, I was pregnant again. Again we took every precaution. Again we prayed every day for the child's good health and safety. I knew Henry prayed for a healthy son, while I prayed the baby's gender be God's will. I gave birth to a daughter 10 November. Henry wasn't pleased and didn't visit us to see his child. My heart broke when she died unchristened only a few hours later. When I did not think I could bear to endure such grief again, I remembered poor Margaret. Then I would thank God I had a healthy daughter and husband.

By early 1519, young Bessie Blount, now sixteen, still at court and unwed, was obviously pregnant. It was no secret she carried my husband's bastard. When she delivered a healthy son 15 June, I privately wept. I knew Henry wondered why I hadn't done the same for him. She named the child Henry, and my Henry openly acknowledged the birth of his son. But Henry Fitzroy could not be heir to the English throne as our daughter Mary was. This was a bitter herb for my husband to swallow. Bessie, of course, remained at court with her son. I could not hold a grudge against her or her child, for they had nowhere else to go. I could also not blame my husband for wanting his son near him, but I was so ashamed.

I sought solace in my faith. My religion comforted me through all the tragedies and loss. While I found comfort in prayer, my husband sulked and pouted. I knew he wanted stability for our kingdom. If Mary was our only heir, she would need a foreign prince for marriage, which would put England under the domination of another country. I prayed Henry would see the wisdom of making a match for her with Spain. He, on the other hand, was leaning toward another match with France for our daughter, Mary, as he had for his sister, Mary.

In February 1520, we attended a wedding at Greenwich Palace for young William Carey and his bride, Mary Boleyn. Mary was the elder daughter of Thomas Boleyn, our ambassador to France, and had been a servant in the French court for several years to Queen Claude. She was brought back to England in disgrace the year before for having slept with the French King. Now she was fortunate to have an English husband, such as he was, beneath her family's position. After the wedding, at my husband's insistence, she came to our court as my servant. Henry was no longer interested in Bessie Blount. Now Mary Boleyn Carey shared his bed.

Henry's behavior was truly shameful. He approved of and attended Mary Boleyn's marriage to William Carey only to take her as his own while the young couple was still newly wed. A king was free to take such privileges, but my husband demonstrated contempt for the sacrament of matrimony. I suspected he did this to show his displeasure for me giving him a daughter, but I had done my best, and I had no proof of my suspicions. I was a faithful wife and good queen. I prayed for strength to endure these small insults. Everyday I silently forgave him, although I knew he neither required nor desired my forgiveness.

Then my nephew, Holy Roman Emperor Charles V, came to England on a state visit. Since Henry wasn't interested in finding a husband for Mary in Spain, I encouraged him to make an alliance with Charles instead of France. But as soon as Charles left England, Henry and I went to France together to visit King François I. The field where our meeting took place was filled with tents made of cloth of gold. The sun shimmered on the tents as the cloth fluttered in the breeze. It was a spectacular sight. We were treated appropriately for our status, but I found the French women immodest and the Frenchmen's behavior toward the women lewd. Of course, I kept silent, as I was a guest of the French court. Henry was more concerned with preventing a French attack upon England, and he negotiated a successful truce.

Jane Seymour
1508—1520

I was born in 1508, a descendant of the Percy
family and of King Edward III of England through
my mother's father. My mother was Margery
Wentworth, and my father was Sir John Seymour of
Wiltshire. King Henry VIII and his consort, Queen
Catharine, were crowned the year following my
birth. The king was my cousin, and my father spent
a great deal of his time at court.

Though descended from royalty, the women
in my family dressed modestly. We each had
several pretty gowns—usually one made of silk or
cloth of gold for special occasions, another trimmed
with fur for the Christmas season, and two or three
of less expensive cloth. We also had warm cloaks
for winter and modest, but fashionable, headdresses
to match our gowns. I had an older sister named for
our mother, Margery, who was six years old when I
was born. I was fortunate to have an older sister to
look after me and share with me what she'd learned,
because my mother was very busy managing the
household. And Margery and I were not her only
children.

I also had three older brothers, John,
Edward, and Thomas. John died 15 July 1510. I was
too young at the time of his death to remember or
understand what happened, but my parents and
siblings talked of it often as I grew, and I knew how
important he had been to them.

In 1512, when I was four years old, my
beloved mother gave birth to my sister Elizabeth.
Though I was just a child myself, I took my duty
very seriously to help our sister, Margery, look after

little Elizabeth. We were a close family, and I dearly loved my parents, brothers, and sisters.

The following year, there was much talk of the Scottish invasion of England while our King Henry was abroad fighting the French. All I understood at the time was that good Queen Catharine saved us all by leading the army north to defeat the Scots. I heard the Scottish King himself was killed in a great battle. I was so proud of our queen. Every day my family and I thanked Our Lord for giving her to us in His great kindness.

As I grew, I gradually became aware of my appearance. My skin was very pale, and my hair was a fair reddish blonde. My nose was long and straight and pointed down to my weak double chin. When I was six, my mother was pregnant again. One rainy day when little Elizabeth was napping and Margery, my mother, and I were sewing, I asked, "Am I pretty?"

My mother looked at me, smiled, and sighed. "My dear Jane, you are precious to all who love you. Be thankful Our Lord has blessed you with a cute but boyish face that will not tempt young men to lead you into sin. You must never wish to be pretty. True beauty is in the soul, not the body."

I smiled and sighed in imitation of my mother. I wasn't cursed with being pretty, which was a temptation for sin, but I was loved.

A couple of months later, my dear mother delivered another son, Henry. As we gathered around her bed to see our baby brother, she told us, "It's very important for a family to have sons. They grow up to protect us, to govern us, to serve the king, to fight in his battles for the honor and safety of our country, and to continue the family titles and wealth. It is women's place to obey the men, manage their households, bear their children, and never dishonor them or the family name."

I obediently listened to every word. My parents were strict but kind. We were well cared for and looked out for each other. I took my mother's loving guidance to heart. I wanted to grow up to be a good, loving mother and wife just like her.

One cold day when I was seven years old, Margery and I were sitting together. She was helping me practice my stitching when Mother came into the room with a bright smile on her face and said, "Our beloved Queen Catharine has given birth to a daughter. We must give thanks to Our Lord for the birth of Princess Mary."

We put our sewing aside and knelt on the floor in the middle of the room with Mother. "We pray for little Mary and her parents," Mother began out loud, "that God will protect them every day and keep them in good health." Then she led us in saying the rosary together. We were grateful for a princess who would bring honor to our country.

The following August, Margery and I went out into a field near our home and gathered flowers to take to church for the celebration of the Blessed Virgin Mary's Assumption into heaven. Margery took a bouquet of daisies, while I took violets, my favorite flower. In the church, next to the altar, we each placed our bouquets at the feet of the statue of our Blessed Mother. "Please watch over and protect the baby Princess Mary," Margery whispered.

"Amen," I answered.

Eventually, I grew to average height, but my figure, such as it was, did not tempt me to the sin of vanity. My complexion was pale, my hair was strawberry blonde, but my face would never catch men's eyes. My charms were more of kindness, patience, and knowing how to keep my tongue still—more appropriate qualities for a lady of my station. It was my duty and desire to honor the family that provided me with such a fortunate position—one for which I was truly grateful.

I was well-trained in household management, and my needlework, after much time and practice, became elaborate and beautiful. I learned to read and write some, but that sort of education was better suited for my brothers. I was raised to be a devoted Christian, a good wife for a nobleman, and a good Christian mother.

Father continued to serve at court, while Mother stayed at home and managed the household. We were strictly supervised and not allowed any mischief. We understood that someday the boys would also serve king and country, and the girls would serve queen and country. Our parents would make good marriage matches for us. They knew best.

I had learned about heaven, purgatory, and hell, but still I was unprepared for actual physical death. At first, Margery was ill and stayed in bed. I sat with her some of the time and tried to cheer her, but after just a few days, I was shocked to see her so still and pale. Her lips turned bluish. She would not wake up.

"She's now in heaven with the angels," Mother said, sobbing as she pulled me from the bedside.

"But I want her here with us." She'd been my constant companion all my life.

"We must not question God's will," Mother answered.

I saw how it grieved my parents to lose another child, and now I understood how it felt. That evening Father tried to comfort us. "Margery is with Our Lord, and we are grateful to have had her with us while we did." My parents guided me through my grief and taught me not to fear such loss.

After Margery's passing, it fell to me as elder daughter to assist Mother in household management. I continued to look after Elizabeth and Henry and practice my embroidery and needlepoint. I remembered all the happy times I'd had with Margery, and I was confident I would be well-prepared for marriage.

Anne Boleyn
1517—1524

As lady-in-waiting to Queen Claude of France, my
fair sister, Mary, caught the eye of King François.
Neither secrecy nor discretion was involved. The
queen wasn't pleased with her lady bedding the
king. Nor was Father happy with Mary's conduct.
Our family could gain nothing by it. We were
English subjects. The French King would bestow no
favors on us; even I understood that. Mary damaged
her reputation as well as our family's. She liked the
flattery and attention King François gave her in
front of the rest of the court, but now everyone
knew she was no longer a virgin. How would Father
find her a suitable husband? She would be fortunate
just to maintain her position. I didn't want to be in
her shoes when she had to face Mother.

     Mary was called home to England near the
end of 1519, and Mother was angry. Mary married
William Carey, a minor noble, the following
February. She was extremely fortunate to have a
husband.

     I returned home with Father for the wedding
at Greenwich Palace. King Henry and Queen
Catharine attended. Mary was given a position at
court as one of Queen Catharine's ladies. Queen
Catharine was very kind, and I was relieved for our
family.

     Mary was at the English court only a short
time before King Henry summoned her to his bed.
She didn't refuse him. In fact, she told me just
before Father and I returned to France,
"Grandfather, the Duke, ordered me to make myself
available to the king. He said I gave myself to his
rival, King François, and now I must make amends

to my own king. Grandfather warned me I could be charged with treason if I did not."

"It's no secret our handsome king is a jealous man, Mary," I commented. "He probably only wants you because the French king already had you."

"Don't be so tactless, Anne," Father scolded.

"I will do as I must," Mary vowed.

"And William?" I wondered aloud.

"William is loyal to the King," Father answered. He grabbled my arm, and we left quickly.

Once we were outside and in our carriage, I turned to Father. "But it's true. She made her bed in France, and now she's forced to lie in it in England, while her new husband is humiliated."

"I know that," he snapped. We rode on in silence.

I was amazed Queen Claude was able to get rid of Mary from her court, but Queen Catharine simply endured the insult and pretended nothing improper went on in the king's bed. King Henry made no secret of his longtime affair with Bessie Blount. It was a favorite topic of conversation at court in France. Maybe because Mary was an English subject, Queen Catharine had nowhere to send Mary.

Mary missed the whole point of being at court, which was to flirt and attract a suitable husband. She had it all backwards. I had at least learned this lesson. How could a woman ever hope to bring about social reforms if she didn't first improve her own status with an appropriate marriage? I vowed not to make the same mistake as my sister.

I came home to England early in 1522. I had lived in France almost half my life, and I felt at home there. I sailed from Calais to Dover, and then traveled by carriage to Hever Castle. I was educated, coy, and charming now. On my next birthday, I would be fifteen, and I was to be married. I hoped the marriage would let me to serve at Queen Catharine's court. I loved court life, but while at Hever, Mother and I made wedding plans.

King Henry ordered Father to settle a dispute about inheritance with our Irish cousin by marriage of James Butler, the ninth Earl of Ormond, to me. I was honored to have my husband chosen by the king. I imagined myself dressed in a white gown with a large bouquet of fragrant, white lilies as I said my vows. The white gown and flowers would compliment my dark coloring, and I would be a stunning bride.

But all my grand plans evaporated when Father and our cousins argued again. Instead, I was given a position at court, where I preferred to be anyway. My duty was to assist the queen in any way she desired, entertain her if called upon, and perform whatever task was required of me by my elder ladies.

I was free to flirt with whomever I chose, and I chose Henry Percy, son of the Earl of Northumberland. He served as a page for Cardinal Thomas Wolsey. I used all the skills I learned at the French court with my delicate figure and five feet three inches of feminine charms. My Henry was as smitten with me as I with him. We had many secret meetings, none of which lasted very long. He professed his true love for me. As I had learned in France, I received his advances coolly at first. Another young lady helped me allow Henry to discreetly discover my fondness for lilies. Just as I planned, I was rewarded with a lovely bouquet. I loved him, but I struggled with myself to not appear too eager. He courted me the rest of the year.

By 1523, Henry Percy proposed marriage to me, and of course, I accepted. Our betrothal was done in secret, but we required permission from both our fathers for it to be official. Father wasn't pleased when he found out. I didn't understand. The Percy family was very old and well-established in the north of England. I had done quite well for myself, but then Henry's father, the Earl, objected to the match. I was shocked.

No one supported our love, and I was sent home to Hever Castle. I found the relative quiet of Hever dreadfully tedious after so many years at court, but mostly I missed my true love, Henry Percy. As soon as I arrived in the courtyard at Hever, Mother came outside. She wasn't smiling. "You will not be allowed to return to court until you are over him."

I silently nodded assent and curtseyed, and she turned and went back inside. I worked hard to hide my feelings. Secretly, I hoped to return to court soon so I might see him again.

My new duty was serving Mother. I was home only a few weeks when Mother told me, "Mary is pregnant."

"She and William must be very happy," I said before I thought about it, and quickly added, "Well, someone must be happy about it."

Tension erupted in the family and among the servants. Much ugly gossip spread, as no one knew if the father was her husband, William, or her lover, King Henry. I wondered if her behavior was the true reason for the Earl of Northumberland's objection to me. There certainly was no flaw on my part. I wanted to be angry with Mary for this, but because of her pregnancy, I was allowed to return to court.

Court was also full of gossip when the queen wasn't present. I pretended not to hear. When asked directly, as I was on occasion, I simply answered, "The child is William Carey's, of course." I had to protect my family's reputation for the sake of my own prospects.

In 1524, I was present for the birthing ordeal in the darkened, dreary room where Mary had taken to her bed. How she screamed and carried on. She was always much more timid than I, but not during labor. I feared it would never end, when finally my niece was born. I suggested she name the child for the wronged Queen Catharine. I hoped to restore our family's standing for my own sake. Queen Catharine was pleased.

I thought the king would've been done with Mary once she was fat with child, but I was wrong. He didn't seem to show favor to his wife again as I expected. After his bastard daughter—or was it really William's—was born, King Henry doted on the child and continued the affair with my sister as soon as she recovered from childbirth. I was amazed the queen kept her composure.

Catharine of Aragón
1521—1525

Less than two years after our state visit with King
François and the treaty agreed upon by our two
countries, my husband declared war against France.
War was such a waste of lives and resources and
brought grief to so many families on both sides.
After all the deaths and losses we had experienced
personally, I couldn't fathom how Henry could
dishonor his own word. I was, however, relieved
Mary would not be betrothed to a French prince.
Instead, Henry planned to promise Mary in
marriage to Emperor Charles V.

But Henry was not careful with his money.
He built and renovated palaces. He was generous
with gifts for me and my ladies, while war was
costly. He expanded the navy. His father had erred
on the side of frugality, a flaw which better served
the country. My daughter and I both benefited from
his generosity, but I was concerned. Overtaxing
one's people was unwise. I remembered my days as
a widow without income, and feared for the less
fortunate.

I diverted myself with academic and
scholarly learning. I loved literature. I wanted to
provide the best training for Mary. I tried to make
education of women acceptable. My husband,
however, still considered women of consequence
only to serve men's needs. Yet I loved him.

Among my friends were the scholars
Erasmus of Rotterdam and Thomas More. I was a
patron of Renaissance Humanism, which promoted
cultural and educational reform and studies such as
philosophy, medicine, law, and theology. Since I
was privileged to have had an excellent education, I

felt compelled to support others in their quest for knowledge. This endeavor could only help my own daughter eventually.

In 1522, Mary Boleyn Carey's younger sister, Anne, came to court to also serve me. She brought with her the French customs and fashions she learned at the French court. Unlike her fair, blonde sister, Anne was dark and very quick-witted. She could be amusing—even charming—but I found her French mannerisms to be out of step with the rest of the court. Then in 1523, we learned she'd made a secret betrothal with one of Cardinal Thomas Wolsey's pages. The page was the son of the Earl of Northumberland, who wasn't pleased and didn't support the match. Anne was sent home to her mother in Kent. Henry and I were amused at the couple's foolishness. They were so young and ignorant to think they could make their own match while serving in our court. But Anne returned once it was obvious her sister was pregnant.

In 1524, Mary Boleyn Carey, attended by my ladies, gave birth to a daughter. The child was christened Catharine, in my honor. I had fallen so low in the esteem of my own husband. I loved Henry, but we would have no more children. We no longer shared a bed.

Then next year, Mary Carey became pregnant again. She still slept with my husband while married to William. I tried my best to forgive, but I too was human. All I could do was hold my tongue and pray.

When Mary was once again large with child, I noticed Henry's eye wandered from her at last. But it didn't turn back to me. I was thirty-nine. I had given him my love, my loyalty, and my all, but he seemed to think time stood still for him, while others aged. When his wandering eye alit, its subject was Anne Boleyn, Mary's younger sister, who had amused us with her failed betrothal to young Henry Percy. My Henry did not seem concerned that he grew older and older than his mistresses. He was almost twice Anne's age.

Anne seemed so different from her sister. Mary was quiet and compliant. Anne was quick, intelligent, and energetic. I wondered how Anne would react to this older man, who so recently had been her own sister's lover, once she realized his intentions. As I watched, I saw she was coy and went out of her way to avoid him. I thanked God she was more virtuous than her sister and prayed she would successfully escape his advances.

Anna von Kleve
22 September 1515—1526

My early childhood taught me that others, who professed to be Christians, were not kind to girls who were not pretty. I was fortunate to belong to a ruling family, since I was not pretty. My father was John III, and my mother was Maria, Duchess of Jülich-Berg. My parents had together the three duchies of Berg, Jülich, and Kleve united. Jülich was in the valley of the River Ruhr. Through the northern part, the Duchy of Kleve was fortunate the River Rhein to have flowing. The Rheinland was on the continent most fertile. The Rhine flowed from Kleve into the Netherlands.

    Our dear father stood against Roman Emperor Charles and sided with all other protestant nations. Papa was also for his love of peace well-known.

    I was Anna von Jülich-Kleve-Berg on 22 September 1515 near Düsseldorf born. My elder sister Sybille and I were not close. She was very pretty and petite. I was bigger boned and clumsy. Sybille was fair and graceful, but I had swarthy skin and dark hair. And as I grew up, hair grew on my chest and abdomen. My arms and legs were also quite hairy, and though my dresses covered my abnormality, I was of being very different conscious. I was fortunate protestant to be raised, because our manner of dress was quite modest. The square necklines of our gowns came up to the collar bone, unlike the stories I heard of less modest Catholic countries—especially France. The large, starched headdresses we wore over our hair were similar to the nearby Dutch and formed a curl just above the shoulders.

My sister Sybille never seemed to have time for me, except for my awkwardness or lack of natural beauty to criticize. I resented her partly for her grace, charm, and nice looks, but mostly for her treatment of me. My younger brother, William, was the year after me born. Amelia, our younger sister, came after William. None of them had my excess body hair, big bones, or ugly face. I felt alone.

Sybille, William, Amelia, and I grew up in Schloss Burg, which was on high ground above the River Wupper. The countryside was pretty, and I liked the river to watch. The land below our castle was green and with flowers in spring and summer decorated. I especially liked the little sky-blue wildflowers. Sybille laughed at me. "They're just weeds," she would say. "They're called cornflowers because they grow as weeds in the corn fields. They're not truly beautiful, proper flowers, but then maybe you like them because you're not truly beautiful either." She was correct. I was a weed in the field of my family. But I loved the little cornflowers all the more for their lowly status as a weed.

As my parents' only son, William would the heir to our parents' Duchy of Kleve become. As daughters, Sybille, Amelia, and I would by our parents be matched to wed. Even though we were older, Sybille and I were our younger brother to serve. We had chores, while William had studies. He was not to be disobeyed.

Amelia did not care. She was pretty like Sybille, and both of them had reason to anticipate the best of matches for their marriages. I could only for kindness hope. Only with Papa at home I found it.

Sybille wed John Frederick, Elector of Saxony and head of the Protestant Confederation of Germany in 1526. Papa escorted her to her new home. There she was wed. Upon his return we would the details of the ceremony learn. The reformed teaching of the Reverend Martin Luther had in Germany over taken, and John Frederick was named the champion of the Reformation. Sybille was in her match with John very fortunate. I was for her happy and for myself foolishly happy. Now I would the elder daughter at home be. Once Sybille left for her new life in Saxony, I discovered she had in many ways from our strict mother protected me. Mama was still Roman Catholic.

Before my sister married, Mama beat me only occasionally. After Sybille left, Mama beat me every day. I was eleven years old when Sybille left.

Amelia was also cruel. She twisted our private conversations into impudence by me when she to William tattled, who then went to Mama and my chastisement demanded. Amelia teased me. She called me the ugly duckling. I soon learned my tongue and my temper to hold.

I sought solitude and said little—except to dear Papa. If not for him, I would no friend in the world have had. He consoled me, "You may be called ugly by some, but you have a beautiful soul, kind eyes, and a lovely smile. I have no doubt you will grow up to be a lovely lady." I adored my Papa.

Anne Boleyn
1525—1526

My Grandfather died in 1524. His title, Duke of
Norfolk, passed to my uncle. He was a very
handsome man with a long face and limbs like my
own, but he struck fear into the hearts of our
womenfolk. He was very stern. I was told that
beneath his fine looks lay a heart of stone.

In 1525 at Richmond Palace, my uncle
pulled me aside from my duties into a secluded
corner. "You've caught the eye of King Henry. His
Majesty is looking for a replacement for your sister,
Mary, as his mistress."

"Uncle, I will not be the king's whore. You
should find me a suitable husband above my own
status."

"Such insolence and ingratitude," he
growled. "Your impudence may well jeopardize
your father's position in the king's service."

"I beg your pardon, Uncle, but I will not be
a whore like my sister."

"Mind your place, woman." He stormed off.

The duke was, of course, much closer to
King Henry than Father, and as such, was quite
powerful. He was the head of our extended family.
What the duke wanted, the duke always got, but he
would not make me a whore. The duke controlled
his relations, but I was more stubborn. Maybe he
and I were a lot alike. There was a family
resemblance between us in more ways than one. I
had his long face, long neck, and wide mouth. Of
course, my eyes were much prettier, and I was
spared his strong chin. His chin helped him express
his anger and intimidate when he wished. But I
would have my way by being clever.

Mother had warned me Uncle could be cruel. I didn't share that trait either. But he should have changed the mind of the Earl of Northumberland so Henry Percy and I could wed. Throwing his flesh and blood nieces at the King of England as whores was unacceptable.

After my conversation with Uncle, I noticed the king watching me, and so I flirted with him as I so aptly learned to do in France. By the next year, he openly pursued me. I hid from him as much as possible, often in Queen Catharine's presence. Even this bold and wayward king dared not court me in the presence of his own wife.

I curtseyed low before Queen Catharine. She looked up from her embroidery and nodded in acknowledgement. "Yes, my child?"

"Forgive me, madam, but I fear the king might trap me as he did my sister."

She answered sweetly, "You may hide with me any time, dear child. You are safe with me, and I shall pray for your continued safety."

"Thank you, madam. I am most grateful for your kindness." At least I had her on my side.

For a time I was safe from him. I even enjoyed our game of flirting and hide-and-seek. I saw the other ladies envied me. I also saw the king's behavior troubled Queen Catharine. She discretely assisted me in hiding from him.

Then, as I prepared for bed one night, a note appeared under the door with my name on it. It was written in the king's own hand and invited me to his rooms. I did not go. I tucked the king's note under my pillow and went to sleep in my own bed. To refuse one's king was a dangerous thing. I knew Uncle would be furious, and I would have to avoid him as well.

The next day, King Henry approached me directly. I found no escape. He had such a fine physique. He really was difficult to resist, but I told him, "Sir, I will not be your mistress like my sister. I am not a whore. I am a good Christian lady, and I will only be bedded by my husband. I would be married to my good Henry Percy, but his father, the Earl of Northumberland, would not allow it. Perhaps you would intercede with the earl on our behalf?"

"I will have you. Whatever it takes, I will have you. I'm most pleased the Earl of Northumberland refused your marriage."

I had hoped for a different response. "No man will have me without the benefit of marriage, sir." I curtseyed and took my leave of him.

I knew I was in danger, so I returned to Hever. Mother greeted me. "The duke is extremely displeased with you, Anne. You must not presume to tell men what to do. A lady must be very discreet in how she guides a man. Under no circumstances should you be so bold as to simply say 'no' to the duke or the king."

I nodded in obedience, and yet, what she warned me not to do was exactly what I had already done, otherwise I'd be ruined. I was obviously the one in favor now instead of Mary. I was being pursued, and the terms of my surrender were mine to dictate. My mother wasn't as clever as I. She would have me give in like Mary and destroy my chance of a decent match. She never appreciated my cleverness, nor could she appreciate that the king had made a fool of himself over me.

While at Hever, I reassessed my situation. Of course the king sent for me, but my service at court was to the queen. If Queen Catharine sent for me, I would return. Otherwise, I would go when I was ready. I thought much about Queen Catharine. Her marriage with the king hadn't been a true marriage for some years. She had given birth to six children, but only Princess Mary survived. The ladies at court were well aware the queen's childbearing years had ended. With Catharine, Henry could have no son. He needed a male heir for his throne, but siring bastards wouldn't give him an heir. What would become of England if the king died without an heir? No one wanted another civil war.

I realized the opportunity before me. The marriage of the king and queen was over for all real purposes. The king was pursuing me. I had already told him I wouldn't give myself to any man unless I was his wife. The king had married his late brother's wife by way of papal dispensation. Surely, as King of England he could find a way to have his marriage to Queen Catharine annulled. Then he would be free to marry me. I was capable of bearing children. I was his obsession. I, Lady Anne Boleyn, could become Henry's wife and Queen of England.

I returned to court at once. I didn't go directly to the king, of course. Once he discovered I'd returned, he was quick to find me.

"Sir, I find it difficult to resist such a handsome man as yourself," I greeted him, "but I will do just that until you make me your wife."

"Lady Anne, you know very well I'm married to the queen, whom you serve."

"But she was first your brother's wife, was she not? The papal dispensation was given on the presumption of truthful testimony."

His look of shock quickly transformed into one of hope. "Could this be why God has withheld a legitimate son from me all these years? Could Catharine have lied to gain my hand in marriage, and now God has punished us for this sin?"

"I would not know, my lord," I answered meekly, my eyes lowered. "How long was she married to your brother?"

"Months. They were married for months."

I could see the light dawn on his handsome face. He kissed me impulsively out of joy. I allowed it briefly, but then gently pushed him away. "Sir, I am not your wife."

"Not yet," he said. "Not yet. Please excuse me, Lady Anne. I must attend to affairs of state."

I curtseyed as he hurried off. I knew I had found a husband of a suitable position. He was eighteen years my senior, old enough to be my father, but the Duke of Norfolk could be damned. He could not deny the king, and I would be Queen of England.

Anna von Kleve
1527

I was twelve years old when Papa at home after a
journey arrived. I was in the courtyard when he rode
up on his fine, black horse. I ran to him to greet.
After returning my smile, hug, and kisses, he
delighted me with good news. "Anna, my child, you
are informally betrothed to François, the son of the
Duke of Lorraine."

"Oh, Papa, what a wonderful surprise!"

"François is only ten years old," he
explained, "so this is just a simple agreement
between parents, but someday you will be the
Duchess of Lorraine. I must inform your mother."
He turned and went into the castle.

Someday I would be married and far away
from my mother, William, and Amelia. Once Papa
told the rest of the family, Amelia taunted me less.
She even pouted. I never dreamed anyone of me to
be jealous. I enjoyed it very much.

Sybille had from our home only a year been
gone, but that year had been horrible. In spite of my
betrothal, terrible William still manipulated Mama
for his amusement and my great pain. He watched
her with a switch punish me. I was humiliated. I
feared my kind Papa to tell. He would on my behalf
have intervened, but my situation would only worse
become, because he traveled frequently for his
duties. I would alone with William and Mama be
left. I stayed close to Papa for protection when he at
home stayed.

But I now had a future life as the Duchess of
Lorraine to anticipate. My day of deliverance would
arrive. Someday I would free become. Someday I
would far away be. My blessed Papa had to me the

gift of hope given.

Jane Seymour
1521—1528

In 1527, I was on my way to serve our blessed
Queen Catharine at court. I felt well-prepared for
this great honor. I was nineteen years old.

My father expressed his pleasure with me
before I left. He told me in front of my mother and
sister, Elizabeth, "I am confident you will serve the
court well and bring honor to our family."

My mother added, "You know how to
behave properly. You're an obedient daughter and
will be an obedient attendant to Queen Catherine.
We know you will never engage in gossip or
flirtation or other temptations that may be a lady's
downfall. You know God is watching and sees and
hears everything. As long as you remember this,
you will not only serve the Queen, but a proper
husband will be found for you when the time is
right."

I reminded myself that pride was a sin, so I
lowered my eyes in respect as I curtseyed to my
parents, smiling slightly. I was delighted they were
so pleased with me. I knew that with such a good
Queen as Catharine, I would be in the best of
company at court.

Things were not as I had expected when I
arrived at Greenwich. The tapestries, tableware, and
ladies' gowns were quite grand and made my
humble family's home seem modest. But after
growing up in such a loving home, I was shocked
by the behavior of others. I held my tongue and did
my best to keep my demeanor pleasant. My parents
certainly told me true about the gossip and
flirtation, but I realized my life at home was too
sheltered to prepare me. I tried my best not to listen

to the gossip about the king by the queen's ladies, but I must confess, it was interesting and exciting. Although I kept my silence, I listened eagerly to the wagging tongues all around me.

I learned King Henry already had a bastard son, Henry Fitzroy, by Bessie Blount, who was still one of Queen Catharine's ladies. Not only had the affair lasted for years, but the King had openly acknowledged the child as his own. When he'd finished with Bess, he'd taken Lady Mary Boleyn Carey, a married woman, to his bed many times. Mary and her younger sister, Anne, who was also one of the queen's ladies, had the same great-grandmother as I, Elizabeth Cheney. The affair with Mrs. Carey had lasted throughout her first pregnancy and didn't end until she was well into her second. Nothing prepared me for any of this.

Once the king was done with Mary, he directed his advances toward Mary's younger sister, Anne. I heard Anne led him on with her flirtations and played hard-to-get. She seemed to think herself a clever girl, but she had been corrupted by prior service in the French court. And yet when the king summoned Lady Anne to his bed, to her credit, she did not go.

Throughout all of this, good Queen Catharine conducted herself as a proper queen and daughter of the church. She never spoke ill of her husband. She endured her husband's shameful behavior with proper Christian patience and faith. She was a most dignified example to us all. I was pleased to work in her service and grateful for my position. I hoped in some small way I might make her days a little brighter—or at least less painful.

During my second year at court, an epidemic broke out in London. It was the dreaded sweating sickness. The king left London for his own safety, which of course, was best for England. But I noticed he did not take his wife or child, Princess Mary, with him. Lady Anne Boleyn left court and returned to her family's home in Kent, but when word was received she'd been taken ill, word also came that King Henry sent his own personal physician to tend to her. The physician wasn't kept at the side of the king, where the good doctor's place should have been, nor was he sent to see to the queen or princess. It was now obvious even to me that Lady Anne was something very special to King Henry. And yet, she was not his wife and had refused to go to his bed. I began to fear for our good Queen Catharine, that she might be trampled as violets in the field so often were. I offered my daily prayers for her safety and that of Princess Mary, for if the king himself was not concerned with them, who would protect them other than God?

Anne Boleyn
1527—1530

King Henry was as obsessed with annulling his marriage to Queen Catharine as he was with taking me to his bed. As he worked to find a solution to his annulment problem, I flirted flamboyantly with him everywhere—even in front of his wife. She was so stubborn. She refused to acknowledge she couldn't give the king the son he needed and just step aside.

"I asked her to go quietly to a nunnery, but she would not," Henry complained to me.

I understood she wanted to keep her title and position at court, but she was old now. In December 1525, before Christmas, she turned forty. She no longer slept with the king, so in that regard, she already lived as a nun. If she only went quietly, I would persuade Henry to allow her ladies to wait on her and ensure her life was comfortable. She was so devout in her prayers and attendance at mass, she would feel at home in a convent. Surely she realized the king simply couldn't afford to wait for her to die before taking another wife.

In 1528, the sweating sickness broke out with great severity all over London. The mortality rate was alarming. I'd never seen such death before, but Henry remembered it from when he was a child. "This disease took the life of my brother Arthur, Catharine's first husband, and it almost took Catharine as well. I cannot afford to die and leave the country without a male heir. I must leave London for England's safety."

I followed his example and went home to Hever, but I took sick anyway. I was too weak to be aware of much. Mother sent word to King Henry of my illness, and Henry sent his own physician to

Hever to care for me. Once I recovered, I was told Mary's husband, William Carey, had died from the sickness. Mary, who was still at court in Catharine's service, was now a widow with two children.

Henry secretly sent William Knight to Pope Clement VII to seek his annulment. Cardinal Thomas Wolsey, the king's secretary, wasn't told of this, because the Cardinal was close to Catharine. He would likely object. Once Henry told me of William Knight's mission, I no longer thought of Catharine as queen. Soon her title would be mine.

I comforted Henry, "You do God's will. You acknowledge the mistake of your first marriage. You cannot be held accountable for any falsehood that brought about the papal dispensation. Surely, once you've corrected the error, God will show his pleasure with you by giving us a son."

Pope Clement did not agree. He was a prisoner of Catharine's nephew, Emperor Charles V, and so he wasn't free to follow the obvious course of action. The king then put the matter into Wolsey's hands. As expected, the Cardinal stalled and even plotted with Catharine. The old man was foolish to communicate secretly with the pope, and Henry found out. I'd never seen him so angry.

Wolsey was arrested. He had dared to plot to have me driven into exile. Catharine should have understood when Wolsey was arrested, it was time for her to go quietly, but she didn't. Wolsey, by this time, was old and ill. His illness spared him public execution. He died in his bed in 1530.

Catherine of Aragón
1526—1531

Mary Boleyn Carey gave birth at court to a son 4 March 1526. She named him Henry. My Henry could not openly claim the child as his own, as he had done with Henry Fitzroy, Bessie Blount's son, because Mary was already married for some time. This didn't lessen my grief, which was no fault of the child's.

Henry had nothing more to do with Mrs. Carey after her son was born. The legal father was William Carey, not Henry. Then in 1528, William Carey died of the same sweating sickness that had taken my first husband. Of course, I kept poor Mary at court with her son and daughter. Her father was in the king's service, and Sir Thomas Boleyn could provide for his family, but she was still, even after all that happened, one of my ladies. I promised her, "Lady Mary, I will see that you and your children are well cared for."

Henry came to my private rooms one morning. He was clearly agitated, and my ladies quickly left when I nodded. "What troubles you, sir, this fine morning?"

"God has cursed our marriage because you were first married to my brother."

"But sir, my marriage to Arthur was never consummated. Had it been, I could not have married you. You know this."

"But did you lie just to win my hand and crown?"

"May God forgive you. I, a true princess of Spain and the crowned Queen of England, have never lied to you. You have my word." He promptly left the room.

Henry began to speak openly with others of his crazy idea. He shamed me and said publicly I had not been a virgin when I married him, which he knew to be a lie. He said this was why we had no son. I was humiliated. I kept to my rooms. I prayed and spoke to my confessor and Cardinal Wolsey. I assured them the papal dispensation for our marriage was based on true testimonials, including my own. But Henry was convinced otherwise. After all I had done to legitimize the Tudor crown, after all I had worked and sacrificed for our successful marriage and the success of our country, and after having lost one of our children from leading his army to defeat Scotland, he dared to blame me.

He came again to visit me in my chambers. After my ladies were dismissed, and we stood face to face alone, he asked, "Will you admit lying so we can annul this empty and wrongful marriage? Then I would be free to marry Lady Anne Boleyn, who can bear me a son. England needs an heir. Quietly step aside and enter a nunnery."

I answered him defiantly but honestly, "God never called me to a convent. I am your true and legitimate wife." My answer did not please him.

His insanity was that young Anne had refused him. He never learned to accept rejection. I knew this, but I never dreamed he would be so arrogant as to mock the sacred sacrament of marriage—the very marriage that legitimized his own crown in the eyes of European royalty. Anne was a mere servant.

At first, I thought young Anne was loyal to me. Henry ordered her to his bed, but she wouldn't go. She even voluntarily returned to her mother in Kent to avoid his advances. But then I realized just how clever Anne was. After over twenty years of marriage, Henry asked Pope Clement VII to annul our marriage on the grounds that the dispensation to marry of Pope Julius II was obtained under false pretenses. Henry didn't think of an annulment on his own, and Anne wasn't loyal to me—she coveted my crown. I prayed with almost every breath I took for Henry to come to his senses. And I prayed I would have the strength to endure his madness. My heart was broken, but I still had a daughter to protect and duties to perform.

Henry sent his request to Pope Clement by William Knight. The king's own secretary, Cardinal Thomas Wolsey, wasn't even told. Cardinal Wolsey knew me, and he knew well I was no liar. He would never submit falsehoods against my honor to the Holy Father. When William Knight failed, Henry put the matter into the hands of Thomas Wolsey. Wolsey stalled and intentionally failed on my behalf. I prayed for Our Lord to protect good Wolsey from Henry's temper. My dear Wolsey plotted instead to have Anne Boleyn forced into exile, while he communicated secretly with Pope Clement. When the plot was discovered, Henry ordered Wolsey's arrest. Wolsey, may God keep and protect him, was found to be terminally ill. Even Henry wouldn't execute an already dying man. The good cardinal returned to Our Lord in 1530.

Pope Clement VII sent word to Henry; he forbade Henry to marry again before a decision was given by Rome. I was sure this reprieve would save me and our daughter, but instead, Henry banished us from court in 1531. He gave my chambers to Anne Boleyn. I, the Queen of England, was banished from my own court. Two of my elder ladies remained loyal and left the palace with me in my disgrace. Princess Mary also accompanied me. Henry provided us with shelter in a much lesser house.

Anne Boleyn
1531—August 1532

In 1531, Henry finally sent Catharine away from court, since she wouldn't go willingly. At long last, I was given her rooms, the ladies-in-waiting served me, and I was publicly escorted by the King of England throughout Greenwich Palace. Henry showed his deep affection to me in front of all. He continued to try to lure me to his bed, but I would not go.

"Not until we are married and I am Queen of England," I told him. "There must be no question of the legitimacy of our children." Of course, he agreed.

I was amazed and troubled that the common people didn't understand the situation. Catharine was foreign born, while I was a native English woman, but their support remained with Catharine. I thought they would be loyal to their handsome king and celebrate his betrothal to a fertile, future queen, who could restore the promise of peace and stability. But they were not quick to grasp this necessity. It seemed to me an opportunity to introduce reform that would benefit the country. "The commoners' lack of understanding of royal affairs," I told Henry, "merely demonstrates a need for more widespread education."

"I have far too many matters of great importance with which to concern myself than educating peasants."

One evening that autumn, I was dining in a manor house on River Thames. The hall was filled with tables laden with food. There were many guests, but I was the guest of honor. I enjoyed myself and my company, but suddenly a crowd of openly belligerent women forced their way into the house, and I was almost seized. Without learning their true intentions, I ran for my life and barely escaped by boat.

Back in my private chambers at Greenwich, Henry blamed Rome for the public outcry. "It is clearly wrong for a foreign head of state, such as the Pope, to be held in greater esteem in England that the King of England himself."

"No one dares disagree with you, sir." I didn't know who was angrier—Henry or the public.

"I must break the power of the Roman Church in England," he vowed as he continued his rant and paced back and forth in front of me.

Sir Thomas More was still the Chancellor of England, even though he had been a friend of Catharine's for many years. He was loyal to Catharine and Pope Clement, and he had made it clear he was no friend of mine. In 1532, Sir Thomas Cromwell brought a number of acts before Parliament to recognize the king's supremacy over the Roman Church. Of course these acts were passed, as the king had made his will known. Once these acts became law, Thomas More resigned as chancellor. He doomed himself with his public disloyalty to the king. More's departure from court left Sir Thomas Cromwell as Henry's primary advisor.

Meanwhile, with Catharine gone from court, I was free to act openly as Henry's consort. I granted petitions, received diplomats, and presided over some foreign policy matters—especially where France was concerned. I had an excellent rapport with Baron d'Entrammes, the French ambassador to England, and I worked with him to secure a much needed alliance with France. It was the least I could do to help the king, but I still would not bed him until we were married. I was no fool.

Katherine Howard
1521—1532

I was a very pretty child. My Grandfather was the second Duke of Norfolk, but my family's power did me little good. I was well housed, but I didn't have the pretty dresses one would expect of my status. I was born in 1521 to Lord Edmund Howard. One would expect a lady in my position to have jewels and pretty things, but I was neglected.

When I was ten years old, my first cousin, Lady Anne Boleyn, had the King of England send his own wife away from court. Anne was given the queen's rooms and many lavish gifts. Anne's mother, Elizabeth Howard, was my aunt. Anne was unusual, because she had become a woman with power. Of course, she didn't lack for jewels and proper gowns. She found my father a job in Calais, across the English Channel. As a result of Anne's generosity, when my parents moved to Calais, I was sent to live with my step-grandmother, Agnes Tilney, the Dowager Duchess of Norfolk, at Lambeth. And the Dowager Duchess was not generous. All I wanted was a jeweled necklace and pretty dresses.

Lambeth, on River Thames, was a very large household. The Dowager Duchess took little notice of me, which was fine, as she was a crabby old lady. Many other aristocratic children with poor relatives lived there as well, so I was never alone. I slept in a big room with all the other girls. We had fun together, but none was as pretty as I.

There were many servants in the household. My step-grandmother was busy—she managed her own household and affairs. She had no time for those of us sent to live with her. I was happy with my companions, but I thought it shameful to belong to such a powerful family and have nothing to show for it. I was of no consequence to anyone, but I was also free from observation. I didn't have pretty dresses or jewelry, but at least I was free to do as I pleased. My fellow boarders and I were spared the discipline many of our station experienced. No one should be mean to their own children, and a beautiful child should never be punished.

The Dowager Duchess was often away at court, so she couldn't possibly know what went on at Lambeth among her wards. I didn't know her very well. She was perpetually ill-tempered. When she spoke to me, she always complained about something—my manners, something I said, or the way I said it, or to whom I said it. I never pleased her.

I didn't mind there was so little concern at Lambeth with education. I was happy to spend my time with the other young ladies. We laughed a great deal. I could already read and write a bit. Surely that was enough. My goal was to catch the eye of a handsome young man or even get a position at court. The latter was the sort of thing always taken care of by someone else. I was the first cousin of Anne Boleyn, so I expected to be called to court to serve her. I made sure my lady companions at Lambeth taught me the dances they knew, and we practiced diligently. Dance, in my opinion, was the most important part of a lady's education.

I practiced my dances, and I practiced all the flirtatious gestures I learned from my companions. Even at mass, I practiced in my mind. I was much too pretty to be a nun, so there was no need to study prayers or religious matters. Those were best left for clergy. Why would we need the clergy, after all, if we kept up with such things ourselves? The Dowager Duchess had grown sour with age and lost any youthful beauty from all her bother with unnecessary matters. I had no intention of following her example.

On 1 September 1532, King Henry VIII gave my cousin Anne the title of Marquess of Pembroke. I was sure gifts of great expense went with this great honor. I dreamed of being called to the royal court, where there would be many handsome young men to court me and give me lavish tokens of their affection.

Soon after, King Henry also granted Anne's father, Thomas Boleyn, the title of Earl of Wiltshire. The king obviously favored my cousin's family. I had no idea what duties the king expected from my uncle or cousin in return for their titles, but I knew that with titles came the king's generosity and gifts. The new marquess and duke bore a family resemblance to each other, which I did not share. The duke was a tall, handsome man, but the new marquess, though she shared the duke's dark hair and long limbs, was neither as pretty as me nor as fair.

In preparation for my anticipated court duty, I practiced how I walked, danced, and presented myself to attract the most attention, and also my many flirtatious gestures and looks. I was blessed with natural beauty. Surely I should strive to draw attention to my one God-given gift.

Catharine of Aragón
1532—1533

By my forty-sixth birthday, my own husband, whom I had loved, defended, and prayed for, had taken away my purpose in life. He broke my heart, robbed me of my position and duties, and banished me from our court. I fasted. I struggled to maintain my composure under the strain of such humiliation. He could as easily have murdered me, but I was still burdened with the pain of life. My residence was no longer a proper palace, but a mere house—small, poorly furnished, dark, and poorly ventilated by comparison—though my physical surroundings were the least of my heartaches. I was afraid to reach out to my many friends for fear of putting them in danger, but I was grateful for the companionship of my dear daughter.

When the Archbishop of Canterbury, William Warham, died, Henry appointed the Boleyn family's chaplain, Thomas Cranmer, to the position. Henry defied Pope Clement, the Church of Rome, and the holy sacrament of matrimony by declaring himself supreme over all religious matters as well as matters of law. Against all standards by which we had been taught, my husband declared our lawful marriage annulled in 1533. In spite of everything, until that time, I was prepared to take him back if he only repented and called me wife. But now I understood he had no love left for me.

I lost my will to live. Except for my beloved Mary, I no longer had any duties. I wrote to my family in Spain, "My tribulations are great, and my life is disturbed by the plans daily invented to further the king's wicked intention. The surprises he gives me through certain persons of his council are so mortal. My treatment is enough to shorten ten lives, much more mine."

John Fisher became my most trusted counselor. He appeared in legates' court on my behalf, and he said he was prepared to die on behalf of the indissolubility of marriage. Thomas More also publicly supported my cause. Even Henry's own sister, Mary Tudor Brandon, the former Queen of France, sided with me. I knew Henry's temper, and all who took my side were in great peril. Emperor Charles V, Pope Clement VII, and protestant reformers Martin Luther and William Tyndale were united in their condemnation of Henry—all to no avail.

King Henry and Lady Anne Boleyn traveled together as king and consort to visit King François in Calais. My humiliation was now international. I wondered on what terms King François received them. And then they returned together to England.

On 23 May 1533 Thomas Cranmer declared my marriage to Henry illegal. On 28 May he declared the marriage of Henry and Anne, which allegedly had taken place in January in secret while he was legally married to me, to be valid. How did a mere Archbishop of the Church have the authority to rule against the Pope in Rome? Henry was repeating the very illegitimacy issue of his ancestors and defying his own right to his own crown. He had publicly admitted bigamy. The world I had known dissolved around me. Henry allowed me, the rightfully crowned Queen of England, with ancestry to the English throne stronger than his own, to use only the title of Dowager Princess of Wales. My servants continued to address me as queen, of course, and no one doubted Mary was a true princess. I taught her to behave with dignity and

Christian charity.

Anne Boleyn
September 1532 – 1533

On 1 September 1532, King Henry granted me the title Marquess of Pembroke. My new title gave me more credibility in matters of state. After all my childish attempts at love, I had found the best match possible for a husband. I was now in a position to help reform English society for the betterment of the people.

Henry was also generous with Father and named him Earl of Wiltshire. I was proud to have brought such favor and prosperity to my family. I was now more powerful than even Uncle, the Duke of Norfolk, who would have made me a whore like my sister. The family now looked to me for favors and guidance.

Henry took me with him to Calais that winter, where we met the Baron Ambassador and the King of France. The last time I had been with the French royal court, I was a mere servant. It was grand to return to French soil as consort of the King of England, but in spite of agreeing to support us as rulers of England, the King of France would not defy the Pope. He would have no religious reformation in France.

We left Calais disappointed and sailed to Dover. Once we were back on English soil, Henry and I were secretly married. My charms had worn down the King's manly resistance, and I gave myself to him in bed as soon as we were wed. He was still the most handsome man in Europe, and with his experience, fine looks, and regal bearing came grace in love-making, which I very much enjoyed.

We had not been married long, when much to my delight, I became pregnant. Henry wanted no doubt about the child's legitimacy, and we married again privately 25 January 1533 in London. But he could not announce the marriage, because the public still thought him wed to Catharine. His ministers, temporarily sworn to secrecy, were witnesses to our marriage. When eventually my pregnancy became obvious, the courtiers would know I carried the king's heir.

On 23 May 1533, Archbishop Thomas Cranmer, my confessor who replaced Wolsey, publicly declared King Henry's marriage to Catharine illegal and annulled. Five days later he declared King Henry's marriage to me valid and legal. Shortly after the Archbishop's declaration, Pope Clement excommunicated both my husband and Archbishop Cranmer. This removed all ties with Rome and left Henry in charge of the Church of England.

On the last day of May, I rode through the streets of London in a litter of white cloth of gold resting on two regal horses clothed to the ground in white damask. I was obviously with child, and all the people of London could see that the king was expecting his long awaited heir. As I rode in my litter, the barons of the Cinque Ports held a canopy of cloth of gold over my head, because our baby, England's future ruler, required it. I wore a white gown with a coronet of gold on my head. I let my long, dark hair flow freely down beneath my crown. I wore a white gown to accent my beauty. I had no bouquet of lilies, but my coat of arms displayed the Lion of England, my husband, and the fleur de lis.

I was surprised when the people who greeted me in the streets were less than enthusiastic.

I expected them to cheer. They'd been liberated from bondage to Rome. Change was in the air, it was a beautiful day, and they now had a queen who would champion reforms on their behalf. But they did not cheer.

In spite of the small crowd's lackluster greeting, I was crowned Queen of England the next day at Westminster Abbey. I was the first Queen of England to be crowned with St Edward's crown. Before my coronation, it had only been used to crown a reigning monarch, but I carried the next King of England. The coronation was followed by a lavish banquet.

I settled myself at Greenwich Palace, which was Henry's favorite, and slipped into a quiet routine. The first week of September, I went into labor. I had never experienced pain like the pain of childbirth. I was grateful Henry was not there to see me suffer and scream. I was even more grateful he was not there that afternoon when I delivered a daughter instead of a son. I knew he would be angry with me. We were so sure we would have a son. All his hopes rested on this certainty, now dashed. I could do nothing. I had risen from a servant in a foreign court to the Queen of England; I had brokered an alliance with France and given the king a way to break free from Rome, and yet I was powerless, because I had given birth to a healthy baby girl. I named her Elizabeth after my mother. Princess Elizabeth was born 7 September. She looked just like her father—fair and beautiful. I promised Henry our next child would be a son and reminded him of how quickly he had impregnated me. He sent our little Princess Elizabeth to Hatfield House accompanied by her own large staff of servants, because he thought the country air was healthier. I was reassured, because Henry was looking out for our happy little family. I visited Elizabeth as often as I could. Her servants took excellent care of her, but I loved my baby and wanted to be with her.

Jane Seymour
1531—1533

King Henry banished good Queen Catharine and
Princess Mary from court in 1531. Only a few of
the queen's favorite ladies were sent with her. The
queen's rooms were then given to Lady Anne
Boleyn, who had become the object of King
Henry's affection. With Queen Catharine gone,
Anne acted in the queen's place. The rest of us
ladies were required to attend Anne. Except for this
strangeness, court life continued as usual. It was not
my place to question the will of a king, but I missed
Catharine and the Princess.

      When King Henry sailed to Calais at the end
of 1532 to meet with King François of France, Lady
Anne traveled with him as his consort. They
returned by way of Dover in January for a brief
stop, and then came back to Greenwich Palace.
Rumors spread quickly through the court of a secret
wedding ceremony at the end of January, even
though the king was already married to Queen
Catharine. A Christian king could not have two
wives at once. No one dared speak against the king,
but he was clearly wrong.

      Then the Archbishop of Canterbury died,
and Thomas Cranmer, Anne Boleyn's confessor,
took his place. Archbishop Cranmer was a tall man
with an unusually wide mouth. In May, Archbishop
Cranmer annulled the marriage of King Henry to
the great Queen Catharine after so many years. My
heart wept inside for our gracious queen and
Princess Mary. They had indeed been trampled like
violets underfoot, and only God could help them. I
wondered where they were and in what
circumstances, but I dared not ask. Then the

Archbishop declared the marriage of King Henry to Lady Anne valid, even though it took place before his first marriage was annulled. For this, Pope Clement rightly excommunicated both the king and the archbishop, but not Lady Anne.

The first day of June saw the coronation of Queen Anne. She was noticeably with child. She rode through the streets the day before her with her hair hanging loose from under a gold tiara without the benefit of a proper headdress or veil. This immodesty did not merit her popularity with the good people of London. Anne's manners were more French than English. The people's loyalty was clearly with Queen Catharine, but then the king proclaimed that Catharine's only legal title was Dowager Princess of Wales. Only Anne was Queen of England, and so I served Queen Anne at court, even though I had been called to serve Queen Catharine. These were such confusing times.

On 7 September 1533 at Greenwich Palace, Queen Anne gave birth to a healthy daughter, whom she named Elizabeth. It was not the male heir King Henry desired, but it was a healthy child. She bore a strong resemblance to her father, which helped to win him over. He provided the babe with her own court in addition to the more than sixty ladies already serving Anne. Anne had kept the ladies at court who served Catharine and then added to them from her own relations. I would never dare say it aloud, but it seemed to me even a king could not have limitless wealth. Even I could see Queen Anne knew little of managing a household. I missed the good sense of the now Dowager Princess of Wales.

Katherine Howard
1533—1534

At Lambeth in May 1533, my friends and I were gossiping in the courtyard when a courier arrived with news. Archbishop Thomas Cranmer had declared the king's first marriage to the Spanish Queen Catharine null and void. He also declared the king's marriage to my cousin valid. We were so excited. Anne had married Henry, and now she was carrying his child. She once served in the French court and favored French fashions, which were much less modest than Spanish and English. The French style would allow me to show off more of my God-given assets. If only I had money for cloth to make new dresses, but I didn't. All I could do was pull down on the shoulders and bodice of my gown to show a little more of my lovely fair skin and push back my headdress to show more of my beautiful fair hair.

We talked of who would be called to court. "Older and more experienced ladies will be called before you, Kate," one of my older friends said.

"But I'm the queen's first cousin. I'll just have to practice more," I said, and everyone giggled.

The Dowager Duchess was not impressed. She called me aside. "Why is your dress slipping down like that? Have you forgotten how to wear your headdress properly? Wherever did you learn to walk and curtsey like that? You are much in need of improvement."

I ignored her ignorance of French fashion, but the rest I understood clearly. "I will work very hard to improve," I assured her. I was bound to be called to court sooner or later.

In September, Anne gave birth to a baby girl. I was delighted. The royal princess was named Elizabeth, after Anne's mother, my aunt. But my friends were not excited about Princess Elizabeth. As we prepared for bed, one told me, "King Henry needs a son for his heir."

Of course, I didn't pretend to understand these matters. I shrugged. "Surely a beautiful princess is exciting enough?"

"Oh, no," another lady said. "The former Queen Catharine had the beautiful Princess Mary, and now they're not even allowed at court."

"But a live, royal child in my own family is cause enough for celebration," I protested. "Everyone knows men desire women above all else. The king is a man, after all. How could he not be thrilled with a beautiful princess?"

The following March, the priest announced during mass, "Pope Clement has condemned the royal marriage of King Henry VIII and Anne Boleyn. The Pope has excommunicated our King."

As if what the Pope thought mattered to anyone, but they fussed about it as if they cared. All I wanted was for others to notice my beauty, and that would be easier with a few pretty dresses and a jeweled necklace.

Anne Boleyn
1534—1535

I had over sixty ladies in my service, wore the finest clothes and jewels, and was the most powerful woman in Europe. My confessor, Thomas Cranmer, was now Archbishop of Canterbury. I was twenty-six years old and in the prime of my life.

Archbishop Cranmer was a large man and a great comfort to me. I was pleased to have someone I trusted in such a powerful position. He towered over me in his kindly manner with his large smile. Physically he was strong, not what I considered handsome, but his demeanor was well-suited for a priest and confessor. He was humble and patient.

In March 1534, Pope Clement in Rome condemned my marriage and then died later that year. While in bed with my husband, I mused, "Perhaps Clement's death was punishment for denying our lawful marriage?"

Henry chuckled. "Do you think the new pope will understand that? Would you like to write him a letter and suggest it to him?" Then he laughed heartily, and I laughed with him. Of course, the new pope condemned us as well, but it made no difference to us.

Then Henry's courtier, Thomas Culpepper, ran up to us one morning in the corridor as we were leaving the chapel. "Your Majesties," he bowed and then continued, "Lady Mary Boleyn Carey has secretly married Sir William Stafford."

We were shocked. My own sister didn't ask royal permission to marry. Henry and I had wed in secret, but he was the King of England and needed no one's permission. Before King Henry, I dared not marry my love, Henry Percy, without permission.

Henry turned to me, his face red with rage. "How dare she!"

"I am insulted Mary defies us," I agreed with him. "I will see that the entire Boleyn family disowns her."

We banished Mary and William Stafford and my niece and nephew from court. I still had my brother George and sister-in-law Jane with me. George wasn't pleased with the match made for him with Jane, but he was loyal to me. Amid the uproar Mary caused, I discovered I was again pregnant.

Near the end of 1534, Parliament declared my husband to officially be the one true head of the Church of England. I expected celebration, but then the pillaging began. I learned from my ladies that Henry, Cranmer, and Cromwell had all sanctioned the looting of monasteries.

"Oh, yes, madam," Lady Jane added, "the king claims their lands as his own."

But this was common thievery, and if Henry had been anyone other than king, he would have been arrested and hanged. We were royals, not burglars. That evening over a private dinner, I said, "Looting monasteries was not the reform I intended."

"YOU intended? I am king, and you are but a mere woman. Do not meddle in my affairs. You'd do well to mind your place," he warned me.

HIS affairs. Were we not king and queen, husband and wife together acting as one? Had he not granted me authority to rule with him, make alliances, grant petitions, and receive diplomats? Now he was saying my very intelligence, which had attracted him to me in the first place, was a threat to him. Or was I mistaken? Had he simply been drawn to my physical charms? I was perplexed. I had thought my king and confessor to be honorable men. I had envisioned our joint rule liberating the common people.

The next day in chapel, Archbishop Cranmer privately advised me, "Attend to womanly matters and leave matters of state to men."

I dared not argue, but obviously the men didn't share my goal of liberating the common folk—certainly not women. I wondered with some fear what kind of future Henry intended for our precious Elizabeth. I wanted her to be educated and free to make her own decisions—with our permission and guidance, of course.

During the Christmas holidays, I prematurely went into labor. It was just as painful as before, but didn't last long. I gave birth to a stillborn infant. It was taken away, and I never saw the child. I wanted to hold it in my arms at least once. Never before had I cried so, as my ladies tried their best to console me. For this tragedy, I blamed Henry. It was wise of him to dare not visit me afterward. I had no desire to see him. I also blamed Cranmer and Cromwell. I blamed my sister Mary. I was devastated.

One of my ladies kindly reminded me, "You still have Princess Elizabeth, madam." And with that lovely thought, my spirits recovered. But gradually I came to fear Henry might plot with Cranmer and Cromwell to banish me from court as he had done to my predecessor. He knew I did not condone stealing money and property from monks and nuns.

I rested through the winter and had physically recovered by spring. Somehow, perhaps for the sake of our daughter—or more likely for the hope of a son—Henry and I reconciled. We spent the summer together as king and queen on progress, traveling throughout our country and meeting our subjects. We were away when Thomas More and John Fisher, my predecessor's friends and defenders, were executed in London.

  One evening, in private quarters at the home of a nobleman, as we sat across from each other in high-back chairs upholstered in red silk, I commented, "I spend so much money on gowns and jewels."

  "It's important for the English people to see us properly attired," Henry explained. "Yes, my lovely Anne, the court is in need of money, but we must keep up appearances. This is why we decided to make use of the wealth hoarded by clerics bound by vows of poverty."

  "Perhaps some of that money could be used for education and charity," I suggested.

  "I've warned you before not to meddle in my affairs."

  "But, sir, I have been involved in your affairs since before we married. Did I not arrange the alliance with France?"

  "Cromwell is my appointed minister, and he handles all monetary and foreign affairs. You, woman, had best concern yourself with bearing me a son."

  I kept my silence and nodded in submission to him. He was clearly in no mood for debate.

  "I've had enough of our alliance with France," he continued. "Cromwell and I will keep England's alliance with the Holy Roman Emperor Charles V instead."

With my head bowed and my tongue silent, I rose and curtseyed respectfully. He waved his hand dismissing me, and I quietly left the room. I understood his veiled threat completely. Charles was his first wife's nephew. I would not be allowed to advise him again or rule by his side until I bore him a son.

While we were on progress, it was obvious the public was not enthused with their monarchs. Henry's decision to pillage the monasteries had been viewed as unwise at best and dishonorable at worst. The people had no way of knowing my opposition to the theft. But by October, I was again pregnant.

Catharine of Aragón
1534—7 January 1536

In the fall of 1534, Pope Clement VII died. His
successor, Pope Paul III, repeated the condemnation
of Henry's actions, the illegal annulment of our
marriage, and Henry's false and unlawful marriage
to Anne Boleyn. Pope Paul restated to the Christian
world that I was the one true wife of King Henry
VIII and the one true Queen of England.

In May, I was sent to Cambridgeshire to live
without my daughter in the decaying and remote
Kimbolton Castle. Henry forced me to live without
Mary in the southwest corner of a dreary building,
which was in a horrible state of disrepair. But he
could not take away my dignity or faith, and I was
grateful Mary didn't have to share my fate. I
confined myself to one room. This was the room in
which I slept, took an occasional small meal, and
prayed. It was adequately furnished with a small
table, two chairs, and a small bed with no canopy. I
left my room only to attend mass. I wore the hair
shirt of the Order of St. Francis under my gown. I
would eat only a few bites of food a day and fasted
the rest of the time. If Henry would not do penance
for his sins, I would do it for him.

My loyal servants and guards kept me
informed of events beyond my existence. My dear
friends, Sir John Fisher and Sir Thomas More, were
arrested. They refused to swear allegiance to Anne
Boleyn as Queen of England or recognize her
marriage to King Henry. For this, they were
imprisoned in the Tower and then beheaded 22 June
1535. My husband had become a murderer. I prayed
for him and continued my fast. Sir John and Sir
Thomas were good Christian men. Henry had been

raised and educated in our true religion to serve the Church of Rome, but he turned his back on his faith, education, and heritage.

I was permitted occasional visitors, but I was forbidden to see Mary, my only reason for living. I knew Henry wished me dead. But Mary and I wrote to each other. Our letters were carried secretly by our loyal servants. I longed to see her face, hear her voice, and hold her in my arms. My husband offered Mary and me better quarters and each other's company if we would defy God, Pope Paul, and our faith by acknowledging Anne as Queen. But we would not deny our duty to God and country. I prayed for those who served him to have the courage to stand up for the truth.

In late December, during the celebration of Our Lord's birth, I wrote to Henry, "My dear husband and king, I beg you to put your own immortal soul above worldly matters. I ask this for your sake, so one day we may be together with Our Lord in Heaven. I forgive you, my husband, for everything. I pray to God daily on your behalf. I humbly ask you to be a good father to our daughter and to make suitable and favorable marriages for her and my three ladies. I ask this of you in the name of Our Lord and Savior, Jesus Christ." I simply signed my name, "Catharine," without any title.

On 5 January 1536, my dear friend, Maria de Salinas, who had been forbidden to see me, forced her way passed the guards and into Kimbolton Castle. Somehow, perhaps with the help of loyal guards and servants, she found her way to my room. She was such a great comfort to me. I was weak and frail from fasting, and the joy of her presence was more than my heart could handle. In

Maria's arms, I took my last breath in this body. I had lived fifty years and carried six of Henry's children in my womb. Only Mary survived. She was seventeen at the time I died of a broken heart.

*   *   *

The pain of life is gone. I'm so glad it's over, but I worry for Mary's safety. Her father thinks so little of women and so highly of himself.

How could I have known when he was so young and handsome and seemed so devoted to our religion that he would treat us so shamefully? I came to love him, as was my duty. How quickly he turned. He made a fool of himself and endangered his own soul. Yes, I worry for his safety too—and his sanity and spiritual well-being. But my part is done now. I did my best. I was loyal to my parents, my church, my daughter, and my husband. And I suffered such humiliation at his hands.

I knew men, even kings and popes, often strayed for sins of the flesh, so I looked the other way when Henry took Bessie Blount and then Mary Boleyn to his bed. Both were young and sweet, though of little moral fiber, but I understood they had no choice. I forgave them both and wished them peace. If there were others more discreet, I forgave them and was grateful for the kindness of their discretion.

I looked the other way when Henry pursued Anne. But Anne was not sweet. She teased and taunted Henry, and then she had the audacity to defy her king, not for morality's sake, nor out of loyalty to me. She defied us both. For this covetous, young upstart, he banished me, his loyal wife and queen, and his own daughter. Mary was bright and

90

capable enough to hold her own, but women were not allowed to act without the permission of their men.

How did men come to hold such power over women who, through the power of God, gave them life? If Henry denies Mary, she won't find a suitable husband. But if he finds her one, she'll escape her cruel father only to suffer a husband. Yes, I once believed in the sanctity of marriage, but no more.

I am at peace with myself. How strange that this world beyond death doesn't resemble my expectations of the heaven promised by the church to whom I was loyal. Perhaps I am in purgatory. I have judged others, and that is a sin. Perhaps I did not do enough for the poor. I will think and pray on these matters, but I suspect I have yet again been betrayed by men. All men are weakened by their egos and their need to control others. I was wrong to have trusted men's wisdom over my own.

Our merciful Lord is invisible where I now am, and yet I feel at peace. Perhaps this peace is the Lord, and as mortal beings confined in fleshly bodies, we could neither perceive nor grasp this. Without the Lord's presence, I surely would not be at peace, but this peace offers me a chance to return to the physical world by birth in a common family. I will be a poor, working man's daughter, and I will choose for myself not to trust a man in marriage again. I will try to fend for myself instead. I understand I will see both Arthur and Henry once again. I also understand I won't remember any of my past once I'm born. I'm determined to be my own person this time. I'm determined to do things differently.

Anne Boleyn
January—May 1536

On 8 January 1536, Henry and I received news that Catharine had died at Kimbolton Castle. While I was truly sad for her, she had lived a long life, and with her dead, no one could deny the legitimacy of my marriage. We celebrated and mourned Catharine's death at the same time by wearing yellow, which was a symbol of joy and celebration in England, but the color of mourning in Spain. It was my idea—a clever one of course. It was the first idea of mine in quite some time that pleased Henry.

I felt sorry for Princess Mary. After her mother's death, I tried to make friends with Mary and welcome her at court, but she was bitter and refused my offers. She was still Elizabeth's half-sister, and I wanted them to know each other. I also wanted to give Mary a chance to be free of her unenlightened servitude to Rome. It was an opportunity lost.

Toward the end of January, Henry decided to ride in a jousting tournament. I looked forward to seeing my handsome husband show off his renowned skills. He was a fine sight in his armor, as he sat on one of his favorite horses. I smiled and waved at the crowd from my canopied platform. I leaned forward in my chair as Henry charged his opponent, but when they met, Henry was knocked from his horse. I felt the breath knocked out of me, as if I took the fall myself. He was unconscious on the ground. I was terrified. My husband was older than I, but I wasn't prepared to lose him so soon. He was carried from the field, and I needed help as well. The doctors explained to me that his head had been injured. My ladies did their best to comfort me, but in spite of their constant company, I felt very alone. What would become of me, Princess Elizabeth, and our unborn child if Henry died? I doubted the male lords would support me as regent.

Henry regained consciousness hours later, but he would not follow the doctors' advice to remain in bed and rest. He appeared to recover, but still I worried. I wondered if he defied the doctors to prove his manhood to his people, who had just seen him lose the tournament. Henry didn't like to lose.

Five days after Henry's head injury, I miscarried. It was the same day as Catharine's burial. Just when things should have been better for us as husband and wife, it seemed all manner of tragedy struck. Henry was like a stranger to me in many ways. He had changed. I saw no joy in his eyes, and he seemed enshrouded by a veil of darkness. I was in bed recovering from the miscarriage, when my sister-in-law Jane came to me. "Henry has publicly declared he was seduced by some evil spell or deception into marrying a witch. Anne, he means you."

"Where does this nonsense come from? Is it his injury?" I had not given him a son. He must have been frightened by his jousting accident of his own mortality, as had I. Catharine was five years older than him. Did he wonder if he had five years left? If he had died of his wound, there would have been no male heir to the throne.

Henry couldn't fathom the idea of a woman on the English throne. I knew my days by his side were limited. I wondered what reason he would find to banish me from court. Before his announcement, I could not have imagined what plausible reason he could find to annul our marriage. But now he was

the supreme head of the Church of England and
didn't need a reason. I wondered if he even realized
on his own that he now had this power. I certainly
wasn't going to tell him. I said no more about theft
from the monasteries. But to suggest he was
somehow deceived or tricked into marrying me,
when it was he who pursued me for so long, was
ludicrous. I was frightened.

By March, my husband courted Jane
Seymour, one of my less attractive ladies. The irony
did not escape me. Henry courted me while I served
Queen Catharine. She was royal by birth, a Spanish
princess, and I was a mere lady. So, he would
banish me in favor of Jane as he had done Catharine
in favor of me. The difference was that Jane was
quiet as a mouse and neither flirted nor offered
ideas of her own. I was the one who had suggested
to him how to rid himself of Catharine. Jane would
offer no suggestions, and Henry wasn't clever
enough on his own to manage anything better than
"by some evil spell or deception." No, Henry would
rely on Cromwell, and Cromwell wasn't my ally.
He favored the old alliance with Emperor Charles,
the late Catharine's nephew. That alliance would be
better served if I, the cause of Catharine's
banishment, were removed from court. It made no
difference that Henry Tudor had pursued me. I
would have been happy with Henry Percy. I
understood the danger I was in, and I was terrified
of burning to death for witchcraft. My rooms were
given to Lady Jane. I offered no protest; I knew this
would happen. My concern now was protecting my
daughter, who was with her own court at Hatfield.
While I waited for Thomas Cromwell to meet with
Henry and concoct the reason for my banishment,

Cromwell was taken ill. But by the end of April, he was back at court in good health.

Then on 2 May, I was suddenly arrested and taken by boat to the Tower of London. Henry had at least offered Catharine a nunnery, but I now realized there would be no such option for me. The ferry rocked as we approached the Tower entrance, and I realized how foolish and naïve I had been. The punishment for any manner of treason against the king by his queen was to burn at the stake. Whatever charge Cromwell made against me would be some manner of treason. Henry never intended to banish me; he meant to burn me alive. The ferry docked, and I tried to stand to disembark, but as I did, I felt the blood drain from my head. I was trembling as everything around me went black.

When I awoke, I was sitting on the ground at the entrance to the Tower, and the ferry was pulling away from the dock. There was no escape. "You fainted, my lady," a guard said. I stood with his help, and was led inside through the corridors of the infamous Tower. We finally stopped in front of a door, which one of the guards unlocked and opened for me. I entered, the door closed behind me, and I heard the key turn in the lock. My room held a plain bed and a small, locked window with opaque glass.

Once I recovered my wits, I realized my entire family was in danger. I begged to know the whereabouts of Father and George as well as the charges against me. I received no answer. As I paced back and forth in my room, I became more anxious. How could I possibly bear the pain of fire? My torture would be witnessed by others, and the English people would never protest my cruel treatment.

Henry had once banished his daughter Mary from court. My last ounce of strength left me when I understood this would now be Elizabeth's fate as well. She would be told her mother was evil. I would never see her again. I threw myself backward onto the bed, sleepless but unmoving.

Finally, Archbishop Cranmer came to visit me. "Your father is well, and your daughter is safe, but your brother has also been arrested. I cannot believe King Henry would actually think you culpable."

Cranmer had pronounced our marriage valid. "Take care for your own safety," I warned him, "at whatever cost to me. See to your own safety."

On 15 May, I was tried in a royal court for treason, adultery, and incest with my own brother. I was astonished at the last charge. George was a handsome man, shared my wit, and was very popular with the ladies, but he was married to Jane Parker, and had loyally served the king as England's ambassador to France, as had Father. Now I understood why George was arrested. Why had Cranmer not prepared me? George had made an enemy of Thomas Cromwell less than two years before over a mere difference of opinion. I wanted to laugh and cry at the same time. Neither George nor I deserved this. Perhaps it was meant to frighten me into accepting whatever banishment or exile he had planned. If that was indeed the plan, it worked. I would gladly and quietly go into exile in France or be banished to the remotest corner of England. I had just convinced myself of this hope, when Lady Jane Parker Boleyn was brought into the room to testify against me and her own husband. Her testimony mentioned a prior trial in which four men, including

George, had already been convicted of adultery with me. I could not be found innocent. One of my judges was Uncle, whom I had surpassed in authority by becoming queen. I realized too late that my kinswomen had been right. But Henry was both king and supreme head of the Church of England, the latter in no small part thanks to me, and could pardon me. My only hope was his pardon.

After only a few hours, I was convicted and sentenced to burn at the stake. I fought with every bit of determination I had left not to faint. Once back in my cell, I fell to the floor and cried uncontrollably.

Later that day I was visited by Lord Kingston, the keeper of the Tower. I knelt before him. "Sir, I assure you I have never committed adultery with anyone. I have been completely loyal to the king. Unlike my sister, I would not even go to the king's bed until we were wed. Once married, I never considered any man but my husband. I could never have thought to perform such acts with my own brother. I accept that I will never again be Queen of England or return to court. I humbly submit to the king's will. If I had known he wished to put me aside, I would have gone quietly. I know he needs a male heir, and I failed to bear him a live son, but I never expected this. If the king will not pardon me and send me into exile, I pray he will be kind enough to spare me the horror of burning alive."

Kingston replied calmly, "My lady, I will send word to the king requesting mercy. You should know that your brother, George, was sentenced to be hanged, drawn, and quartered."

The look in my eyes as the tears poured forth had to speak for my heart, since my voice was speechless. I buried my face in my hands.

"I assure you, my lady, I will also ask for mercy for your brother."

He quickly excused himself, and I was alone in my bitter anguish. I was already destroyed along with my brother. I spent the night on the hard floor and cried until there were no tears left. Then I felt nothing but darkness, emptiness, and numbness. I dared not move. I clung to the lack of feeling and hoped I would feel no more.

The next morning, Lord Kingston came to my cell with a kind smile on his face. "I have news, my lady."

I waited on the floor in silence. I was still numb. I did not think I could move of my own volition.

When he saw I wouldn't speak, he continued, "The sentences for your brother and the other gentlemen convicted of adultery with you have been commuted by the king to execution by beheading."

I breathed a small sigh of relief. "Well," I said as I finally found my voice, "beheading at least is quick, if the executioner has a good aim and sharpens his axe."

"This is true, my lady. And the king, in his mercy, has commuted your sentence to beheading as well. He has hired a French swordsman for your execution."

My body came back to life in relief. This time, I cried tears of joy. "Now I can find peace," I told Lord Kingston. "Thank you, my dear sir."

He turned and left me to my thoughts. A sword was quicker and surer of its aim than an axe.

It would all be over soon enough, and I was glad of it. I would die in the French style of execution. This pleased me. Nothing more concerned me. I had done all I could. I felt a great weight lift from my shoulders that I had not before noticed was there— and then I laughed out loud when I realized this was to be literally true very soon. I was free to smile and laugh without fear, for there was nothing left to fear. The whole world could tell lies about me, but I wouldn't be around to hear any of it. "I will have no ears to hear their lies," I shouted.

Henry would trouble me no more. I would say nothing against him or those who judged me or testified against me, for they were under his spell, and he still had the power to withdraw his mercy from me. No, I would have no more to do with worldly matters. My life was over. I was twenty-nine years old.

Lord Kingston came to my room 17 May. "Your brother George and the other gentlemen have all been beheaded today."

"Thank you for telling me, kind sir."

"Your execution will take place in two days."

I nodded as he left the room. I heard the key lock the door behind him.

Shortly before dawn 19 May, I called for Lord Kingston. Together we heard mass. Just before taking communion, I swore to him, "Mr. Kingston, I've always been faithful to the king. I've had no man but him. I am innocent." When mass was over, I said, "I'm sorry, but I thought by this time my pain would be over."

"But there should be no pain," he answered.

I smiled. "Then the executioner must be very good." I laughed as I put my hand around my long, slender neck.

I wore a loose, dark grey, damask gown trimmed in fur and a mantle of ermine over my red petticoat. Accompanied by two ladies, I was led to a scaffold and climbed the scaffold steps without assistance. I smiled. It felt good to breathe fresh air. At the top of the scaffold, I turned toward the small crowd and said to them, "I am here to die according to the law. I will not speak of being accused, but I pray God save the king. To me he was kind and gentle. I leave this world now. I ask for your prayers. Lord Jesus, receive my soul."

My ladies removed my headdress, gown, and necklaces. Then I knelt upright, in the French manner. A blindfold was tied over my eyes and around my head, as I continued to repeat, "Lord Jesus, receive my soul."

I felt a slight breeze on my face, which was pleasant. I heard a man's voice nearby say loudly, "Where is my sword?" All went black.

*   *   *

I awoke as if from a long, deep sleep. I didn't know where I was. I remembered breathing fresh air and feeling a slight breeze on my face, but I could feel nothing now. I realized there was no pain—only peace. I looked around to see where I was. I saw blue sky around me. Was I in heaven? All was quiet.

Then I looked down and saw a strange sight far below me, as if I hovered in the sky. I could see the scaffold. There were no people around—just one small body in a red petticoat. Her head with its dark hair soaked in blood was lying nearby—what a strange sight. I knew it had been my body, but I wondered why it was still there with no one around. There had been a crowd of people, a swordsman somewhere, and two ladies attending me. I felt strangely numb and at peace, but I found it curious that my body was neglected so. I felt very sad. It seemed unkind.

I kept a silent but peaceful vigil above the scaffold, as I watched over what I had once identified as myself. Eventually a man I did not know, dressed as a common laborer, appeared from inside the Tower with an empty arrow chest. He gently placed my head and body inside. I was grateful for this stranger's kindness—and he was but a commoner. If I had been able, I would have wept at the sight. I did not bother to follow to see what the kind commoner did with my coffin, the arrow chest. I preferred to picture it laid to rest somewhere with a bouquet of sweet, white lilies on it. How odd that this kind commoner had more decency than the entire king's court.

Jane Seymour
January—May 1536

During the first week of 1536, the English royal
court learned of the death of Catharine, Dowager
Princess of Wales and once a great queen. Instead
of giving her a royal funeral appropriate for the
Queen of England and Princess of Spain, both King
Henry and Queen Anne wore yellow, the color of
celebration. They offered the explanation to the
court that yellow was also the color of mourning in
Spain, which made their behavior more palatable.

Still, I was a mere servant in no position to
judge. Secretly I grieved for the loss of Queen
Catharine and prayed for the safety of Princess
Mary. It was such a tragedy to witness how the
royal family had been torn apart. I prayed God
would protect us all as He did all the flowers—
especially the violets so easily tread upon.

Later that month, King Henry was
dreadfully wounded in a jousting tournament. He
was knocked from his horse and found to be
unconscious. Everyone feared the worst, but he
recovered later that day.

By February, King Henry was disillusioned
with Queen Anne. He began to seek me out for
conversation. I was flattered to be noticed by him.
Of course, I welcomed His Majesty's company. I
was concerned about the recent sacking of the
monasteries, though I dared not ask him about this.
I held my tongue as I was taught.

On the second day of May, Queen Anne was
arrested and charged with treason, adultery, and
incest. I was appalled, shocked, and wondered if she
was capable of such despicable acts. The incest of
which she was accused was allegedly with her own

brother, whose wife, Lady Jane, was also one of the queen's ladies. There was much talk among the ladies at court, but I did my best to stay quiet and uninvolved. I believed we should leave judgment to God and the proper authorities. I could not imagine Lady Jane's humiliation. The entire Boleyn family was in disgrace.

With Queen Anne in the Tower, King Henry now sought my company more often. It was my opportunity to try to cheer him up and offer him solace. He was somber and burdened by recent events. He confided in me, "I fear I have been under a spell of some kind. I feel as if I am waking from a bad dream."

"All will be well, sir," I assured him. "The good people of England love you and will support you through your difficulties. Dare I mention, sir? Queen Anne has never been very popular with the people."

He smiled for the first time I had seen since before his dreadful accident. I was happy to be of service to my handsome king.

Less than two weeks after Queen Anne's arrest, a trial of four men, including her brother George, was held. They were all accused of adultery with her. Anne's own uncle, the Duke of Norfolk, sat as judge at their trial. Shockingly, they were unanimously convicted. Even George's own uncle was convinced of their criminal behavior, so it was no surprise when Anne was also convicted. Strangely, public opinion then turned in her favor and against King Henry.

On the evening of 18 May, the day after George Boleyn and the other men were beheaded at the Tower, Thomas Cranmer, Archbishop of Canterbury, once loyal to Anne, and who just a few years ago had declared her marriage to King Henry valid, now declared the same marriage dissolved. I realized the king played a cruel game, and I did not like the many games I saw at court played at the expense of others.

The next day, Anne was beheaded by a swordsman in the Tower courtyard. I was relieved I was not required to attend. Nor did Henry witness her execution. I could not blame him. He had made no preparations for her funeral or burial, and he would not be bothered to do so. He said, "She is no longer my concern."

I silently hoped he still considered Princess Elizabeth and Princess Mary among his concerns. I was grateful to not be a monarch who had to deal with such affairs. I thanked God I was born female.

Anna von Kleve
1535—1536

"I'm sorry, my dear Anna," Papa said to me one afternoon in 1535. He had to me into his study invited and asked me to sit. I felt my heart into my stomach drop. "The arrangement of marriage between you and François of Lorraine has been cancelled for political and religious reasons."

"But how can this be?" I gasped. "We've been engaged for eight years."

"No, no, not engaged. It was an informal arrangement. You know that. I told you it was just informal."

"But I was only twelve," I protested. "All I understood was you promised me to him in marriage. That was eight years ago, and now you break your word? Papa, please!" I dropped to my knees to beg. This was a disaster. The marriage was my salvation to have been. All hope was away from me taken.

"No, Anna, the marriage promise was informal, but it has been cancelled just as informally. François is Roman Catholic."

"So is Mama."

"Yes, and we will find you a suitable protestant husband."

At this time, I was almost twenty years. I feared no match for me would be found. Most ladies younger than me were already wed. But most young ladies had charm, beauty, or grace. I had no such privilege. I wondered if perhaps Lorraine knew, and if that was the true reason—with politics and religion the polite excuse. Maybe fair Lorraine did not a weed in the cornfield of a duke's family desire.

Amelia was quick to tease. "Spinster, you've failed at marriage without even a wedding. No one of our station will have you. You will end up being a peasant's wife or William's servant."

I burst into tears and ran to Papa, who assured me, "Amelia is still young and doesn't understand the hurt she causes you," he explained.

But I was devastated. What was of me to become? I was very frightened. I was certain great humiliation to suffer, because Amelia would before me marry. I needed escape. I thought of far away to run, but I could not my dear Papa's heart break. He truly loved me.

I envied Sybille, because she had a good husband of fine reputation and a new life with him. I also regretted when we were younger and lived together, I was not to her kinder. What cruelty had she from Mama endured? Or was Mama only to me cruel because I was ugly? Did farmers not burn weeds? The thought terrified me for my precious blue cornflowers.

I still had in life two joys. One was my little blue cornflowers; the other was my dear, kind Papa.

Katherine Howard
1536

In January 1536, the former Queen Catharine died. I
didn't know much about her, but my friends said
she was well loved by the English people. Pope
Clement had bothered himself to no avail. Both he
and Catharine were dead, and King Henry and
Queen Anne were still married in spite of the papal
condemnation. Everyone had been upset over
nothing.

But then in May, Anne was arrested and
charged with treason, adultery, and incest with her
own brother. I'd never heard of such a thing, but I
was grateful to be at Lambeth instead of court. I
was told she was taken to the dreaded Tower of
London as a prisoner and put on trial like a common
criminal. She must have been so humiliated. Then
her judges found her guilty of all charges, and she
actually was a common criminal.

My own cousin was guilty of treason. I had
nightmares and cried out in my sleep. The other
ladies tried to comfort me, because they wanted to
get back to sleep themselves. But the punishment
for treason by the Queen of England was to be
burned alive, so how could I not have nightmares?
Fortunately, King Henry commuted her sentence to
death by beheading. I thought he should commute
the death sentence itself, but he didn't. Anne was
beheaded. Surely nothing like this had ever
happened before or could ever happen again.

My cousin George was also beheaded. Only
their sister Mary had been spared, but Mary's
daughter, Catherine Carey, was forced to watch
Anne's execution. If I'd been there, I believe I
would have fainted. Everyone at Lambeth talked of

all the events, and I was just as eager for news as anyone, but it was truly the stuff of nightmares. Dreadful things happened at court that month. I was glad to be safe at Lambeth and free to do as I pleased.

King Henry remarried right away. "He's getting old and can't afford to waste time," one of my companions explained. "He still needs a male heir."

"I think he should be happy with his two daughters," I responded.

"You just don't understand such matters. Now he's married to Lady Jane Seymour, and she's banned the French fashions from court. So we'll all have to be more modest."

"And I heard Queen Jane's favorite flowers are violets," another friend added.

"Violets are hardly a proper flower for the Queen of England," I argued. "Even I know the proper English flower is the rose." My friends nodded in agreement. Needless to say, we no longer talked of going to court, and I had to readjust the way I wore my gowns and headdress.

That summer, the Dowager Duchess sent for me. I found her inside stitching her embroidery. She smiled when she saw me, and I curtseyed. "You are much improved, Kate. It's time you study music. Musical ability is important at court. A lady at court must be able to sing pleasantly or play a musical instrument to entertain the royals. I have hired a teacher for you. His name is Henry Manox."

"Thank you, my lady." I curtseyed and left to find a friend with whom to share my news.

When the time arrived for my first lesson, I went happily to the music room. The curtains were pulled closed even though it was mid afternoon. As soon as I entered the room, Mr. Henry Manox closed the door behind me and locked it. He motioned for me to sit in a chair beside the virginal, and then he sat in the chair in front of the virginal facing me. He was quite handsome and just enough older than me to know many things. The prospect of private lessons with this handsome man was most titillating.

He explained, "A proper understanding of music would be beneficial in the matter of dancing, and every proper lady must be able to dance well."

"Yes," I readily agreed, "dance is very important to me."

"Good. Then we shall include practice of dance as part of your musical training, but you must give me your word that you will share nothing I teach you with anyone."

I was delighted. "You have my word, Mr. Manox."

"I cannot overstress the importance of secrecy in this matter. What I teach you is for you alone. You must not even tell the Dowager Duchess. She will be pleased enough with your results. She need not know the details of how you achieve your skills."

"Oh, I agree with you, sir. She has so many things to manage already. She needn't bother herself with the details of my lessons. I will be a good student and practice everything you teach me."

"Without telling your friends about your lessons," he added.

"Without telling my friends about my lessons," I repeated. "I will tell no one. You have my word."

"Very well then, let us begin."

He taught me a great deal about a woman's body. No one had taught me these things, even though they were clearly important. He also taught me about a man's body. He assured me these things were necessary for dance.

"My dear Kate," he told me, "your body is like an exquisite musical instrument made of rosewood, but it has never been played. For an instrument to make the sweet sound of music, it must be made to vibrate—to blossom. You are like a rosebush that has not yet blossomed. I will teach you how to vibrate the rosewood of your instrument so it will sing sweetly. I will help you blossom."

He recognized my beauty as equal to a rose. I loved it when he touched my private parts. Then he explained how I could give him the same pleasure by touching his. I thought I had found heaven on earth, but then he showed me even more. From my dear Henry, I learned how the man's private part fit so ecstatically into the woman's, and how this tremendous pleasure could be prolonged. I was in love with him.

Jane Seymour
May 1536—October 1537

The day after Queen Anne was beheaded, King
Henry and I walked together in the courtyard of
Greenwich Palace. "Lady Jane," he said, followed
by a brief pause. He stopped, turned to face me, and
asked, "Will you marry me?"

I was quite surprised. I dared not refuse. "I
am humbly honored, sir." He smiled at me, and we
continued to walk. I was twenty-eight years old
with no other prospects for marriage. With my plain
looks and no well-defined waist to form a feminine
figure, I had accepted that no man would have me. I
added, "I am also well trained in household
management, and I will bring the court under strict
supervision. I'm not given to extravagance like the
French court."

Henry nodded. He understood my meaning.
He could have any woman in Europe, but he chose
me. I accepted his gifts graciously. I was
determined to bring great honor to my family.

King Henry and I were married 30 May
1536. I was publicly proclaimed queen consort on 4
June. My coronation was scheduled to take place in
London, but there was a plague spreading through
the city, so the ceremony was postponed
indefinitely. It was the only prudent thing to do. I
was happy enough to be wife of the King of
England. I told Henry, "The expense of the
ceremony should be spared in favor of the health of
your court, sir."

"We are pleased."

Where Anne was clever and bold, I was
formal and strict with my ladies. I concerned myself
only with their management. I instructed them to

remove all trace of French fashion from their wardrobes. There would be no foreign influence in my court.

I brought my sister, Elizabeth, and my brother's wife to court to attend me. I invited Princess Mary to return to court. She had grown into a beautiful lady. As her step-mother, I developed a close relationship with her.

Later that year, there was an uprising in the north of England over the king's break from the Roman Church and dissolution of the monasteries. A riot ensued, and many were arrested. They were good Christian men with families to support, and they were rightly upset with the pillaging. It was the king's business, and their behavior had been rash, but I begged him, "Please, Sir, show mercy on behalf of their families, who otherwise will be left to starve. Most of the men arrested have wives and children to feed. Without these men, who will work the fields or provide for your people?"

Henry responded sternly, "Never again meddle in affairs of state as your predecessor did."

And so, I never did again. However, I tried to ensure Princess Mary's place in the line of succession after any children Henry and I might have. Henry was not in favor of this, but Princess Mary was aware of my efforts on her behalf. "We are all Christians, after all," I told Henry, "and all of us reared in the same faith."

"My marriage to Princess Mary's mother was illegal, because she was my brother's wife. Therefore, Princess Mary is a bastard."

"But you are still father and daughter," I reminded him, "just as you are still father of your other bastard children." And so King Henry and Princess Mary were reconciled. Family loyalty was most important to me, and I was satisfied with what I accomplished.

By spring, I knew I was pregnant. Henry was so happy, and he catered to my every whim. I craved quail, so he sent for quail. I began my confinement in September in a dark, quiet room. King, court, and country were all praying God would finally give England a male Tudor heir.

It was a difficult and painful labor of two days and three nights. I expected pain—I remembered witnessing the birth of my younger brother—but nothing prepared me for the struggle. During my difficulties, my ladies told me the child was not well positioned in my womb. I felt so weak. I sensed I might not survive. Then on 12 October 1537, I gave birth to a son. I was vaguely aware Henry visited shortly after the birth. He was ecstatic, but the ordeal left me dreadfully weakened. I was too exhausted to focus on anything. Henry named our son Edward. My ladies told me the child was healthy. I must have fallen asleep. I didn't remember Henry leaving my bedside.

I was in a perpetual fog after that. I thought the delivery would be the end of the pain, but it continued and even increased. My sister said, "Our little Edward was christened. Both Princess Mary and Princess Elizabeth were present. They carried his train."

I was greatly pleased that his sisters attended him. It brought me one brief moment of joy in the midst of agony. My son was brother to his two elder sisters. I had united the family. I managed a smile with great effort, and then I slipped into a feverish sleep.

When I awoke, I was unaware of how long I'd slept. I felt I was being stabbed over and over again in the tenderest parts of my lower abdomen. These sharp pains would not stop. I could not seem to relieve my distress by changing positions in my bed, and I did not have much strength to move my own body. A lady, I don't know who, tried to prop up my head. She wanted me to sip or swallow something, but I was overwhelmed with pain. "Make the pain stop," I said as I pushed the spoon away.

I became afraid I would not die. I cried out to God. "Lord, have mercy on me. Show me pity, and let me die." I used what little strength I had to speak. But the constant torture did not abate; indeed, it worsened. I could not live with this—I had not the strength. I spoke again, "Please let me die."

A woman's voice answered, "Please, do not say such things. You must fight for your life. You have a child."

What was the child's name? Oh dear, I've forgotten. Fight with what? I have no more strength. It was too much to bear. I felt my mind slip away from me. At long last, I drew my final breath. It was 24 October 1537. I was not yet thirty years old.

*   *   *

The pain has ended and I am quiet. If absence of physical pain is peace, then I am at peace, but this is not what I expected. I obeyed my parents. I performed my duties with patience and held my tongue as I was taught. I remained true to my faith and my husband. I reconciled Henry with his daughters. I gave him his male heir, but in the end, I was alone in my suffering.

My life was much hard work, occasional happiness, and a torturous death. I'm glad it's over. Was it worth the suffering? I honored my family, but it all ended in agony after so little happiness. I never expected to be damned or to become a saint. I was right on both counts. There is no devil here, nor any angels, and frankly, I couldn't care less, because there is no pain.

In a way, this place seems distantly familiar. I remember things from a distant past—yes, I have been here before. And I lived on earth before I was Jane Seymour. It's very strange, but I realize I will return to earth in yet another body against my will. I want no more suffering. I will live again, but why? I don't want to be trapped in such a rigid lifestyle with no choice but to hold my tongue and do as I'm told. I want to be carefree and happy.

I was surprised when Henry pursued me. He was my only love—or at least I loved my position. But he was very handsome, and he clearly wanted me. I'd come to believe no man would have me, until Henry asked for my hand. He could have had any lady in Europe, but he chose me. If only we had more time together.

I must be with Henry again in my next life. This time I want to be Henry's first love and survive when I give birth to his son. I may also see Queens Catharine and Anne again. I will still live in England, but times will have changed. I'd like to be able to be myself instead of working so hard to be what's expected of me—especially if life is so short.

Katherine Howard
1537—1539

My dear Henry Manox and I continued our lessons in love and music. I was in love with him for almost two years.

In October 1537, my friends and I heard the news that Queen Jane had delivered King Henry's long sought-after male heir, Prince Edward. Like everyone else, I was happy for them at first, but by the end of the month, Queen Jane was dead. She was given a proper queen's funeral, unlike my cousin and her predecessor. I was already aware of the danger of childbirth, but I hadn't realized it could kill a queen.

The next year, one of the secretaries to the Dowager Duchess caught my eye. His name was Francis Dereham, and he was more handsome than Henry Manox. Once I knew Francis had noticed me, I was no longer in love with Henry. I was, after all, now a proper woman who knew how to flirt and make love. I let Francis pursue me. He had to earn my affection to appreciate his prize. Like Henry, he was several years older than I, and an experienced man. We became lovers.

My companions looked the other way when Francis came to my bed and spent the night with me. Henry had never come to my bed. Francis and I didn't have a home of our own, but he called me wife, and I called him husband. We'd had no ceremony, but we exchanged our own private vows in secret. He gave me a red rose, and it had such a sweet scent. I kept it, without the stem and thorns, inside my gown, deep between my breasts, until it wilted and its petals fell apart. We slept together as husband and wife in my bed.

I knew my good friends could be trusted with our precious secret. After all, marriages were only done publicly with the permission of the family elders, and since no one had arranged ours, no one needed to know about it. My parents had left me at Lambeth years before. If they ever remembered me and made me a good match, things might be different, but meanwhile, there was no harm in me secretly having the handsomest young man I'd ever met as my husband.

Francis gave me his money to keep safely for him whenever the Dowager Duchess sent him somewhere on business. Until Francis, no man had ever given me a flower, though Henry Manox had talked about making me blossom. No one had ever trusted me with anything of value until Francis. Without Francis, I had nothing of value of my own.

Francis had neither title nor property, but he told me often, "I plan to travel to Ireland and make my fortune there. Then I will return for you when I've earned my fortune, and we will publicly be husband and wife. I'll pay for a place for us to live."

It was all I thought about, as well as Francis' fine body of course, since I had nothing of my own without him. No one else made any plans for me, so I let Francis.

Then in 1539, my step-grandmother somehow found out about me and Francis. I was surprised that one of my very own roommates told her. One of them was jealous and spiteful, though I didn't know who. The Dowager Duchess wasn't pleased, and she begrudged me my happiness—sour old lady. I never pretended to understand, but she insisted, "You have acted most inappropriately for a lady of your position."

I never had a true position of my own until Francis called me his wife. But my marriage was over all too soon, thanks to a jealous tattle-tale and a meddling old lady.

Anna von Kleve
1538—January 1540

In 1538 my beloved Papa died. My grief was
sincere and deep. He was my only friend. Now
William inherited Papa's title and position. I was at
the mercy of my cruel kin. I was trapped.

But it was not long before I learned William
negotiated with Sir Thomas Cromwell, Chancellor
of England, to marry me to the most powerful man
in the protestant world, King Henry VIII. William
wanted the alliance with a powerful friend. I prayed
this match would not fail. Since Henry was a king,
these negotiations were official. If an agreement
was reached, it would be binding. I heard King
Henry was very handsome, and his court was rich
and grand. I could hardly my good fortune believe.
Papa must from Heaven have arranged.

England had a strange road to protestant
reformation taken. King Henry was first to a
princess from Spain married for at least twenty
years. They had one child, a daughter. The English
did not women to rule allow. Since the Spanish
princess was first the wife of Henry's brother, her
marriage to King Henry was annulled. The Roman
Pope condemned them, and so the Church of
England was from Rome free.

King Henry then married a lady who the
freedom of the English church championed, and
they also had a daughter. After three years of
marriage, she was of adultery with her own brother
accused and beheaded, as was her brother. I could
never such a foul act with William consider.

As soon as the second queen was executed,
King Henry married again. She was devoted to the

protestant cause and faithful to King Henry. She bore a son and died soon after.

Now King Henry was for two years a widower. He had his son and two daughters. All three children had different mothers. They needed a mother. I vowed a kinder mother than my own to be. But I was very nervous the Queen of England to become. I spoke no English. I knew nothing of English customs. I knew nothing of how the English people about their previous queens felt. I had so little information and feared how the English people would a German lady as their queen receive. William and Mama admonished me to be modest. They said, "Modesty is all you need to be a proper Queen of England."

King Henry VIII was throughout Europe for his fine looks and manners well known. I was not pretty by any standards. I was, however, a proper and modest lady.

"Modesty is a lady's most valuable trait," Mama said many, many times.

I wondered if she thought me stupid, since she repeated herself so much. I listened to her caution, as I wanted the British Isles, far from Kleve, to reach. With her excessive repetition, I put my worries aside. I would a fine queen for the English become. Once I reached England and was married to my handsome new husband, I would be safe.

The marriage treaty between Kleve and England was on 4 October 1539 signed. It was official. A little blue weed would on the throne of mighty England sit.

And then reality began to dawn. I was to one of the most powerful rulers in Europe betrothed.

The Queen of England did not very long appear to live. I must careful of my actions be.

I must learn English to speak. I had no formal education. I spoke only German. How hard could English be? I did excellent needlework. I enjoyed cards. I would manage.

When finally I left Kleve, I traveled farther than I thought possible. Sir Thomas Cromwell escorted me. I was to see strange lands excited and then the coast and the sea—so much water! The farther I traveled, the safer I felt. I exchanged humiliation for the crown of a wealthy country.

We sailed to England. At last, I would my husband meet. Along the way, I practiced English. What was said to me was very difficult to understand, and so I just nodded. But Sir Thomas responded when I in English to him spoke. The ladies in England dressed quite differently from my custom. But my new husband would his wishes in this say.

And then we met in Rochester. I was shocked. He was not handsome but old and obese. I turned away from his bad odor and my nose and mouth covered. He stomped out of the room. I had erred. I tried through Sir Thomas to apologize. I did not the king intend to offend. I begged,"Bitte, mein Herr Thomas, entschuldigen—excuse, please—Sie meine Bescheidenheit to King." I suggested I was modest being. I wanted not to Kleve to return.

I was in the English manner of religious worship instructed, and I learned this quickly. I dared not again the king offend. I needed flowers near my nose from the king's odor to divert, but it was winter. I scolded myself for intolerant being. I must endure.

I expected a grand, royal palace, but I did not imagine. The gentlemen were all so finely dressed, and the ladies' gowns were of beautiful cloth—silks, furs, and cloth of gold. I felt in this rich land humbled. I vowed the best wife possible to become. This elderly man was a good Christian to have not by my less than pleasing face, my stocky figure, my dark complexion, and my dark hair been deterred. I would return his kindness by his smell no more to notice.

King Henry and I were at Greenwich Palace on 6 January 1540 wed by a very kind priest, Archbishop Thomas Cranmer. Archbishop Cranmer was tall and pleasant looking. The ceremony was good, and I spoke my vows in English. I would a good Queen of England become.

That night, the servants accompanied us to our wedding bed, undressed us, and then left us alone. I was modest above all else. I lay in our bed and waited for my husband his wife to take. I braced myself. I would not any sign of pain to him show, no matter how much he hurt. He climbed on top of me, and he was very heavy, but he did not the act complete. Instead, he rolled off me and turned his back on me. I waited. Perhaps he was gentle being or perhaps was tired after the long ceremony and banquet. He ate heavily at the banquet. Soon, he snored loudly. I would my ladies ask what sort of fragrant bouquet in England in winter might be found to decorate our bedroom.

Katherine Howard
January—June 1540

My uncle sent me to King Henry's court as lady-in-waiting to Queen Anne of Cleves. I'd been told my whole life King Henry was handsome, but I found him old, fat, and repugnant. And Queen Anne was simply ugly. Her manner of speech was appalling. I couldn't stand to hear her voice. She sounded like she was choking every time she spoke. Her clothes were hideous. Someone should have told her to dress like the Queen of England, but it wasn't my place. I decided it was appropriate for an ugly old man to be married to a woman who didn't even try to be fashionable.

I was careful not to mention my relationship to the Boleyns, but everyone already knew. One of the other younger ladies asked me if I was frightened to be there. I assured her I was not. After all, I was nothing like my late cousin, and much too young to be of interest to the king. I was glad to finally be at court for the dancing, courtship, and gossip. I knew my uncle had sent me so he could arrange an appropriate marriage for me.

There was much talk among the ladies about the royal marriage. Apparently, King Henry wasn't happy with his bride. One lady whispered, "I've heard that the match was made by Sir Thomas Cromwell to secure an alliance with the rest of protestant Europe."

I didn't understand, so I just listened and giggled with the others. Then another lady said, "Well, it will be a much stronger alliance if she gives him another son."

"Even better if she survives it," someone added.

"Oh, this one's of much sturdier stock," the first lady reassured us. "She'll hold up better than poor Queen Jane."

"But what would the children sound like?" I asked. Everyone laughed and then scolded me for such a shameful comment, but it was an honest question.

Several nights later at dinner, the king clapped his hands and announced that there would be dancing after we had dined. I was delighted for the opportunity to show off my dancing skills. I was surprised when King Henry danced with me. Of course, I used all my well-practiced charms, and he smiled. If my charms could make this dour old man smile, I was sure to attract a handsome husband.

The next day, while Queen Anne was doing needlework, she motioned for me to come over to her. She waved away the other lady next to her. I went immediately, bowed my head, and curtseyed deeply to her.

"Lady Katerine," the Queen said, mispronouncing my name. "You are young and pretty. You be more like lady, yes?"

"Yes, madam," I answered and smiled sweetly at her. Of course I was a lady, or I wouldn't be at court attending her.

"Gut," she said. It was all I could do to keep from giggling. She looked and sounded like a pig. Then she dismissed me with a wave of her hand. What in the world was that all about? Poor thing couldn't even have a proper conversation.

That night at dinner, I was seated at a table with some of the other younger ladies, when King Henry caught my eye from across the banquet hall and nodded to me. I covered my mouth with my hand and batted my eyelashes at him. He said something to one of the food servers, so I turned my attention back to my meal. Moments later, the same server appeared at my table and offered me meat from a dish. "His Majesty bids you enjoy this, my lady," the man said.

I knew the other ladies would be jealous. I took a large portion and then turned my head to look at His Majesty. He smiled at me again, so I gave him a little wave of thanks.

Later, one of the older ladies came to me and whispered, "Be careful, Lady Katherine. You've caught the eye of King Henry. He will expect you as his mistress, and you must not deny the King, for that would be treason." Then she quickly walked away.

At first, I was shocked at the thought of bedding such an old man. But then I realized if I had found favor with the King, there would be more gifts like the special meat at dinner—maybe even a wealthy husband when he was done with me.

And I was right. Soon I received a necklace of pearls with a ruby pendant from the king. At last, I had jewels of my own. I was summoned by my uncle. I went to him proudly adorned with my beautiful necklace.

"I see you have found favor at court," he greeted me.

"King Henry is a generous man," I responded.

"Sit down, Kate." He gestured to the large oak table and chairs that occupied the center of the room. I sat obediently. "With favor comes responsibility," he lectured me. "You must do whatever His Majesty says."

"Of course, Uncle, I intend to."

"But you must also be on your best behavior otherwise. You must not make Henry jealous under any circumstances. You remember what happened to your cousin, Anne?"

I shuddered at the thought. "I will do as the king wishes. All I ask is that when he is done with me, I be wed to a wealthy, handsome husband."

"As it should be," he agreed. "But you must also be very careful and discreet." He noted my puzzled look. "You must only wear the necklace when you are alone with King Henry, unless Queen Anne is away from court. Just as you must not make Henry jealous, you must also not make the queen jealous, or she may dismiss you from her service. If you're sent away from court, there will be no wealthy, handsome husband for you."

"I shall be very…" I searched for the word he had used.

"Discreet," he offered with a sigh. "See that you are careful. And hold your tongue around the other ladies. You must not talk of your affair with the king."

"They will surely know."

"No matter what they say or ask you," he said sternly, "you must not say a word about it. Our family needs King Henry's favor."

King Henry sent me expensive cloth for new and better gowns. I was careful not to talk about it, but the ladies knew I had no means of buying it myself, and I obviously had no other courtiers. Yet he did not send for me to come to his bed. By June, Henry had given me my own land, and all I had to do was flirt with him.

Anna von Kleve
1540

Henry and I slept together a few weeks, but no
more. I wondered if, since he already had three
children, he had no more interest in physical lust.
He was an old man. I noticed during this time the
source of his bad smell was a wound on his left
thigh—a very big, inflamed boil—that gave him
great pain. When it swelled up, his pain was intense.
Then the doctor lanced it and drained the pus. I
never was present for these treatments. Henry
wanted no witness. The smell must much worse
have been while draining, and he must as the king
suffered humiliation. Now I understood the source
of his torment. I was kinder to him and made
excuses to others for his foul moods.

     Sir Thomas confirmed, "His Grace injured
his leg in a jousting accident during the reign of
Anne Boleyn. It seemed to have healed quickly, and
everyone was much more concerned with his head
injury, as he was unconscious for hours. But since
the passing of Queen Jane, the leg has begun to
trouble him again."

     I thanked Sir Thomas for the information.
After one of Henry's treatments, I asked his
physician, "Vill his leg heal?"

     "No, madam," he answered. "It does not
appear that it will. All that can be done is to drain it
from time to time."

     "Tank you for dis," I said. "Perhaps you do
more often."

     "If His Majesty allows." He bowed and left
the room.

I hoped if the doctor drained the wound before it so painful became, my husband's temper and smell would ease. I prayed for him.

I noticed one evening as we disrobed for bed two other smaller boils on Henry's right leg. He caught me looking, but I turned away and said, "Please forgive my immodesty, sir." I wanted him to flatter by saying he still had fine, manly legs, but I knew not how without immodest appearing.

The next day, one of the king's men came to me. "His most generous Majesty has made a present to Your Majesty of your own chambers. They are being prepared for you now."

I knew not how to respond, so I just nodded and said, "Tank you." I was relieved, but I also understood Henry wished not to share his bed with me. I was too obvious his boils to notice. At dinner, I tried to speak my respect for him, since he was clearly more modest than I, but he seemed not to understand.

"You're most welcome, Anna," he replied.

I just smiled and nodded. I really wanted my own rooms to have for the first time in my life. I wondered when my coronation as Queen of England might take place. Then as spring arrived, I received a letter from William in Kleve. Mama had died. Henry postponed my coronation for grief, and I dared not argue.

I noticed one evening at dinner that Henry watched one of my newer and younger servants, Katherine Howard. She was really just a child, but fair and beautiful. She was for him a temptation.

The next day, I cautioned her about her behavior. She agreed with me, but soon after, Henry danced with her in front of me. I failed as a wife, and Henry failed as a husband. And I never got to be step-mother to his three children, since little Prince Edward had his own court, and Henry's daughters lived away from us.

In mid June, Sir Thomas came to me with a very concerned look on his face. "Was ist los?" I asked him, and put aside my needlework.

"I have bad news, madam," he said. I motioned for him across from me to sit, and he did. "Duke William von Kleve has made an open disagreement with the Holy Roman Emperor. This does not please the king. He has no desire to make an enemy of the Holy Roman Emperor."

I nodded my understanding. My brother William was trouble on the continent causing.

Sir Thomas continued, "The king cannot be married to the duke's sister and be neutral in this matter."

"Ah," I smiled and nodded. I understood. Henry felt he must my honor defend. "My Henry is most important," I told Sir Thomas. "He need not mit Villiam in dis be."

"You are most gracious, and I will convey your sincere loyalty to the king, but the king cannot be married to the duke's sister and be neutral. And he must be neutral." He stood, bowed, and left me to consider his words.

I sat still in my chair in silence. A lady came into the room to me, but I ignored her. I was not queen to be crowned. Henry fancied a mere child five years younger than his elder daughter, Mary. Lady Katherine Howard never was modest. I laughed out loud. My servant looked strangely at me. I tried Lady Kate to caution. I laughed until I tears poured from my eyes. I feared for Lady Howard's safety with the king, the Supreme Head of the Church of England, but he wanted immodesty. No wonder he gave to me a separate bed.

Then my laughter abated. I also understood the seriousness of my situation. Henry could not young Katherine marry while I was his wife. I must not back to Kleve be sent. Henry's first wife did not willingly go, and I was told she was put into undesirable circumstances. His second wife had no choice—she was arrested and beheaded. He married his third wife before his second wife's body was even cold. My life was now in danger, and I must very careful be.

On 24 June, I was with two of my ladies playing cards in one of my private rooms, when Henry suddenly entered. We quickly rose and curtseyed. With a wave of his hand, he dismissed my companions. I offered him the most comfortable chair—my favorite. He sat, and I hurried a footstool to bring to prop up his left leg and make him more comfortable.

I was still on the floor kneeling, when he said quietly, "Thank you. You were betrothed to François of Lorraine."

I was dumbfounded. "Dis matter vas not formal," I protested, and sat back on my feet, "and papers vere from Kleve sent."

"No," he contradicted. "There were no papers from Kleve."

I gasped. "My brother has me betrayed. He said the papers he sent."

"He did not," Henry insisted. "This is most serious. If you were betrothed before, then our marriage is not valid."

I nodded. When he did not any more speak, I asked, "What is to be done, sir?"

"You must leave the court," he answered. Then, when he attempted to rise, I helped him to his feet.

"Sir, I cannot to Kleve return after my brother has betrayed me. I am your loyal servant and vish to stay in England, but, please, sir, vhere am I to go?"

"You may take your ladies to Richmond Palace."

"You are to me most kind." I curtseyed and bowed my head. I was greatly relieved. No charges were against me to be brought, and I would not back to Kleve be sent.

My ladies and I quickly made our household in Richmond Palace. It was a delightful building with many windows and comfortable furniture. On 6 July, I received a letter from Henry:

> *Madam,*
>
> *We have decided to reconsider our marriage in light of your previous betrothal to François of Lorraine. We ask you to consent to an annulment on the grounds of your previous betrothal and non-consummation of our marriage. You will be properly compensated with your own lands and household here in England. You will no longer retain the title of Queen of England. Instead, you will be called The King's Beloved Sister, and you will keep a position over all other English women except the Queen of England and our own daughters, Mary, Elizabeth, and any yet unborn. We require your answer to this matter immediately.*

It was, of course, by Henry signed. I asked the courier, "Please vait," while I penned my response. He nodded his assent and bowed. I wrote:

131

Your Grace,
You have truly like a brother to me been,
even more than my brother from Kleve. As our
marriage never has consummated been, I consent to
an annulment. I am most grateful for your kind
settlement and as The King's Beloved Sister to be
known. I am your faithful friend and loyal servant
and most honored to be.
    The King's Beloved Sister,
    Anna von Kleve

After the letter was sealed, I gave it to the courier to King Henry return. I had arrest and execution escaped, and I now had my own household in England. I never would be free to marry, because of the question of a former betrothal, but it was a small price for my freedom to pay. At my age, with my looks and foreign ways, and rejection by the king, no man would want me. But I was safe.

On 9 July 1540, my marriage to King Henry VIII was officially annulled. I laughed to myself every time I was addressed as "The King's Beloved Sister," while smiling pleasantly to the person who addressed me. I found comfort that I would never directly by another man be mastered. My settlement was grand. I was not only Richmond Palace given, but also Hever Castle, and a house in Lewes in Sussex. I was richer than my brother. I dared not to court go, unless I was by the king himself invited. I preferred not to court go. I was as the master of my own home very happy.

Once our annulment was officially announced, Henry began openly to court Lady Katherine Howard. I felt sorry for her. She was not very clever, and one so young should not into a marriage with a man in Henry's condition be forced. I wondered how she with his age, ugliness, and boils would deal.

I also felt very badly for Henry's children. Now they would no step-mother have. Princess Mary must further insult endure. She must a woman five years her junior address as Queen of England. And I felt badly for the terrible example all of this would for Prince Edward and Princess Elizabeth be. I consoled myself that, although I had treated as a weed been, I had quite well for myself done—much to my surprise. And I was delighted, because my favorite little blue cornflowers on the grounds of Richmond Palace grew.

Henry married young Lady Katherine 28 July—less than a month after our annulment. Of course, I pretended for them to be overjoyed, but dear Sir Thomas Cromwell, who had my ill-fated marriage to Henry arranged and escorted me from Kleve to England, and had such a good friend been during my short time as Queen of England, was not fortunate. Sir Thomas was beheaded the same day Henry and Katherine were wed. How easily I also could on the scaffold have been. Perhaps Sir Thomas was Henry's whipping boy, and Henry expressed his true feelings for The King's Beloved Sister on Sir Thomas' neck.

I put aside the past and enjoyed my freedom. I visited the house in Sussex, but did not stay. Instead, I went to Hever Castle. I liked the latter very much. My household moved to Hever. I wrote to Henry:

My Most Beloved Brother, King Henry,

> *Of all your generous gifts, I have my home*
> *at Hever Castle made. Richmond Palace is too*
> *grand for a simple country lady. At Hever, I may at*
> *once to court come when Your Majesty commands. I*
> *will at Hever enjoy the country air and wildflowers.*
>   *Your Most Grateful Beloved Sister,*
>   *Anna*

My life was simple and peaceful. I had new gowns and headdresses in the English style and in the color of my favorite sky blue flowers sewn. I had horses and the freedom in the fresh air on my own lands to ride. And I managed my own household. I did not allow ladies in my service to remain unless they behaved like ladies. And I was careful who I asked me with English—such a complicated language—to help. I was safe if I trusted carefully.

Katherine Howard
July 1540—1541

King Henry annulled his marriage to the second
Queen Anne 9 July 1540, and it was about time.
The poor woman was a simpleton. She'd been
betrothed before, and apparently she and Henry had
never consummated their marriage. Even I knew
how to do that. She wasn't pretty and her English
was terrible. She made even me look clever.

It was a hot day, and all the windows were
open inside Greenwich Palace. I was summoned to
King Henry's private chambers. Well, at least I'd be
able to take off my clothes.

When I walked into the king's chambers,
Henry was seated before me, and Archbishop
Thomas Cranmer stood behind him. I paused,
surprised by the Archbishop's presence, but then I
remembered my manners and curtseyed low until
the king said, "Come closer, Lady Kate." He held
his hands out to me, and I gave him mine. Then
once again, I awkwardly remembered my manners
and kissed his ring. He laughed. "You are such a
sweet rose without a thorn, Kate. I would like you
to be my own."

"I am yours, sir," I agreed eagerly. "I will do
whatever you wish."

"Ah, dear Kate. We would have you as our
queen."

My jaw dropped, as I felt the world spin
around me. When the spinning stopped, I was aware
the Archbishop supported me by the arm. He smiled
kindly and stepped away.

"Will you marry me, Kate?" the King
repeated.

I fanned myself as I searched for the right words. "Yes, of course, sir, your wish is also mine."

"Then we shall be husband and wife. I'm sure you have many things to do to prepare." He nodded, and the Archbishop motioned for me to leave. I curtseyed and backed out of the room.

Once outside with the door closed behind me, I exhaled and caught myself before I slumped over. I hurried back to where the other ladies played cards and embroidered. Then I stopped myself. Instead, I went to the former queen's private rooms. I sat in the window seat. A pleasant breeze welcomed and refreshed me. King Henry meant to marry me. I deserved someone young and handsome, but I'd be the next Queen of England. The silly man called me a rose without a thorn. Even I knew all roses have thorns.

There certainly was much to be done, but it was all done for me. By now, the world truly was spinning around me. Even Uncle was surprised. Henry and I were married 28 July at Oatlands Palace in Surrey. Afterwards, he was smelly and heavy on top of me in bed, and in spite of my best efforts, he seemed incapable of finishing the task inside me. After that, several nights in a row, he made a mess all over the bed clothes. But he gave me wonderful gifts—jewels, expensive cloth for new gowns, and more lands.

I decided to overlook his lameness— sometimes he couldn't walk unassisted, and I had to help him in and out of bed, as well as in and out of me. He'd never have been able to maintain an erection without my experienced hand and tongue.

Henry was repulsive to look at—he weighed at least twenty-one stone. But he had some handsome servants. Thomas Culpepper was his favorite courtier—and mine. In January, Lady Jane Boleyn Rochford, who was my friend and widow of my late cousin George, began to arrange for me to meet with Thomas. He was also attracted to me.

I invited my friends and former roommates from Lambeth to court to serve me. I missed all the fun we had together. I even invited Lady Mary Hall, who had served as chambermaid to the Dowager Duchess at Lambeth. She knew my family secretly kept the old Roman faith, but she and her brother John were protestant zealots. It was all the same to me.

Our court went on tour in the summer of 1541. I happily wore my finest gowns and jewels in public and saw Thomas on the side. But the one thing I didn't have yet was my coronation. "When will I be crowned, sir?" I asked Henry one night in bed.

"When you become pregnant," he answered. I hadn't expected that. He had three children already, but I became determined to get pregnant, since that's what he wanted. After all, it wouldn't matter by whom. Among his many problems, Henry had poor eyesight. He wouldn't likely notice.

As my affair with Thomas continued, my friends from Lambeth began to ask for special favors. I brought them to court for fun, and now I had to buy their silence with appointments for their relations and lovers. Then I received a letter from Henry Manox. He wanted to come to court as my musician. He was an excellent musician, and he taught me so much. I had to keep his silence.

After our tour ended that autumn, Francis Dereham appeared at court for a position. It was too much. "Go away, Francis," I told him. "Go back to Ireland."

"A position for me that pays well, or I'll tell everyone we were married."

"We never married," I corrected him. "There was no priest. There were no witnesses."

"Your roommates saw us sleep together as husband and wife," he answered coolly.

"Well, of course, I'll give you a good position. No need to get us both in trouble." He became my personal secretary. I did my best to grant everyone's requests and get pregnant, so I could be crowned. I dodged people I didn't wish to see or be seen with and met secretly with my true love, Thomas Culpepper.

On 2 November 1541, Henry and I attended All Souls' Day mass together at our private chapel in Hampton Court. Archbishop Thomas Cranmer gave Henry a letter with communion. Immediately after mass, Henry opened and read the letter. "This is a forgery," he said accusingly to the Archbishop.

"I'm afraid not, sir," Cranmer answered.

I pretended to say more prayers while I waited for them to finish their business. I assumed it didn't concern me.

"I want proof," Henry demanded and then left the chapel.

I followed after him, but he shut himself in his rooms. I wasn't allowed in, so I went to my own rooms. Lady Jane was waiting for me. She was upset. "Thomas Culpepper and Francis Dereham were arrested," she whispered.

Suddenly I was frightened. "What should I do?"

"Beg for mercy," she advised. "For treason, you could burn at the stake. If you ask for mercy and the king grants it, your death will be quick by beheading."

I instinctively clutched my throat and thought of my cousin Anne. My blood ran cold. Henry would kill me?

Days of terror passed. I tried everyday to get into Henry's rooms to beg for mercy, but he wouldn't see me. Then on 7 November, Archbishop Cranmer and a delegation of councilors came to question me. All my ladies except Lady Jane were ordered to leave us.

"You are charged with treason and infidelity against King Henry VIII," Cranmer said solemnly. "You are confined to your rooms with Lady Rochford."

"I must speak to the king," I insisted.

"That will not happen."

I felt my last hope fall beyond my grasp. I fell to my knees and begged. I burst into tears. Lady Jane tried to quiet me, but I could not be consoled. The Archbishop asked his questions.

"I beg you for mercy. I beg the king for mercy. I don't understand."

"Were you under precontract to marry Francis Dereham?" the Archbishop asked.

"No," I cried. "He raped me. Please, have mercy on me, sir."

Cranmer turned to his men. "Remove anything with which she might hurt herself." They searched my things. Then Cranmer turned back to me. "Madam, Thomas Culpepper and Francis Dereham have both confessed to committing treason with you against the king. The king has in his possession a love letter in your handwriting written to Thomas Culpepper. Unfortunately, if there had been a precontract with Mr. Dereham, it would invalidate your marriage to the king, as with Anna von Kleve, but since you deny any precontract, you must be tried for treason." The Archbishop and his men left us locked in.

What was happening? I was condemned for denying Francis was my husband, but it had seemed so clearly the right thing to do. I didn't understand.

Jane said, "Thomas and Francis testified against you because they were tortured. I'm sure they truly love you."

I shuddered. I didn't know the pain of torture. My beautiful jewels and gowns were taken from me. I had no more lands. All my relatives, except Uncle, the Duke of Norfolk, were imprisoned in the Tower of London. I was so confused.

At my trial, Thomas and I both insisted we engaged in sexual conduct, but not sexual intercourse. The judges didn't believe us. On 23 November, I was no longer the Queen of England, and I was taken from Hampton Court as a common prisoner. I was so ashamed and confused. Guards took me to Syon Abbey in Middlesex, where I was imprisoned.

I was cast down so suddenly. The abbey was cold and damp, and it was winter. I now had only simple, plain clothes to wear and no furs. I had plenty of time to think and nothing to do. If I'd told the truth, I would have been treated like the simpleton, Anne. She was free on her own lands, and I was in prison. I'd been tricked, and I was very jealous of her. The Archbishop should have explained what would happen before I answered him. It was his fault.

In mid December, I was told that sweet Thomas had been beheaded. I felt queasy, but then I learned Francis had been hanged, drawn and quartered. I couldn't imagine how such a gentle

soul could have endured the ordeal. He should have
stayed in Ireland. I was told that both their heads
had been put on spikes and mounted atop London
Bridge. They haunted my dreams. I was alone in
such a cold place with images I couldn't bear. But
at least I was alive.

Anna von Kleve
1541

My life was happy. I had everything I needed, and I was in charge of my home. I wanted no ladies in my service unless they behaved properly, but I was cautious in dismissing. I did not need enemies. If I was careful, I was safe, so I kept my true feelings hidden.

  That summer, King Henry and Queen Katherine married. They went on tour to the northern part of the realm. I did not envy them. I noted Katherine had no coronation either. Maybe England had enough money on coronations spent, since so much on royal weddings was spent. Maybe the next coronation would little Prince Edward be. But I did not conversation about such matters permit in my household.

  I received a letter from my younger brother. He would Princess Jeanne d'Albret of Navarre wed. She was only thirteen years old. I did not congratulate, as I did not wish falsely to write. I also declined the wedding to attend. I would never England leave.

  King Henry and Queen Katherine returned from their tour in autumn. I only went to court if by King Henry invited. Otherwise, I kept away.

  Near the end of November, I heard the shocking news that across the country went. Young Katherine Howard was no longer Queen of England. She was in an abbey in Middlesex. The marriage was not annulled. That meant only one fate for the silly little girl I had tried so long ago to caution.

Katherine Howard
February 1542

I was cold and lost track of the days. Suddenly, I heard a commotion outside my cell. The door opened and guards stepped inside.

"We will escort you to the Tower of London, madam," one of them said to me.

"The Tower?" I repeated, dumbfounded. I felt the blood drain from my head. I fought not to faint.

"We have orders to escort you to the Tower of London," the guard repeated. They took me straight away, totally unprepared. The abbey was cold, but I was taken outside without warning in the middle of winter. I was put into a carriage, and we left the abbey.

"Please, sir," I asked the guard who had addressed me, as he seemed to be in charge, "what is today's date?"

He looked amused and answered, "10 February, madam."

"I didn't know it was February. Please, sir, what amuses you?"

"Usually prisoners on their way to the Tower want to know why rather than the date."

"But I've been tried and imprisoned in the abbey." I was truly frightened and confused. I thought I'd already been through the worst and all that was left was for me to live in my cell.

"Madam, last month Parliament passed a bill, which made failure of a queen consort to disclose her sexual history to the King of England within twenty days of their marriage, or to incite someone to have adultery with her, treason punishable by death."

I said no more. I sat quietly in the carriage
and pondered what I'd just heard. I didn't
understand, except the guard had clearly said
"punishable by death." I realized I was being taken
to the Tower of London to be put to death. I did not
want to know how. Jane told me long ago I could
burn at the stake. I didn't want to know. I decided to
ask nothing further. I'd already begged for mercy
once. I thought it had been granted.

I was so cold I was numb, and I no longer
had any sense of time. Finally, we arrived at the
Tower of London. I was full of dread. The guards
escorted me to a room. The man with the keys
asked, "Do you require anything, madam?"

"Mercy," was all I could think to say. I was
locked in alone.

The next day the same man returned to my
cell. "Madam, I've come to tell you that today the
bill passed by Parliament received the king's
assent."

I hesitated before asking, "What does it
mean?"

"The day after tomorrow you will be
beheaded." He waited patiently for me to respond.

I wouldn't be burned. I exhaled and took my
time to form my words carefully. "How does this
happen? What must I do?"

He looked surprised by my question, but
answered kindly, "You'll be escorted to a scaffold
in the courtyard. You'll climb the scaffold. If you
are unable to climb, someone will help you. You
may speak to the crowd with any last words. Your
outer garments will be removed, and you will be
blindfolded. You will put your head on the block.
When you are ready, extend your arms outward as a

sign to the executioner. The executioner will do the rest."

"Thank you, sir. May I have a block with which to practice, so I may get it right? I like to practice before ceremonies."

"Of course," he said quietly.

After he left, I exhaled a long, slow breath of relief. I would be beheaded, which would be quick. I repeated the guard's kind instructions over and over in my mind so I wouldn't forget. Eventually I fell asleep.

I was awakened the next day by men entering my room. They dropped a large block of wood with a loud thump and left. When I awoke fully, I practiced according to the guard's instructions. I thought what my last words would be—something others would think appropriate. I wanted to play my part well, as this would be how others remembered me. When I'd removed my outer gown and sleeves, I knelt directly in front of the block. I closed my eyes and imagined a blindfold tied around my head. I leaned forward to feel the block under my neck, and I extended my arms. I repeated this again and again. With repetition, the block came to feel comfortable and familiar. As I put my neck on it and extended my arms, I remembered the words, "The executioner will do the rest."

The next morning when they came for me, I was terrified, exhausted, and still didn't understand, but it no longer mattered. I knew what to do. Guards escorted me out into a courtyard. In front of me was the scaffold with a block upon it. Beyond it was a small crowd of onlookers. I wondered if they understood why this was happening. Tears welled up in my eyes. I trembled terribly. By the time we reached the scaffold, I needed help to climb the steps. I turned to the onlookers and said my rehearsed words in a shaky voice, "I ask only for mercy for my family and prayers for my soul."

A lady waiting on the scaffold removed my outer garments. I knelt directly in front of the block. I was relieved it was just like the one with which I had practiced. A blindfold was tied around my head. I laid my neck upon the block. As I extended my arms, I thought, *I'm glad I practiced.*

.

*   *   *

Gradually the numbness wore off. I was no longer trembling or cold. My eyes were still closed, but I could no longer feel the block. I opened my eyes as if waking from a bad dream. Just below me was the familiar block covered in blood. Slumped behind it was my headless body. I could not find my head.

Anna von Kleve
1542—July 1557

At the end of January 1542, I heard the expected but
dreadful news. Parliament had a bill passed, and
now Henry could young Katherine execute. Henry
gave consent for the child's death 11 February. The
poor dear was only twenty years old. Her entire
family, except the sly Duke of Norfolk, was also
imprisoned. On the morning of 13 February, she
was beheaded with one stroke of the axe. I was for
her relieved. It was quick, and her troubles were
over. The Lord was surely more merciful than
Henry, and whatever foolishness she may have done
in her youth was due to lack of proper guidance.
God would forgive. She asked for prayers for her
soul. I called the ladies of my household together,
and together we knelt and prayed for the soul of
young Katherine.

 Not long after this tragedy, I received word
of my brother's latest insanity. He dared to King
Henry write and tell Henry to remarry me. I was
happy when Henry quickly answered, "No." I sent a
letter to the king:

> *My Dear Beloved Brother, Your Grace,*
> *I write to thank you for your kind and just*
> *wisdom in saying no to William. He has much*
> *unnecessary trouble caused, and I am grateful for*
> *your patience. You have most kind and generous to*
> *me been, and I am sorry he has more trouble*
> *caused.*
> *Your faithful and humble Beloved Sister,*
> *Anna*

The rest of the year passed without incident. Henry invited me to court for a few special occasions, and I went. He did not to me look well. He was not happy, and he was bigger than ever. He required assistance to walk. He would never again dance or ride a horse. Surely this man would never again marry.

The next year, my presence at court was less requested. I was not happy to see Henry decline, so I missed not the intrigues of court. I cherished my solitude in the country above all else.

Much to my surprise, Henry married again in July 1543. Lady Catherine Parr was no child. She was a direct descendant of King Edward III, and a wealthy widow. She would not the same mistakes as young Katherine make. She would Henry's nurse be in his old age. They were at Hampton Court Palace married. I attended happily and smiled during the entire ceremony. I smiled for my safety.

Back at Hever, when I was alone, I chuckled to myself. Henry was most fortunate to king be. Another man would have which date was his current wedding anniversary to remember.

Later that year, the new Queen Catherine reconciled Henry with his daughters. Perhaps they would better get to know their father. Queen Catherine also had a good relationship with Prince Edward. I was happy. She also had been courted by another when Henry took her as his wife. I laughed to myself that even such a great lady could not a true love have.

In July 1544, Henry made Catherine Queen Regent, so he could war with France one last time. England was safe under her. But by September, France defeated Henry, and he came home. Henry did not like to lose. I was happy he was not my problem.

The great queen must take care of the smelly, invalid king who took her from her chosen one. Henry must submit to a woman. I was delighted at the vengeful thoughts I had. Henry had once been handsome and active. Now he was old, lame, and to a woman's care confined. Such bitterness must inside him grow.

I received a letter from William in 1545. I read it and laughed out loud. His marriage to the child, Princess Jeanne d'Albret of Navarre, was annulled. Perhaps I would King Henry ask to tell him to remarry her. My brother's marriage also was not consummated. He too was childless. Perhaps Sybille's husband or children would rule Kleve when William died. This was a happy thought, and it would have also my dear father pleased.

28 January 1547 King Henry VIII was of his massive body relieved. He was in Windsor Castle buried next to Prince Edward's mother. Edward was crowned King of England 20 February. He was nine years old.

That summer my household learned King Edward secretly gave permission in May to his step-mother, Catherine, and his uncle, Thomas Seymour, to marry. Catherine and Thomas had courted before Henry proposed to her. She wisely married her king and finally brought together his separated children. Still, her marriage to Thomas was a scandal considered, because she was expected to mourn.

The next year, Catherine became pregnant at the age of thirty-five. I feared for her safety. I felt she deserved some happiness. She gave birth to a daughter, Mary Seymour, 30 August 1548. But my fear was realized. Catherine died a week later.

During the reign of the child, King Edward, England was by a Regency Council ruled. This council was led by the Duke of Somerset, Edward's uncle, Edward Seymour. Economic difficulties and social unrest plagued England in 1549. I kept myself from notice removed. I lived in only one house, and had no attachment to my other lands.

England lost a war with Scotland and forfeited land in France. Young King Edward encouraged Archbishop Cranmer to align the Church of England with the earlier continental Protestant Reformation. I was awkward with the new prayer book, but I was more comfortable with English words now, and so I adapted.

In 1550, the Earl of Warwick, John Dudley, ruled the Regency Council. When England began to recover and enjoy peace and quiet needed for prosperity, young King Edward VI became ill. It was winter, and he was only fifteen years old. He named his cousin, Lady Jane Grey, as successor, and removed his own sisters from the line of succession. He died in summer before he was sixteen. Peace died with him.

Queen Jane Grey of England was the granddaughter of Henry VIII's younger sister Mary, who was once Queen of France. Queen Jane's parents were Lady Frances Brandon and the Duke of Suffolk, Henry Grey. Queen Jane was seventeen and married to Lord Guilford Dudley, son of John Dudley, now the Duke of Northumberland. She gave her husband the title of duke, not king. What would Henry think? So much trouble for a son, but a woman would rule England after all.

Nine days later, when the Duke of Northumberland left London in search of Princess Mary to imprison, the Privy Council turned against

Queen Jane in favor of Princess Mary. Mary was Queen of England, and Jane and her husband were imprisoned. Oh, my dear "Beloved Brother" Henry, the daughter you thought not to rule is on your throne. England was again in chaos. Men fought instead of working the fields. Children would starve, and many would die. But still, I laughed until I cried at the senselessness of it all.

Jane, her husband, and two of his brothers were tried and found guilty of treason in November. They were all beheaded in February 1554. When I heard the news, I joked to my stable boy, "For all the forests of England, they still make coffins too short."

"I don't understand," he said as he helped me into my saddle for a ride.

I laughed, "They bury the body without the head." I trotted off for my afternoon ride. The English lack humor, I chuckled.

Queen Mary was thirty-seven years old and still unmarried like me. I thought it senseless at her age to marry. She had her own cousin killed, but she still had her half-sister, Elizabeth, to succeed her. Instead, Mary reversed Edward's protestant reforms and returned England to the Roman Church. I was German and could not escape suspicion, so immediately my household and I converted to the Catholic faith. I would keep my head.

When Queen Mary married the King of Spain, I wrote to her my congratulations. It was not Christian of me, but I resented other ladies and their fancy marriages. I never would a kind husband have, and Mary never would at her age a child bear. Only chaos to England would come.

A couple of years passed, while all around people were burned for the protestant faith. Then my old friend, Archbishop Thomas Cranmer, with his broad smile, was arrested. He was to me so kind. He also was the author of King Edward's prayer book, and for this he most painfully died 21 March 1556. I had nightmares of him in flames. I felt no more pity for Queen Mary. She surpassed Henry in cruelty.

After the Archbishop's horrible but brave death, my joy for life failed. I now understood I had left the cruelty in Kleve only to find cruelty in England. I realized cruelty was everywhere, and so I lost hope. I was bitter in my isolation.

I fell ill in 1557. A dull pain was in my bones. Queen Mary invited me to Chelsea Old Manor, near Chelsea Palace and once the home of Sir Thomas More, so I might by a doctor be attended. I accepted because I dared not refuse. I was my own room provided with a comfortable bed. A window was nearby, but the curtains were always closed.

In July I dictated my will. I asked Queen Mary and Princess Elizabeth to please employ my servants. They were all I had. My entire life was at the expense of so much suffering, but I protected myself. I was comfortable while others perished of foolishness, and they all had thought me stupid. I heard them talk when they thought I could not hear or could not understand. But on 16 July, I fell asleep in my bed.

*   *   *

I dreamt I floated peacefully. I floated in Chelsea Old Manor. I drifted effortlessly to my bedroom, where I saw myself asleep in my bed. My skin was very pale. All my life I was plagued with a dark complexion, but now I looked quite pale. One of my ladies entered the room and gasped. She touched my face, quickly pulled her hand away, and began to cry. I watched her pull the bed covers over my face.

So this was my end. All I accomplished was to die alone in my own bed. They could laugh at me all they wanted now. I was still alone, but I had died in my own bed. Was life just a game to control how one died? Was it about learning to stay safe when everyone else died? Or was living about learning to make the most of what you had? In that case, I did quite well. Once I left Kleve, I lived quite comfortably. And I was now quite comfortable. I wanted to sleep here for a very long time.

PART II

Delusions we swallow
Can lead to downfall
Or keep us from feeling the pain
We cannot control
What others may choose
But holding on leads to more shame

Try something different
Try something new
But change whatever it is that you do
That leads to the unpleasant
That clings to you

Like moss to a stone
It only grows thicker
Unless you move on
And change the picture
Within is the dawn
Outer darkness is quicker

Anna von Kleve

I had a long, peaceful sleep. When I awoke, I looked down at London. It had grown so much, and styles had changed. I drifted a while and enjoyed my peace, but soon an angel appeared before me. "Have you come to take me to heaven?" I asked him.

"I'm your friend," he answered. "In time, you'll remember me. I'm just here to guide you. This is for you." He handed me something flat and shiny. "It's a mirror, but not in the earthly sense."

I took the mirror. It was unlike anything I remembered. I looked up to ask him about it, but he was gone. I held it up in front of me, but I didn't see a bodily reflection. I saw the angel telling me to remember to be kind, and I'd promised him I would. It seemed to have happened a long time ago, before I was born.

I thought back over my life. I hadn't been kind to my older sister, and I could have been kinder to Papa. I certainly wasn't kind to Henry at our first meeting, but I'd thought he was a stranger acting inappropriately. I tried to be kind to my ladies, but I still treated them as servants, because they were. Maybe it was easier to be kind if one was pretty. I sensed that wasn't going to happen. Maybe it was easier to be kind if one had no servants. I would be reborn as a commoner in England. I didn't want to go back to Germany. Maybe as a commoner I might use my embroidery and sewing skills.

*　　*　　*

Annie Chapman

The Paddington district of Westminster, England, was the place of my birth in 1841. As Ann Eliza Smith, I had a simple childhood, but as I grew, my parents argued constantly. They fought about money and which of them worked harder. I felt caught in between them. I helped my mother with all the household chores, so I was inclined to take my father's side, because he went off by himself to work everyday and brought home money. He was also nicer to me. My mother resented me for taking his side.

"I help you here at home everyday," I reminded her, but she slapped my face.

"Don't talk back to me, girl. It's your duty to help out. You're not doing anyone any favors." I ran to my room and cried.

Still, I knew Papa loved me. He'd tell me how pretty I was. I had dark hair and what I thought was an unattractive face, but Papa always said, "You'll catch a fine husband someday, Annie. You're my pretty little girl, you are."

I played with the other girls from my neighborhood in the narrow, cobblestone streets and alleys around our apartment buildings. They didn't think I was pretty at all. I was big boned and large for my age. Often when we played, they pretended I was a monster. At first, when I was little, I thought it was fun to act the part of the monster and run after the others while they screamed and pretended to be scared. Then one day I tired of it and said, "It's someone else's turn to be the monster now."

They laughed at me. "But you're the only one who looks like one."

They hurt my feelings badly, and I ran home crying. When my mother asked, I sobbed, "The other children said I look like a monster."

"Don't you pretend to be a monster and chase them?" she asked as she wiped away my tears with her hand.

"Yes, but they said I look like one."

"Well, they were just pretending. If you don't act like one long enough, they won't pretend you look like one."

After that, I refused to play monster anymore, and we moved on to other games. When we played royalty, I was always told I had to be a servant. "You're not pretty enough to be a princess."

"I could so be a princess," I insisted, but they didn't let me.

One day when I was ten years old, the girls I played with teased me and called me "bastard." Of course, I denied it, because I didn't know what it meant, but it didn't sound nice. I didn't like being called names. I knew they all thought they were better than me.

Then one of them told me, "Your parents weren't married when you were born. They didn't get married until after. That makes you a bastard."

I ran straight home crying. I didn't like being told I was different.

"What's wrong, child?" my mother asked.

"My friends say I'm a bastard," I told her.

"Your friends have foul mouths, and you're never to use that word again."

I bit my lip and continued to cry. After that, when anyone called me "bastard" I ran home, but said nothing about it.

As an adolescent, I was painfully aware only my parents saw me as pretty. The boys always noticed the other girls, but never me. I felt like a weed in a cornfield.

When I confided my feelings to my father, he said, "Well, then, you've nothing to worry about. Cornflowers are pretty little things, aren't they?"

I had to smile. He could always make me smile. The next day, he brought me a bouquet of little, bright blue cornflowers. And I had to agree with him—they were pretty. As long as I had Papa, I felt safe.

I lived with my parents after I passed the age of twenty. We lived in Westminster in a flat with a kitchen, living room, a bedroom for my parents, and a pantry just large enough for my bed. I helped my mother with household chores and ran errands for her. I'd learned to keep quiet around her and hold in my tears when my feelings were hurt. I had no boyfriend, because I wasn't pretty. I worried no man would want me, and I'd be stuck at home with my mother every day for the rest of my life.

"You can't afford to be choosy when it comes to men," my mother told me, as if I had anyone to choose from. I didn't tell her, but I thought about how she'd only married because she was pregnant. I didn't dare say it out loud, even though it was true. At least I was modest and proper.

By the time I was twenty-four, all my childhood girlfriends were married and had no more time for me. I suspected they laughed at me behind my back. I imagined they called me names like "ugly duckling" and "old spinster." Then my mother introduced me to one of her relatives. He was pleasant and employed, but had not yet found a wife.

I was so happy when Mr. John Chapman courted me. I imagined the disappointment of my former friends. They would have to find someone else to gossip about. There was a man for me after all. I talked about him to my mother incessantly.

Mr. Chapman was a coachman, a respectable occupation, and a gentleman. I was proud to be seen in public with him with my hand on his arm. And then he proposed marriage. He was very proper about it. First, he asked Papa's permission, which of course, Papa gladly gave. My parents knew how pleased I was with him by the way I talked about him all the time at home.

Once Papa gave his blessing, Mr. Chapman knelt in front of me in our own living room and asked, "Annie, will you marry me?"

"Of course I will." I was overjoyed. John Chapman and I were married on the first of May 1869 in a small church in Knightsbridge, south of Westminster. We moved into our own apartment in Knightsbridge. It was about the same size as my parents' flat, but it had a row of windows on the south side, which made it bright and cheery. Since there was little else about the London area that was bright and cheery, this seemed a good omen for our future life together.

The very next year, on 25 June, I gave birth to a daughter. We named her Emily Ruth Chapman. She meant the world to us. John and I were very happy with our life and our baby girl. John teased me when I put a pale blue ribbon in her hair.

"Blue is for boys," he laughed. "Girls should have pink ribbons."

"No, this one is special." I told him about Papa and the cornflowers.

"Oh, well, that's just silly," he scoffed. "You're the most beautiful wife a man could ever hope to have, and that's all there is to it. But now that I take another look, Emily looks even prettier in her blue ribbon than she would in pink."

I couldn't have been prouder of my little family.

John, Emily, and I welcomed another little girl into our family 5 June 1873. Emily was delighted to have a sister, and John and I were just happy she was healthy. We named her Annie Georgina Chapman. I was glad my little girls had each other to play with. I taught them, "Never call other children bad names or make fun of anyone, no matter what others do. Look out for each other, and if ever other children are mean to either of you, you both come and tell me at once." I would not stand for my girls being made fun of as I had been. We were a close, devoted family.

In the spring of 1880, I was pregnant again. Emily was nine and Annie was six when I told them the news. We surprised John at dinner that night. As soon as he came home, our daughters made a fuss over him. They made him sit in his favorite chair, brought his slippers, took off his boots, and put the slippers on for him. We were all smiles, but none of us would say why until dinner was finished.

Then I brought out a cake the three of us had baked together and set it on the table in front of him. I stood behind John with Emily and Annie on either side of him. I counted, "One, two…" and we all at once yelled, "Baby!" There was a brief moment of silence before he understood. Then he jumped up, and we danced around the room with Emily clinging to John's leg and Annie to my skirt.

The next day, John came home late from work. When he finally arrived, he proudly presented me with a big bouquet of sky blue cornflowers. "I knew this was your favorite color," he explained, "but I had a devil of a time finding them."

"And they're lovely. I'll put them in a vase." I was delighted.

That November, I gave birth to a son, John Alfred Chapman, Jr. Our family was complete. Emily and Annie loved to fuss over little John. They were eager to help with their baby brother. That Christmas was special. Papa John and I watched the girls play and open baby John's gifts for him. I couldn't have been happier.

But my fairytale family life began to dissolve when baby John didn't grow and develop like my daughters had. I began to worry. Had he been my first child, I would never have suspected so soon, but I knew all was not right. Late that spring, Papa John agreed I should take the baby to a doctor. I did with great trepidation, and our fears were confirmed.

"I'm very sorry to inform you," the doctor said, "but your son will never learn to walk or be able to take care of himself. He will never be a normal child, and will always require special care for as long as he lives." I burst into tears, but he continued, "There is a special facility in Berkshire—a charitable school that can care for him properly." He handed me a card with the name and address of this charitable school printed neatly on it. Then he patted me on the shoulder and said, "Mrs. Chapman, there is nothing you or your husband could have done differently to prevent or avoid this. No one is to blame for his condition. He is simply what he is—a baby who will grow into a boy who will require constant, specialized care. You and your husband won't be able to manage his needs. Be thankful you have two healthy children." He and his nurse kindly showed me and my baby out to the street.

John tried to be stoic when I gave him the news, but he was clearly crushed by it. "Well, then," he said, "if it's best for him, we shall have to move to Berkshire so we can at least visit him. I won't have my son grow up and not know who his parents are."

I nodded in agreement. I couldn't bear the thought of my own baby being plucked from society like a weed from a field. I explained as best I could to Emily and Annie that their little brother was very sick, he would have to live in a special hospital, and we would have to move too, so we could visit him.

Papa John collected letters of reference, as I packed our belongings. I'd never been to Berkshire, but nothing mattered anymore except keeping the family together. Papa John traveled to Clewer in Berkshire, where he found a modest home for the four of us and arranged to have little John admitted to the charitable school. When he returned to Knightsbridge, we moved to Clewer, near Windsor.

The Berkshire countryside was lovely, but not lovely enough to absorb our sadness. The brief happiness we'd enjoyed was forever shattered. The girls played as girls would, but they too grieved. Papa John found work, and I got by as best I could. I remembered the doctor's words that it was no one's fault, but I feared when word got out, my daughters would be teased for having a defective brother. I didn't know how to handle my own grief and protect them too. I was glad they had each other. I'd grown so accustomed to keeping my feelings to myself from growing up with my mother; I just didn't know how to deal with the loss of my baby boy. I let my daughters console each other, and I had no idea what to say to Papa John.

When I was forty-one, my beloved Emily took sick with a high fever. The doctor who came to our flat said, "I'm sorry, but this is meningitis. If the fever breaks, and she survives, you absolutely must keep her in bed. This is very serious. If she lives, there could be permanent brain damage."

I dared not ask him what "permanent brain damage" meant. I only wanted her to live, but she didn't. I felt as if I died with her. My world shattered. I didn't know what to say or how to express my feelings.

Papa John was also devastated. Little Annie cried constantly. At Emily's burial, I felt like we buried our little son, John, as well. For the first time in her life, little Annie was an only child. I didn't know what to do. My biggest comfort had always been that Emily and Annie could look out for each other.

Papa John and I talked to each other less and less. There was nothing left to say. Hope was gone. We went through the motions of each day simply out of habit. I envied him his work, because staying home in the flat was a constant reminder of the emptiness. We visited little John less frequently, and as time passed, he didn't seem to know us. It was just too much to bear. Annie didn't even want to see him anymore. The visits probably reminded her of Emily. I knew I should spend more time with Annie, but she reminded me of the two children I'd lost, and I couldn't cope. I tried to clean house, but everywhere I turned, I saw the ghost of dear Emily. I did less and less.

Papa John and I both drank to lift our spirits. A few drinks after dinner evolved into binges. And when we were drunk, we talked again, but we only complained of our unhappiness. Complaints grew into arguments. John rightly accused me of falling behind with the household chores while he still worked. Finally, too many unkind and unmeant accusations were spewed at each other.

He ordered me out of his house, and I was glad to go. I left little Annie with Papa John, since he had income. I didn't know what else to do with myself, so I replied to an advertisement in the newspaper and joined a traveling circus in France. I ran away from my misery and joined the circus.

The French circus traveled throughout Europe. I made and mended costumes and helped cook the meals. France was a republic, unlike the monarchy of England, and customs differed. The language was different, but most of the performers and staff spoke more than one language. I had difficulty with French, but found German easier, and many in the circus spoke English. It was all new and exciting. Being busy took my mind off my losses. I put the past behind and lived in the moment. The circus people were high-spirited. They didn't mind if one had a few drinks, as long as the work was done. I enjoyed the rehearsals and performances and met many people. Everywhere we went there were cornflowers in the fields.

Eventually though, the newness wore off, and I settled into my duties and the rituals of travel. I helped pack props and costumes. Then we'd move to a new site and unpack everything again. I enjoyed the happy children entertained by the performers. Once in a while, I'd spot one who reminded me of Emily or Annie, but then I'd turn away and find a chore to do. I wasn't able to escape my sadness, and I began to feel disoriented. I felt the years of my life weighed down on me like a burden I no longer wanted to carry.

By 1886, I'd tired of life as a nomad. I returned to England, and found a cheap room in Whitechapel, in London's East End. I wrote to Papa John, gave him my address, and asked about little Annie. He wrote back she was fine and included money. He promised me a monthly allowance. He was a good man. I knew he'd never leave our lost children in Berkshire. John intended to see our son buried next to his sister someday. But those were the same reasons I couldn't bear to go back to Berkshire. I missed Annie, but she'd only remind me of Emily and baby John. I stayed in Whitechapel.

I met other women in pubs, but I had only one close friend, which was more than I expected. If I'd been an ugly duckling in my teens, I was certainly the worse for wear now. But I met Polly Nichols near the end of 1887. She was sweet to me. She introduced me to Long Liz, who had an odd accent similar to German, and Nelly Holland.

I found occasional work as a seamstress, but I wouldn't have survived on my own without help from Papa John. At least the circus had fed me and provided costumes and a tent. Life was hard, but I took comfort in drink, my freedom, and a room of my own.

Then in June 1888, Polly introduced me to young Mary Kelly. Like me, she seemed very sad. She and Polly both worked the streets as prostitutes. I never knew what to say to young Mary, but I complimented Polly on her good taste in clothes.

That summer, my allowance didn't arrive. I wrote Papa John a short letter. Instead of receiving money from him, a letter came from little Annie.

Papa John Chapman was dead. He was my last happy memory, and my source of survival. I didn't know how to survive on the pitiful wages of a part-time seamstress. I didn't have the energy to go back to the circus. I felt weak and broken. Now little Annie wanted to know if I'd come home. At first I cried, but then my tears turned to hysterical laughter. *The poor child thinks I have a home.* I couldn't even remember little Annie's face or how old she was now. I laughed, and then I cried, and then I laughed some more until I cried myself to sleep.

I felt deep grief for my loss of Papa John. Then the reality sunk in—there would be no more allowance. Little Annie needed a mother, but I only had work as a seamstress, and I certainly couldn't provide for the child. I didn't reply to her. I didn't know what to say.

My world had collapsed again. I didn't have much money left, so I chose to save what I had for drinks. Gin helped me remember the good times when I was happy. When I wasn't in a pub, I either walked the streets alone taking in the sooty, city air, or stayed home and cried. And when I cried, I often coughed up blood. I was too tired to work. I wasn't well, and it didn't matter. There were permanent shadows under my eyes. I preferred to go out after dark, so no one would notice my ugliness.

On the evening of 7 September, I went out for a walk and found myself at my favorite pub. Long Liz and Nelly were there. As if I wasn't sad enough, Liz said, "Did you hear? A week ago, Polly Nichols' body was found. Her throat was cut."

"Don't tell me such a terrible thing unless it's true," I warned Liz.

"No, it's true," the bartender spoke up.

167

I almost fell out of my chair. "Not sweet
Polly. She can't be dead."

"It's true," the bartender repeated.

"I told you," Liz added. "Had her throat cut,
she did."

I ordered another drink. I passed a few hours
and spent my last coins. When my money was gone,
I stood up. As I did, I said to Liz, the bartender, and
the other patrons, "There, you see? I'm so much
lighter now that I have no money." I laughed
heartily as I left the pub, until I began coughing
again. Out in the street, I coughed up blood, but I
didn't mind as I had no more burdens. I felt light as
a feather. I went back to my room, but when I got
there, I was turned away.

"You haven't paid," the landlord said, "and
it's two in the morning."

"But I have no money," I laughed, "so I
can't pay."

"If you have no money, then you have no
room," he said and slammed the door in my face.

I chuckled at being left outside. *I have
nothing to weigh me down. I'm light as a feather.* I
strolled down Hanbury Street. A nice looking
gentleman walked up to me. He had dark brown
hair, a mustache that curled up on the ends, and
crystal clear blue eyes. He carried himself like a
man of great importance. I couldn't seem to resist
him. "You look familiar, sir. Do I know you?" I
asked.

I failed to catch his response as he took me
by the arm. "Oh, you are a gentleman," I said and
patted the hand that firmly gripped my arm. He led
me into a backyard. "How nice of you to take me to
your home, sir."

He pushed me up against the fence and held a hand firmly over my mouth. I felt a sharp pain in my neck.

*   *   *

Suddenly I was at ease and truly light as a feather. I felt nothing at all. I looked down and saw my poor, ugly body. It looked as though my head had been tied onto it with a handkerchief soaked in blood. *Did I cough all that up?* My dress was pulled up over my breasts, and my legs were spread apart in a most indecent display.

But just then, I was distracted by a familiar voice. I turned around and saw John Chapman. "Why did you leave me, Annie?"

"You ordered me out of your house," I reminded him.

"But you knew I didn't mean it. You knew that, didn't you?"

"I guess if I'd known you didn't mean it, I wouldn't have left. Why didn't you come with me?"

"We had a daughter to take care of and a son to visit. 'For better or worse,' remember? We could still have been a family."

"Well, we weren't," I laughed. "I was a terrible mother. Poor little Annie has no one, and now I have nothing, and I'm light as a feather."

"Are you a fool?"

"Ah, but the fool is the joker," I said, "and the deck was stacked against us. Didn't you know we were just little blue weeds in the cornfield?" Then, as his appearance slowly changed, I realized John Chapman had been the friend I'd taken for an angel. "I'm so sorry," I told him. "I wasn't very kind."

169

Polly Nichols

My parents named me Mary Ann Walker when I was born 26 August 1845 in London near Fetter Lane. I never liked the name Mary Ann. It was plain. My father was a locksmith, but my parents didn't have any imagination when they named me. Victoria was a grand name. After all, it was good enough for a queen, even though it was a mouthful. But I just wanted a pretty name that wasn't so common. I was fair skinned with dark brown hair and a pretty face, so I deserved a pretty name.

When I was ten years old, I chose the name Polly. It began and ended like "pretty" and rhymed with "jolly." People would smile when they said my name. I felt clever as I'd thought of it myself. I told my parents and friends, "My new name is Polly."

"That's a ghastly name," my mother reacted, "and it isn't even a saint's name like Mary or Ann. At least with Mary Ann I gave you two holy saints to watch over you."

"I don't understand about saints," I said. "Besides, I'm not a saint, so I don't need a saint's name. But I'm pretty."

"You ignorant child," she answered, shaking her head.

I didn't understand why she was upset. I was the only Polly I knew. My mother continued to call me Mary Ann, but I ignored her. We grew further apart after that. I was pretty, which should have been enough for my mother. She was interested in church and housework, but none of that was any fun.

As I got older, I became interested in getting boys to notice me. I had a very feminine figure, so I practiced walking to show it off.

"You walk like a slut," my mother scolded me one day as we walked down the street together to the market.

"Well, our name is Walker," I sassed her back. "I should have a special walk."

"You don't have to walk like a whore."

I didn't bother to answer her. I never understood why she was always upset with me. I'd already practiced my new walk to attract the attention of handsome young men. I smiled and batted my eyelashes as I swung my hips from side to side while my breasts proudly led the way.

"How will you ever find a decent husband when you behave like this?" she said with disgust.

But I didn't want a husband who would make me do all the housework, if I could attract the attention of wealthy or ambitious, handsome men. I was too pretty to work.

In spite of my mother's dire predictions that I was headed for a life of prostitution, at eighteen I married handsome, fair-haired William Nichols 16 January 1864. He courted me with pretty gifts, and I fell in love with him. Just before the wedding, he gave me a bunch of pretty posies to carry with one red rose in the center as a token of his love for me. I blushed when he gave me the bouquet and sniffed it as we said our vows.

William earned our living as a printer's machinist. I didn't understand what that was, but he was a good and reliable man. I tried to keep the house tidy for him, and I waited for him to come home from work every day, because we were in love. He made sure I had pretty dresses to wear, and we liked to stroll down the street with my hand on his arm.

During the second winter of our marriage, I took sick. I got up one morning to make breakfast, but I collapsed on the floor before I reached the kitchen. William found me and carried me back to bed. I was sick for several days with a painful throat. William sent for the doctor, and I got better, but the weakness clung to me for months. I felt like I was dying, but I was only twenty. I couldn't concentrate or take part in conversation. William had to help me finish my sentences and remind me of my chores. He made a list of things I was to do every day. I'd struggle to complete one chore, and then sit, rest, and catch my breath before the next, but I muddled through. By summer I had some of my strength back. I'd never been so ill before, and I was never quite the same again.

"I feel as if I've lost my former self," I told William, "and I have to start all over again."

"You're just confused, Polly."

"I am," I agreed. "There's so much I don't understand." I wore a bright dress each day and did the best I could.

Once I was well, pregnancy came along and drained my energy again. Over the years, we had five children. Our eldest was a son named Edward, a proper English name fit for a king. William was so proud, but the baby only added to my confusion. I had even more chores. With the next pregnancy, I gave William another son, Percy, but I had to do all the work for my husband and sons. I was pleased my next two children were daughters, Alice and Eliza. I hoped they'd know how to help me when they were big enough.

By the time our youngest son, Henry, was born, I had more than I could handle. I no longer had my youthful figure and felt exhausted all the time. No one paid attention to how I felt. The children were all so demanding. I no longer felt pretty. With no other adults around during the day, I kept my spirits up with an occasional extra drink.

I visited my mother with the children and asked her to help with them. She laughed at me. "You're their mother," she scolded. "They're your responsibility." She laughed louder. "I'd say you've gotten your just desserts. At least William insisted on sensible names."

She was cruel. She never said anything nice to me. William turned out no better. He fussed at me every day when he came home from work. "Keep the children quiet. I've had a long day."

"At least you weren't stuck with them all day. You never take care of them. I'm worn out."

"You don't even keep this house clean," he shouted.

"You try to clean a house with five children running about." I began to cry.

"It's your place to teach them to behave properly. Instead, they run and scream like a bunch of hooligans. They're not even cleaned up. I expect them to greet me respectfully when I come home," he insisted.

"They're young children, for heaven's sake," I said. "Children don't act like adults—they run about and play like children. At least I play with them. You never do."

"You need to raise them properly."

We went on like this for a few years. From time to time I thought about our wedding. William had given me a bouquet with a rose. Now all I had were children and the thorns of his insults. I didn't understand why he'd changed.

William didn't care much for Eliza. The other four all favored his looks in some way—Alice and Percy more than Edward and Henry. I was fond of little Eliza. She took after me in both looks and mannerisms. She was such a pretty girl. And the resemblance between Edward, Henry, and Alice was clear enough. Percy, though, was the spitting image of his father.

One day when I was twenty-eight, I visited a neighbor just to chat—for all the good it did me. The neighbor women were rude and unfriendly. I understood they were jealous of my beauty, but they said many unkind things to me. One even asked, "Do you intend all your children to be scoundrels?"

Well, on this particular day I tried very hard not to complain. I smiled and talked pleasantly about dresses. She continued to hang her laundry as I talked. When she finished, she said, "Pardon me, but I have duties that require attention inside." And off she went.

So I was in no mood for William's criticism when he came home that evening. I tried talk to him. "You won't believe how our neighbor treated me today," I said the moment he walked in the door. "I feel totally alone in this neighborhood."

He stopped in the open doorway and answered, "Is that any way to greet your husband, who puts food on the table and a roof over your head?"

"In all our years of marriage, I've never seen you cook a meal," I yelled back, lost my balance slightly, and dropped the plates I was carrying to the table.

"You're drunk," he accused and walked past me without closing the front door.

I knelt on the floor with the shattered plates and wept. Of course I was drunk. How else could I manage? Then he reappeared before me. He grabbed me by both arms and pulled me to my feet.

"There's the door," he pointed. It was still open. By this time, the children were quiet and crouched behind the inner doorway to the kitchen. I sensed their presence.

"Yes, I see the door you forgot to shut," I said.

"You drink all the time. You can't manage your household chores, much less the children, and you've had an affair with another man."

"What? After all this, how could you say such a thing? I don't know any other men, and I don't have time."

"Look at Eliza," he shouted.

"Eliza's beautiful," I answered. "I'd be pleased to look at her forever."

"She's not my child. She has neither my looks nor my family's. You say you have no time. You certainly haven't taken time to teach my children proper manners, and your chores are never finished. Maybe you've been working on your back. Maybe that's why you drink so much. Maybe that's why the neighbors have nothing good to say about you."

I noticed a small group of neighbors gathered in the street a short distance from our open door. They stood there silently and watched us. I didn't know how to defend myself. I knew no one would take my side. I'd tried my best, but William was the man of the house and head of our family. He forced me to leave, and our marriage was over. Even though he accused Eliza of being another man's child, he kept all the children. I was turned out onto the street alone with no friends and nowhere to go. I was humiliated as I walked out the door past the gawking neighbors, while my children were left behind.

William was wrong. Eliza was his child, and I was no prostitute. He and the neighbors were no different than my cruel mother. I went to the London's East End to get away from all who knew and hated me. I found work as a maid. After all, that's what I'd been all those years of marriage. The work wasn't bad. I missed all the hugs and smiles from my little ones, and I missed playing games with them. But I didn't miss the noise, chaos, exhaustion, and constant criticism from everyone around me. At least as a maid, I only had household chores. My employers hired a nanny to take care of their own children. I realized William should have hired a nanny for our little ones. My grief and shame were his fault, and I hated him for it.

I lived in my employers' home. I worked hard, and they were kind to me. I was able to rest at night, but I wasn't part of the family. Sometimes the Mr. brought the Mrs. roses. I loved to smell them and pretend they were mine. I made friends with some of the neighbors' hired help. Sometimes in the evening when chores were done, I'd stroll with my lady friends about the neighborhood. It was dark, and there was nothing to see, but we gossiped and giggled. Life was pleasant, quiet, and somewhat monotonous, but I felt better.

Then in 1876, I began to have strange dreams. My husband had shut me out, but he wasn't William in the dreams. We were in a large building with many rooms, but his room was locked. I was desperate to speak to him, but he would neither hear nor see me. I pounded on his door and demanded to speak to him. I'd wake up terrified in a cold sweat. I felt trapped, and something terrible was going to happen to me.

After a few nights of this horrible dream, I spoke to one of my friends, also a maid, in the evening when we took our stroll. She was several years older than I and a widow. I told her about my dreams. "I'm sure in the dream my husband isn't William, but he's the only husband I've ever had. And he shut me out of his life, but why in the dream is something terrible about to happen?"

"Oh, it's just a dream, Polly," she said. "Weren't you frightened when he turned you out and you had nowhere to go?"

"Well, of course, I was terrified."

"There," she reassured me. "You were banging on doors in your dream, because you were terrified."

I felt much better after our talk. That night I settled in for a sound night's sleep and slept deeply. As I awoke slowly, I felt my neck resting on cool wood. I sat up suddenly, startled. My neck was on a block about to be chopped by an axe.

I tried to distract myself with my chores. The dream seemed so real. I stayed busy all day and tried to put it out of my mind. After supper that evening, as I tidied the parlor, the Mr. and Mrs. discussed the daily newspaper he was reading.

"How very odd and after all this time," he commented.

"What's that, darling?" she looked up from her knitting.

"Men have been working on the restoration of the chapel of St. Peter ad Vincula, and they've exhumed two bodies from the chapel. Both were young women who had been beheaded."

177

"How gruesome," she gasped, instinctively putting her hand to her throat. I felt chilled to the bone as I realized I'd made the same gesture and remembered the feel of cool wood under my neck.

"Ah, but they've both been identified," he continued. "The older woman was Anne Boleyn and the younger was Katherine Howard. Just think," he said as he lowered the newspaper and looked at his wife, "no one had remembered where they were buried. Well, now they've been found. I'm sure they'll be reburied properly."

"Those were dreadful times," his wife commented.

"I believe I need some air," I said, anxious to get out of the house.

"Of course, Polly," the Mrs. answered. "You've worked very hard today."

"Thank you, ma'am. I'll just take a short stroll." Outside in the street, I walked quickly and felt myself gasping for air. The dank, sooty air was anything but refreshing, but I needed time alone. *Anne Boleyn and Katherine Howard*—two wives King Henry VIII beheaded over three centuries ago. Somehow, I knew it was King Henry, not William Nichols, who'd shut me out in my dream. Somehow, I must have become haunted by one of ghosts—but which one?

The following evening, I sought out my older friend with whom I'd already discussed the dreams. I knew better than to tell her my fear of being haunted. I was frightened people might burn me as a witch.

"Did you hear the news?" she greeted me. I shook my head, and she continued. "They've found the lost bodies and heads of Queen Anne Boleyn and Queen Katherine Howard. Isn't that interesting?"

"It must have been dreadful for them to have their heads chopped off," I said.

"As I understand it," she corrected, "it was very quick. Anne's was cut off with one stroke of a sword in the French manner before the guillotine was invented. Katherine's was chopped off with one stroke of an axe on the block in the English style."

I shuddered as I realized it was the ghost of Katherine Howard in my dream. "What do you suppose happened to their souls?" I asked.

"Some believe the souls of those executed are doomed to walk the earth as ghosts," she said, "and some believe if they were contrite, they'd go straight to heaven."

I considered that for a moment. "What do you believe?" I asked.

"I don't know, although I'm sure the priest would tell you heaven. I've read that people in India believe in the transmigration of souls."

"What's that?" I didn't understand.

"When a soul leaves the body at death, it's reborn into a new body."

I thought quietly as we turned the corner back toward our homes. "So," I ventured as we approached my front door, "if Katherine Howard's soul was reborn and alive today, do you think she might dream about what happened?"

My friend laughed. "I daresay she would think someone had uncovered her grave."

It was a lot to take in. I tried to understand how I'd lived first as Katherine Howard, had my head chopped off with an axe, and then was reborn as a commoner—only to be thrown out by my husband and find work as a maid. Katherine's

179

husband had locked her out too. I supposed being a maid was better than being beheaded, but I didn't understand why I should have to work, since I had been Queen of England. It wasn't fair.

I became more and more disgruntled with my position once I knew I'd been Queen of England. I only knew my husband had my head cut off with an axe, but I didn't know why. I didn't understand why I was now a servant. I wanted people to know my true status, but I was afraid I'd be accused of witchery or insanity.

The more I thought about it, the more I realized my mother should have been grateful to have given birth to a former Queen of England. The least William Nichols could have done was to hire servants, but instead he'd treated me like his servant. Who did my common employers think they were to withhold my hard-earned money to pay for uniforms, room, and board? They'd been stealing from me all along. In the summer of 1888, I stole as much money and clothes as I could wear and carry and left behind the maid's uniform in exchange. I took back what was rightly mine.

I went to London's Whitechapel district and rented a room. Rent was cheaper there, and no one would look for a former queen in a low rent district. I enjoyed walks around my new neighborhood clad in my new dresses. It was even dingier than the places I'd lived before, but I was less likely to be caught. I saw quite a few attractive men in the area who appreciated a pretty lady. They not only bought me drinks, but paid me for my company. I finally found my true position in life as an independent lady, and I had many lovers.

I made new lady friends too. I frequented a pub in Spitalfields, where I met my friends, Nelly

Holland, Annie Chapman, Liz Stride—Long Liz we called her—and young Mary Kelly. Annie was the eldest of our little group. She often complimented me on my pretty dresses.

In mid June of 1888, Annie told me, "You won't believe what Long Liz said now. You know she's got a reputation as quite a liar."

"So I've heard. What did she say?"

Annie took a sip of her drink and then giggled. "She claims she lived before this life and was Queen of England." Then she broke into laughter and slapped the table top with the palm of her hand.

"Really?" I smiled as I shuddered with chills. Two beheaded queens' bodies had been found. I wondered if Long Liz might have been Anne Boleyn. How strange. After that, I never gossiped about Long Liz. The least I could do was respect her as a fellow former queen. I looked for an opportunity to meet with her alone to talk about my dreams.

On Thursday night, 30 August, I went out and had a good time with Nelly. I turned forty-three several days before, and I was still celebrating. I'd celebrated on my birthday with young Mary and my good friend Annie, but Nelly wasn't there that night, so the two of us celebrated together Thursday night. I had a lot to drink and spent time with a gentleman, who paid me well. Afterward, I walked down Bucks Row toward my room. It was about two-thirty Friday morning, when I encountered another very attractive gentleman. This one was strikingly familiar with his dark, stylish mustache and piercing blue eyes. I wondered where I knew him from—I had definitely looked into those eyes before—when he pushed me up against a wall.

Naturally, I pulled up my skirt—I thought we were
going to have sex—when he held his right hand
over my mouth as his left hand stuck a knife into
my throat. I couldn't breathe.

*   *   *

I awoke as if from a bad dream. But then, I saw the
same man I'd just been with nearby. I recognized
my dress, now covered with blood, on a woman's
body on the ground beneath him. I didn't
understand what was happening. He had a knife in
his hand, and he was slashing and stabbing wildly at
the poor woman's stomach. Then he placed her legs
tightly together, pulled down her skirt, and ran
away.

I gasped. I saw my body on the ground
covered in blood. At first, I didn't understand, but
then I realized I'd been murdered. I remembered I'd
stared into those piercing blue eyes before, only
then they were in the body of a mean, old, fat man.
First, I had my head chopped off, and now, I'd been
murdered again, only my head was still attached.
Well, I supposed that was progress.

Liz Stride

Although I was Swedish, as a child I always had a fascination with England—London in particular. I was born Elizabeth Gustafsdotter on 27 November 1843. I daydreamed of visiting romantic places like London and Paris, because I dreamed at night of being in London and Paris in my sleep. My dreams were very real to me. I even spoke a bit of English and French at a young age. My parents just thought I loved to learn.

"I plan to travel when I grow up," I told them.

"You'd best marry rich, girl," Papa laughed.

"Oh, but I shall."

I dreamt at night of being a fine lady in a royal court. I dreamt I wore the finest clothing and beautiful velvet gowns. My surroundings in my dreams were always wealthy and rich with color, all the best tapestries and furnishings, and bouquets of fragrant lilies. The sights and smells were more vivid than when I was awake. I often talked about my dream memories and my fantasies. My parents, friends, and school teachers didn't take me seriously. I was often scolded for lying or too much time spent daydreaming, when in fact, I told the truth of my dreams.

By the time I was sixteen, I was tall and slender with a long face, long neck, long limbs, and a wide mouth. I considered myself quite attractive. I tried to present myself at my best—as the fine lady I knew I was—so I would find a good husband. I only wanted to improve my circumstances, but instead I was called a liar. It wasn't fair the way others talked about me. Everyone lied, but I told the truth from my dreams.

At eighteen, I charmed a handsome young man into marriage. Bjorn was tall, slender, and fair. He was gracefully long and lean with bright blue eyes. I knew we would have the most beautiful children together. Even though he proposed to me in February, I made him wait for a summer wedding, so I could have lilies as my bouquet to match my fashionable but simple white dress.

Months after our wedding, we argued. "You spend my hard-earned wages on expensive dresses," Bjorn accused.

"But your wife deserves to be fashionable. I need a minimum of six everyday dresses in different styles, prints, and colors—not to mention at least three finer dresses for church on Sundays and special occasions. And each dress requires matching shoes, gloves, and hat. You're supposed to provide for me properly."

"You just put on airs and try to be above our station in life," he argued.

"I'm trying to improve our status."

He didn't understand, and he simply wasn't ambitious enough. Our marriage lasted almost three years, and then he left me. My parents blamed me for him leaving. I couldn't bear to be around them after that. I was on my own and found I was pregnant. I stayed in our two-room apartment, but I needed money for rent and food—and I would soon outgrow my clothes. I couldn't be someone's servant after having been a proper wife—not in my condition. I didn't have the energy for so much hard work which paid very little. I needed higher wages than were offered to women, and I wanted to better my status. There was only one high wage job available to me, and I'd soon have a child to support, so I became a prostitute. I was smarter than

184

Bjorn, and I proved it by earning more money. I put a good bit aside, because I had limited time before my pregnancy was obvious. I wouldn't be able to work during the last trimester, and then, I'd need to provide for a baby.

I gave birth to my daughter 21 April 1865. She was stillborn. My heart broke. No one grieved for her but me. I was so alone. I went back to work as soon as I was able. I was never lazy, and I wasn't about to go through my savings when I could work and earn more. I occasionally had to spend some of it on doctors for the treatment of venereal disease.

When I was twenty-two, I escaped drab Sweden, which was a constant reminder of my losses. The memory of my little daughter was too painful, so I moved to London, England, in 1866 to start over. London was darker and dingier than Sweden, but for me it was a fresh start. I was always a dreamer with a great imagination. I knew I could rise to meet many situations of which no one else thought me capable. I considered it a big accomplishment to have escaped to England.

"Long Liz" they called me in London. I took it as a term of endearment. I had a long face and a long, slim neck. There were so many Elizabeths in London, I was lucky to be distinguished from the rest. Still, some I thought of as friends had fun at my expense behind my back and hurt my feelings.

English seemed to come naturally to me. I always loved English things and stories ever since I could remember. And it was hardly a stretch to say I'd been to Paris. I'd certainly been there many times in my dreams, but no one believed me. Again I was called a liar. No one understood. And yet here I was in England conversing in English. I could just as easily have lived in France.

In my dreams, I was an English Lady in a French royal court. It was so real in my mind, only there was no longer a French royal court and hadn't been for many years. So I was careful not to mention royalty or courts when I talked about my French memories. I was smarter than most. I tried to work it out—to make sense of it all—but even I was confused. Even if I had been in France when I was a child (my parents insisted I had not), I was no English lady. I felt and behaved like a lady, and now I lived in London, but nothing explained my dreams. Perhaps I was secretly a seer of the future, and someday I would be an English lady in France? Perhaps I would become an actress and portray a lady in a French royal court? But I knew I'd already been to France. When I first arrived in London, I discovered my dreams of London had been quite accurate. I just couldn't explain it.

In spite of it all, I found a fine Englishman to be my husband. John Stride was a ship's carpenter. He was thirteen years older than I, but employed with a good wage. My dreams had come true. He was tall and long limbed with a strong chin. In fact, had we not come from separate countries, we might have been mistaken for kin. John also had a square face and wide, square shoulders. He was a very good provider and very determined once he'd set his mind to something. I knew he'd be more ambitious than Bjorn. I knew John would provide for me properly. We were married 7 March 1869.

I was happy as I could be—at first. John didn't appreciate my dreams or imagination. I told him everything, of course, because a good wife didn't keep secrets from her husband. He told me often, "Woman, you need to focus on the real world instead of what's in that flighty head of yours."

186

"Oh, but I have such grand ideas." I smiled at him.

"Well," John answered, "I'm not so much interested in grand ideas as the real world, especially when we're with other people. You know, Liz, sometimes you embarrass me."

"I certainly don't want to do that," I protested.

"Now, lass, I don't mind your grand thoughts so much when we're alone. That's different. I just want you to be more demur around others. I promise I'll protect you and provide well for you as long as you mind your tongue around other people."

I made my best effort. I loved him dearly. I accepted that he could be quite bossy, especially since he was more than a decade older. I might have preferred to be treated more as a partner in the marriage, but with the age difference, I just accepted he was in charge. I tried my best to love, honor, and obey him. I believed he truly loved me too. He was extremely protective of me. I knew a man needed to feel in control.

Christmas Eve of 1872 was a happy time. We decorated a beautiful Christmas tree together in the living room of our flat, and I cooked a lovely meal with plump goose for just the two of us. That evening, I went alone to the kitchen to fetch the carving knife for the dinner table. When I picked up the knife, I saw a flash of reflected light on the blade just as I heard John call out, "Where's my sword?"

When I awoke, I was in bed. The curtains were closed but daylight peeked through. When I tried to lift my head, I felt a bandage on the right side of my neck. I touched it with my hand. As I stirred, I saw John, who sat in a chair next to the bed, reach for me.

"That was a very close call," he said. "How do you feel?"

"Weak, strange, confused."

"What happened?" he asked me, though I was about to ask him the same thing. "Do you remember what happened?"

I had to think for a moment. "You asked for your sword," I said.

"What? What sword?" He sounded very concerned.

"Knife," I corrected myself. "I meant to say knife. You asked for your knife. That's all I remember." But I was sure he asked for his sword. He was right though—he had no sword. I was confused.

"Yes, the carving knife. You went to the kitchen to fetch it for the goose. Then I heard a crash. I called to you, but, when there was no answer, I ran into the kitchen and found you on the floor bleeding."

I touched the bandage on my neck again. "What happened?"

"You must have fainted with the knife in your hand," William explained. "The doctor said the cut was very dangerous—that you could have died from your throat being cut. Yet here you are— our very own Christmas miracle."

John insisted I stay in bed and rest, and I didn't argue. As I rested, I remembered seeing a flash of reflected light in the blade of the knife. I wondered if somehow the flash had caused me to faint, but I couldn't quite make sense of it. I might have died, and I was barely twenty-nine. It was a strange feeling.

My marriage began to fall apart when I awoke from a nightmare during the middle of the night in 1876. I screamed, and John woke up from his own sound slumber. He came to with a start, jumped out of bed, and demanded, "Who's here?"

"No one but me," I told him as I sobbed and shook.

"Have you lost your mind, Liz?" he asked.

"I had a bad dream," I explained, hugging my shoulders and rocking myself. "Please come back to bed."

He got back into bed, calmed down, and put his arm around me. "Now what could trouble you so as to cause you to scream like that? It made my blood curdle."

"I was dead, and my bones were being dug up and looked upon," I told him.

"Aw, now, that's just a bad dream," he said, giving my shoulders a squeeze. He gently kissed my cheek. "You're clearly not dead, and even if you were, no one would dig up your bones and look at them. It was just a silly dream."

"But it seemed so real," I weakly protested.

"Aye, you've always had that problem, haven't you?" he reminded me. "Now we'll go back to sleep, and we'll speak no more of this." We both lay back down. Soon John was fast asleep.

I knew in my heart the dream was real, but I couldn't make sense of it. I had vividly seen my own skeleton viewed by strangers in a chapel where they'd found it encased in a very old arrow chest. I'd seen them open the chest, and I knew what was inside. But what shocked me and caused me to scream was what I saw when they opened it. My skull was next to the rest of my skeleton. It wasn't attached.

Eventually I drifted off to sleep. I found myself praying in my sleep, *Lord Jesus, receive my soul.* I was aware that everyone I knew had told the most horrendous lies about me, but I didn't care. I just wanted to be done with it all. I wanted to be far away from where I was. I was kneeling and praying, but it was no church I knelt in. I felt a slight breeze on my face and hands, and I was blindfolded. I heard a man's voice say, "Where's my sword?" I awoke in my own bed once more.

John was already gone to work. He was kind not to wake me. I knew I couldn't discuss this latest dream with anyone else, or John would be angry. Our agreement was for me to hold my tongue about my dreams, and for that favor, he'd never leave me. He said we'd speak no more of this, but that was before the second dream. Since he wasn't home to talk to, I went out for a walk. I thought it might be better to have some other topic of conversation prepared to share when John came home from work. It was the least I could do, since I'd disturbed his sleep. I stopped by the market for a few things for our dinner, and then I saw a boy on the street selling newspapers. I bought one to read the current events for our dinner conversation that evening.

When I got home, I sat down at the table with the paper and began to read. There were many topics of interest, and I made mental notes to remember these items for discussion at dinner. Then I turned another page and read the strangest article. Chills came over me. I began to cry uncontrollably. I was thirty-two years old, and this sort of thing just wasn't supposed to happen. The article described the progress of the renovations of the Chapel of St. Peter ad Vincula. The skeletons of two wives of King Henry VIII had been discovered and identified. Both had been beheaded. One was the skeleton of Queen Katherine Howard. The other, which was found not in a casket, but in an arrow chest from that time, was the skeleton of Queen Anne Boleyn. I recalled the arrow chest in my dream.

The article summarized the lives of the two women. Anne had first served the Queen of France as a lady-in-waiting, and then served Queen Catharine of Aragón at the English court. Anne was beheaded not by an axe with her head on the block, as was the custom, and as was Katherine Howard, but in the French manner of the time—by a sword while kneeling upright.

I remembered clearly hearing a man's voice say, "Where is my sword?" I'd prayed and wished to be far away from there. I was blindfolded and knelt upright.

Now I knew once and for all what was happening to me. I wasn't mad, nor was I seeing the future. My dreams were real, and they were memories of my past. I didn't understand how, but I had clearly lived before. I'd been Anne Boleyn, Queen of England and mother of Queen Elizabeth by King Henry VIII. I had in fact been a true and real English Lady in both French and English courts. And my bones had been unearthed and looked upon. It was real, but no one else understood.

I did my best as John's wife, but he just couldn't understand why I was so emotional. It really seemed to bother him that he couldn't control my feelings. I carried several centuries inside me, and I could talk to no one about it. I felt so alone. I worried I would say something accidentally. I took an occasional drink to calm my nerves, but when I drank a wee bit much, it was impossible to keep my secret past quiet.

"I was Queen of England once," I told John.

"You're a damned boldfaced and incorrigible liar." Still, he stayed with me. I didn't fault him for his reaction. He tried to protect me. Were it not for my sweet John, I'd probably be in an asylum.

A few years passed before I realized John was ill. He developed a cough. Too much exertion left him short of breath. He also became more irritable. I knew he wasn't well, but I found it difficult to live with him. "I swear to you, John, I feel I'm on the verge of coming unhinged every time you mock me."

John could only respond with a deep, hacking cough. I worried about him. We argued more and more. I tried to care for him, but he was stubborn and wouldn't rest. He wouldn't listen and no longer talked to me. I knew he fought to remain in control, but his strength waned. It was so very frustrating for both of us.

I was glad we had no children. We each had enough to deal with. I forgave him his promise to stay with me forever, and we parted ways at the end of 1881. We remained friends and tried to take care of each other.

I found a room of my own in Spitalfields, and John gave me money as long as he was able. I kept to myself a great deal. I cried frequently, so I stayed home. I didn't know why I was so different from everyone else in society. I pondered the memories of my dreams, and how I should know such things. I'd been the Queen of England and was glad to be rid of it. Increasingly, I came to realize the past belonged in the past.

John's health deteriorated. One day when he came by to give me my allowance, he had a coughing fit much worse than I'd ever seen. I saw blood on the handkerchief he'd held to his mouth as he coughed.

Eventually, he was no longer able to work. He was diagnosed with consumption. He died 24 October 1884. I bought white lilies and laid them on his grave. We were married fifteen years, though we didn't live together the last three. I took comfort in the thought that if I'd lived before as Anne Boleyn, perhaps he too would live again. Maybe we'd even see each other again in some future life. Maybe he'd been somewhere in my life as Anne Boleyn, but I knew he wasn't Henry VIII. He'd taken such good care of me in this life, I couldn't imagine him otherwise, but I had the strange thought he protected me in this life because he hadn't then. And now he was gone.

Meanwhile, I was forced to sew and clean houses for others. I no longer had delusions I could improve my status in life or travel to France. I was alone now. I skimped on meals to pay the rent. It was safer for a woman to have a safe place to sleep, even if it was just a room. Then I moved to a house of common lodging. I could afford to go without a few meals. My lower front teeth were tender, so I preferred soft food and had no need for expensive meat. One by one, my lower row of teeth loosened and fell out, but I'd lost much dearer things in this life and before.

Several months after John Stride died, in 1885, I moved in with a dock worker. John had introduced us some years back. His name was Michael Kidney, and I met him again at John's funeral. Michael had a smile almost too wide for his face. He was a kind man, and looked in on me from time to time. Once Michael and I moved in together, I had no more money worries. He was very generous. I attributed his kindness and gentleness to his sincere faith. His favorite book was the King James Bible, and he often read to me from it. I especially liked it when he read from the Psalms.

I knew by this time not to speak of certain things, such as my dreams and my life before as Anne Boleyn. I didn't want Michael to question my sanity or be embarrassed by my conversation, and I feared he'd think it blasphemy. Michael spoke kindly of John, and of course, so did I. We lived together in a small apartment in the East End near Whitechapel. I continued to sew occasionally for pay to help with expenses, but life was so much easier with Michael. He was kinder to me in bed than John. John had been a forceful man, but Michael took time to be sure I also enjoyed our intimate encounters.

I still had occasional crying spells, which I kept secret from Michael. There was no need to concern him with moods I experienced while he was at work. He'd never lost a child or felt like a social outcast. I drank to calm my nerves, because I didn't want Michael to think I was hysterical. I didn't normally have a temper—except when I was drunk.

Michael cautioned me to cut back on spirits. He said drink could ruin a person's health. He was so considerate—much sweeter and less demanding than John. I knew I shouldn't compare them, but Michael was my favorite husband. When he sometimes went out with his mates for the evening,

I'd go to my favorite pub in Spitalfields to see my lady friends.

By June 1888, I'd been with Michael a little over three years. I was at the pub with Annie Chapman and young Mary Kelly, when the drink got the better of me. "I was once the Queen of England in a former life," I told them. I hadn't intended to—it just slipped out.

"A former life," Annie laughed. "What's that supposed to mean?" The two of them erupted with laughter.

"Well, there it is," I said, finished my drink, and went home. I was glad I got home before Michael. I went straight to bed to sleep it off and hoped he didn't notice. After that, I didn't frequent the pub as often. When Michael went out with his mates, I either stayed home or took a short walk in the dark.

The end of August was Polly Nichols' birthday. I passed her on the street the day before. "Tomorrow's my birthday, Liz. Will you come to the pub and celebrate with me now?"

"No, I'd best not," I answered, afraid I'd give in to temptation. "I'd best go home to my husband, but you have a happy birthday, Polly." I knew Polly and young Mary Kelly were prostitutes, but they didn't have men to provide for them. I'd once been like them.

A few days later, Michael came home with bad news. "There's been a murder in Whitechapel. A prostitute named Polly Nichols was found with her throat slashed."

I screamed and covered my mouth and throat with my hands. I closed my eyes, caught my breath, and said, "I know little Polly. I passed her in the street just the other afternoon. She invited me to celebrate her birthday in the pub, but I declined."

"Well, it's a good thing you didn't go," Michael said. "She was found with her throat slashed, poor woman. 'The wages of sin is death.'"

"But we all die."

"Aye," he agreed, "because we're all sinners."

I felt sick. Polly was the only woman I knew who didn't mock me or call me a liar, and now she'd been murdered.

About a week after Polly's last birthday, I told Michael I was going out for a walk. I went by the pub. Annie Chapman was there. She hadn't heard about Polly's death, so I told her. At first she didn't believe me, but the bartender confirmed it.

The following evening, Michael came home from work and said, "There's been another murder." I quickly sat down. I covered my mouth so I wouldn't scream, closed my eyes, and waited. "A woman named Annie Chapman," he continued. "They say she was slashed up something awful. Apparently there's a murderer loose in Whitechapel targeting prostitutes."

I opened my eyes. "I know Annie Chapman. She's no prostitute. Her husband died recently, and I felt sorry for her, but she always made fun of people. She made fun of my accent." I didn't dare tell Michael I'd said I'd been Queen of England.

"Well then, at least you made a poor widow smile before she was killed." Michael always found something kind to say.

"First Polly and now Annie," I said in disbelief.

"Their reward will be great in heaven," he tried to comfort me.

"I hope so," I said, but I didn't believe it.

30 September was a good day—nothing out of the ordinary. I was forty-four and would be forty-five in less than two months. Michael went out with his mates for the evening, so I didn't need to cook dinner. I went out by myself for a stroll in the dark. Of course, I went by the pub and had a drink to relax.

Nelly Holland was there. "I drank with them both," she said.

"I beg your pardon?"

"I drank with Polly the night she was murdered, and I drank with Annie the night she was murdered," Nelly explained.

"Well then, perhaps you drink too much," I said, as I got up and left the bar. I was finally at ease and didn't want to think about the murders. I continued my stroll. I enjoyed being alone to think about what strange lives I'd lived. I'd only had one child, my stillborn daughter. I often cried for her, poor little dear. As Anne Boleyn I'd only had one daughter, but I didn't have her long either. Still, I'd escaped Sweden and made it back to London, just as I'd planned. As Anne, I was keen to be far from London, but I came back. I recalled the dream where I saw someone discover my bones. The Christmas Eve prior to that dream, I'd fainted and accidentally cut my own throat. I realized my throat was cut when I was same age Anne was when she died. I walked along, thought about how odd life was and wondered who Henry VIII was now. Just then a gentleman with a fashionable, dark mustache approached me. He was charismatic and attractive, but we'd never met. I saw no one else on the street.

"Might I have the pleasure of your company this fine evening?" he asked me.

I laughed. "I'm sorry to disappoint you, sir," I told him, "but I'm already spoken for."

He smiled at me charmingly as he walked alongside me and matched my stride. "And where is your gentleman, if in fact you are already spoken for?"

"He's out with his mates," I told the friendly stranger, "and I'm simply having a stroll."

He smiled and continued to walk with me, as if he was considering what to say next. Finally, he broke the silence. "Well, then, since your gentleman is with his mates, might I have the pleasure of your company this fine evening?"

"No, sir, you may not. Goodnight to you." I quickened my pace to get away from him, but I wasn't quick enough.

He grabbed me tightly by the arm with his left hand, and forced his right hand over my mouth as he shoved me into an alleyway. It happened so quickly. He pressed me up against a wall with his body, and kept his right hand tight over my mouth. As I looked into the blue eyes of this stranger, I gazed into the eyes of a madman. My last thought, as I felt a stab in my throat, was, *so here you are, Henry.*

*   *   *

He killed me again, and left my body lying in an alley just like Anne's body was left on the scaffold. The coward ran away. What's wrong with him? Surely he had whatever vengeance he wanted the last time. This lunatic could simply not take no for an answer, and he'd learned to kill with his own hands. At least this time he left my head attached.

I realized Michael had been a kind priest, who'd given me religious counsel and heard my confessions when I was Anne. He was the archbishop who'd come to me when I was arrested. I'd warned him to protect himself. I wondered now if I'd talked to him about my strange dreams, would he have remembered. Well, it was too late for that conversation, but he'd know to put lilies on my grave.

I also saw John Stride had been my deceitful, treacherous uncle who did some of Henry's bloody work. No wonder he didn't want me to talk about that life. I was attracted to him because he was familiar. Of course I was happier with Michael. I wondered how poor Michael would feel when he learned I'd been murdered. I feared he'd blame himself for being out with his mates, but I couldn't console him. And poor Nelly had a drink with me just before.

So this was how it really worked—we were born, our bodies died, but we went on, and then we were born again, only to die again. There really was eternal life; it just wasn't the way it was taught it in church. Good people died to be reborn just like murderers and madmen. I needed to learn not to put myself above everyone else. I wanted to go far, far away from London, from England, and from Europe—to the far side of America. Maybe the madman who had been Henry wouldn't find me there.

I also wondered what became of the queen I deposed, Henry's first wife. She must have hated me. I realized I would see her again—a frightening thought. It was no small matter to steal a kingdom and a king from a queen. I'd rather pay that debt than have it hang over my head, so to speak.

Kate Eddowes

My parents were decent people. My father worked hard, but he also drank a lot of gin. I was born 14 April 1842 as one of ten siblings. "There's not enough money for food and clothes for all of us and the gin too," my mother often said.

I grew up learning to read and write and fend for myself. I knew that, in their way, my parents wanted the best for their children. I didn't judge them. They did the best they could with what little they had. I felt it was up to me to learn to take care of myself.

When my father drank, he'd pinch my cheeks and say, "There's my little princess. Your cheeks are as rosy as ripe pomegranates."

The first time he said that, I asked, "What are pomegranates?"

"They're very sweet, red fruits from the Bible, my little angel," he told me.

"Like apples?" I asked.

"Like apples, only sweeter." It always made me smile. Of course, as I got older, I realized that my cheeks were only rosy because he pinched them. As time passed, his gin led to foul moods when he'd slap my mother around.

I grew to only five feet tall, but I was smart enough to know marriage could neither make a woman happy nor provide for her physical needs and wants. I sensed there was something more I should search for, but I didn't know what it might be. "There must be something more to life," I told my mum as she put away the dishes I dried after my sister washed them.

"Something more? There's nothing more, foolish girl. This is all there is."

"But don't you want to be happy someday?"

"Rubbish. You just do your chores and concern yourself with finding a decent man to look after you."

"But why should only men have the right to make decisions?" I asked her.

"It's just the way it is."

I knew if I trusted a man to provide for me, he'd make me his servant or put me aside as he wished. Marriage certainly hadn't worked out well for my mum.

I was often told I was pretty. I had pleasant face, dark auburn hair, and hazel eyes. I was bright and liked to read, but there was no place in this world for a literate woman, unless she was queen. I wanted to make my own way without being legally tied to any man, so I read as many books as I could find. I was small, but both strong and strong-willed. I understood most men were unwise, and I had little patience for dull men who hurt women. My mum wasn't woman enough to stand up to a drunk. Instead, she'd take out her frustrations on her children. Our family had no peace. Mum was my father's servant. If a man ever hit me, I vowed I would hit him back. Sometimes I wondered why I had to keep my opinions to myself. I felt strongly that I never wanted to be submissive to men as was expected of me.

My family attended church. I liked it when I was a child, but as I got older, I realized it was just another institution that took what little money our family had. Rich folks hired common people to work but barely paid them enough to live on. A woman could get into real trouble for talking about social wrongs. I was angry at injustice. I wanted to change everything that was unfair, and I wasn't even allowed to talk about it. But first, I had to change my own circumstances. I knew if I repeated my mother's mistake with marriage, I would end up like her. I couldn't let that happen, but I wasn't supposed to go out on my own as a single woman either.

I was twenty-three when I visited a relative in Birmingham and met a soldier, Thomas Conway. He didn't ask me to marry him, so I stayed with him. Tom liked me just the way I was, and we were happy. I wanted to please him, because he didn't demand anything of me. I left my parents' world behind. I decided for myself I wouldn't be a servant, a whipped wife, or indebted to a church run by men.

Tom and I left Birmingham and moved to London together. We were happy, and I got pregnant. I gave birth to a little girl, Annie, when I was thirty. She was my darling. Tom took good care of us. I was luckier than most women. We were a happy little family. I would pinch Annie's cheeks, just as my father had done mine, and then tell her they looked like ripe pomegranates. When she asked what those were, I explained to her just as my father had to me.

Then Tom and I had two more children, both sons. Things began to change. Tom treated Annie and I like the house-servants, while he spent his time at home with his boys. He considered little Annie old enough to help with the boys, but she was a child too. He made it clear housework was women's work. The boys would be taught a trade, but not expected to help at home. Annie would not be taught a trade. She was to depend on men her entire life. She and I had somehow become servants.

Tom and I hadn't married, and we weren't supposed to end up like my parents. Tom drank gin from time to time, so I did too. Only I began to prefer the gin to Tom. When I drank, I lost my temper over the injustice of how women were treated by men. "You've no right to treat me and Annie like servants," I told him.

Then he got angry, and we fought. "You're not a good mother," he told me. "A good mother doesn't drink."

"A good father doesn't drink," I retorted. "I only drink because you do."

"I'm a man. I have a right to a drink when I want."

"Then so do I. Maybe I'm not a good mother, but I'm not your soldier to command. You think you can make decisions for me just because you're a man. You never ask my advice or consult me about decisions that affect us all. You're not any smarter than me just because you're a man. I drink because I'm unhappy. If I stay, soon enough my own sons will think they're my masters as well. It's wrong."

I was never a whipped wife, but I hadn't changed anything. I'd tried. I couldn't stay—not even for my Annie. I couldn't help Annie if I couldn't help myself, so I left Tom and the children. It broke my heart to leave Annie, but she was old enough to find her own way, and I had nothing better to offer her. Tom would train her to serve him and her brothers, so she could be a good wife to some other man. If I found a better way, I'd come back and help her.

Tom gave me money every month. "It's the proper thing to do," he said. "You're my wife, even though it's just common-law." I was never his wife, but I took his money. Without it, I was penniless. It was hard for a woman to earn a decent wage, much less afford gin. I'd become dependent on the gin. Still, if I'd known he'd thought of me as his wife, I'd have left him sooner. He never even asked me if I wanted to be his wife. Just like a man, he decided for me, and I didn't even know. I felt like a fool. And then he stopped giving me money, so I stopped eating. Fasting was a futile, silent protest, but I spent what I had for gin. I didn't want to face my failure with myself and my daughter.

As I walked past a store window, I saw myself in the reflection. I no longer had the rosy cheeks my father used to compare with ripe pomegranates. Instead, I was pale and drawn. I wondered what a pomegranate tasted like or if it held some magic elixir to restore my health. But I was fasting, and I'd never seen a pomegranate. I'd just have to settle for gin.

It was early in1886 when I first met Jack Kelly. I fell in love at first sight. I felt so comfortable with him, and I foolishly couldn't resist him. Even I didn't understand why I was so drawn to him. He had dark brown hair and beautiful blue eyes. He seemed honorable, and he carried himself with grace like a true gentleman. Men earned more money, and I was exhausted from work as a maid and seamstress which paid so little. I told him, "I hope you and I might be good friends or partners. I've no interest in marriage, and I don't expect you to account to me for your actions, as long as you don't expect me to account for mine."

He just smiled and replied, "So be it, Lady Katherine." He was the only one who ever called me that. He was an upholsterer by trade, and had a collection of knives.

"Are you good at your job, Sir Jack?"

"Aye, I wield a sharp blade. I aim and slash with fine skill."

It was my turn to smile. After I teamed up with Jack, I broke my fast, but I never seemed to regain my appetite. Jack Kelly and I liked to drink together. I knew there was something a bit off about him, but for all his fantasy and delusions, he treated me like a lady.

Jack and I never seemed to have much money, because when we did, we drank it away. For me, life was about independence and fairness rather than wealth. Jack and I talked like equals. Sometimes he'd laugh and say, "You don't think like most women."

But I'd found a man who didn't want to own me. I knew how rare that was. I knew he was different, and there was strangeness in him. Sometimes his pretty blue eyes would change into a very odd look, and then he'd leave. I wouldn't see him for a few days or a few weeks, but we were both free. When he came back, I never asked him to account for himself, because I'd promised I wouldn't. I knew he probably had other women. I fancied he might even have a home somewhere, but liked his freedom. So, when he wasn't around, I felt free to make easy money by selling my body. I never told him, because I didn't have to account to him either. I didn't like resorting to prostitution, but I was too tired to struggle with hard work that paid so little.

Jack and I always celebrated our birthdays together, because we were both born in April. The first one we shared was my forty-fourth. "We're diamonds, the both of us," he would say, "like our April birthstone."

I enjoyed Jack's occasional disappearances. I kept our rented room when he was gone. Jack never treated me like a servant. I was finally free, but I couldn't support Annie, and I couldn't bring myself to return to her only to tell her to become a prostitute.

I was lucky I had little need of food. It often made me sick. Gin eased the pain in my lower back, which only grew worse over time. Sometimes my hands and feet would swell—another reason for prostitution. I couldn't sew or clean with my fingers swollen and my feet painful to stand on. I had spells when I was short of breath. I no longer dwelled on my failure as a mother. I just dealt with physical pains day to day.

Meanwhile, my little Annie had grown up and married a gun maker. Her new name was Annie Phillips. I sent her a note of congratulations, although I feared for her future. She and her husband settled on the south side of the Thames.

In the summer of 1888, Jack said, "Let's go to Kent. We can spend time in the fields and fresh air."

"I knew you were a worldly man, Jack, but what about the cost of the journey? We'll have to give up our room." I wondered if he was actually an eccentric gentleman from Kent. He was kind to me, but I'd also wondered about the mood that caused the strange look in his eyes right before he'd disappear for a while. I looked closely, but it wasn't there now.

"The country air will do you good," he insisted. "We'll split the cost of the trip with Emily."

Emily was a friend of ours. She often joined us in the pub, but she was more my friend than

Jack's. We found her and asked her. She was delighted with the idea. "It'll be good for us all—an adventure."

So, the three of us went to Kent. We found work picking hops. The Kent countryside was lovely. The air was sweet and pure, unlike Whitechapel. I was happy again for the first time since Annie was a baby. I felt the sun on my face. The three of us were equals working for the same wage—a dream come true for me. It was hard work, and I felt faint most days, but the fresh air was wonderful, so I kept quiet and worked. I finally found what had so eluded me as a child. I hoped I could someday tell Annie about the bright, clean country outside London, and I was relieved to not have to work as a prostitute for a change. I'd always felt Jack was an honorable man, and now I felt my own honor somewhat restored.

At the end of August, we returned to London and Whitechapel. Emily went her own way, but Jack and I kept each other company. London was dark and gloomy after the hop fields of Kent, so I wasn't surprised when Jack got that strange look and disappeared for a few days about a week after our return. I took advantage of the time for a much needed rest, but the money we'd worked hard for was easily spent over the next few weeks. The work had been as hard on my body as the fresh air and sunlight had been good for it.

Jack and I split our last sixpence for rooms in male and female boarding houses 28 September. We met again the next morning. We had no money. We strolled about all morning in search of work but found none. Jack didn't know I sold myself when he was away, so I only looked for domestic jobs that day, even though I didn't think I could work much with the pain in my back, hands, and feet.

As the morning wore on, Jack became tense and agitated. "I have a right to work," he grumbled. "These employers don't appreciate my skills as a craftsman."

By afternoon I had an idea. "I could get money from my daughter, Annie. I'll go down to Bermondsey on the south bank of the Thames. Annie Phillips is her name now. She's the wife of a gun maker—so appropriate, as her father was a soldier. She'll give me some money, and I'll come straight back to Whitechapel."

"Good," Jack agreed.

I went to Bermondsey. I badly wanted to see Annie, but she greeted me with, "Mum, what have you done to yourself?" She made such a face.

"Oh, I know I've lost weight, but food doesn't agree much with me. I need to sit down, darling. I need to catch my breath." She took me in, fussed over me, and insisted I stay the night. When her Mr. Phillips came home from work, we sat down to dinner, but my appetite failed me. "Annie, you're an excellent cook," I told her, and I did my best to swallow what I could. "I had a lovely summer in Kent working in the hop fields. The fresh air did me good. You should see how lovely, bright, and clean it is outside London. Not only was the air fresh, but I was paid the same as a man for equal work."

Annie listened intently, but Mr. Phillips was silent as he concentrated on his supper. After I poked at breakfast the next morning, Mr. Phillips himself gave me some money. "You take this now, Kate," he said. "Try to take better care of yourself."

"Oh, I will. Thank you, sir. I'll be just fine. Don't you worry. Thank you for everything and for taking good care of my Annie." Then I turned to Annie and said, "And thank you for the good food and for being such a good daughter. There's no need to fret about me, dear. You really should visit the country sometime."

I went back to Whitechapel. By late afternoon, the pain in my back was bad, so I stopped for a sip of gin. In the pub, I talked to young Mary Kelly.

"Haven't seen you lately," she said. "Can't say as I blame you for laying low with such dreadful happenings lately."

"What dreadful happenings?" I asked. "I haven't been 'laying low,' as you say. I'm just not well."

"First Polly Nichols was murdered, and then Annie Chapman. Just dreadful. I heard they were all slashed up, and Nelly Holland had drinks with them each the nights they were murdered. I'm frightened."

"Oh, that's terrible," I said and ordered another drink. I forgot I was supposed to share the money with Jack. I felt the need for more drinks to relieve both the sadness and the physical pain. Mary Kelly went on about some other woman she'd known who'd been stabbed somewhere else, but I didn't understand what had happened. The next thing I knew, I was in the street and arrested for drunk and disorderly. At Bishopgate police station, I told the coppers, "My name is Mary Ann Kelly." I didn't want word to get back to my Annie and her Mr. Phillips I'd been arrested as a common criminal. I laughed in my cell when I realized I still cared about my reputation. Sometimes, Jack called me other women's names without seeming to notice, and I ignored it. I knew he had other women, but he always came home to me.

I was released later that night. I looked for Jack and finally found him. He had pawned his boots the night before for lodging, but then he'd stolen another pair. I never stole, but I didn't judge him, since I'd spent the night at Annie's and left him penniless. I was short of breath, and the pain in my lower back was worse. We walked to nearby Mitre Square, which was surrounded by warehouses. I stopped to lean against a wall. "My back's killing me, but Annie's husband gave me some money. I spent most of it at the pub to stop the pain, and then I was arrested. You're awfully quiet tonight, Jack."

"I've searched for you for hours," he said and just stared at me. His blue eyes had the crazy look he'd get before he disappeared, but I didn't want him to leave. I'd just been freed by the police and only just found him. I didn't like the look in his eyes, so I looked the rest of him over more closely.

"What's that splattered on your clothes? It's red like pomegranate juice."

"Never you mind," he answered. "They took you to jail, but obviously they didn't keep you. You were supposed to bring the money back, not drink it by yourself."

"My back hurt badly, Jack. And the coppers kept me just long enough to sober up a bit. When they picked me up," I laughed, "I told them my name was Mary Kelly. I don't know why—"

He suddenly shoved his right hand over my mouth and held it there. I thought I was going to faint from lack of air. We looked directly into each others eyes, and I knew he was going to abandon me for good. Then he jabbed something sharp into my windpipe. I fainted.

*   *   *

When I awoke, I felt no more pain. I was floating above the square looking down at Jack below me. I watched as he slashed his knife across the right side of my face and my right ear lobe fell off. What had been my face was already covered in blood, but then he underlined both my eyes with his blade and cut through my upper lip. I watched with a strange mixture of horror and amazement as he cut out my kidney. He held it up in his bloody hand and whispered, "Now there's the end of your back pain."

Had my kidney caused me all that pain? He was right. Both pain and weakness were gone. I was forty-six and would grow no older. My Jack had killed me.

I followed him for a short time and watched him cook and eat half my kidney. Was he that hungry? Then he wrote a letter and put it into a package in which he'd wrapped the other half of my kidney. Curiously, he signed the letter, "Jack the Ripper." How had I been so deceived by this madman?

I floated away and enjoyed my freedom from pain. I had no more worries about money or where to sleep. I was glad for the time in Kent with the sunlight and fresh air. I was happy I'd seen Annie, but other thoughts crept in. Maybe I should have been better to the children. Tom was a good father. Even Annie was his faithful daughter, and Mr. Phillips provided well for her. I wasn't a good mother. I'd kept my part of the agreement with

Tom, but he'd treated me as the wife I never agreed to be.

Then there was Jack. Had I really been a murderer's companion? Did he murder the women Mary Kelly told me about? Why didn't I see his madness? I remembered right before he killed me I'd asked him what was splattered on his clothes. I knew now it was blood. He killed someone while I was looking for him.

I recognized him from another life. He was my husband then, but he put me aside for another woman. I was his wife, partner, and mother of his child, but he put me and his own daughter aside. I was so afraid of being put aside I never married. Instead I ended up with him. He was the problem to start with. He was always charming. I vowed to remember this when I found myself in another body. I vowed to hold him responsible for his actions. Twice he turned on me. Twice I saw his insanity too late. I vowed the next time I met him I'd protect myself and others from him. I was more determined than him, and I wasn't crazy.

Mary Janet Kelly

I was born in Wales in 1863. My parents and I left Wales when I was a child, so my father could find work. We spoke Welsh at home but had to speak English everywhere else. We were a good Catholic family. My parents loved me and doted on me, and I loved them too. I never gave them any trouble—at least not until I met the man I knew would be my husband.

I was short and slim with a straight nose that pointed down to my double chin. I was fifteen years old when I met Mr. James Kelly. I was instantly drawn to him. He stood straight and always seemed taller than his actual height. Of course he was handsome and eighteen years old, but it was more than just that. I'd found a missing piece of myself. I was attracted to him beyond my free will. I couldn't say no to him. I knew better—I was too young according to what my dear parents taught me—but he was the one I just couldn't say no to. I loved my parents, but I felt James and I had known each other forever. I trusted him. I knew he'd take care of me. Any warnings I may have heard from my mother about young men couldn't possibly apply to my James Kelly.

I didn't have the most eye-catching figure, but I was petite with red hair and blue eyes. James said he loved me. I knew I was meant to be his wife. He always knew what to say and do, and I followed his lead.

By the time I was sixteen, I was pregnant with his child. Of course, he asked me to marry him, and of course, I agreed. James worked as an upholsterer and was very skilled with his knives, so I knew he'd provide for me and the baby. I told my dear parents, "Don't be upset with me. James Kelly has asked me to marry him, and I'm pregnant with his child. James will be part of our family as well as the baby. May I marry him, please?"

They agreed. I believed they'd be as happy with James as their son as I'd be with him as my husband. I didn't see they only agreed to the wedding because they were too ashamed of me pregnant and unmarried. They made no pretense of happiness for me, the baby, or James, but I told myself we'd all be fine. James would marry me, and we'd be a happy family.

James assured me, "Your parents will come around once the baby arrives. It'll be their grandchild. I'll take care of us. You're going to be the mother of my child. We'll be a good Catholic family. Your parents will come around."

Of course, I believed him. He always took charge. I was so happy. I went with my parents to the church. I wore my favorite violet dress. My parents forbade me to tell anyone else, so I didn't. I was eager to make everyone happy, and if no one else knew the date of our wedding, it wouldn't be so shameful. James met us at the church with a pretty posy of violets for me. I was thrilled—no man had ever given me flowers before, and they matched my dress. We were married in the church by a priest with only my parents there.

My mother cried throughout the short ceremony. Once we said our vows, and the priest pronounced us man and wife, my father turned to me and said, "You've brought shame on us, Mary. Good Catholics get married first, but you refused to live as we taught you. You're his now. We'll have nothing more to do with either of you. Don't ever come back to us. You've dishonored us, and we disown you."

WHAT JUST HAPPENED? I thought my parents loved me, and I trusted James. "But I'm going to have your grandchild." I looked desperately at my mother, but she'd turned her back.

"We're moving," my father continued. "You come back, and you'll see. We won't be there." They walked away as quickly as they could.

I was devastated. How could they could be so cruel? We'd been so close, and I was their only child. I thought they loved me. We came to the church together, but they never told me this would happen. I thought they'd be happy for me, but they disowned me, and James said nothing—not a word in my defense. My wedding was the last time I saw my parents.

"Well, that's the thanks we get for doing the right thing," James finally said after my parents had gone. "They're not even going to give us a wedding gift or welcome their own grandchild with gifts? The least your old man could've done was offer me a job."

I couldn't believe they'd abandoned me. I was crushed to hear my father say such things and watch them walk away. They just cut me off, and we'd been so close. I was their little girl—their only child. James never said he planned to provide for us through a job from my father. I trusted him take good care of me. I was his wife. It was all too much to take in. I cried the entire way as James and I walked back to the flat we'd call home—where we would welcome our baby into the world. It was supposed to be a happy occasion. I clutched my posy of violets and watered them with my tears.

"All right, that's enough now," he said once we were inside. "You're not allowed to cry all through our wedding night." He smiled.

How could he smile after what just happened? Why hadn't he defended me? But he was all I had left. I looked up at him, wiped away my tears, and said, "Let's talk about how we're going to raise our child. Let's promise never to treat our own son or daughter the way my parents just treated me."

"Or me," he added. "We'll never turn our back on our child, unless of course, he or she takes up with a Jew."

"Fine. The child will marry another Catholic, of course, but it could also choose a protestant instead."

"As long as the spouse is Christian," James agreed. "It wouldn't be right to associate with Jews."

James wasn't educated or anything fancy like that. I'd thought he was a working man. I soon learned he was very moody. His reactions always surprised me. Before we married, everything he said and did seemed so appropriate, but after the wedding, I saw a different James. He only took work as an upholsterer, but his jobs didn't seem to last long. When he didn't work, he moped around the flat, sharpened the knives he used for his work, and blamed my father for our circumstances. I was always nervous when he sharpened those knives. He always got an odd look in his eyes when he did, and I didn't like it. When he'd get paid, he'd disappear for the night. I knew when he came home the next day he'd been drunk.

I kept my posy of violets long after they'd wilted and dried, but they were all I had left from my wedding—except for my violet dress. But it was also the only dress I had from my former life, and I soon grew too big to wear it. James bought me two oversized maternity dresses, both yellow. I was grateful enough as I had nothing else to wear. I couldn't bring myself to tell him how embarrassed I felt in them. I needed him, but I felt so betrayed. I'd thought I loved him, but was this really true love? After my parents and James, I began to doubt love meant much. I realized I wasn't lovable.

I felt so alone. I had no money of my own, and James didn't bring home enough to buy baby things. I was lucky if I didn't go to sleep hungry. My slim figure wasn't slim anymore. James no longer found me attractive. He probably stayed with another woman when he was gone. I hoped things would change when the baby arrived, but instead, his overnight disappearances stretched to several days at a time. I knew I'd lost him. Eventually, he never came home at all. I was on my own with a baby on the way, no money for the rent, no food in the cupboard, and nothing at all for the baby. I went to church and asked the priest for help.

"You should find your husband," the priest told me. "Your husband's responsible for you. When you find him, you can bring him to me, and I will instruct both of you on how to make a good marriage."

"But I've looked everywhere, and I can't find him," I said. "I don't know where else to look. I'm all alone, and I'm hungry. Isn't there somewhere I can go for help?"

"You can't go to a home for unwed mothers," he answered, "because you're married. You can't join a convent for the same reason, and you can't give the baby up for adoption, because you'd need your husband's consent. Surely you have relatives you can ask for help?"

I left the church in tears. If my parents were good Catholics, I was a good Catholic, James was a good Catholic, and this good Catholic priest couldn't help me, because I'd gotten married like a good Catholic, what was so good about being Catholic? If I hadn't gotten married like my parents and James insisted, I could have gone to a home for unwed mothers. At least the baby might have had a chance of finding a good home, but I'd so wanted to marry James.

When the landlord evicted me, I swallowed my pride and went back to my parents' house. They were no longer there. The neighbors didn't know where they'd gone. They kept their promise to never see me again. I was abandoned by my parents, my husband, and my church. The thought of childbirth frightened me out of my wits, but I'd expected to have my parents and husband to look after me. I slept in alleys at night and wandered the streets in the daytime. My sleep was fitful and full of nightmares in which I writhed in agony and prayed for death. I carried my violet dress bundled in the spare dress I wasn't wearing at the time. I begged for spare change, and people were often kind to me in my condition. I was terrified to have the baby alone, but I had no choice. Labor began one afternoon in one of those dirty alleyways. I was in pain, but fortunately my son was delivered before sunrise, and the pain subsided. I wiped his nose and mouth and cleaned him with my dress. Then I tied off his umbilical cord, wrapped him in a rag, and cleaned myself up as best I could before I left him in the doorway of a protestant church. As I walked away, I remembered how James and I said we'd never abandon our own child unless he married a Jew. When I remembered that, I shook my head. I'd been so stupid. I was tired and weak, but I walked away. I wept bitterly. I had to abandon my son, because I couldn't feed or clothe him, but why had everyone abandoned me?

I chose to abandon my past. I told people I was Irish rather than Welsh. I reinvented myself, and hoped the new me was more lovable. I even learned to sing Irish songs. I invented new childhood memories. I also told people my only living family member was a stage actor to explain his absence and lack of financial assistance. I told people a lot of things, because I was so ashamed. I even said my husband was killed in a mining accident. I had no one, so I invented a socially acceptable explanation, but I knew my life was a lie. I hated myself.

Once my belly shrank back to normal, people weren't so generous when I begged for spare change. All I had left to wear were two dresses. One was yellow and way too big now, and the other was my violet wedding dress that was too snug. I took work as a servant in a household. They took money from my wages for my uniform, the food I ate, and the bed I slept in. Nothing was left for me, but I had a place to sleep, food to eat, and a dress that fit. I felt the uniform disguised me and hid my shame.

One day while I was out running an errand for my mistress, I overheard a conversation in the street. My ears perked up at the sound of my husband's name, James Kelly. It was the middle of June 1883, and I was twenty years old. Two gentlemen walked by me, and one of them said it clear as a bell, "James Kelly." Of course, I followed them. They took no notice of a mere servant like me. One of the gentlemen had a daughter, Sarah. He talked about her and her husband, James Kelly. I thought it might be a different James Kelly, but I still followed them. The other gentleman addressed the first as Mr. Brider. That was how I found him— my husband, James Kelly. And that was how I found her—Sarah Brider, who was also my husband's wife. But I'd been his wife first.

Late one afternoon, I met her on the street in my oversized, yellow dress. "Pardon me, Sarah," I called out.

She stopped and turned to look me in the eye. She had kind eyes and a kind face. I felt sorry for her. "How do you know my name?"

"I don't think you really want to know," I said, "but I need to know, please, if you are Miss Sarah Brider."

"I used to be Miss Sarah Brider," she answered, "but now I'm Mrs. James Kelly."

"Well, I'm also Mrs. James Kelly. We were married by a Catholic priest in a Catholic church in 1879. My James Kelly is an upholsterer from Liverpool." The poor woman's face went pale. I knew we shared the same husband.

"That can't be," Sarah insisted.

"My James has piercing blue eyes," I said confidently, "and they get an odd look in them when he's sharpening the knives he uses for his work as an upholsterer. He loves to handle those knives."

Sarah gasped. I could see in her face we were married to the same man. "I don't blame you, miss," I assured her. "My parents disowned me and disappeared, because James Kelly got me pregnant when I was sixteen. I loved him, but they turned their backs on me the day we were married. Then

James left me when I was big with child. He left me
with no money to pay the rent and no way to feed
myself or the baby. The church wouldn't help me,
because I wasn't an unwed mother, nor was I able
to join a convent—not that I wanted to. I've got no
one now. James Kelly married me first. He's still
my husband as long as we're both alive. I'm sure he
didn't tell you. You wouldn't have married him if
you'd known, and I'm sorry, but he's with you now,
and I don't want him back. But I'm dreadfully
hungry. Could you spare some money to help me
out? If you could, I'll just disappear and not say
anything. But it's not right he provides for you,
while I'm penniless, on the street, and hungry—
that's just not right since I'm his true wife. All you
have to do is give me some money, and I'll be on
my way."

Poor Sarah cried, but she reached into her
bag, pulled out some bills and coins, and gave them
to me. "It's all I have," she said.

"Well, it's not much, is it? I can see by your
fine dress you can do better." I looked down at the
yellow rag I wore.

"It's all I have with me," she repeated, "but
if you meet me here in two hours, I'll bring back
more."

"Oh, that would be fine," I told her. "I'll
wait here, but mind you, if you don't show, I'll
make a nuisance of myself. I'll ask all over the
neighborhood about my husband, James Kelly."

"No, that's not necessary," she promised
me. "I'll be back. Just meet me right here. Wait for
me, please. I'll bring more money, and then you
promise you'll disappear, right?"

"Yes, Sarah, I promise," I said. "I don't
want to make trouble. I just desperately need the

money." She kept her promise. She came back two hours later, even though it was after dark, and brought me a good sum.

I knew I couldn't depend on the other Mrs. Kelly to support me, and if I returned for more, she might wise up and have me arrested for blackmail. I had no skills other than household chores. I didn't want to clean someone else's house while I had to live on the street, and I didn't want to hide away in someone else's house as a servant. I was tired of always living by other peoples' rules—the church's, my parents', James's, or employers'. My employers had been nice enough, but with my shame and painful memories freshly revived, I realized it was just a matter of time before they'd find an excuse to put me out on the street.

I decided there and then I was through living by other people's rules. I was through with my fairytale belief that others would take care of me. I no longer believed anyone could love me. I had to look out for myself. I wanted to just be myself.

I bought food and a new dress with the money Sarah gave me and kept the rest hidden on my person. I found a good paying job in a brothel in London's West End. I used my body to keep my body alive, because no one else cared. I soon learned there were cheaper rents and less trouble from the coppers in London's grimy East End. So I moved.

I laughed bitterly at what my parents would've thought of how I'd turned out, but it was thanks to how they'd treated me I'd found my new lifestyle. Nobody else cared, so I lived as I pleased. When those thoughts didn't keep up my spirits, I'd go for a drink at a pub. And sometimes, I'd just cry myself to sleep at night. I knew I'd have been a better mother than my own, if only James hadn't deserted me. I figured out he'd expected to be part of my family, but when my parents threw me away, he was ashamed of me too. I hated the church I was raised in, because it was the source of my betrayal.

I heard Sarah Brider Kelly was murdered—stabbed in the throat. It was in the papers, and people talked about it in the pubs. James was arrested and confessed to the crime. He'd murdered the kind lady. I'd been his wife. He was sentenced to death. I was horrified. Might I have unwittingly played a part in the sordid affair? What if she'd told James she gave me money? Had she confronted James about his first marriage? Did he kill her because she threatened to charge him with bigamy? I never meant to cause her harm. I didn't know just how cruel people I trusted could be.

I realized James was cold-blooded to have married Sarah when he already had a wife, who'd been pregnant when he left. I thought about the way he'd always sharpened those knives and the strange look in his eyes. He stabbed her in the throat with one of his knives. The thought gave me shivers down my spine, but I was very glad he'd left me, and I was happy to have moved since I'd met poor Sarah, as James would be unable to find me—not that he could, since he was in jail and sentenced to death.

Then the papers announced James Kelly was officially insane and committed to the Broadmoor Asylum. I wept, because I was lucky to have been abandoned by the man I loved. How I wept.

But I was still alive, so I had to carry on. I used my charms with men for money. I answered to no one except my customers, and I had no one. All that mattered to me was how I felt in the moment. I drank gin to drown out thoughts of poor Sarah, mad James, and the baby boy I'd left on a church doorstep. I could no longer remember where the church was or what day or year he'd been born. I felt so sad that I'd never even given him a name. I should have loved, protected, and taken care of him, but how? I did all I knew to do. I didn't even know if love was real. Besides, what if he grew up to be insane like his father?

     I often wondered what life might have been like if I'd obeyed my parents. The thought always gave me a laugh. I would have continued to believe they loved me, when they didn't. I would have continued to go to a church which had no place for me. And I would have married someone as false as my parents and priest and believed we were happy. At least in reality, I didn't live a lie.

     I knew James Kelly was locked in the asylum, but only gin stifled my irrational fears of him and our son. I couldn't shake the feeling I hadn't seen the last of James. I rented a room for a month and then moved. I tried to disappear in the black soot and dark streets of Whitechapel. In early 1888, I rented a room at 13 Miller's Court. After I paid my rent, I spent the rest on gin.

     By November, I paid for gin first and rent if anything was left. Rent fell behind. Terrible things happened in Whitechapel. Four women I knew from the pub I frequented were murdered. All of them were stabbed. It was dreadful. People called the murderer "Jack the Ripper" and said he killed prostitutes. Kate and Polly were prostitutes like me, but not Annie Chapman or Long Liz. Annie and Liz were both married women, even though Annie was separated from her husband. I had the oddest sense that Sarah's murder and the murders of my friends were connected. I expected he'd soon come for me.

Just after midnight 9 November, I ran into James Kelly in the street. I knew I should be afraid, but I was drunk, and I froze. He smiled at me like he had when I was young and in love with him. He was still the charmer, my James.

"Mary," he called to me, "I've looked everywhere for you." He was so handsome. He wore a gold watch chain and a stylish mustache. "I was released from the asylum, and I now earn my way as a violinist."

With most of my friends dead, I found it impossible to resist talking to anyone who cared to know me. "I didn't know you could play the fiddle."

"It was part of my therapy in the asylum. Music soothes and heals the soul. It calms even the most agitated of men."

I smiled and walked alongside him. "Oh, I'm so glad to hear they found a cure for whatever ailed you."

"I realize now I was wrong to leave you. Since we're still legally married, I thought we should be together. I'd love to play for you."

"Well, it's safer these days for a lady to have a man."

"You've been drinking," he commented.

"Of course I have," I laughed as I led him to my room at 13 Miller's Court. We went inside. I lay down on the bed and waited for him to have sex with me. I laughed to myself and wondered how he'd react when I asked for my fee.

"Where's our child?" he asked as he climbed on top of me.

"You mean our son."

"We have a son," he acknowledged happily. "Where's our son?" He forced his right hand over my mouth so I couldn't answer. I felt a sharp pain in my neck.

*   *   *

I floated near the ceiling in a corner of the room. I hardly recognized it. Blood was everywhere. What happened? I was twenty-five years old. I felt no pain, but this was my room at 13 Miller's Court, and James was below me with a knife in his left hand. If that butchered body on the bed was mine, then I was dead. It was over. He really was Jack the Ripper, but what was he was doing? He leaned over my abdomen, which was cut wide open, and held something small and bloody in his hands. It was a tiny child—or what would have become one. I didn't even know I'd been pregnant. At least I wouldn't have to endure childbirth again or have to abandon another baby. I'd given my heart and soul away the first time. I'd have gone insane to do it again.

So what was the point? I was trampled like wild violets underfoot. I was outcast by everyone whom I believed loved me. Images came back to me of another life and time. I saw Sarah Brider as a great lady waiting to marry the husband I left widowed. Images of the past engulfed me. James had been King of England, and I'd been his wife. I laughed at how ludicrous it all seemed after the life I'd just lived. As king, everyone thought he was charming, but he was insane. I began to see faces of all the innocent people whose blood he'd shed, while I obediently held my tongue to protect myself. And now I'd learned how not to live by

anyone else's rules. Now I valued the truth instead
of appearances.

I saw we'd come back to live together yet
again. I couldn't escape. All I wanted was to be
loved by someone who'd tell me the truth—
someone who'd keep their promises and not
abandon or hurt me. But somewhere was a little boy
I abandoned. Life on earth was insane and very sad,
but I still wanted to be loved. Whatever happened,
I'd only tell the truth. I didn't want to betray anyone
else like I'd been betrayed. I wanted to be able to
protect little violets.

PART III

Emotions cling to us
We dress ourselves in our pain
The burdens we carry
Are what is remembered
When we dream

Choose to stand alone
We seek comfort from others
When inward lies home
The direction is independence
As we become one
In stillness we find love

Choose to let go
Of pain that haunts
Choose to let go
Of what others want
Contemplate what you truly want most
Recognize the past that keeps you from it
And choose to let go

*   *   *

The symbol of a flower
The message of a dream
Is to be interpreted
To hold what it must mean

The Universe encoded
By patterns given reign
There to be deciphered
In the letters of a name

229

Mary Janet Kelly

I thought a lot about everything that was wrong
with my lives. I needed to learn to not be totally
submissive to others, to think for myself, and to get
past my fears. I'd only attempted it once. I was
determined to openly be myself. I'd try again.

A lot of time had passed in the physical
world. I missed the little violets. I could make my
own choices. I wanted to protect Mother Nature and
creatures with no defense against humans, and I
wanted to be loved.

*   *   *

Tommy Feltener
22 October 1948—1967

My mother came from rural Minnesota, and my
father was an aeronautical engineer from New York
City. He was overbearing and controlling—more
than just a bully. He was scary and cruel. Mom was
afraid of him. She was quiet, and he mocked her by
calling her "mousy." He liked to call people
derogatory names. He wasn't tall, but he was husky
and loud. Mom was petite. Dad made a good salary,
but he kept it all for himself. Mom wasn't even
allowed to drive the car without his permission. He
had college degrees and thought he was better than
everyone else. I just wanted to be loved.

I was born just before dawn 22 October
1948 in Santa Monica, California. I had red hair,
and pale, freckled skin. My eyes were deep blue
like the Pacific Ocean. Dad wanted a son. He
named me Tommy, like he'd planned to name his

son. Mom said it was cute. She was afraid to contradict him.

When I was only fourteen months old, Mom gave birth to my brother, Ricky. In 1951, Dad bought a new house in Westchester, another Los Angeles suburb just south of Santa Monica. I kept dreaming Mom and Dad would take me to church and just leave me there. I was scared they'd abandon me, so I kept quiet about my dreams. As time went on, the dreams got worse. I'd wake up suddenly, having been stabbed in the throat. As young as I was, I understood being stabbed in the throat meant I was supposed to be quiet. I tried to not be noticed. Then my little sister, Tina, was born in September 1956. I helped her learn to be quiet when Dad was home. Mom was "mousy" for good reason. Fortunately, he was a workaholic and not home much. Still, home life was like walking on eggshells. As I made friends in the neighborhood, I learned they didn't want to come to my house, but I really liked going to theirs.

I don't know why Dad was so angry, or why he yelled or punished me so much. I just accepted if he was home, I'd be punished and not know why. All he liked was his work. He was unhappy and made everyone around him unhappy.

I loved nature, flowers, and animals. I adored our pet beagle. I felt loved by flowers and animals. I identified with wild violets. They were small, like me, but very pretty. Somewhere I heard the phrase "shrinking violet" and felt sorry for the violets. "Shrinking" sounded like scared. I wanted to stand up for flowers, animals, little violets, and myself if ever I could. I couldn't feel scared if I had to protect something important.

My parents let me take dance lessons. I got to tour with a dance troupe. I was the youngest and smallest member, but I was no "shrinking violet" on stage. I had talent, and I loved to dance. I loved the attention of being on the stage and being liked. My teacher said I could be a star someday, because I was a natural performer, but Dad didn't like that. Mom let me stay with the troupe anyway. We did folk dances from all over the world and everything else from square dancing to contemporary dance. And when we got to sing, my teacher found out I really could sing, so I got some fun parts.

A lot of kids in the troupe were jealous, because I got lead parts and they didn't. They made fun of me and teased me. It really hurt, so I tried to be extra nice to them so they'd like me. But when that didn't work, I just tried to ignore them. I made friends with the older kids in the troupe.

My parents weren't interested in my performances. Dad made me eat meals in the kitchen, while the rest of the family ate in the dining room. He didn't like me to talk during meals. He didn't want me to have a life outside of home where I had fun. All the other kids in the neighborhood were scared of him. I heard some of their parents say he was hostile and pushy.

With the troupe, I was on television shows like Lawrence Welk, Dinah Shore, and Art Linkletter. When we performed at Disneyland, I met Walt Disney. We also went on tour all over the continent. We rode in a bus together, slept on the floor together in places like school gyms, and saw a lot of cool things—up to Alaska and all the way to the East Coast. We performed at the White House in Washington, DC. The head of the troupe, my teacher, used to play his guitar and sing with us on the bus. Sometimes he told us, "The United States will eventually fall just like the Roman Empire. No great empires last forever."

"Will you adopt me?" I asked him.

He started to laugh, but then just smiled at me. "Not possible," he said.

By the time I was in junior high school, Dad didn't let me go on any more tours. He had no control over me when I wasn't home. Other kids' parents offered to pay my way, even though Dad had the money. On my last tour, we performed at the Seattle World's Fair.

Back home, Dad started to lock me in my room. By this time, I hated him more than I feared him. He didn't want me to hang out with dancers or performers. Everything had to be his way, but I noticed once he'd lock me in, he never checked on me. I figured out how to get out through the window. I'd go to friends' houses.

I still went to dance class and local performances, but I was sad I didn't get to go on tour. At school, I hung out with creative kids. We listened to Bob Dylan. We were considered to be some sort of counter-culture, and that was okay with me.

I started high school September 1963. I dated older boys I knew from the dance troupe, but we were just friends. My parents didn't know who I hung out with, because they thought I was locked in my room. Sometimes, I just didn't bother to go home after school. Then when I did, nobody mentioned my absence, but Dad would lock me in my room again.

I was never comfortable in churches. They always seemed cold and judgmental to me, like my father, and I'd grown up afraid my parents would abandon me at one. Church didn't feel good like dance class. I went to different churches with friends, but they all felt like being at home, and I didn't like it. So I explored other aspects of the spiritual—stuff people called occult. I liked to make up ghost stories and tell my friends. I liked to imagine what it felt like to be outside my body. One evening at a friend's house, I got everybody to join me in the bathroom, where we held a séance. It was cool, but the friend whose house we were in thought it was creepy and said we couldn't do it again. I got a Ouija board. It worked too, but again I scared the other girls. I didn't know why they were scared. Ghosts, by nature, couldn't do physical harm like people in bodies.

Then Dad bought another house in Redondo Beach, and we moved. I had to go to a different school. We only moved six miles south, but I had to quit the dance troupe, because Dad wouldn't let Mom to drive me to class. So I joined the theater group at my new school. I got a lot of supporting parts, but I gave them my all. I was happy to not be the star, because I remembered from dance how the other kids were jealous of stars and didn't like them. So I tried to be supportive.

I wrote poetry. I needed to express myself. At home, Dad announced I wasn't part of the family. I expected Mom to stand up for me, but she was scared. Dad was gone most of the time, Mom hardly ever talked to us, and Ricky and Tina went their own separate ways. We stayed away from home as much as possible. We avoided each other and found our own ways to escape Dad. When Dad was home, nobody else spoke out of fear. I don't know how much he beat up on Mom, but he sure liked to hit me. I didn't expect a reason. He never

234

said much to me. When we spoke, we always argued. "Stop talking back to me," usually ended it, whatever that meant. He didn't know how to discuss. I didn't wear cosmetics, except to cover bruises. I used poetry to pour out my emotions and disappointments.

I slept at friends' houses as much as possible. I took a part-time job a couple of hours right after school three days a week at a hamburger joint, so I could stay away from home longer. When things were bad or I couldn't hide the bruises, I skipped school. I smoked cigarettes. Sometimes I deliberately burned myself with them to externalize my pain, but nobody ever noticed.

By my senior year, which started in the fall of 1965, I went to work for the mother of a school friend. She was an artist with her own studio. I stretched the canvas and stapled it to the frames. It was fun, she paid me, and was nice to me, but Dad beat me up when he found out I had my own money. I didn't quit the job; I just avoided home.

That year I also had a great English teacher, but I had to miss classes for days—sometimes weeks—at a time. Sometimes, when I couldn't find anybody to stay with, I just slept on the beach near the boss' studio. Everybody around me must have known something was wrong in my life, but they looked the other way. I wasn't their problem. I knew no family would ever want me, and no guy in his right mind would ever love me. I didn't believe in marriage. Marriage had nothing to do with love and everything to do with secrets.

When I slept on the beach, I had nightmares about having a baby. Sometimes I dreamt I was in a big bed in a dark room, and the pain was horrible. Then the baby was born, but the pain only got worse until I died. Other nights I dreamt I was in a dirty alley in a big city in the middle of the night. I was all alone and homeless when I had the baby. Then, since I had no way to take care of him, I left him at the door of a church. It was always one of the two dreams, and they never changed. I always knew in the one where I left the baby at the church, my parents had also abandoned me at a church. It was the dream from my early childhood that often ended with me being stabbed in the throat. When I'd wake up from one of the dreams, I'd sit on the beach, listen to the surf, and try to make sense of things. If I was abandoned by my parents in a past life, was that why I was all alone? Maybe, if I hadn't abandoned my baby, I'd have better parents. Maybe I'd been stabbed in throat, because I just wasn't good enough to live. I was just another leech on the planet. Maybe if I found a way to make the world a better place, I might earn the right to live.

During the day, I was just my honest self. If others saw me as defective or weird, it was fine, because I was. I talked to friends at school about how to change the world for the better—like Dr. Martin Luther King, Jr., was doing with the civil rights movement. I wanted to make the world better, but I didn't know how. I knew the problem was people, and I was one of them.

Things never got better at home, but at school I was recognized for my poetry. I still skipped a lot—more after each of my suicide attempts. I wasn't good at suicide, and that only made me feel like more of a failure. I tried to overdose on barbiturates, and I cut my wrists. My life was a disaster, and so was the planet. All around me, people manufactured weapons of war and death for money. I figured maybe I'd try to live again in a different time, place, and family, but I blew it, and no one noticed.

I was seventeen when I graduated high school. I tried to find another place to stay for the summer of 1966. The mother of a friend asked Dad if I could live with them for the summer. He said, "No." Since they didn't have his permission, I couldn't stay with them, but I found a house-sitting job. I liked having my own place, even though it wasn't mine. I drank alcohol when I wanted. I invited friends to stay, and they did. We listened to folk music and talked about how to improve the world.

The owner came by. "This place is a mess," the old lady yelled at me. "You're supposed to take care of it, not trash it, and you've got a boy staying here with you."

"He's just a friend," I tried to tell her.

"Pack your things, and get out of this house NOW."

So we had to clear out. It was fun while it lasted. Not paying rent had let me save for college. I had to find a job and a cheap apartment.

Meanwhile, my family moved to a condo in Redondo Beach. I got a friend to drive me back one last time to get the last of my things. I tried to confront Dad. "Why don't you love me?"

"How dare you question me." Then he hit me. As I gathered up my things, I got an earful from him—a litany of what was wrong with me. When I left with my stuff and got back into my friend's car, it rained like the earth cried with me. My friend and I just drove away in silence.

I couldn't really afford an apartment on the money I made, and when I looked for one, I found landlords were a lot like Dad with all their rules and judgments. I took a room in a boarding house near the beach. I didn't like to swim, but I watched the surf come and go to relax. When I sat on the beach, I felt one with nature again. By this time, I'd realized my nightmares about childbirth were probably from past lives. To have a baby, I must have had a man. I wondered if it were possible for a man to ever love me. If one had in past lives, maybe I'd meet him again. Life would be easier if I wasn't alone. I thought about what I could do with my life. I needed to go to college, but I couldn't manage. I had to pay for the basics, like my room, cigarettes, booze, and marijuana. I couldn't work full time, go to class, and study. Other college kids had families who supported them. If I wanted to go to college, I had to go home.

  In December, I went to my parents' condo. Dad said, "I'll pay for you to go to El Camino Junior College in Torrance, but you have to live by my rules."

  I pictured life at home as a performance. If I didn't talk to Dad and stayed in my room and studied when I was home, maybe it would work. I already knew about the working world—everybody lied, and no one cared about the planet or other people—only money. Society was an ugly, messed up place. I didn't have delusions about money, but I thought maybe I could find a way to change society.

  I wrote poetry. I related more than ever to the little violets trampled, ignored, and killed by buildings put on top of them. Man took over the earth and turned it into metal, concrete, and trash. The country wanted men to go to the moon so they could trash it too. Guys were sent to be killed and maimed in some unheard of place in Southeast Asia. I was tired of the destruction and waste. I cried for the decline of beauty in what had been a beautiful world. Everywhere people were polluting the earth. Where would the violets grow?

I started El Camino College in Torrance spring semester of 1967. I was eighteen. I signed up for dance, theater, psychology, and French. I hoped for a good year. I was terribly lonely, but I had hope.

I did well in school and broke out of the shell I'd put around myself to help me survive at home. I should have known better, but I had to be myself. I didn't keep my mouth shut at home. Unfortunately, Dad disagreed with my use of a word. He always had to be right. He didn't care what I knew. I got out a dictionary to show him there was more than one definition for the word.

"It's my way or no way," he insisted.

"That's just dumb. I can't just agree with you when you're wrong. It's here in the dictionary. We're both right."

"GET OUT OF MY HOUSE."

In just three weeks I'd finish my first semester of college, but I had nowhere to live. I saw no point in going back to school. I knew there was no future for me in society. I knew people lived more freely in Venice, about ten miles north, so I hitchhiked there. I needed to be around other people who weren't rigidly stuck in their own rules like Dad. I needed a place where I could be myself. All I had with me was my books, the dictionary, and some cosmetics.

As I sat on the Venice boardwalk and watched the ocean, I heard a male voice say, "What's the problem?"

I looked up and saw he was talking to me. He was different, but familiar, even though I'd never met him before. He hadn't shaven or bathed recently. He had dark hair and magnetic eyes. Magnetic—that was how he felt. He wore a cap and carried himself like an elegant hobo—poor and regal, physical and ephemeral at the same time. He was a charmer, and the idea popped into my head that we were soul mates. "How did you know?" I asked.

"I'm a gardener. I tend flower children."

I didn't want someone to put me in a flower box and make me grow a certain way. I reminded myself I didn't know this guy. I lowered my head and hoped he'd go away. After a little while, I looked up, and he was gone. I looked all around to see which way he went, but I didn't see him. I felt desperate he'd gone. I was terribly lonely.

Then I heard his voice again. "Your father kicked you out?"

I looked behind me, and there he sat. I was glad to see him. "Yeah, I was about to finish my first term of college. I wanted to learn how to make the world a better place. Nature's under attack with pollution and ugly, artificial walls everywhere. I just want to be myself and find a way to protect and live with nature."

"The way out isn't through a door," he said. "If you don't believe you're in, you won't need out."

That actually made sense. I liked this guy. "I spent a whole semester in college looking for answers, and you give me one in just a couple of minutes."

"I've been penned up a lot. I had a lot of time to think about things in solitary confinement. I've spent twenty-two years in prison—long enough to think right through the walls. The warden told me

I could get out early if I worked. But get out of where? The warden was there too. I was in my head. Why get out of my own head? So I played my guitar."

He was honest. Most adults I'd known would never admit they'd been in prison. He was different, but he was honest, and I wanted to trust him.

"I have to go back up north. You can come with me if you like," he invited. Then he got up and walked off.

I thought about it as I watched him leave. I hesitated, but I was too curious and too lonely. I grabbed my books and ran after him.

In the Haight-Ashbury district of San Francisco, I learned that Carl Hoessmann really took care of flower children. The flowers he took care of, of course, were female. He had a special girlfriend he stayed with, Ruby Marner. She was a librarian and older than me, but not as old as Carl. Ruby was smart, and I liked her. I was also in awe of how many people there were on the streets and how casual and individual they were. The old societal rules I grew up with didn't apply here. It was a relief. I could be myself.

Carl wanted Ruby to quit her job. She hesitated, and I understood. She was self-sufficient, but eventually she quit, Carl got permission from his parole officer, and the three of us went north. We stayed in a cabin and communed with nature. The trees were awesome. I felt restored.

One day Ruby went to the store and left Carl alone with me in the cabin. He was lying on the bed and said, "Take off your clothes. I want to look at you."

"No." I was appalled.

241

"You're too inhibited. You think you're ugly, don't you? Well, you're not. You're beautiful."

He saw me as beautiful? Still, I didn't take off my clothes. Instead, I left the cabin. When I walked outside, I saw Ruby on a bench. She hadn't gone to the store, and she was crying. I realized Carl sent her out to leave us alone, and she knew why. I sat down next to her and put my arm around her. "It's OK, Ruby. I didn't take off my clothes. Nothing happened. I know you're in love with Carl." She hugged me back.

Carl was quirky, and I liked that about him. Like a lot of guys, he always carried a knife. Sometimes he'd take it out and very gently stroke my neck or Ruby's with it. He always smiled when he did it. He meant to be sensuous, but it was weird.

Another time, Carl and I were in the car. "You never swear," he said.

I looked over at him and wondered what he'd say next. I didn't bother to answer.

He looked sideways at me, smiled, and said, "Go on. Say 'fuck.' Say it."

"Don't tell me what to say."

But he kept on, "Say it. Say 'fuck.' Say it."

Finally, I said, "Fuck you, Carl."

He laughed. "That felt good, didn't it?"

"Yeah, it did," I admitted. We both laughed.

Carl traded Ruby's car for a Volkswagen bus. Ruby put a mattress in the back, so the three of us could sleep together. She and Carl helped me overcome my inhibitions.

By that summer, Ruby was pregnant. "It scares me," I told her.

"It scares me too—the childbirth part. Like maybe I died in childbirth in a past life. But that was then, and this is now. We live in the now."

Eventually, I let Carl make love to me, but I was still afraid. It was my first time. I was terrified something really bad would happen, like maybe I'd get pregnant too.

He sensed my fear and kept saying, "Give up your fear, Tommy. Give up your fear."

I repeated to myself what Ruby had said, we live in the now. My fears evaporated, and it felt really, really good. He touched places I never realized I had, and I had my first orgasm.

We found a spot on the beach where ownership was in dispute, so it was literally a no man's land. I was amazed at how somebody or some government agency owned every inch of land. Even the campgrounds where we'd camped were owned. There were so many boundaries that nature didn't know about or understand. The boundaries and ownership seemed to me a form of fear, insecurity, and inhibition. But Ruby, Carl, and I lived without those fears, so when we found an abandoned little red trailer, we put it on the beach that was in dispute. We had our own place beyond the boundaries, and I could sit and watch the ocean. I felt we were three equals, and I felt at peace with myself.

A family moved in nearby on the beach— young parents with a few kids. They lived in a tent. One morning, I got up and went out on the beach. A heavy fog had rolled in. I realized I still needed to make amends for my past lives by making life better for others. I thought about the family in the tent. I went back to the trailer and told Carl and

243

Ruby, "It's time to go south. Let's give the trailer to the family."

We went back down the coast. Carl wanted to find some people near Redondo Beach, my old haunt, so I drove us around. We went down to Manhattan Beach and came across Katrina Pricewinkle. She was unhappy. She'd gone to Alabama to go to school, but it wasn't right for her. So she'd come back, moved in with her sister, and taken a job for an insurance company. But that wasn't right for her either, and her sister was a junkie.

"Come with us," I said. "Leave it all behind. Give up your unhappiness and be free."

"I can't just leave, and I know my sister and Dad will tell me not to. I have to give notice at my job, and without my income, how will my sister pay the rent?"

"Not your problem," I told her. "I've been there. The confrontation isn't worth it. You deserve to be happy. If you give up your unhappiness, you give up the need to take care of a junkie, to give notice at your job, and argue with your Dad. So you could just give it up and be happy, but it's your choice."

She joined us. All she had were the clothes she wore, her purse, and her Dad's credit card. The four of us drove back to San Francisco in the VW bus. At night we all slept together. We competed for who slept next to Carl. We'd all been programmed to think a relationship was only one man and one woman, but we were a real family. Carl made love to each of us while the other two watched, and it was beautiful.

Kat was intelligent and well-read. I liked her. She'd worked hard to fit into a world that didn't want her, and she'd learned to bury her feelings. I understood.

Back in the Haight, we moved into a brown house with a lot of other people. We met a guy named Mike, who was easy to get along with. We also met Billy Bowson, who led the group we lived with. He played guitar better than Carl, who was pretty good, and we all sang together. We smoked a lot of pot.

Then one day while Carl was singing and playing his guitar, a dancer named Anna appeared and danced to his music. She had big doe eyes. She wasn't very bright, but she was confident. When we moved out, she came with us. She'd done time and a lot of drugs and was uninhibited.

Carl traded the VW bus for an old yellow school bus, because there were more of us, and we needed more room. His parole supervision was transferred to L.A., so we moved back south. Again, Ruby made the bus comfy with mattresses, pillows, and carpet. So Carl, Mike, Ruby, Kat, Anna, and I drove to L.A. I noticed by the time we left for L.A., Carl had only made love to Anna a total of three times. I guessed she didn't turn him on, but I felt like I had a family now. We took care of each other, and I belonged.

Anna Stukiss
7 May 1948—1967

Dad was already crazy about my older brother when
I was born 7 May 1948 in San Gabriel, California,
east of Los Angeles. Then a younger brother joined
us, and my mother was crazy about him. I was in
the middle, but no one doted on me. I was just a
girl, and I was left-handed. My parents weren't
thrilled about having a left-handed daughter, even
though I was pretty.

When I was five years old, we moved north
to San Jose, south of Oakland and San Francisco.
We all went to church as a family, and my brothers
and I attended Sunday school. Then one day I
watched my babysitter's father die right in front of
our house of a stroke. The babysitter cried and
prayed out loud the whole time. "Why did God take
my daddy?" she asked over and over.

No one answered her. After that, I refused to
go to church. What was the point? My parents
punished me—I couldn't have dessert or watch
television, but they finally gave up. Mom gave me
and my brothers each our own Bible.

Five years later during a thunderstorm at
night, the electricity and all the lights went out. We
lit candles so we could see. I set my Bible on fire,
but my brother helped me put the fire out before it
spread. Dad yelled, "You could have burned down
the whole house."

"But I didn't. It was an accident." Actually,
I was excited until the fire was out.

Dad and big brother had each other. Mom
and little brother had each other. I had a Siamese cat
named Miss Kiss. Miss Kiss and I had each other.
Sometimes I'd shoplift treats for Miss Kiss, but

246

nobody noticed. My grades in school were low. I failed and had to repeat the fifth grade. I didn't like it when others said I was stupid. But I was pretty as a rose—thorns and all.

When I was twelve, we moved to another house in another neighborhood. I made friends with the girl next door and went to the Baptist church with her, because we were friends. When she wanted something but didn't have money to buy it, I'd steal it for her. She needed a bra, but her mother wouldn't buy her one, so I stuffed it under my shirt. I liked stealing. It was a thrill, but I got caught when I tried to leave the store. That was my first arrest. I just wanted my friend to like me, even though I was prettier than her.

My parents were upset about me getting busted. "If your friend's mother didn't want her to have a bra yet," Mom said, "you shouldn't have interfered. It's none of your business."

"I don't like how much you drink, but that's none of my business," I said as I walked away from her. My parents liked to drink a lot.

I was petite with straight, dark brown hair and dark eyes, and I could sing. I sang in the school glee club, and I joined the church choir to sing. I was ready to be popular and have fun. I knew high school was where I was meant to attract handsome boys.

I was fourteen when Dad told me, "Anna, you're mother is sick. She has cancer."

In my family, alcohol was the best medicine, so Mom drank. Dad always went to the bar before he came home from work. They took turns yelling at me for not doing all the housework. I learned that cancer meant dying instead of getting well. I didn't understand why my brothers didn't have to clean house, wash dishes, or do the laundry. It wasn't fair, and it made me mad. I didn't like being the maid.

I came home from school one day and found Miss Kiss asleep under my bed. I petted her, but she wouldn't wake up. I realized she was dead. I cried as I got Dad's shovel and buried her by myself in the back yard. Nobody else even noticed.

Dad was upset about Mom's cancer, but he still worked and drank after work. He told me, "Anna, it's your responsibility to make sure Mom's comfortable."

I didn't understand what that meant. "Of course I want Mom to be comfortable," I said, but how was it suddenly my responsibility? How was I supposed to go to school dances and have dates, if I had to be at home with Mom? "Why can't my brothers help?" I asked.

"They have schoolwork to do," was the answer.

"What about my schoolwork?"

"You've never worried about it before," he said. "And housework is women's work."

That fall, my older brother enlisted in the Navy. So I went to school, came home, did chores, and looked after Mom. The cancer spread to her brain. She lost the ability to walk by herself, to feed herself, and to use the toilet by herself. I complained to Dad, "I can't handle all of this and go to school."

"She's your mother," he shouted back at me, like I had done something wrong. "You take care of her. I don't want to hear any more complaints. Keep her clean. Bathe her, wash her hair, and change her diapers. It's time for you to grow up."

"But what about dating?"

He slapped me in the face. "Grow up."

I ran to my room in tears. I was fourteen. When he first told me she was dying, I had no idea it would come to this. I thought she would just die like my babysitter's father and Miss Kiss.

I wasn't grown up. I hadn't been able to date or go to a prom. I was pretty, but I didn't even have a boyfriend. I was five feet five inches tall and weighed 115 pounds. How was I supposed to lift her and move her to bathe and change her? I didn't even know how to do that for a baby yet.

I was trapped. While other kids my age were out having a good time, I watched my poor mother slowly die. It was a horrible death. I didn't know it would be like this. She was in and out of the hospital, and when she was in the hospital, I was relieved. I was scared she'd come home from the hospital. I didn't understand how to deal with it, so I went to school.

As Christmas approached, I was stuck at home. One night, the church choir came by the house, stood outside my mother's bedroom window, and sang Christmas carols. She smiled. I cried. I wanted to sing with them. They were out having fun. Two weeks later, Mom went back into the hospital and died there 9 January 1964.

At Mom's funeral, I mentally told God to get lost. Life sucked. By that time, I knew more about death than anything else. For me, school was only for sports and fun.

Soon after the funeral, Dad moved us southeast to Los Banos in Merced County. It was due east of Monterrey Bay in the center of the state. My younger brother and I had to go to different schools, while Dad worked on the San Luis Dam and left us alone in Los Banos. I lost my friends in San Jose and still had to be Dad's maid.

I sprained my knee jumping on the trampoline at school. I was prescribed codeine for the pain, but I didn't need all the pills, so I saved them.

I failed my junior year of high school, so I dropped out, which made Dad angry. The end of that summer I took a part-time job at the International House of Pancakes (IHOP) and rented a cheap room near my job. I was done being Dad's maid. I stayed there until April, when I quit my IHOP job and went up to San Francisco. I found a job as a telephone surveyor that came with a blue Rambler station wagon and a studio apartment on Market Street with no windows. I was supposed to get paid commissions, but I didn't understand I had to sell something to earn a commission. I wouldn't earn any commissions as a telephone surveyor.

When I realized I wouldn't get paid, I swallowed a dozen codeine pills I still had from when I sprained my ankle. Then I called 911, told the operator, and talked long enough for the call to be traced. I was taken to the hospital in an ambulance, where I told the nurse I was lonely. I gave her the phone number for my boss. When he picked me up, he asked, "Why did you do this?"

"I feel trapped in that tiny apartment with no windows."

He moved me upstairs to a bigger apartment. I'd learned how to take care of myself.

Then I met a really nice guy in a bar. Zachary was tall and blond. He bought me drinks and dinner. We slept with each other in my new apartment the first night we met. He appreciated me, so I didn't have to worry about cash. A few weeks after we started our affair, he went mountain climbing.

Later, I saw one of his friends in the bar. "He fell," Zachary's friend said. "It was an accident. He didn't make it."

I just stared at him. Finally, I said, "What do you mean, "he didn't make it?""

"Zachary's dead."

Not long after Zachary died, I was driving the blue Rambler when I got stuck in traffic on the streetcar tracks. Before I knew what happened, my station wagon was hit in the side by a streetcar. The car was a wreck, and I was shaken up. I had to see a medic as a result. His name was Sean. He helped me find a job as a waitress in a coffee shop, so I quit the job that didn't pay, which meant I also lost my free apartment. I moved into an old hotel. Most of the residents were old too, and I had to share the bathroom down the hall with everyone on the floor. But I had a job, a place to stay, and a boyfriend.

One day when I was home in my room, a private detective knocked on my door. "Your family hired me to find you and bring you home."

"I don't want to go home. I'm better off by myself." He couldn't force me, and I wouldn't go, so he left.

About a week later, Dad showed up. I was surprised. "Please, come home, Anna," he begged.

"No way. You just want me to do your housework for free. I have a job. Get out." I held the door open for him, and he left in tears.

I met Don at the coffee shop while I was working. He came in with a male friend. Don was tall, husky, and reminded me of Zachary. He was very soft spoken and polite. I fell in love with him as soon as I saw him. His friend Pete was a few inches shorter with dark hair and a beard. Pete didn't say much.

251

"When do you get off work?" Don asked.

"Eleven," I told him. He smiled, and I smiled back. I knew he'd be back.

About ten minutes to eleven, both Don and Pete showed up. I was expecting Don, but not Pete. They both walked me back to the hotel, so I invited them up to my room.

Once inside, Don said, "I knew the minute I saw you that you're the one for me." He looked into my eyes and smiled. I could see in his blue eyes he was telling the truth.

"I knew it too," I told him.

"We're on our way to Oregon," he continued. "I want you to come with me. Pete's cousin has a place up there in the country where we can stay while we find our own place. We can get married and live in the Oregon countryside."

The next day I worked my shift at the coffee shop. On my break I called Sean on the phone. "I'm moving to Oregon."

"Why?" He didn't sound very happy for me.

"Just am. I'm happy about it."

"I don't understand," he said.

So I hung up. I didn't tell him about Don or marriage plans. At the end of my shift, I told the boss, "I'm quitting. I'm getting married, so I won't be back."

Don walked me back to the hotel. Pete was napping in my room. I grabbed my stuff, and we woke up Pete. The three of us went back downstairs, got into their car, and left for Oregon. Pete drove, and I sat in the front seat between him and Don. Don said, "I've been in prison, and now I'm out on parole."

"Well, I'm glad you're out," I said, snuggling up to his body. Then he and Pete talked, and I gathered that Pete was also on parole. They wanted to go to Oregon to get away and start over. But first, they planned to rob someplace. They needed guns, so they could pull a bigger heist to get money to buy land in Oregon. I was excited. Work at the coffee shop and Sean, the medic, had been boring. Don mentioned they stole the car we were in. I was even more excited.

On the way to Oregon, we made a couple of stops. Don and Pete stole some guns and camping equipment. We made it to Pete's cousin's place late in the afternoon in southern Oregon east of Crater Lake. We camped out in the woods. Pete had a tent for himself, while Don and I shared. They taught me how to shoot the guns they stole. I had fun.

Then the sheriff's men showed up at his cousin's place. They almost caught us, but we saw them first and escaped on foot through the woods. I was thrilled to be on the run with Don.

We ran through the woods mostly at night and slept during the day. We followed the highway but kept under cover. After a couple of days, we thought we'd lost the cops, so we walked closer to the highway. We didn't see the deputies until it was too late. They came from behind, and we were surrounded. They pointed guns at us, and we had to lie down on the pavement while they cuffed and searched us. I looked over at Don while I was being cuffed and saw he was crying. I realized his parole would be revoked, and he'd go back to prison. I'd never see him again, much less get married.

I spent three months in the county jail waiting for my trial. When I was convicted, I was sentenced to two years probation and some suspended jail time. I was released to go back to

San Jose to my Dad and aunt. I stayed with my aunt for a month, before I went back to San Francisco.

I got my old job back at the coffee shop and moved into a different hotel. I reported to my parole officer as I was supposed to and even found Sean again. I don't know why, but he wasn't very nice to me. I started bar hopping. When I tired of the hangovers, I tried marijuana. I liked it better than alcohol. I even tried LSD. It was exciting, and I wanted more. I liked the thrill of danger—it made me feel alive.

I also liked pretty things. While Mom was sick, no one thought about my needs. Once I was in San Francisco, I didn't have money to buy the pretty things I saw in stores, so I stole them. Nobody ever thought I was smart enough to take care of myself, but I was, and I solved my own problems all by myself. I had beautiful treasures— pretty jewelry, fashionable shoes, stylish clothes, cosmetics, and sexy underwear. I needed these things to be cool and attract men.

In January 1967, I was at a bar when a man announced, "We're having a topless contest. The woman who wins will get a job as a dancer."

The guy I was with that night said, "Go on. Do it. You'd be good at it. You'll win."

So I entered, and I won the contest. At eighteen I was a go-go dancer on the North Beach, but I used a fake driver's license, because I was supposed to be at least twenty-one to drink alcohol. I liked to dance. I was good at it, it was fun, and I had an audience. I had energy, all the right curves, and I knew how to move them. I danced, flirted, and took off my clothes. I felt liberated. I really liked being on stage with everyone looking at me. I'd found the perfect job.

I made up for all the time I lost when Mom was sick, when I was Dad's maid, and when I was in jail. I was overdue for parties, and I knew about drugs. I'd sampled my mother's drugs to see what they were like. I had pain too, just a different kind. Drugs were necessary to dull the pain of dying, and we were all dying—it was just a matter of time. The whole point of life was to party as much as you could while you were still alive.

I worked my dance job from four in the afternoon until two in the morning. I danced a half hour and took a fifteen minute break before dancing another half hour. One afternoon, a man dressed in black came in, and my boss had me dance for him.

After I danced, my boss said, "You just auditioned for a big show here. He's the producer, and he wants you in it."

"Whatever," I said.

"No, really, it'll be good for the club, and you'll get paid."

"OK, what do I have to do?"

The man in black was high priest of a satanic church, and the production was a staged Witches Sabbath. All I had to do was wear blood-red lipstick and matching fingernails with very little costume and lie in a coffin with my arms crossed over my chest for most of the show. Then at the end, I'd rise up suddenly and point at the audience. The Satan stuff didn't scare me. I knew all about death. The devil's bondage game was how Dad treated me. So I said, "Bring it on." I got paid.

I took LSD before the show. Then I lay in my coffin and imagined I was dead but still able to hear everything around me. It was cool. But then I got sick and had to see a doctor. I was hospitalized

255

for four months for a wicked case of gonorrhea. I lost my job.

When I got out of the hospital, I moved in with Sam, a guy in the Haight-Ashbury district who'd introduced me to LSD. He took me in as his maid. He had a big house overlooking the beach and lots of drugs. I met Rudy at Sam's house and liked him better, so I moved out of Sam's place and in with Rudy, who didn't want me to be a maid.

I ran into a girlfriend I'd known in school. Judy was straight back then, but not anymore. She took me home to her communal family—several couples who lived together and shared everything, except each other. It was a brown two-story house. The singer Janis Joplin lived next door, and we listened to her rehearse.

Judy introduced me to the one guy who didn't have a woman, Jason. The guys dealt drugs, and the girls handed out samples on the street to drum up business. We knew the FBI watched us. We even waved to them. Jason was busted for drug dealing and went to jail.

One afternoon in November, I came home and heard a man's voice upstairs accompanied by guitar. I was stoned, barefoot, and wearing a short skirt. I followed the music and found a strange man on the couch with a guitar. Others were there too, but he caught my eye. He had dark hair and magnetic eyes. I fell in love at first sight and danced to his music.

When he finished the song, I put a record on the stereo and danced some more. I felt him come up behind me. He put his hands on my hips and directed my movements. "No two moves are alike. Every move is new," he whispered in my ear.

I felt like we became one in a cosmic dance. "I'm Anna," I whispered back. "Who are you?"

"Carl."

Carl was five feet seven inches. I went home with him. He lived just down the street with a different group of people. Three of the women were at Judy's house when we danced. Tommy, a small waif of a girl, was fiercely loyal to Carl. Ruby had been with him the longest. Kat was a snob who made fun of everybody else. Carl was moody, different, and older than all of us. He'd been paroled from prison. He and I were like cosmic, timeless lovers, even though we hadn't yet had sex.

A couple of days later, Carl and I began to make love. "I'll teach you a new game," he said. "We'll pretend I'm your daddy and you do what I say."

I laughed out loud. "Yeah, you're older than me, but you're not my daddy."

"I call it the papa game." He smiled as he caressed my crotch.

"Okay, I'll play along." I climbed on top of him. He pushed me back under him, and I laughed again. Carl's papa game reduced dear old Dad to any mere male. I became a sex goddess, and Carl and I had a cosmic romance. If I was a goddess, then Carl had to be a god. He even had his own group of followers.

Several weeks later, Judy's house down the street was raided by the police for drugs. The neighborhood didn't feel safe anymore. Carl said, "My parole supervision just changed to L.A., so we have to go."

He had an old school bus, and he and Ruby had remodeled the inside. It was plush. Carl, Ruby, Tommy, Kat, two other women, and I went on a road trip to L.A. Along the way, we picked up two more guys and a girl hitchhiking. We stopped by the side of the road, and all of us took LSD. Carl said, "You're all going to die."

I laughed. "It's true—every word."

Then Carl repeated to the younger hitchhiker, one of the boys, "You're going to die." Carl grabbed him and hit him hard. The kid crawled and ran to the front of the bus. He and his two friends got off and ran away. I couldn't stop laughing.

When we got to the San Fernando Valley, we picked up another hitchhiker, who took us to his place in Malibu on Topanga Canyon Lane. We had orgies there. I told Carl, "I'm in love with you."

"You just want to be the queen bee," he answered.

Katrina Pricewinkle
3 December 1947—1967

My father was an insurance agent, and I was a daddy's girl. My mother was a housewife. We were Roman Catholic. I was born 3 December 1947 in Los Angeles, California. As a child, I attended catechism classes and sang in the church choir. I liked stories about angels, and I tried to make my parents proud of me. I also had a sister, Jenny. She was pretty. She was Mom's little girl.

    I had straight, auburn hair and blue eyes. The other kids made fun of me a lot. I had a lot of body hair—hairy arms and legs and hair on my chest and abdomen. My mother said it was just the way I was made. But I was also overweight, and that didn't help. I didn't like being called Fatty Katty. I was ashamed of my body.

    By the time I stopped growing, I was five feet six inches tall, and I eventually slimmed down to 120 pounds. But I could see in the mirror I wasn't pretty. I didn't get asked out on dates. I thought about becoming a nun. I didn't see a lot of options in my future, so I talked to Dad about it. "No guy will ever ask me out. I feel like a weed in a garden."

    "To be pretty, you only need to smile," he answered. "Besides, all the flowers we have now were once wildflowers or weeds."

    "That doesn't make sense," I responded.

    "I know you like blue cornflowers," he continued. I nodded—they were my favorite, because they were the color of the sky. "Cornflowers got their name centuries ago, when they were just weeds in cornfields."

    "So I'm like a cornflower?"

He smiled and nodded. "Just as pretty as a cornflower."

By high school, I tried to stick to my studies. Even though we were Catholic, I attended public school. My parents argued a lot. Divorce wasn't an option they would consider. I didn't have any girlfriends. I seemed to make friends easily with guys, but none of them asked me out. One of the guys I knew introduced me briefly to a small girl with red hair. She was quiet but intelligent, and I liked her. She was a year behind me in school, and her name was Tommy. She had a masculine name, but she was pretty and feminine. I thought we might become friends, but I didn't know how to talk to her, so I didn't get to know her. It was the same with other girls I met. I never liked to show my feelings. I had to protect my feelings from being trampled.

We moved before my junior year, so I had to go to a different school. I hoped against common sense things would be better there. I met some new people, but I was never asked out. My parents separated, and I stayed with Dad so I wouldn't have to change schools again.

In December 1964, I turned seventeen. The following year, I graduated high school, and my parents finally divorced. I started teaching catechism to the younger kids at church. I was considering being a nun, a teacher, or both.

My mother moved to Alabama. My aunt lived in Mobile, and I went to live with her, so I could attend Spring Hill College, a Catholic school. But after one semester, I went back to Los Angeles and shared an apartment with my sister, Jenny. I didn't think I would make a good teacher, because I worried too much about sick and sad children. I decided not to be a nun.

When I moved in with Jenny, I found out she was addicted to heroin. Some of the people she knew scared me, but she was my sister. I didn't know what to do without getting her into trouble. One of us had to pay the rent, so with some help from Dad, I got a job with an insurance company. I didn't like or dislike it. I needed an income. I took one day at a time. I knew Dad loved me, but I was afraid no one else would ever love me for myself. I knew deep down I'd never marry, so I'd have to take care of myself. My sister's lifestyle scared me. There was no happiness in my life—just a sense of obligation.

Then in September 1967, I was sitting on Manhattan Beach contemplating my lack of future, when I saw two young women and an older man. I recognized the smaller woman from somewhere, but I couldn't remember where. So I waved, and they came over. "Do I know you?" I asked.

They looked at me quizzically.

"I remember," I explained. "You're Tommy from school." She obviously didn't remember me, so I added, "I'm Kat."

"These are my friends, Carl and Ruby."

I thought she meant Carl and Ruby were a couple. We talked, and I mentioned I'd gone to a Jesuit school in Alabama for a term. Carl started quoting the Bible. I was impressed.

"Come with us," Tommy invited. "Leave all your misery behind, and come with us."

I had doubts, but I really was miserable living with my junkie sister, so I decided to just do it. I felt I deserved a chance to be carefree and do what I wanted. We drove up the coast in a VW bus.

I felt like I'd run away and joined the circus. I was free of possessions, routine, and obligations. I was light as a feather. Along the way, Carl made love to me. "It's my first time," I told him.

"That's OK. Just pretend I'm your papa."

That was an odd thing to say, but he made me feel comfortable. We used Dad's credit card for food and gas. When we got to San Francisco, we moved into a two-story brown house in Haight-Ashbury with some other people. Carl made friends with Mike, a guy we all liked, but Billy was in charge. We sold drugs for money. We also met Anna. She was dark haired, flaky, and worked as a topless dancer. She tried to seduce Carl, but by then, I knew Carl only took women when he was ready.

The first time I smoked pot, I felt more relaxed. My senses seemed stimulated in a positive way. The first time I tried LSD, I thought I'd left my body, my inhibitions, and my pathetic attempt at life behind. I entered another world where there were no judgments. The faith I'd grown up with seemed so small and confining. I realized I'd been taught I had few choices in life, but I was so much more than something to stuff into a box. On LSD, there were no boxes. There was no burden of obligation. There was no attachment to a physical body or social status. It was very primitive and liberating at the same time. It was also illegal.

The police watched the house constantly, so we moved down the street—Carl, Mike, Ruby, who was pregnant, Tommy, Anna, and me. We'd take LSD together, and Carl would lead a conga line. We'd follow him and do whatever he did. He'd take off his clothes and we would too. No one laughed at me. It was fun, and it really was like a circus—colorful, spontaneous, and entertaining. For the first time in my life, I had friends and was having a good time. Life had become a party, only this time I was invited.

I asked Ruby one day, "Are you excited about having your baby?"

"Of course, but," her face clouded over and her voice dropped to a whisper, "I have dreams over and over that I die from childbirth."

"I think that's probably normal." I really had no idea but wanted to reassure her.

"Tommy said she has the same fear. She promised to get me to a hospital if anything goes wrong. Don't tell Carl."

"I won't," I promised. "We'll take good care of you." I gave her a big hug.

"Thanks, Kat. I also have nightmares about being stabbed in the throat with a knife by someone I knew. Tommy told me she believed she was killed that way in a past life, and that maybe she died from childbirth in another life. What are the odds we both died the same way in two different past lives?"

"I have no idea." I shuddered as a chill ran up my spine. I knew well the nightmare of being stabbed in the throat. I didn't know about reincarnation, but I'd always wondered about that line in the Bible, "Who sinned, this man or his parents, that he should be born blind?" Could we have all been stabbed by the same person?

Then Carl's parole officer transferred him to L.A., so we had to move. "I've got a chance of recording my music in L.A.," he told us.

In October, Carl traded the VW bus for an old school bus. We removed the seats, and there was room for all of us. Ruby took charge of redecorating. "It's my nesting instinct," she laughed. She included a stereo, lots of pillows and peacock feathers, a table suspended with wires like it was floating, and an icebox. Again it reminded me of a circus.

We headed south. We kept getting stopped and cited by the police. Only actual school buses were allowed to be yellow, so we painted ours black.

Sheila Von Lueten
23 August 1949—1967

I already had an older brother when I was born in Los Angeles 23 August 1949. Then my parents adopted two Korean children, so my brother and I had a younger brother and sister. We got along better than our parents, who divorced when I was fourteen. The same year, I got pregnant by my older boyfriend, Mac. I didn't know what to do, and with my parent's divorce, marriage wasn't a desirable option. So, when Mac offered to pay, I had an abortion. I felt I was on an emotional roller coaster.

In both my freshman and sophomore years of high school, I was elected homecoming queen. All the attention was like manna from heaven. I loved my popularity and tiara. I felt so elegant. I felt I had a responsibility as school queen to be nice to the other girls who weren't as fortunate. I used my clever sense of humor to cheer up anyone I saw at school who looked down. I'd gone from the depths of despair and humiliation to being queen of the world. I was a slim five feet six inches tall with long arms, long legs, and a long, slender neck. I had a broad smile, brown eyes, and dark brown hair. The school paper described me as effervescent.

The first year I was elected, I was given a bouquet of roses. But before the second year's election, I let it be known that fragrant lilies would be so much more elegant. I used the fact that roses had thorns to justify the change of bouquet to my favorite flower. At my second coronation, I was presented with lilies. I knew then I was a force to be reckoned with as long as I was diplomatic.

Disaster struck in my junior year; I wasn't reelected. I thought all the students at school were my friends and subjects, but they put my crown on another girl's head. How could they continue to smile to my face when they'd voted against me? I was angry with everyone. I couldn't bring myself to go back to school.

My boyfriend, Mac, had already finished high school. He wanted to go up to San Francisco. Since I'd dropped out of school, I went with him. Mac often said I was beautiful. He frequently complimented me on my big brown eyes and big, beautiful smile. I trusted Mac, and I really cared about him. I wanted to start a new life with him, but the things I saw in Haight-Ashbury scared the hell out of me. So I went back home to L.A., swallowed my pride, and finished high school. I still resented the rejection by the other students, so I just concentrated on the classes and earned my diploma. Once I graduated, I took a year-long secretarial course, so I could get a job.

By the time I finished the course, Mac had returned to L.A., where he joined the followers of Paramahansa Yogananda at the headquarters for the Self-Realization Fellowship on San Rafael Avenue. He became a novitiate priest. I was in love with him and wanted to be with him. So I joined the Self-Realization Fellowship and learned the meditation techniques and philosophy which Mac practiced. Before long, I became a novitiate nun. I took a vow of celibacy. It was a beautiful, peaceful place, and everyone seemed happy. We meditated, and practiced kriya yoga, which involved use of a mantra and visualization with the breath. Everyone exercised, did chores, read the teachings of Paramahansa Yogananda, and attended services.

I felt very comfortable among all the bouquets of lilies inside and the lilies growing outside on the grounds, but after eight months, I realized I didn't want to spend my life as a kriya yogini. I was only there for Mac, but we could never marry, so I left.

Katrina Pricewinkle
1968

We all moved to Topanga Canyon in L.A. We got
fake IDs with fake names. Carl had Trina Lopez put
on mine, and everyone laughed. I didn't tell them it
hurt my feelings. Trini Lopez was a famous male
musician. When anyone called me Trina, I ignored
them, so they only called me Kat. And I ignored the
names Carl gave the others.

On April Fool's Day, Ruby gave birth to a
baby boy. We all delivered him. Everything went
well. "His name is Peter Rabbit," Ruby announced.

Carl laughed at the name and said, "The
Hopi say when the end of the world comes, it can be
survived by hiding in a bottomless hole in the
desert. Peter Rabbit can dig us that hole." It
sounded to me like we were all Alice in
Wonderland, which was better than a circus.

More people joined our group. Billy
Bowson and his girls came by sometimes. They
lived with a music teacher. Billy starred in a movie
about Lucifer and played guitar. He was talented,
but he was also cold and bossy. He and Carl were
friends and competitors on many levels. Both
wanted to be in control. Eventually, we were
evicted, because too many of us lived there.

So, Carl, Mike, Ruby, Peter Rabbit, Tommy,
Anna, and I went on a road trip in the black bus to
New Mexico and Texas. I felt so free. I mentioned,
"I'd really like to see my Mom again. She's in
Alabama."

We drove to Mobile. When I saw Mom, I
immediately regretted coming back. She obviously
disapproved of my friends, the way we dressed, and
that I'd quit my job and wasn't working. So many

268

judgments! "I thought you could just be happy to see me," I told her as we left. "I clearly don't fit in your world anymore."

We left and headed west. "Are you OK?" Tommy asked.

I smiled at her. "I'm glad I'm with all of you instead of back in that little boxed in world."

"We're family now." Tommy gave me a big hug.

We were back in California by the end of April and moved to a ranch in the desert. It had an old western movie set, saloon and all. I imagined we were all entertainers—weeds that snuck into other peoples' gardens and bloomed. We were wildflowers.

Carl played sex and mind games, but mostly he played with others' fears. I noticed when women stood up and belittled him, he cringed and ran like a child. He had us women do the chores. Anna was a good cook, and she complained if she had to do anything else, so we let her cook. Ruby and Tommy were good at cleaning. I liked children, so I took care of the kids. I felt very protective of them. Carl wanted us to change jobs so we each did every job, but we stuck with what worked best.

Diana Lisa Bank
21 June 1949 – June 1969

I was born to the Drew family on the summer
solstice of 1949 in a small town in Maine. I grew up
in Milford, New Hampshire, with my mother,
younger brothers, and sisters. We were a large
family. Divorce was still considered shameful but
had become more common. My parents divorced
when I was a young teenager. My father moved to
Florida, but my mother and I stayed in beautiful
New Hampshire. Mom worked. I went to school
and helped take care of the younger kids. I grew to
be five feet and one inch with dark blonde hair and
green eyes.

Everyone told me I was smart. I loved to
read, especially stories about Native Americans,
because they respected girls and women. In the
Native American stories, women had a say in what
happened to them, unlike my reality. I was told at
home and at school that women had to get married
and be wives. I liked stories about the Hopi in the
southwest. They were strange, earthy, and magical.
I read a story about a hole in the earth. You could
go through it from one world to another. I was
intrigued by the possibility of escape.

I also loved to read Bible stories that
mentioned pomegranates. I never actually saw one,
but they seemed special. I asked a librarian to show
me what one looked like. It was beautiful. Once I'd
seen the picture, I always thought of it as a magical
fruit. The flower that produced it was pretty too.

I was shy when I was young, but I had to get
over it. I didn't see much of Mom, so I felt like I'd
lost both my parents and become a single parent
myself. I felt trapped. I wanted to have a choice

about my life. I had dreams at night of being a queen dethroned. I felt like my childhood had been stolen instead of a throne. I had dreams of being an independent woman working in a field. I wanted to be a free woman. And, yes, I wanted to be loved.

I had no delusions about marriage, but I knew I had to get away from my situation, or I'd go crazy. Mom remarried, and my stepfather was abusive to her. I was angry. Their marriage wasn't about love. She just needed a man to help her feed and clothe her kids.

Then I fell in love. I was only sixteen, but he was my way out. He wasn't abusive. He promised he wouldn't leave me like my father. We got married and moved to California. We found friends, marijuana, and real pomegranates. People called us hippies, but we were just kids looking for freedom, love, and peace. We tried lots of drugs. On psychedelics, I realized I'd missed something in my life. I called it God. We found lots of communes and wandered from one to another, but somewhere along the way, I discovered my husband and I didn't share the same quest. He was into all women, not just me. He was too materialistic for me, so we split up. Then we divorced.

I hooked up with another hippie. Toby's parents were from Eastern Europe. Unlike us, they were good American capitalists. They had one of those long, unpronounceable names with too many consonants, so they changed it to just the last syllable, Bank. Toby and I married when I got pregnant. I took his name, so we'd all have the same name. We had a baby girl in 1968. We named her Annie. I loved my sweet little Annie so much. I thought Toby and I were better off than our parents, because we were free spirits. I wanted us to be a happy family. I wanted Toby and me to be equal partners. I was idealistic.

Toby and I separated in the summer of 1969 when he took up with another woman. I kept Annie. I knew how to take care of kids, and Annie was my own. Toby moved to another commune in Taos, New Mexico. Suddenly, I was a teenage single mom again. I needed to support the two of us, but I couldn't take Annie to work with me. I did the only thing I knew; I went home to Mom in New Hampshire. I was unhappy, and I missed California, but Mom was glad to meet her granddaughter. I let Toby know where we were, since we were still legally married.

I hadn't been back east long before Toby called me. I hoped he missed me and Annie and wanted to get back together. "I want you to come back to L.A.," he said. "I met this guy with his own sailboat, and we plan to sail to South America. I want you and Annie to come too." Annie and I went back to Toby. I was glad to be back in California and with Toby and hang out with other hippies, but Toby sailed without us. I'd just found out I was pregnant again, and he left. I didn't begrudge him his freedom, but I was angry, because I thought we were a family.

I needed a way to cope. I was a single mom with no income or daycare for my baby, when a girlfriend of the guy Toby sailed off with told me, "There's a commune at a ranch with an old movie set on it. Everybody helps each other, and the women take care of the children. You and Annie would be safe there."

"Sounds wonderful."

"The hippies at the ranch are making a paradise to escape to through a hole in the earth.

Social turmoil is coming, and they plan to escape that way."

"Seems to me the social turmoil is already here." But what intrigued me was the idea of escaping through a hole in the earth, like in the Hopi stories I'd read. "I was planning to go to a Fourth of July love-in in Malibu, but maybe you could introduce me to these people."

"Sure, I'll take you." So she drove me and Annie out to the ranch, where she introduced me to a man named Carl Hoessmann. Carl was small and older than I expected, but he was soft spoken with big, deep, brown eyes. There was something familiar about him that made me feel comfortable.

Carl said, "Women are my flowers, and my job is to tend my flowers." So Annie and I stayed. I met a girl there, who was petite, bright, and honest. Her name was Tommy, and she reminded me of an elf. She was intelligent and well-read. She wrote poetry and knew more than anyone I'd ever met about nature, animals, and flowers.

"What's your favorite flower?" she asked me.

"I love pomegranate flowers, but I've never actually seen any, except in pictures. Of the flowers I know, I like crape myrtles best. They bloom all summer. What's your favorite?"

"I like violets," she answered. "Did you know crape myrtles are related to pomegranates?"

Tommy Feltener
1968—July 1969

After we lived in a house in Topanga Canyon with a lot of other people, we found our own place and moved out. Billy, from San Francisco, came by with some of his girls. He'd sung harmony with Frank Zappa and done some acting. Carl was interested, because he wanted to get into the music business with songs he wrote.

Ruby gave birth to her son the first of April. We were all there, and I was so happy there were no complications. She named him Peter Rabbit, which was cute. I was proud of Ruby. She had the courage to have the baby at the house. I told her afterward, "If it was me, I'd have gone to a hospital. I'm terrified of childbirth."

"I was too, but Carl said I had to face my fear."

Anna clung to Carl while Ruby was occupied with Peter, but Carl preferred sex with me. She had a curvy figure, but I felt radiant. Then Carl got an appointment to see someone at Universal Studios. It was important for him to make a good impression, so he cleaned himself up, and I cleaned up the bus inside and out. The two of us met two guys who talked about a movie in which Jesus reincarnated as a black man in the old South.

"I think Jesus' message can be summed up in one word," one of the clean cut men in his thirties said, "surrender."

"Or submission," Carl suggested

"But surrender or submission to what?" the other man with glasses asked.

"Love," Carl answered, "submission to love. That way no one dominates anyone else. Tommy, kiss my feet."

I knelt on the floor, kissed Carl's feet, got back up, and sat down in a chair. Then Carl knelt on the floor and kissed my feet, turned to the men and said, "Hey, maybe I could help you guys work on your movie."

The guy without glasses answered, "Sure."

On the way back to the house, I told Carl, "Wow, you made a great impression."

"Now I'll get my start in the entertainment business. I'm on cloud nine."

"You'll make it big," I said, and smiled.

Carl went back to Universal several times to consult on the black Jesus movie. He also got to make some demo records of his songs. Then we were thrown out of our house, because there were too many of us. Some went to live on beaches and other places, while Carl, Ruby, Anna, Mike, Katrina, a guy named Lawson who'd joined us, and I went on the road in the bus. We drove across the southern part of the country as far as Alabama, where Kat's mom and aunt lived. When we got back to L.A., someone had found a place for all of us, so by the end of April, we lived on a ranch in the desert with a movie set where westerns had been filmed. We played a lot on the sets. Carl taught us to dissolve our identity. "We're all one," he repeated. He led games where we mimicked everything he did, so we'd realize we were one.

An old blind man owned the ranch and lived in a separate house. He needed someone to take care of him, so I moved in with him. I cleaned his house and spent time with him. He was a nice, but lonely, old man. He told me stories of his life. I hugged, petted, and made over him. He said he liked my high pitched giggles and occasional squeals of delight.

One night in October, I dreamt someone crashed through a window, jumped into a fire, and yelled, "I'm the devil." I woke up and felt like my subconscious was trying to warn me of something. As the day went on, I remembered more of the dream. Lawson was the one on fire who shouted, "I'm the devil," as he held up a prayer book. Then there were knives, and someone I knew, but couldn't see, stabbed me and the other women in the throat. I kicked and screamed to get away. I didn't tell anyone I still had repressed fears I hadn't surrendered.

I worked hard cleaning the old man's house, but I didn't mind. It was a nice place to stay, and I enjoyed his stories. He was kind of like a grandfather, except for the sex, and I liked sex.

19 April 1969 I was arrested on suspicion of grand theft auto. The police didn't have a clue, but they seemed to really enjoy their power trip over prisoners. It was just like one of Carl's games, only they didn't understand. After my Dad and then Carl, they couldn't humiliate me—but they tried. I worried about who'd take care of the old man. I was caged for three days. They had to release me, because they had no evidence against me. I knew people who stole cars, but I'd never taken part.

About a month later, Carl and Anna left for a couple of weeks. Carl liked to move around a lot. I was glad he took Anna with him this time. I hoped she might give up her ego along the way, but I really expected she'd come back more puffed up than ever—which is what happened.

In July, Ruby was arrested in L.A. for credit card fraud. She was held for trial. I knew she'd be OK, but I missed her. Carl said to live in the now. I wondered if maybe there was something he didn't want us to remember about our past lives.

Things happened fast. Carl taught us about guns and knives. I saw it as an opportunity to face my nightmares. I heard talk that Carl shot someone, but I still lived with the old man, and I didn't believe it. Bikers moved onto the ranch, and the old man didn't like them. "I need to get somebody to throw all these hippies off my land," he grumbled. That pissed me off after I'd taken good care of him. Then Kat told me a music teacher I'd only heard of from Ruby had been murdered. I felt like violets were being trampled.

Anna Stukiss
1968—July 1969

Kat and I had bonded on the bus when we moved to
L.A. We became close once I joined her in making
fun of the others. I guess she realized how smart I
was. She wasn't pretty, but I was nice to her
anyway. Carl had new fake IDs made for all of us.
He put the name Sara Ann Kissup on mine. I
thought it was cool. So sometimes Carl called me
Anna, and sometimes he called me Sara Ann. He
chose the name Mary for Ruby and called her Mary.
He said, "I'm Jesus and she's Mary Magdalene."

I didn't like it. He only acknowledged our
special cosmic love when we were alone together,
but in front of the others, he made me feel small.
And we weren't alone much.

The same satanic high priest who staged the
Witches Sabbath in San Francisco was in L.A. too. I
took Carl and a couple of others to meet him. I
thought he was cool. His church used torture,
whips, chains, bondage, and simulated virgin
sacrifice. I was thrilled, but Carl felt humiliated
with the whips and chains. After all, he was a god.
But as time passed, he started whipping women's
asses and slapping us around. "Women have no
souls," he said.

"What's a soul?" I asked, and we both
laughed.

Meanwhile, Ruby gave birth to a baby boy,
Peter Rabbit. Carl gave all his attention to her and
the baby—the holy family: Jesus, Mary, and Peter
Rabbit. Rejection from Carl really hurt. I wanted to
die. I thought about suicide, but I knew he wouldn't
rescue me. My life had crashed down around me. I
cried a lot and wandered around the streets, until I

278

was arrested for vagrancy. I used my fake ID and name. I was released before they discovered my real name and past record. I went back to Carl.

But the group grew, and we moved to a ranch outside the city that had been used for old cowboy movies. The movie set was still there. Carl preached about love and the ever-present present moment. He encouraged us all to sing. Billy competed with Carl for leadership. When Billy joined us, he brought his own followers, but Carl always won as the leader, so Billy and his girls came and went.

I realized I was pregnant. I didn't know who the baby's father was. It couldn't be Carl's, but since I was the goddess romantically involved with a god, the baby had to be Carl's. I told him, "I'm having your baby." He grinned ear to ear.

The women shared chores. They cleaned, cooked, did laundry, and made beds. It reminded me of when I lived at home. "I don't like it," I said. "A goddess shouldn't have to do chores."

"Why don't you just cook?" Kat suggested. "You're a good cook."

So I cooked. But I found out later she was being sarcastic and didn't like the way I cooked. At least I got out of doing the other chores.

For income, some panhandled, some used their parents' credit cards, and some of us stole. I didn't understand why the women had to earn money *and* do all the chores. Otherwise, we did pretty much as we pleased. We played games and cards, took lots of naps, did lots of drugs, had lots of sex, gossiped, and argued. But we always had dinner together on the movie set. We also had a radio and a TV, so we knew about Martin Luther King, Jr., being shot and killed in April 1968 at a hotel in Memphis, Tennessee. Then Robert Kennedy was shot and killed the first week of June at the Ambassador Hotel in L.A. Carl preached a lot about reincarnation and said, "We never die."

I wondered if Mom had been reborn, and I wondered who my baby had been. Maybe Carl really had been Jesus. He played the papa game with all the women. If Carl was my father in a past life, he had sex with me, I laughed to myself. Then Carl told us, "The world's about to end, and we need to live off the land."

"I don't want to be a farmer," I said, and everybody laughed, including Carl.

A very tall, slim, handsome guy named Lawson Tascher stayed with us. He had dark hair and blue eyes. His huge smile was very attractive. Billy rejoined us with a new girl, Sheila Von Lueten. She was smart and emotionally strong. I had to share both Carl and Lawson with her, but I was prettier.

At the end of the first week of October, when I was about seven months pregnant, I took some acid. Carl was angry. He yelled at me, "You shouldn't be doing stuff like that, Sara Ann. You've got to think about the baby."

"I'm cool," I told him, but then the contractions started. It really hurt. I didn't like it. The other women helped deliver my son while I screamed, but the baby was finally born on the floor. They tied off the umbilical cord with a violin string. Then Carl came into the room, knelt down on the floor next to me, and gently picked up the baby. He held up our son with pride. "This is Krackz," he announced. "My son's name is Krackz, and he's officially the new leader of this group."

Everyone applauded and smiled. "Krackz is our leader," they shouted.

Carl leaned over and whispered in my ear, "You did real good, Anna. You gave me another son."

He was very tiny, and the other women were worried about his size. I was very weak. When Carl wasn't around, Ruby told me, "You need to go away with Krackz to recuperate, because Carl will expect you to help out with the chores."

"I don't have anyplace else to go."

"You'll need help. A music teacher I know, Harry, helped me after I had Peter Rabbit. Billy used to live with him. Harry gave me money, food, and baby food. He saved me, so I found a place for you. There's a mission that's used as a retreat house near here. They'll take care of you, and in return, you'll need to do some light housework for them when you're able."

Krackz and I stayed at the retreat house until the end of the year. He grew, and I got my strength back. While I was there, I had dreams about having a bunch of children, feeling weak and confused, and Carl getting mad at me for not cleaning house. I knew it wasn't really Carl in the dream. It was a different time and place. I guessed maybe it was from a past life.

By the time I got back to the ranch with little Krackz in January, everybody was listening to the Beatles' White album. Carl said it spoke to him. The men still sold drugs, and Carl had made friends with a famous rock star. Carl said he had his start in the recording business.

Mothers in the group didn't take care of their own children. Kat didn't have any kids, so she spent a lot of time with them. She said she wanted to be sure they were OK. I was free to party. I knew since Carl was really Jesus, he'd take care of us, but he talked about the end of the world coming and how we'd have to survive. I didn't understand how a recording contract squared with surviving the end of the world. I was confused.

Carl always had some sort of blade on him, but in April, he taught the rest of us to use knives and guns for self-defense. I really impressed the other women with my knowledge of guns. In mid May, Carl took me on a trip with some bikers. We went east, and I finally had him all to myself. We went to see Carl's uncle in Kentucky. "He used to treat me pretty bad," Carl confided in me, "and now I'm going to give back what he gave me."

The two of us knocked on his uncle's door. It opened, and the man was clearly surprised. "Carl, I haven't heard from you in so long."

Carl pushed his way passed him. "Aren't you going to invite us in?" I smiled at the uncle and followed Carl inside. "This is Sara Ann, my girlfriend. She's a real good cook. She'll go in the kitchen and fix us up something." He sat down on the couch as his uncle closed the door.

"That's not necessary," his uncle said, and followed me into the kitchen. I turned around and saw Carl right behind him. Carl made a motion with his hand across his throat, so I grabbed a butcher knife from the knife rack over the counter and pointed it at his uncle. Carl hit him over the head with his pistol. He fell to the floor. He was just dazed, so I held the knife to his throat to keep him down. I expected Carl to rob him, but instead, he pulled out his own knife and stabbed his uncle in the chest several times. An image flashed through my head of an axe coming down hard on the back

282

of my neck. We grabbed what money we found, cleaned up, changed clothes, and left. I hadn't had that much excitement in a long time, and I shared it with my true love.

When we got back to the ranch in California, Carl announced, "We have to move to the desert."

"We're in the desert," I answered, and several others nodded.

"You dumb bitch. Weren't you listening? Armageddon is coming, and to survive, we need to move."

Lots of runaway teenagers had joined us, and one of them said, "My grandmother has a ranch in Death Valley. The ranch next to hers is vacant, but we'd need dune buggies to get around on it. There aren't any roads, and it's rough terrain, but it has caves."

"Sounds perfect," Carl smiled. "Let's get some money, some dune buggies, and check this place out."

Lawson was a mechanic and really good with cars. We stole cars so he had parts to build buggies. We got more guns and took turns on guard duty. It was cool.

There was another woman, Diana Bank, who'd recently come to live with us with her baby. Carl called her by her middle name, Lisa. When he wasn't around, we called her Diana. She and I bonded, because we were both mothers. Together we robbed people's homes. We called it creepy-crawling. We dressed in black, crept up to an empty house, broke in, and took whatever money or jewelry we found. Diana was really nervous, but I had fun.

One day Ruby asked me, "Do you remember that music teacher I told you about who helped me out with Peter Rabbit?"

"Sure."

"He's a nice guy," she continued. "His name's Harry. He's gay, and I think he's got a thing for both Carl and Billy. Maybe that's why he helped me. He's very gentle—practices transcendental meditation."

"Yeah, I've heard of that," I said. "That's the Maharishi Mahesh Yogi's trip."

"Right," she acknowledged, "just like the Beatles. Well, he's inherited some money, so Carl wants to send someone to get him to share with us."

"No problem," I told her. "Thanks."

I walked to the movie set and sat on a big rock in front of the saloon until Carl came. "Sara Ann, you belong in the kitchen, but you're always try to get into the living room. You want to do something important?"

I smiled. "Sure, Carl."

"Go kill Harry and get his money." I thought Harry was a friend, so I just stared at Carl, and he stared back. I wanted to be as tough as Carl. Finally Carl broke the silence. "Harry inherited more than twenty thousand dollars. You, Ruby, and Billy go and get it. He'll give it to you."

It was late July. The three of us got a lift to Harry's house. It was two stories set back from the road on the side of a hill with the living quarters upstairs. As we approached, I saw we weren't likely to be noticed. We went up the stairs, and Billy knocked on the door. Harry opened it and let us in. He was husky and about six feet two inches with his hair cut short. He took us into the kitchen and

invited us to sit around his table. Ruby was right—
he was a nice guy.

We sat down, and Billy said to Harry, "We
need all your money and your cars."

Harry looked stunned. "I don't have any
money in the bank, but you can have the ten or
fifteen dollars I have here. I'm glad to give you
what I have."

"We know you've got money," Billy
insisted.

"You should leave now," Harry said as he
stood up.

As Billy leaned across the table and hit
Harry in the face, he pulled a revolver out from
under his shirt. Harry fell to the floor. As Billy
came around the table, Harry got up, and they
fought. Billy passed me the gun. I set it down on the
table and watched them fight, but Harry lunged for
the gun, picked it up, and pointed it at the three of
us.

"You dumb bitch," Billy barked at me.

But then Harry handed the gun to Billy and
said, "I don't believe in violence. You know that.
I've always shared what I had with you, but you're
angry. Just leave now."

Billy took the gun and motioned Harry into
the living room. Ruby and I heard Billy try to
convince Harry to give us all his money. We
cleaned up the kitchen. We heard Harry say, "I
don't have any more money. I'm tired."

Billy came back into the kitchen and told
me, "Watch him while I call Carl."

I went into the living room. Harry was lying
on the couch. I watched him like I was told. When
Carl arrived, Harry got up and yelled, "I thought
you were my friend."

But Carl had his twenty inch sharp sword. He slashed Harry across his right ear and the right side of his face. Blood spurted everywhere, as Harry fell back onto the couch.

Carl ordered quietly, "Make him comfortable. We need his money." Then he left.

Ruby brought a towel from the kitchen for Harry to hold against his wound, and he slid onto the floor. The three of us watched him and listened to the radio. We stayed up overnight and through the next morning. I figured Carl was going to kill Harry once he gave us his money.

That afternoon, Billy fell asleep. Harry tried to get to the door to get away, but Billy woke up in time and beat Harry up. This time, Harry didn't fight back. He seemed to have given up.

By the third morning, Harry signed over both his cars to Billy. That afternoon, Billy stabbed him in the stomach. We watched him bleed on the floor a while, and then Billy stabbed him again. A sort of gurgling sound came from Harry's throat.

"Clean this place up," Billy ordered. "Wipe everything." While we did, Billy put on a glove, dipped his finger in Harry's blood, and wrote "political piggy" on the wall. After we cleaned up and locked the door behind us, we could still hear Harry gurgle and try to move. Billy went back in through an unlocked window and came out a few minutes later. "I smothered him with a pillow."

We drove away in one of Billy's cars. We stopped at a restaurant and ditched all our bloodstained clothes. We got back to the ranch after dark. I was too excited to sleep, but I crawled into bed with one of the girls and whispered, "Harry's dead." The next morning, that girl left with her man and didn't return.

Billy got a lift back to Harry's house, took the other car, and didn't come back to the ranch. Ruby and I hid from the others during the day so we wouldn't talk to them about what had happened. I didn't tell Ruby I already told someone.

Sheila Von Lueten
1968—July 1969

I met Billy Bowson. He came from San Francisco and shared a house with a music teacher, Harry. Harry was at least ten years older and gay, but he meditated and was a really nice guy. Billy was very talented as a musician and an actor. He was tall with long legs, long arms and fingers, and a very strong chin. He'd been in a couple of movies. He always seemed to have lots of connections and know the right people. He was also very stubborn and liked to be in charge, but I understood I just had to let him think he was. I really liked him and thought of him as my boyfriend. I felt a strong bond between us the moment we met. "I think we've known each other in a past life."

"Yeah," he agreed, "I feel it too."

In June 1968, a couple of months before my nineteenth birthday, Billy took me to a ranch east of L.A. with an old movie set on it. "Sheila, this is my friend, Carl Hoessmann. He's also a musician. We've known each other a while." Carl was older, but I felt a strange attraction to him—like magnetism. I sensed he, Billy, and I had been together before this life.

Carl lived on the ranch with a lot of other people. I noticed one of them, Ruby, was special to Carl. I thought she was his girlfriend. "Carl and I have a son together," she explained, "but everyone shares everything here. It was just the two of us before all the others came. Now we share."

Billy and I decided to stay, but there were no monogamous couples. In a way, it was like living at the fellowship, except with sex—and drugs substituted for meditation—but there were no lilies.

288

Carl told us he was Jesus Christ and Ruby was Mary Magdalene. I took it as a metaphor. I felt like I fit in. I was also drawn to a man named Lawson. He was tall with dark hair and a very wide mouth, but kinder than Billy, and I felt comforted near him. I knew I'd found where I was meant to be.

Anna was a year older than me, but she felt like a kid sister. She was very self-centered. She was pretty, knew it, and flaunted it. She just wasn't very smart. Still, I felt a connection. I told her, "We were family in a past life."

She answered, "We're all family here. Carl says to live in the now."

I would have liked a deeper discussion with her, but Anna didn't go very deep. I also wondered about my past relationship with Carl, but I didn't dare mention it to him. Carl liked to preach, but mostly Carl, like Billy, just liked to be in charge. The more drugs we took, the more I felt one with the group. I decided that whatever happened in the past, we were all together now.

The police hassled us a lot. Some people were arrested for stealing, some for drugs, and some for disorderly conduct. Carl told us, "Armageddon is coming. We can only survive if we find the bottomless pit in the desert." He was talking about a Hopi legend. I thought it was just a myth at first, but everyone else believed it and searched for it.

"Is it real?" I asked him.

"There's a place called Devil's Hole in Death Valley," he explained. "It's actually a bottomless pit in the middle of a barren desert that leads to a huge aquifer—underground water that will keep us alive out there."

I nodded. "It's real."

Carl decided we'd move to a ranch in Death Valley to get away from the law. The only access was by foot or dune buggy. We went back and forth between the two places. Lawson built dune buggies, and others stole cars for parts and money.

Meanwhile, bikers showed up at the ranch where we'd been. With the bikers came speed, which replaced LSD as the drug of choice. The whole mood of love and peace changed to tension and fear. Carl said, "The bikers are here to protect us, so give them whatever they want."

I didn't like sex with bikers. They were rough and crude, but I felt I had to do my part. Carl taught us how to use guns and knives. He had a knife collection he liked to play with. "We have to defend ourselves in the coming chaos. We all feel the tension of the chaos in society. Someday soon there'll be a race war—blacks against whites."

In April 1969, Tommy was arrested for grand theft auto, but the charge was dropped. Toward the end of May, Carl and Anna left with some bikers. They were gone a couple of weeks. Then in July, Lawson stole a lot of money from a man he thought was a Black Panther. Carl shot the man, and then told us, "We're all in danger from the Black Panthers. I've just begun the race war. The blacks will rise up and take over the whites."

Near the end of July, Billy left. Then, I heard Harry, the music teacher Billy once shared a house with, was murdered. Things happened too fast. I didn't want us to fall apart. Carl disappeared, and no one knew where. If I just lived in the present moment, I could shut out all the chaos around me.

Diana Lisa Bank
July—August 1969

Annie and I were greeted with wishes of love and
peace. Everyone promised me we were safe.
Lawson Tascher seemed to be close to Carl.
Lawson was big, lean, and strong with straight,
long, dark brown hair and a mustache over his wide
smile. He was intensely serious and passionate. The
very first night at the ranch, I slept with him.

Sex with Lawson was profound. I felt we'd
just found each other from a past life, where we
were adversaries, and he'd conquered and converted
me to his cause at last. I'd never experienced sex
this way before. Afterward, he told me, "You've got
nothing to worry about. You and your baby are safe
as long as you're loyal. Loyalty is everything to
Carl, and whatever's important to Carl is important
to all of us." I felt safe as I fell asleep, but in my
dreams I was warned to keep my distance from
Carl.

At the ranch, the children were kept
together, so little Annie had lots of playmates.
Whenever I saw her, I told her she had rosy cheeks
like pomegranates. I wanted her to grow up
knowing she was special to me.

Adults played games too. There were lots of
drugs, and Carl was in charge. He decided who used
which drugs when and who would score more. I no
longer needed to look for daycare, much less a job.
Still, Carl was different from any other hippie I'd
known. He was bossy and wouldn't put up with
being contradicted. He was kind to me, but I kept
my dream in mind. I was careful to make a show of
being loyal. Sometimes he called me Diana, and

291

sometimes he called me Lisa. It didn't matter, because I felt Annie and I were safe.

The women did different jobs. Some took care of the children, but according to Carl, a mother wasn't supposed care for her own child. I knew that wasn't right, but I didn't contradict him. Annie was looked after, but I missed her. Most of the other women were mothers too. Sometimes some would go into town to rummage through garbage for food. I fantasized we'd find pomegranates. We all had to help out and be loyal to each other.

One day Lawson said, "It's time for you to do your part."

"Sure," I said. "What do I need to do?"

"We need money," he answered. "Carl needs you to get us some money."

"So I need to get a job?"

He laughed. "No, you need to do a job. Who do you know with money?"

"Nobody," I said. I thought it was the truth.

"Yeah, you do," he said as he stroked my chin. "The woman who brought you here—her old man has money. The guy you're old man sailed with has money."

"I don't know him, but he's gone with Toby, so how would I get money from him? You want me to ask her for money, after she brought me here?"

"No," he smiled sweetly and shook his head, "don't say a word to her. Go to his place and take it. I'll make sure she's not there." So I did as Lawson asked, and I didn't feel bad about it either, since her old man had taken away my husband as soon as I found out I was pregnant again. Besides, if she needed a place to stay, she could join us.

The first time I slept with Carl, he asked, "You got a problem with your daddy?"

"Yeah, I do. My father left my mother, and I hate my stepfather."

"I knew there was a problem," he said.

None of the other men I'd slept with ever said anything like that to me. Carl seemed to sense things no one else did. That's why he was in charge. Maybe he was just older and more perceptive. Before anyone did anything on their own, they usually asked Carl's permission. He liked to direct orgies and decide when anyone took LSD. It didn't stop anyone from doing what they wanted. I'd done drugs and been at other communes, but I'd never experienced his control games or orgies. It went against my belief that everyone should be free.

The other women told me they were all witches. I answered, "I'm a good witch, and I can communicate with animals." We were like children playing pretend.

Sometimes they talked about how black people were going to rise up, but we would escape through the hole in the desert. I asked, "Why aren't any blacks with us?"

"Carl doesn't tolerate whites fucking blacks."

That was just wrong. Carl was a racist, but I'd found a safe place for me, Annie, and the baby on the way. I didn't want to go back to New Hampshire.

I learned a lot of new songs written by Carl. Some said a big record producer sometimes came to the ranch, and they knew members of some of the biggest rock groups. Carl planned to be a rich and famous rock star. I wondered why he was with us instead of touring and recording. Maybe if he recorded, we'd all sing together, and then we wouldn't have to steal or search through garbage.

Carl said he was Jesus Christ, and then he said he was the devil. I didn't take him literally. But he also said, "A revolution's coming, and blacks will rise up against whites. It was prophesied in the Book of Revelation in the Bible."

I doubted that was what the Bible said, but blacks had every right to rise up. Everyone should be free.

But then Carl added, "Even though the blacks win, they're going to need a white man to lead them, and I'm that leader." That didn't make sense, but Carl was on drugs.

I loved all the hippies, but then bikers moved in. Carl said the bikers had come to protect us from the Black Panthers. But if Carl was going to lead the blacks when the revolution was over, why should we be afraid of the Black Panthers? I kept my mouth shut to protect me and Annie. When the bikers came around, I went somewhere else.

If a biker wanted a girl, Carl ordered that girl to strip and do whatever the biker wanted. They did, and I was appalled. I never wanted Annie to be treated like that. I knew she was safe, because only the women looked after the kids. But I didn't want to stay after I had my second baby.

I liked the dogs that lived on the ranch with us. I always loved animals. I had a natural rapport with them. At meal times, the dogs were fed before the women. I didn't want the dogs to go hungry. They were well cared for. I never saw anyone abuse them.

Carl said, "Everything belongs to everyone. It's ours. We live together and share everything, but we don't have enough, because others keep what's supposed to be ours. So we'll take it." Some of the group went into town at night and robbed houses.

Sometimes I went with them. No one got hurt. People who lived in their own houses had extra money. We needed that money, so we took it.

Carl left the ranch 3 August and didn't come back until the eighth. While he was gone, Lawson gave me a thousand dollars. "Go to this address to buy some MDA from the hairdresser there," he said.

So I did, but when I got back, Lawson said, "This stuff is worthless. You got burned."

"No, that can't be. A thousand dollars is a lot of money. I let you down." I didn't want to have to go back to New Hampshire.

"It's not your fault, Diana," Lawson told me. "Carl will handle this when he gets back. You did good. There's nothing for you to worry about."

When Carl got back, he had a new girl with him. Chrissie was seventeen and pregnant. "I'm never leaving her side," Carl said, smiling at Chrissie. Chrissie smiled back at Carl.

The other women who'd been there longer than me were really upset. We all shared, and there were no exclusive couples, but Carl didn't explain. He just went off to be alone with Chrissie. The others were jealous, but I wondered why Carl was so out of character. That afternoon, he called a meeting with Sheila, Kat, Anna, and me. "Bring me up to date on what's happened while I was gone."

Anna said, "Billy was arrested for murder, and Diana got burned a whole grand trying to buy drugs."

Carl scowled as his face turned red. "Just look at how society treats us." He stomped off and came back with Lawson. Carl gave me the keys to one of the cars. "You drive." I was the only one of us with a valid driver's license.

295

"Wait here," Lawson said, so we did. I didn't know where I was supposed to drive or why. Finally Lawson came back with black clothes for all of us to change into and some other stuff he put into the car. After we'd changed, he gave each of us a knife. Then I got into the driver's seat while the others got into the car. Carl leaned in through my window and said, "Be witchy."

"Drive to the same house where you were ripped off," Lawson told me. It was nice to be going out at night. I thought Lawson would straighten things out with the hairdresser and get our money back.

When we got there, the gate was closed. I parked the car, and Lawson got out. He climbed over the gate and out of sight. We chatted quietly in the car and waited until Lawson came back. We all got climbed over the gate. Just then another car came up the drive from the guest house. Lawson motioned us to get back. I crawled into the bushes and stayed quiet. The car drove up, and the driver rolled down his window to push the button to open the gate. Lawson walked up to the driver's side of the car. I heard four gunshots and practically jumped out of my skin. *What the hell?* I saw Lawson reach in through the driver's window. The car lights and engine went off. Then he motioned to us, and the four of us pushed the car back down the drive. I saw the driver, a teenager younger than me, bloody and slumped over. I felt sick. He looked dead.

Lawson pointed to the main house and whispered, "Diana, go find an open window to crawl into, and then go open the door so we can get in."

296

But you just murdered that boy. What are we doing here? I heard music inside. I went around the house, pretended to check windows, and came back. "Nothing's open," I whispered. "Let's get out of here."

"We're not leaving," he answered. He disappeared and then reappeared from inside and opened the kitchen door. He motioned for us to come in. I shook my head and backed up a few steps. He was insane. The others went inside. I heard screams and another gunshot. A woman in a nightgown covered with blood ran out through the front door and collapsed on the ground. I covered my ears and yelled, "Make it stop!" Then a blond man covered in blood staggered out onto the porch. Our eyes met briefly, and I said, "I'm so sorry." Lawson came out and stabbed the man over and over. The blond man dropped to the ground dead.

I ran inside and begged Anna, "Please stop. Make it stop."

"Give me your knife. I've lost mine."

I gave her my knife and went back outside. I remember being told Carl was obsessed with knives. "There are people coming," I yelled. I just wanted us to leave.

"It's too late," Lawson answered.

Katrina was outside on top of the woman in the nightgown. I watched Kat stab her over and over. I looked inside and saw Anna stab a pregnant woman and lick blood off her fingers. I ran back to the bushes by the driveway and hid. I sobbed hysterically and curled up into the fetal position. *I'm pregnant too, and I live with murderers. I drove them here. They're all crazy, and I can't stop them.*

The others came and got me. I was too scared to even run away. My baby girl was back at the ranch, so I went back with them. Lawson drove. No one talked. They were strangers to me. I thought they were into peace, but this was pure violence.

When we got back to the ranch, Carl was dancing nude in the moonlight. We got out of the car. Anna threw her arms around him and said with pride, "We did it."

I was disgusted. *What is wrong with these people?* I didn't sleep much that night. I cried a lot. When I drifted off, I saw people covered in their own blood, and Anna licking blood off her fingers. Kat came at me wildly swinging her knife, and I ran and ran and ran, until I woke up.

The next morning, Kat told me to come watch TV. I went to see what was on. I felt numb. The others were already watching the news describe a familiar, horrific multiple murder scene. *I was there.* I cringed, but I sat down and watched with them.

"Her husband makes kiddie porn," Carl said about the pregnant woman.

I'm pregnant, I thought. *That could have been me. What do I do now?* "Loyalty is most important," Lawson had said. *If I don't act loyal, they'll kill me too.*

That evening, Carl got me, Kat, Anna, Sheila, Lawson, and a kid named Nate together. "You're going to do it again tonight," he said, "but this time you're going to get it right." He gave us all LSD and came with us. He gave Lawson an automatic .45 and brought a bayonet for himself. I knew I had to keep my cool in spite of the acid. I had to not freak out if I was going to get out alive and save Annie and the baby I carried. When everyone laughed, I laughed. When they sang, I sang. Carl drove us around for several hours. I forgot why and got into the singing and laughing. I totally forgot.

    We stopped at a house where the others knew someone, but Carl went to the house next door. When he came back and got Lawson, they whispered to each other. Then Carl said, "Sheila and Kat, you go with Lawson." They got out of the car smiling and followed Lawson up to the house.

    "This time," Carl said as they left, "be more gruesome than before. Make sure the pigs connect this to the others. We'll find another house. When you get done, hitchhike back to the ranch." They took their extra clothes with them. Carl got back into the car with me, Nate, and Anna. We drove around some more. Finally we stopped at a gas station. He handed me a wallet and said, "Go hide this in the ladies' room."

    I took it into the ladies' room, dropped it in the toilet tank, and then splashed some cold water on my face. I realized people were being killed back at that house. *Don't freak out. Remember the baby and Annie. Be cool.*

    When I got back to the car, Carl was in the passenger seat. He said, "Drive us to the apartment of that actor you know."

    I drove to the apartment complex. Nate and I got out of the car, and I deliberately went straight to the wrong apartment and knocked on the door. Some guy I'd never met answered. "Sorry," I said. "I guess I've got the wrong place." He shut the door. I shrugged at Nate and said, "He must have moved."

    So we went back to the car where Anna and Carl were waiting. I smiled at them and said, "He's moved." *No, Carl, I will NOT kill for you.* We drove back to the ranch.

Two days later, I told Carl I needed to go into town on an errand. He gave me the car keys. I went to where I thought the children were. I hoped to find Annie and take her with me, but they weren't there. I didn't want to arouse suspicion, so I quickly went back to the car and left. I drove toward Taos, New Mexico, where Toby went when he came back from his trip a couple of weeks before, but the damned car broke down. So I mailed the keys back to Carl with a letter, for Annie's sake. I hoped he wouldn't hurt her or come after me. Then I hitchhiked the rest of the way to Taos.

I told Toby what happened and where Annie was. He was with another woman, but Annie was his daughter, and I carried his child. He called somebody he knew in L.A. and asked for help. I was with Toby about a week when we heard the L.A. sheriff raided the ranch, arrested over twenty people, including Carl, and took the children into custody. I called my father on the phone, and he sent me some money. I went back to L.A., got custody of Annie, and took her to Miami to see Dad. Then Annie and I flew back to Mom's in Concord. I never thought I'd be so glad to go back there, but we were safe from crazy Carl. Still, I knew it wasn't over.

Katrina Pricewinkle
1969

We foraged for food. Some sold drugs, and some robbed houses at night. We survived by our own rules. I had friends. No one cared about my body hair. None of the women shaved anyway. I felt feminine and accepted as a woman for the first time in my life. Sometimes Carl had us strap him to a cross like Jesus and then have an orgy with him on the cross. It was a just a sex game. I liked being included.

Carl told us, "A big race war is coming, and the blacks will overcome the whites. Since we're white, we need to hide in the desert."

OK, this was different. We learned self-defense for survival. Carl had always liked playing with knives. This was just another excuse—another game.

Carl left with Anna and some bikers for a couple of weeks that spring. Then in July, he and Lawson Tascher robbed a Black Panther. "I killed him," Carl said. "I've started the race war. Bikers are moving in with us, and someone has to be on watch all the time in case the Black Panthers come for revenge."

Even I got paranoid. I wondered why Carl would kill someone. Maybe it was an accident or self-defense. Maybe it was a metaphor. I wondered if Carl was trying to destroy the judgmental concept of black and white, right and wrong, good and evil. But if good and evil were passé, then none of it mattered anyway. I kept the knife anyway, just in case.

Then Carl left by himself the first week of August. While he was gone Diana, a young, pregnant mother who recently joined us, was ripped off in a drug deal. When Carl came back, he had a pregnant teenage girl with him. "Everybody, this is Chrissie," he introduced her. "We have a special and exclusive relationship."

An "exclusive" relationship? Where did that come from? Sheila didn't like it either. Anna was pissed and clearly jealous. Ruby was hurt and angry. I felt for her.

But more important things happened. Harry, the music teacher and Billy Bowson's former roommate, was murdered. Billy was arrested for it. Carl said, "We need to do some copycat kills and make it look like racial stuff, so the cops will know it wasn't Billy. They'll drop the charges against him."

I didn't know much about how Harry had died, so I didn't know how we could copy anything. I didn't imagine we'd actually kill anyone, so Carl didn't make much sense to me. He was just paranoid. I was upset that Harry had died, but death was part of life. I was pissed that Billy had been blamed for murder. We weren't murderers. We were just society's scapegoats. Now I was even more paranoid.

A couple of days later, Carl got me, Lawson, Diana, and Anna together. "I've got a mission for you. Lawson's in charge. Do what he says."

"No problem, Carl," I answered. Carl's missions were usually breaking into homes when nobody was there.

We dressed in black and had our knives. We were all on LSD. Anna and I rode in the back seat while we drove to some house near where we used to live. Lawson left us waiting in the car for a while. When he came back, we climbed over the gate to

the driveway one at a time. We quietly followed
him up the drive toward the main house, but
headlights came toward us. Lawson motioned us to
get down, but Anna and I had already dropped to
the grass. Diana hid in the bushes. I figured Lawson
had already checked to make sure no one was home.
Something had gone wrong, but there was no more
right and wrong. I clutched my knife to ease a rising
sense of panic. I smelled the grass under me, and
felt how soft the earth was.

Gunshots or explosions startled me. I looked
up and saw the car with its headlights turned off.
Anna got up, so I got up and got Diana out of the
bushes. We helped Lawson push the car up the
drive. I remembered we'd come in a different car.

The main house had multi-colored stars all
along the roof. I realized they were Christmas lights
and got excited about finding presents to open.
Lawson let us into the house. I was barefoot. We
walked into the living room, where a man slept on a
couch. I thought we were Santa's elves, but when
he woke up, Lawson leaned into his face and said,
"I'm the devil, and I'm here on devil's business."
Then Lawson hit the man on the head with a
handgun. "Find something to tie him up with," he
told Anna. She tied the man's hands behind his back
with a towel. Lawson said, "Check the house for
others. Bring them here." I flashed back to another
time and place. People were being rounded up and
executed for crazy reasons. I saw Lawson engulfed
in flames.

Anna went down the hall. I followed her so I
wouldn't catch fire. She waved and smiled as she
passed a bedroom door and kept going to the last
bedroom. I stopped at the first bedroom and told a
dark-haired lady, "Come with me," as I pointed my

303

knife at her. I kept her in front of me in case Lawson was still on fire. Anna brought another man and a very pregnant blonde lady. When we were all together in the living room, I thought maybe we were all going to have sex, but the man from the back saw Lawson's gun and rushed him. The gun was so loud. The dark-haired lady screamed, the pregnant woman started to cry, and Lawson put a rope around their necks. "Prepare to die," he said. I thought of Carl's mock crucifixions, and we were executioners. The man from the back was bleeding on the floor, like Santa's red suit and the devil— except Lucifer was a fallen angel. The man on the floor was a fallen angel.

The man from the couch got his hands free from the towel and ran for the door. Lawson pulled his knife and ran after him. The dark-haired lady ran outside after them, and I followed her. I stabbed the air with my knife like Carl had taught us and tried to catch up to her. It was a fast-paced creepy conga line. Diana yelled, "Stop," as I caught up with the woman and knocked her to the ground. I stopped her by practicing self-defense with my knife and stabbed her. As my knife entered her flesh, I remembered yet another time when I was stabbed in the throat. I realized my arm had repeated the motion over and over. There was so much blood. I wondered if I'd really stabbed myself, but it didn't matter.

I went back inside. The pregnant woman was down and covered in blood. Anna was licking the blood off her fingers. Diana was nowhere around. There was no Christmas tree. Lawson said, "Write stuff in blood, and then clean everything up. Don't leave anything behind."

I looked at Anna. "Right stuff?"

"Pig, revolution—stuff like that," she said. I looked for stuff in the blood. It really wasn't the same color as Santa's suit. It was too thin—not plush enough. Then I saw Anna writing in blood on the wall, so I wrote on the door.

When we left the house, Diana was in the bushes crying. She didn't get any presents. We climbed back over the gate, got back in the car and left. I felt a really strange rush of fresh air mixed with acid, and thought it smelled like blood.

I got up early the next morning and watched TV. I couldn't sleep. The news came on and reported murders from the night before. Until I heard it on TV, I wasn't sure it was real. The TV said the pregnant woman was an actress, and her husband, who was out of town, was a movie director. They had attended a dinner with Robert Kennedy the night before he was killed. I woke up Carl, Anna, Lawson, and Diana. "Come watch TV," I told each of them. I wanted to see their reactions. I wasn't sure if we were OK or not. Apparently we had really stabbed people. Lawson had shot a couple of people. I knew now it wasn't Christmas.

The next night, Carl told Diana, Anna, Lawson, Sheila, Nate, and me, "We're going to get it right this time. I'm coming with you."

Obviously, we'd done something wrong. I thought he meant we weren't supposed to have killed people. In the car I remembered Carl said we'd do copycat killings. That's when I realized what was happening. It was a little late to turn back. I felt the stab in my throat. I was stabbed in a past life, and now I'd stabbed a woman.

Carl drove us to the house of a friend and parked. He left us in the car and went to the house next door. When he came back, he whispered something to Lawson. Then Carl told Sheila and me, "Go with Lawson."

We followed Lawson into the house next door. I told Sheila, "I was stabbed once, and it hurt." Then I showed her how it was done. My arm went into motion like it wasn't attached to me, and I watched. We stabbed a middle-aged lady in the bedroom, and then I went back to the living room. Lawson had stabbed her old man. He told me to write "pig" in the man's blood, so I went to the kitchen, got a fork, and stuck it in him. It made about as much sense as anything else.

By October, a lot of us moved to an old mining claim in Death Valley. I was glad we had no more murderous outings. Inwardly, I tried to deal with it. I rationalized that I'd been murdered, so I got to murder others, but I didn't like it. I knew it wasn't something I'd ever wanted to do. I didn't even know those people. They didn't murder Harry, so why did we murder them?

Outwardly, most of us cut our hair short because of the heat. We found some little caves where we could get out of the sun, so we camouflaged them to hide them. At the ranch, our numbers had grown, and people got on each others' nerves, but with all the space in Death Valley, I felt free again. I could just walk away from anyone who bothered me. I didn't want to talk. I'd find a shady spot, like a cave, and take a long nap in the heat of the day. I had time to think about how much had changed. A long time ago, I was impressed by Carl's knowledge of the Bible. Now I'd killed for him. I'd look up at the blue sky and think about cornflowers. At one time, they were just considered weeds. So was I.

Then the deputies came. I don't know how they found us. Lawson escaped. From jail, I called Dad, who had moved to Florida. He arranged my bail and sent me back to Mobile, Alabama, to live with my aunt. I was happy to be there, but it was hard to readapt to her expectations. The creature comforts of living in a house were nice, but I felt like I put on a costume when I dressed the way I used to. I was back in the land of boundaries and rules.

I realized safety and freedom were opposites. My aunt wanted me to reevaluate my life, but I no longer belonged to her society. She didn't know I was a murderer. I didn't want to talk about school or career. None of that mattered anymore, but she didn't understand. I just didn't want to go back to jail. I tried to make sense of the things I'd seen and felt on acid—being stabbed in the throat, Lawson on fire, people being rounded up and executed.

My aunt let me drive her car to look for a job, but a cop stopped me for speeding. I was afraid if I told him my name, he'd arrest me. "I don't have a driver's license, officer."

He arrested me for speeding and driving without a license. At the police station, I was fingerprinted. Locked in a cell, I knew my prints would give me away. I was also charged with giving false information to the police, and taken back to California in shackles. Anna had talked to the police about the seven murders. I knew she was stupid, but I never thought she'd betray us. I believed we could all trust each other. I heard Lawson was in jail in Texas. I remembered he had family in law enforcement there. I hoped they would protect him, but Sheila, Anna, Carl, and I would be tried together for the murders, and I knew I was guilty.

Anna Stukiss
August—December 1969

Rumors spread at the ranch about murders, and a lot of people left. Even Carl disappeared somewhere. Billy called the ranch 6 August, said he was arrested driving Harry's car, and was in the L.A. County jail charged with Harry's murder. He had the knife with him he'd used to stab Harry when he was busted.

Two days later, Carl returned with another teenage girl. "Hey, everybody," he shouted, "Gather around. I want you to meet Chrissie. Chrissie's my new girl, and we have an exclusive relationship, so be nice to her."

WHAT? He can't just forget we're cosmic lovers. I didn't get it. Then I realized he'd never told anybody about our special relationship. I felt betrayed. I didn't like the new bitch. He blew it. I was angry. "Billy's been busted," I said. "He's in jail for Harry's murder."

"Well then, we need to kill or be killed," he said. "Guilt doesn't exist. Guilt isn't real. I have to stop society before it destroys the planet."

Somebody said, "What? You don't make any sense."

"No sense makes sense." More people left the ranch. "Let them go," he said. "They'll be destroyed in the coming chaos."

Lawson and I had a private stash of speed, so as the commune fell apart, we used it. We snorted speed for over a week.

It was a Friday night when Carl called both of us together with Kat and Diana. Each of you get a change of clothes and your knife and go with Lawson. Do what he tells you."

We all dressed in black and went in the old
Ford to Cielo Drive in Benedict Canyon. Lawson
was in charge. He'd come a long way from Texas,
where he was a star athlete in school. Needless to
say, we were high out of our minds, but I was
excited. I was Carl's blood-red rose, and my knife
was my thorn. I'd watched Carl and Billy kill, and
now I was angry enough to prick someone.

Lawson cut the phone wires to the house.
The place was pretty secluded and surrounded by a
fence. We climbed the fence. Lawson carried a coil
of rope over his shoulder. The main house was
about a hundred feet from the fence and lit with
colorful Christmas lights. There was another small
house further away.

A car came down the driveway. Kat, Diana,
and I flattened out on the grass, but Lawson walked
up to the car. I heard him say, "Halt."

Then a different male voice said, "Please,
don't hurt me." That was followed right away by
four gunshots. Lawson came back, and we pushed
the car back up the driveway to the garage, which
was to the right and rear of the main house. Then
Lawson broke into the house and let me and Kat in.
He told Diana, "Stay outside and keep watch." In
the living room, Lawson pulled out a gun, pointed it
at a guy asleep on the couch, and said, "Wake up."

He woke up startled. "Who are you? What
do you want?"

Lawson answered, "I'm the devil, and I'm
here on devil's business." Then he turned to me.
"Get something to tie his hands."

I looked at the rope Lawson had but wasn't
using. I shrugged, went to the kitchen, and grabbed
a towel. I tied his hands with the towel as best I
could, but none of it made sense. The rope would

have been more practical. Then Lawson said, "See if anyone else is in the house."

I walked down the hallway. Through an open door, I saw a woman with dark hair and glasses in bed reading a book. She looked up and smiled at me. I waved and smiled back as I kept going. She seemed nice. I came to another bedroom where a very pregnant blonde woman was in bed, and a man sat on the bed next to her. They talked to each other and didn't notice me, so I went back to Lawson. "There are two women and a man."

"Use your knives and bring them here," he answered.

I went to the furthest bedroom, jumped in pointing my knife, and said, "Come with me or you're dead."

The man stood up and said, "What?" as he grabbed the pregnant woman by the hand and led her through the door. We went back to the living room, where Kat had the lady with glasses. The man stepped between Lawson and the pregnant woman and reached for Lawson's gun. Lawson shot him twice. He fell in front of the fireplace as the pregnant lady screamed and then sobbed. Kat turned the lights down.

"Where's your money?" Lawson demanded.

The dark haired lady answered, "I have some credit cards."

I grabbed her from behind, held my knife at her throat, and jerked her back toward the bedroom. She offered no resistance and went straight to her purse and pulled out a wallet. Back in the living room, she handed Lawson the wallet. "You can have everything," she said.

"Is this everything?" he asked her.

"Yes, it's everything."

Lawson tossed one end of his rope over the ceiling beam, tied it around each of their necks, and then picked up the other end of the rope and pulled it tight. He turned to me and said, "Kill him."

I went to stab the man whose hands I'd tied with a towel, but he'd freed himself and fought back. He grabbed my hair, and we fell to the floor struggling, pulling the rope loose at the same time. He pulled my hair out by the roots as I flailed and stabbed him in his legs. Blood spurted and my head hurt. Lawson hit the man on the head with his gun, and I heard his head crack, but he broke free and ran out the open front door. I realized I'd lost my knife. I couldn't be a true rose without a thorn, but Diana was just outside. "Give me your knife, Diana. I lost mine."

I was alone in the living room with the hysterical pregnant woman She still had the rope around her neck. "Shut up, you bitch," I ordered, but she wailed. "You're going to die," I said as I stabbed her with Diana's knife. Then there was silence. I had blood all over my hands, so I instinctively put each finger in my mouth to suck it off. I looked up and saw Lawson.

He caught his breath and asked, "Did anybody write anything? And we need to clean this up."

We dipped a towel in the woman's blood, and wrote "pig" on the front door. When we were done, I was the last one out of the house. I had Diana's knife and forgot I'd lost my own. We climbed back over the gate. Diana was sitting in the driver's seat of the car crying. Lawson pushed her over and got into the driver's seat, as Kat and I got in the back, and we all changed clothes. We made a big wad of the bloody ones. I was pissed at Diana.

She was such a cry baby. Nobody said anything as we drove, until Lawson pulled the Ford over by the side of an embankment. "At least get rid of these," he said as he shoved the pile of bloody clothes at Diana. She threw them out the window.

Carl was waiting for us at the ranch. "Did you go to the next house?" he asked.

Lawson glared at him. "No."

I was still angry. Carl should have been with me. Lawson and I finally crashed from all the speed we snorted. The next morning Kat woke us. "It's on TV," she said.

Diana and Carl were already watching the news with some of the others. We joined them. The man on TV talked about five murders the night before in Benedict Canyon. He said, "Someone wrote on the door and walls of the house in the victims' blood." The man Lawson shot, who fell in front of the fireplace, was a famous hairdresser for movie stars—the same guy who'd ripped Diana off. I flashed back to my role as a vampire and remembered sucking the blood off my fingers. I wanted some more speed, but then I remembered I left my knife behind in the house. I didn't tell anyone. They'd think I was stupid.

That night, Carl called me, Lawson, Diana, Kat, Sheila, and young Nate together. Nate was new at the ranch. We got into the Ford, and Carl drove to a house. Lawson, Kat, and Sheila went up to the house, and the rest of us drove off. Carl said, "I need to plant this wallet near some blacks." We stopped at a gas station next to a black neighborhood. Carl gave the wallet to Diana. "Hide it in the ladies' room."

She took the wallet, went into the ladies' room, and came back a few minutes later. "I put it in the water tank."

Carl drove us to Venice. He pulled into an apartment complex parking lot. "You know somebody here, don't you Diana?"

"Yeah, I do."

"Nate, you and Diana visit him." Nate had a gun. It was almost dawn. We didn't wait. Carl drove the two of us back to the ranch. It was the first time I'd been alone with him in a while, but we didn't talk. I was still pissed about Chrissie. The others all came back later that day.

I lost track of time. I woke up one morning to the sound of a metallic click. I opened my eyes to a police rifle in my face. Twenty-five of us were rounded up in front of the movie set, while the cops searched everything.

I was charged with grand theft auto and taken to the women's prison, held for seventy-two hours, and released. I went to the Death Valley ranch. I found out my son was taken by the police and placed with a family, so I got Lawson to drive me to the house where Krackz had been sent. I went in through a window, found him, and walked out the front door with him. The three of us went back to the Death Valley. We waited there for Billy to be released, but he wasn't.

Instead, we were raided by deputies 10 October. I hid in a cave with some friends, but we were all arrested, and my son was taken again. I was charged with grand theft auto and arson. I was in jail two days before I was taken out of my cell to an interview room, where I met two detectives.

"Tell us what you know about Harry's murder," the younger one said.

"I was there when he was beaten up by some black men," I lied. "But he was alive when I left him."

The next day I was booked on suspicion of Harry's murder. Then I was sent back to my new home, the women's prison. The cell doors opened at four-thirty every morning, and we had breakfast at five. Lights out was at nine. On the first day of November, I checked into a dormitory, which housed over fifty women. I was assigned to carry messages between prison authorities. I made friends with two former prostitutes on the same work duty, Jill and Angie.

Jill asked, "What are you in for?"

"Murder." I smiled at her.

"Did you do it?"

"Sure, I stabbed him over and over again." I wanted to be important in prison.

Two days later, I told Angie, "You know, there's a case right now that's unsolved, and the cops don't have a clue—the murders in Benedict Canyon."

"Really?" Angie was interested alright. "You know something about that?"

"Yeah, I killed the pregnant woman. The first time I stabbed her felt so good. Then I tasted her blood."

In less than a week, I was moved from the dorm to isolation. It was the mental observation unit made of steel and concrete. The lights were dimmed at night, but never turned off. I was given a lawyer. "You're not in your right mind," he told me. "We can use that in your defense."

So I made a taped confession about the Benedict Canyon murders. I also agreed to testify against the others to avoid the death penalty. I testified in front of the grand jury. Carl should have told the others about our cosmic romance and not humiliated me with that little bitch he brought home.

Sheila Von Lueten
August—December 1969

Carl came back at the beginning of August with a
seventeen year old pregnant blonde. "Everybody,
this is Chrissie. We're together—just the two of us."

The mood on the ranch was already tense
without Carl suddenly going back on everything
he'd said. I didn't like it. Nobody did. Then on 6
August, Billy was arrested in L.A. and charged with
Harry's murder. I was angry. Billy wouldn't do that.
Carl said we needed to stage some copycat killings
to get Billy's charges dropped. I didn't stop to think
about what that meant. I was too angry about Billy's
arrest.

A couple of nights later, Lawson, Kat, Anna,
and the new girl, Diana, left in the car. They wore
black, so I knew they were going to break into
houses where no one was home. Sometimes it was
to steal, and sometimes it was just to move people's
furniture around and mess with their heads.

The next morning, we all watched TV.
There'd been a mass murder the night before. Five
people were killed—one of them was eight months
pregnant. As the day went on, I pieced together that
the murders were done to copycat Harry's death and
get Billy out of jail. I began to catch on that maybe
Billy really had killed Harry. I couldn't make sense
of it. Harry was a friend. Maybe it was an accident.

With Billy gone, I felt I needed to prove my
loyalty to Lawson and Carl. I wanted to fit in and
not be left out, so I went to Carl. "Whatever you
have planned next, I want in. I want to be part of it."

He smiled at me and said, "Get Lawson,
Kat, Anna, Nate, and Diana, and bring them to me."
After we were all together, Carl gave us LSD and

317

told the six of us, "Tonight we're going to do it right."

Carl drove us to the house of someone we knew. "Stay here," he said. He went to the house next door. I was tripping and couldn't focus. When he came back, Lawson got out of the car. They whispered, and we couldn't hear what they said. Then Carl turned toward the car and said, "Sheila and Kat, go with Lawson. Do whatever he says. Then hitchhike back to the ranch."

We followed Lawson up to the house. I heard the car drive away. We went in through the back door. I thought no one was home, but in the living room on the sofa was a middle-aged man with his hands and feet tied with lamp cord. Lawson said, "There's a woman in the bedroom. Take care of her."

I followed Kat down the short hallway. We found the woman gagged and tied up on the bed with another lamp cord. I guessed she was the man's wife. Kat pulled out her knife. I was mesmerized by the fear in the woman's eyes as Kat plunged the knife into her abdomen. The woman, moaning through her gag, rolled onto her side and drew her knees up into a fetal position.

"Stab her," Kat said, "like this." And she stabbed her again in the side.

I pulled out my knife and tried some stabbing motions. *But Carl said the knives were for self-defense.* Still, I wanted to be part of the group. I stabbed the woman's buttocks half-heartedly.

"No," Kat corrected me. "Like this." And she plunged the knife deep into the woman's back.

So I made an effort to stab more deeply. I kept practicing on the woman's back and buttocks. I realized Kat had left the room. I stepped back and

318

saw that the woman was still and pale. I'd stabbed a real human being. There was blood all over her and the bed. I went back to the living room. Kat's back was to me as she leaned over the man on the sofa. When she stood up and went back toward the bedroom, I saw a fork sticking out of the man. He too was covered in blood and was dead. Lawson came in from the kitchen. "Clean this place up." So I did. In spite of the drugs, I was numb. After I cleaned the living room, I went back to the bedroom. Kat had written all over the walls in the woman's blood.

We hitchhiked back to the ranch. I went to bed but didn't sleep. I was depleted—like I was lost in a heavy fog.

About a week later, the police raided the ranch. Two dozen of us were arrested. I was held for a few days and released. They didn't know we'd done the murders. They wanted car thieves and drugs. I went back to the Death Valley ranch in a daze. The police didn't know, but we'd killed people. I wondered if the woman I stabbed was still alive when I stabbed her. She was dead anyway after Kat did her. Everyone died sometime. I wondered if anyone would put lilies on her casket. There were no lilies in Death Valley. I laughed out loud at the name.

I lived in the heat in a daze. I tried not to think or remember. I did as little as possible. I don't know how much time passed, but the law came to Death Valley, and I found myself back in jail.

"We know your people were involved in the Benedict Canyon murders, where the pregnant woman was killed," the older detective said. "So, Sheila, tell us about the other women at the ranch."

"Well, Kat, Ruby, and Tommy are my friends. I don't know Diana's last name; she's only been at the ranch a short time. As for Benedict Canyon, I was never there."

"We've released Katrina and Diana," the younger detective said. "We haven't arrested a Tommy."

"Tommy wasn't there either. She took care of the old blind man who owns the ranch with the movie set."

"But we know Anna was there," the younger man said.

The first detective added, "She already told us."

I showed no surprise. "Anna's crude. Did you arrest Carl and Lawson?"

The older detective seemed annoyed. "We don't have Lawson yet, but we've got Carl. He's not going anywhere, and neither are you. So tell us what happened."

"I wasn't there." I was glad I wasn't housed with Anna. The rest of us had been loyal, but not Anna. If I never saw her again, I'd be happy.

Then in December, Kat was caught. I learned she, Carl, the snitch bitch, and I were going to stand trial together for seven murders, even though I'd only taken part in one. But I didn't tell the police. I wasn't like Anna. I thought maybe if I kept quiet, they wouldn't be able to prove I was there. I wondered where Lawson was, but I took it as a good sign he wouldn't stand trial with us.

My lawyer tried to get my trial separated from the others, since I wasn't involved in the first night of murders. Carl didn't like that. He sent word through Tommy, who visited us, to stick together. She reminded me, "Carl wasn't at any of the murders and we need to protect him." I fired my lawyer and visualized laying white lilies on his casket.

Tommy Feltener
August 1969—1971

The old man talked to one of his friends about us
no-good hippies. I warned Carl. Then the old man's
friend disappeared. I figured Carl scared him away.
In August, the ranch was raided by deputies. I was
really upset, because I suspected the old man had
called the sheriff after I'd been so good to him—
even worried about him when I was in jail before.

    Carl had told us he wouldn't allow
interracial marriage, but there was one black and
white couple. They lived at the ranch before we'd
arrived, but Carl got all worked up about race stuff.
"It's not right," he said, "but that's what
Armageddon's about. The whites oppressed the
blacks, and the blacks will rise up. I shot a black
man. He may have been a Black Panther. The Black
Panthers will come for us."

    So it was true. Carl shot someone, but he
was honest. It seemed to me we should be helping
non-whites, but Carl hadn't surrendered his fear of
race. Maybe it was the speed he used since the
bikers showed up. Everyone that switched from acid
to speed got paranoid. Then the mixed-race couple
was murdered, and a lot of people left the ranch.

    After most of the jailed people were released
and came back, Carl said, "We need to move to
Death Valley."

    Somebody said, "I know an abandoned
place in Death Valley next to my grandmother's
ranch. It's an old mining claim."

    "That's perfect," Carl declared. "We can
find Devil's Hole, a bottomless pit. It'll provide
water, and we can hide from the chaos."

322

Not everyone went, but I was ready to move. I cut my hair short like a lot of others. We could only travel by car so far, and then we had to either walk in or use dune buggies the guys built. It was a long walk. Once we were there, everyone spread out. We carried knives to protect ourselves in the desert. It was just us and nature. There were no woods, violets, or beach, but I was free again.

In October, the law came. They went out of their way to find us. Lawson got away. Katrina's Dad bailed her out, and she left. Some of us were released soon after, but not Carl, Sheila, or Anna. They were all charged with murder. I didn't understand. We weren't killers, but Carl had said he shot a man. Ruby was still in jail on the credit card charge. Billy was charged with Harry's murder. I just wanted to keep my family together, but it all fell apart.

Before the trial, I befriended one of Carl's lawyers, who arranged for me to come with him so I could visit. In March 1970, Carl asked me to find Chrissie, the newest girl he'd brought to our family in August 1969. So I did.

"Carl wants you to come back," I told her.

"No, thanks," she said. "I believed him when he said he loved me and I was his special girl. I didn't know until I met all of you that he slept with anybody but me. Besides, I already told the police he taught a class in murder at the ranch, and on the nights of the murders, he had told me to go to sleep. Then he left and didn't come back until almost dawn. I have a job as a dog groomer. I don't want to see him."

So I left her alone. I was sad and angry. When the trial started in June, a few friends and I went to sit in the courtroom to see our jailed friends

323

on trial, but we were served with subpoenas by the prosecution. They didn't want us to testify. They just didn't want us in the courtroom. Since we were now on their witness list, we weren't allowed back in, so we camped out on the street corner outside. When the defendants carved an X in each of their foreheads, I did too.

In September, my friends and I were arrested on the street corner for loitering. I was in jail four days before I was tried, convicted, and sentenced to time served. When I was released, I went back to the street corner. When passersby asked me about the murders, I told them. "What we do to each other is what we do to ourselves. Just look in the mirror. We all die over and over. Look at what we're doing to our planet. Society kills the earth's creatures." But no one seemed to understand.

Then in mid October, I was arrested again for trespassing. Eventually, the charge was dismissed, because I hadn't been read my rights, but while I was under arrest, I testified for the defense in Carl, Kat, Sheila, and Anna's trial. "To save the earth, we have to become one. We have to let love flow freely," I testified.

But the judge yelled at me, "Just answer the questions."

"You need to understand. We were all rejected by the establishment."

But again the judge yelled, "Only answer the questions."

"Can I just talk to you directly?" I asked.
"No."

One of the lawyers asked, "What was life with Carl Hoessmann like?"

"He took care of us and was one of us," I
answered.

Again the judge interrupted. "Just listen to
the question and answer it."

I was frustrated. I just looked at him, held up
my hands, and shook my head in bewilderment.

Diana and several other women I'd been
friends with testified for the prosecution. Most of
them just told the truth, and Diana was given
immunity. She had given birth to a baby boy in jail
in February. I knew she wanted to be with her kids,
and everyone agreed she'd never stabbed anyone.

I thought a lot about my fear of being
stabbed in the throat. I was glad I hadn't been at any
of the murders. I didn't think I could do it either. I
didn't hate Diana, but Carl was my best friend, and
I didn't know why he'd done all this. I wanted my
friends out of jail so we could be a family again, but
I didn't believe in violence. We were supposed to
be about love, and I loved my friends, so I had to be
there for them, no matter what they'd done. I
focused on all the bad things society did to the
earth. I tried to keep my friends in touch with each
other.

In the middle of it all, a wild fire broke out
east of the city and burned down the old man's
ranch with the movie set. I knew death was just a
transition, but I was sad, because some of his horses
died, and other wild creatures must have perished.

Carl, Anna, Kat, and Sheila were convicted
and sentenced to death in April. A special isolation
unit had to be built for the women at Chino, because
California had no death row for women. Then
Sheila and Kat were sent there while Anna, Ruby,
and Carl were tried and convicted in Harry's
murder, like Billy had been. Nate was convicted for

killing the old man's friend I'd warned Carl about. I was shocked.

I got out of jail that summer. I went back to the street corner with the few friends I had left. Lawson went on trial in August. He was found guilty 12 October and also given the death penalty. Except for Carl, Anna was convicted of more murders than any of the others. That was ironic, since she was the snitch that caused the trials. Five of my closest friends were going to be executed, and I had nowhere to go.

Carl was transferred to San Quentin. He made a deal with the Aryan Brotherhood: if they would protect him in prison, Carl's girls would take care of the Brotherhood on the outside. I found an apartment in Hollywood for the few of us left. Some of the Aryans came by and stayed with us when they got out of jail, but I had to educate them. "We're individuals," I explained. "We have to give our love freely. It's our choice."

Meanwhile, I started to write a book. I needed to record what happened and what we were really about. My roommates did speed, but I preferred marijuana. It was natural. People came and went and got on each other's nerves, while I worked on my book.

Diana Lisa Bank
October 1969—1972

Carl and the others were arrested for murder in
October 1969. I debated with myself about what to
do. I wanted to be sure they were held accountable
and didn't go free. I found a lawyer. I wanted to just
go to the police and tell them everything, but he
advised me to keep my mouth shut until I was
granted immunity. Since I was still pregnant, and I
would soon have two children, I followed his
advice. He made the arrangements, and in early
December I surrendered to the police in New
Hampshire and agreed to extradition back to L.A.
Mom took care of Annie. I didn't mind jail as long
as I was kept away from Carl's group. I wanted to
testify against them. I knew it was up to me to end
that group.

    I accepted immunity in exchange for my
testimony. I was the chief witness for the
prosecution and kept in solitary confinement. My
son was born in February 1970 while I was in jail.

    During the trial, I testified for seven days. It
was hard to talk about, but I felt I had to. I looked
out from the witness stand at Carl, Anna, Kat, and
Sheila. Lawson was in jail in Texas. I cried on the
stand, but I had to stop Carl from hurting more
people.

    I was officially cleared of all charges 14
August. I went back to New Hampshire, but after all
the publicity from the trial, I took the children to
Santa Fe, New Mexico. I tried to keep Annie happy
by reminding her of her pomegranate cheeks. I
found passages in the Bible that mentioned
pomegranates and read those to my kids. Then I'd
make up stories from what I'd read. It helped me

remember I was a mother who had given life—not a murderer who took it away.

When it was all over, including the sentencing in 1971, Carl Hoessmann, Sheila Von Lueten, Katrina Pricewinkle, Anna Stukiss, and Lawson Tascher were all convicted and sentenced to death. Ruby and Billy were also convicted of murder. I didn't regret testifying, but I regretted I couldn't find a way to prevent the murders. I did my best. I lived to testify and protected my children. The lawyers told me there were a lot of other murders I hadn't known about. In February 1972, California abolished the death penalty, and their sentences were commuted to life in prison, which meant a chance of parole.

Toby and I got back together. We completed our family with a third child born near the end of 1972. We changed our names and moved back to southern California, but we were a family, and the nightmare was over. That summer I turned twenty-three and started a new life.

Anna Stukiss
1970—1974

I was taken to the L.A. County jail 5 March to see
Carl. I walked into the room. Carl sat at a table. I sat
down across from him, and when I saw him, I felt
the cosmic connection again. I realized he didn't
have Chrissie anymore. He'd asked to see me. He
must still love me, and I had to make things right
with him.

"Are you afraid of the gas chamber?" he
asked me.

I smiled at him. "No, not now." The next
day I sent word to the judge that I wanted a new
lawyer and I'd lied in my grand jury testimony.

Trial started 15 June for Carl, Sheila, Kat,
and me. Lawson was home in Texas. Diana, the cry
baby, testified for the prosecution, but Sheila and
Kat weren't happy to see me. "You just had to run
your mouth," Kat bitched. "We're on trial because
of you." Sheila nodded in agreement.

"I'm not testifying for the prosecution," I
protested. "That's Diana. Besides, I already told
them I lied to the grand jury."

Sheila rolled her eyes, and Kat just glared at
me, but I knew Carl accepted me back. We did
everything we could to disrupt the trial. When Carl
shouted obscenities, we shouted obscenities. When
he came to court one day with his head shaved, then
we shaved ours. When he ridiculed the judge,
lawyers, and society out loud, we did too. When he
fired his lawyer, we fired ours. We still played
games together.

Diana told the court everything. I was mad
at her, because she never killed anybody. We yelled
at her too. Carl yelled, "There's no place for you to

hide. I'll find you." But then she told them I'd asked for her knife, because I lost mine. The prosecution entered my knife as evidence. It had my fingerprints. It made me look stupid.

One morning, as I walked to my place at the defense table, I knocked the prosecutor's big stack of papers onto the floor. "You bitch," he yelled at me. So I walked my sexiest walk back and forth across the front of the courtroom. I swung my hips and savored my moment in the spotlight.

One Friday, Carl showed up with a bloody X carved into his forehead. "I've Xd myself from your world," he said. That weekend, Kat, Sheila, and I used matches and hot bobby pins to burn Xs into each of our foreheads. I enjoyed my performance for the courtroom audience. Carl and I were still in love.

Lawson was extradited from Texas to California 18 September. He had to stand trial separately, but I was with Carl in the courtroom. To prove my love to him, I testified in his defense. "There's nothing wrong with killing if it's done with love."

"Did you feel any remorse in stabbing a woman who was eight months pregnant?" the prosecutor asked.

"She cried, begged, and annoyed me. I stabbed her to shut her up." I felt so important when I was on the stand.

In mid January, my case went to the jury. I realized they would decide my fate. I'd either go free and could find my son, or I'd probably face death in the gas chamber. I fantasized what it might be like. I wasn't afraid of death, but I still wanted to live and have fun. Carl taught me about

330

reincarnation, so if they killed me, I'd just come back. The jury took ten days to decide.

Monday, 25 January 1971, the verdict was read. It took over thirty minutes, while we stood there and listened. Carl, Kat, and I were convicted of one count of conspiracy to commit murder and seven counts of first degree murder. Sheila was convicted of one count of conspiracy to commit murder and only two counts of first degree murder. It wasn't fair. I should have had eight counts of first degree murder since I'd done the blonde and her baby. Sheila wasn't as important as the rest of us, and I was most important to Carl, because I'd killed two in one.

We went back to court to be sentenced 29 March. We all got death in the gas chamber. I yelled back, "Better lock your doors and watch your kids," as they led us out of court for the last time.

Kat and Sheila were sent to the women's prison near Chino, where a death row for women had just been built. I followed about a month later, after I was sentenced again for Harry's murder. I was definitely more important than the others. I'd been in prison twenty-two months.

As I was processed in at Chino, the guards talked about if I'd be safe from the other two women, since I was the snitch. I wasn't a snitch. Before the trial, Carl had signaled to me he still loved me. But Carl wasn't here—just Kat and Sheila. I didn't know what to expect when I got to death row. It was a narrow corridor with four cells on one side. The cells were nine feet by eleven feet. On the opposite side of the corridor were a shower, a visiting room, and a cell used by the guards. They walked me past the first cell. Kat sat and glared at me. She wore a scarf over her shaved head. In the second cell, Sheila also wore a scarf. I smiled at her, but she didn't smile back. I felt uneasy. The guards took me past the third cell, which was empty, and put me in the last cell.

"Is this it?" I called out once I was locked in.

Kat's voice answered, "This is the last stop."

"Where did you get the scarves?" I wanted one.

"Our parents," Kat answered.

There would be no scarf for me. I wondered if they'd seen their parents. "So, you're allowed visitors?"

Kat's voice came back, "Only parents and lawyers."

Then Sheila added, "Shut up."

I wasn't likely to get any visitors. I was alone. We were allowed to walk alone with a guard in a narrow fenced yard. We planted flowers along the fence. I wanted to plant roses, but we didn't have any. Roses would have been appropriate with all the thorns and barbed wire on top of the fence. Kat planted sky blue cornflowers. Sheila planted petunias. It was as close as she could get to lilies. I planted moss roses, succulents with rose-like flowers.

There was a TV mounted opposite our cells. Otherwise there wasn't much to do. Later we were each given our own TV, and we took up embroidery. My teeth were bad and needed dental work. The prison doctor said, "You have gonorrhea."

"It's not the first time."

"You should have a hysterectomy."

"What's the point? I'll die in the gas chamber anyway. I won't let you cut on me."

332

Toward the end of summer, two more women joined us on death row. Cathy was short with short blonde hair and blue eyes. Rachel was tall with brown hair and brown eyes in her early twenties. They were both in for murder.

We listened to the radio and embroidered. It was early in 1972, and I sat on my bed and worked on a bedspread. We'd been on death row for almost a year. The radio announced California's death penalty had been abolished.

Sheila shouted, "That's us. No gas chamber."

I slipped off my bed onto the floor and sobbed for joy. "What happens now?" I asked out loud.

Sheila answered, "They have to put us with the other inmates. They can't keep us here now."

Three weeks went by, and then Cathy and Rachel were moved out. As the guards were taking them away, Kat asked, "What about us?"

One of the guards answered, "You'll stay here. The three of you are too famous and too great an escape risk." Cathy, Rachel, and the guards left.

We were devastated and bitter. Our sentences were commuted to life in prison, but we were still on death row. "We need to protest this," I said. "It just isn't fair."

"We can shave our heads again," Kat suggested. So we did, but no one cared.

One day a teacher arrived from the University of Santa Cruz. We had a chance to sign up for classes, so we did. We had class in our cells with textbooks and typewriters. The most important class was a course in women's studies. We learned about male oppression and how sexual degradation was one of the tools men often used to keep women oppressed. It hit home hard.

An occupational therapist came in twice a week from the psychiatric unit to help us work on handcrafts and sewing. At least now we had plenty to do, but I still felt shut out by Sheila and Kat. I got my GED in lieu of a high school diploma.

We were joined by two old friends from the movie set ranch, Ruby and Gina. They were convicted of armed robbery after they tried to steal guns to get Carl out of prison. I still felt a kinship with Ruby. We both lost our sons to the system, but she wouldn't talk to me.

Gina pointedly asked me, "Can I trust you?"

I responded, "I'm not sure I trust myself or you."

"Well, you're either with me or against me, so which is it?" she persisted.

"I don't know, but I'll help you if you need me."

"Ruby and I are getting out of here. We're escaping. Are you with me?"

I answered, "I'll help you get out, if that's what you want." I needed a friend.

"Then stay up tonight and time the guards out driving the perimeter."

I stayed awake that night. While I listened for the guards outside, I couldn't think of a way to escape, but maybe Gina knew how.

The next morning, Gina asked, "Are they consistent?"

"No." But I wanted to help her, so I drew a map of the prison in invisible ink and slipped it to her.

"Do you want to come with us?"

I really did, but Ruby interrupted, "I don't want her along."

"Well, I don't think you'll make it," I said, "so I'm won't come with you."

A man from another California prison, Terry, wrote me, and I fell in love with him. He told me how much he admired me, and how he hoped we could meet in person when one of us was paroled. Finally, I had someone who recognized how important I was. I wrote him back and said I wanted to meet him too. The letters became more intimate. I dreamed of someday being with Terry. Maybe we'd even get married in prison, so we could have conjugal visits.

In the fall of 1973, the fog season, Gina announced, "We won't need to go over the fence, because we have a brand new set of wire cutters. A visitor hid them in her vagina and snuck them in. You know, Anna, you could help a lot. Just distract the male guards. It gets cold at night anyway."

I didn't answer. I was too creeped out by the thought of wire cutters in a vagina. I didn't want to get cozy with the male guards. I was in love with Terry.

One day as I read my philosophy textbook, Gina asked me, "Why are you so serious? It's decision time. You coming with us or not?"

"No."

"OK. Tonight I need you to type as loud as you can on your typewriter. Kat, will you turn your stereo up loud?"

"Sure," Kat answered.

"Okay, this is it." Gina sounded happy.

I thought, *good luck not getting killed.* I stayed up typing for two hours. Suddenly Kat's stereo was turned down. A guard said, "Don't move. You're done."

All lights went on. They'd been caught, and they hadn't even left their cells. I got mad when I realized we were going to lose privileges.

By that winter, Kat and Sheila had nothing to do with Ruby or Gina. The tension was horrible. Kat, Sheila, and Ruby were still mad at me. The only friend I had was Gina, and I didn't like her. I worried about going crazy. Gina was the only one I had to talk to. "I'm going crazy, Gina."

"You have to let go. You're not a good convict. You were already a snitch before you got here. You've only got two choices. You can rot and die in here, or you can join the Jesus freaks and preach your way out. They're the only ones left who'd accept you."

Ruby and Gina tried to escape again and got caught. Eventually, they were moved to the main prison population, while the three of us, who didn't try to escape, stayed. Then Gina was paroled. The only friend I had was Terry, my lover-by-mail.

In early January, I eagerly opened another letter from Terry. The envelope was addressed to me. The handwriting was Terry's, and the signature at the end of the letter was Terry's. The words were Terry's and the promises of love and a future together were Terry's. But the letter started out, "Dear Maria,"—he'd put a letter to someone else in the envelope addressed to me. I felt so stupid. I'd been such a fool. Terry probably had pen-pal lovers all over the California prison system. At least I hadn't told anyone about him.

In February, I got a letter from Mike, who'd been at the movie set ranch with us. Mike was in Folsom prison. We were allowed to write each other as long as the letters involved legal matters. I was more cautious this time, but I wrote back. In May, I opened a letter from him that read, "I've always felt you were special, and I deeply wish you realized it. I love you for yourself."

At last! Someday we'd be free together, as long as we remembered to include legal matters in the letters. Later that month, I got another letter from him. "I hold out hope for innocence reborn of love and grace. Read the Bible, especially the New Testament. You'll find some answers, and you'll find out not everything we were told before was true. Take care, beloved sister. Mike"

Beloved sister? I wasn't anybody's beloved sister. I thought his letters were about love, but he wanted me to read the Bible. I read lots of other books, so I got a Bible. But I didn't start with the New Testament. I started at the beginning, and it was interesting. I remembered Gina had told me the only group in the prison population I'd be safe with was the Jesus freaks. Mike seemed to know that too. Now I had a real chance of parole—I just had to be saved.

I read the Ten Commandments and was surprised I'd broken every one of them. I kept the Bible under my pillow. I actually felt sorry for God. His people turned their backs on him. I knew how he felt. I also knew Sheila and Kat would make fun of me if they knew I wanted to be saved.

Then my junior high school counselor came all the way from San Jose to visit me. "You'd feel right at home in San Jose," he told me.

"I don't think so, Mr. Martin. School and I didn't get along."

"I know. I remember. Call me Marty. It really wasn't that bad in junior high school, if you think about where you are now."

"No, Marty, but I was headed this way. Why did you come so far to see me?"

"I felt I needed to tell you about Jesus Christ. He loves you and can help you put your life back together."

"I'm with God." I knew this was my chance. "Jesus taught a lot of good."

"That's true," Marty agreed and smiled at me warmly. "But he's also our savior. He took away our sins. All we have to do is believe." He stood up to leave and repeated, "Jesus loves you."

I thought a lot about what he said and Mike's letters. Jesus loves me. I'd had a cosmic relationship with Carl. Could this really happen to me? He loved me, and he wanted me to love him back. I'd finally found my true love. I dreamed that night Billy's and Carl's ways led to death. Now I had four choices. I could stay in prison alone and go crazy. I could try to escape and get killed. I could commit suicide, which would hurt. Or I could accept Jesus as my true cosmic lover, be accepted by the Jesus freaks, make new friends, and be paroled. I was only twenty-six. I wanted to live and have fun. I didn't need drugs or booze back in my life, but I could still sing, so I made up my own songs of praise for Jesus.

I sang them out loud. I asked to see the prison chaplain. He arranged for me to receive more Christian books and attend his Sunday service. My secret was out, and I didn't care if Kat or Sheila made fun of me. I was in love with Jesus, and he loved me too.

Katrina Pricewinkle
1971

So this was the end of the line. In April the four of
us were sentenced to die in California's gas
chamber. I was twenty-three. It seemed fair. Sheila
and I were transferred to a brand new women's
death row built just for us. Since we'd shaved our
heads, Dad and Sheila's parents brought us colorful
scarves to wear. Sheila and I had our own cells next
door to each other. Every day a guard took us
separately for a walk in a fenced area, where at least
I got to see the sky. I had no future, only the
moment. I was light as a feather, but numb. I'd been
having a good time, but somewhere I got lost in
another world. I was too weary to try to make sense
of it.

We wouldn't see Carl again. Anna was on
trial for Harry's murder. Why would she kill a
music teacher? Sheila and I talked to each other
through the wall.

"We killed people, and now the state's going
to kill us," Sheila said matter-of-factly.

"Everybody dies sometime," I answered.
"At least we won't be around for Armageddon."

"Is there really a Devil's Hole with a giant
underground aquifer in the middle of Death
Valley?"

"Carl said there was. Too bad we didn't find
it. Still," I laughed, "I couldn't see all of us together
stuck in a hole for who knows how long."

"It would have to be a pretty big hole." I
could hear the smile in her voice.

"So now we have our own hole. How does
the gas chamber work anyway?"

Sheila laughed. "First they shave your head, except we saved them the trouble. Then they strap you in, close the chamber, and you keep breathing until you stop."

"Sounds simple."

"Or I suppose you could sing until you can't," she added. "I'd like to go out singing. You know we come back after that."

"You think we can haunt as ghosts? That would be fun—a different kind of creepy-crawling."

"No, I mean we'll be born in another body somewhere. We've all done this before. You, Carl, and I can be together. And we'll get to be with Billy and Lawson. I just hope Anna's not there."

"If she is, we can just kill her." We both laughed.

Then Sheila said, "No, she'd just come back again." And we laughed some more. Then there was silence. I realized some of what I'd seen on acid was from past lives. In one of them, Lawson burned to death. In another, I was stabbed in the throat. This time I'd be executed. I wondered why it kept happening.

Finally Sheila said, "Killing's a waste of time." There was another silent pause, and then she added, "There's been enough killing."

Tommy Feltener
1972—1974

Some of my friends got busted trying to break others out of jail. The police watched our apartment. Ex-cons came and went with drugs. I moved to another apartment up on a hill and worked on my book. I wanted to get back to nature.

Then California abolished the death penalty. I was so relieved. My friends weren't going to the gas chamber, but they were still in prison. But society wasn't any better. Its core was still money and greed. The U.S. was clearly headed downhill. I didn't want to go to the desert by myself. Ivy, a friend in San Francisco who had an apartment and a job as a nurse, let me move in with her. I was closer to Carl, who was in San Quentin. I tried to visit him, but the prison wouldn't let me, so I worked on my book.

In October 1972, Carl was sent a hundred miles away to Folsom Prison. I traveled around the state a lot to visit my other imprisoned friends. Some more were arrested in Stockton, so I went there. I called their house from a payphone and asked them to come get me. The police arrived. I was arrested and charged with murder. I didn't even know two of my friends had been killed. It was a nightmare. I called a lawyer in San Francisco I'd become friends with, and he told me not to worry. "They have nothing on you, Tommy. I'll get them to drop the charges."

He was right. The charges were dropped, but not until January. While I was locked up, I was transferred south to testify for one of the Aryan Brotherhood. Dad visited me, but nothing had changed. He didn't want me, and I didn't want him.

341

At the trial, the defense lawyer said, "Please describe for the jury what the defendant was wearing on the day he was arrested."

"I have no idea." It was the truth. So they sent me back to Stockton.

I was released in early January 1973. I walked outside and was arrested by detectives from L.A. They took me back to L.A. and charged me with armed robbery. I was mystified and frustrated. My San Francisco lawyer friend attended the preliminary hearing. The eye witness described the woman who robbed her at gun point, but she never mentioned that her robber, whose face and forehead were uncovered, had an X on her forehead, because there wasn't. There was an X on mine. I was freed in mid January.

When I got home, I learned Gina and Ruby, who were in prison at Chino, had sworn allegiance to the Aryan Brotherhood instead of Carl. They and others wanted me to do the same, but I refused. Ruby, the mother of his son, deserted him for a member of the Aryan Brotherhood. I'd hoped we'd convert the Aryans to the path of love—surely that was Carl's reason for the deal with them—but now our people embraced violence. I even got a note from Kat saying it was all over.

I received death threats from the Aryans. I was near the end of my book, but now it seemed pointless. There was the world of love and the world of violence; I had a foot in each. I wanted the world of love, but my friends were in the world of violence. I didn't like their world. I cried a lot. I felt my life, like my book, was near its end.

Ivy didn't want to move closer to Folsom. She didn't want to give up her job. I understood. I had one other girlfriend from the ranch days that

342

wasn't in jail. Together Cindy and I found a cheap apartment in Sacramento near the university. I enrolled in classes and went back to school. Cindy did whatever I asked. I felt she'd protect me. I didn't want to be all alone in this ugly, hateful world. I'd found some happiness and a group where I belonged and could be myself, and now it was over.

Cindy and I went on welfare in August 1974. I met an old man named Adam on a park bench. Adam was lonely, but he had money. We slept together. He bought me a used VW beetle, but by October it broke down, so he lent me his Cadillac. Cindy and I drove to Oregon, but on the way back, I wrecked Adam's car. We weren't hurt, but the crash was so jarring, I felt like I'd suddenly died. It left me disoriented.

After we got back, I got a letter from Carl. When Carl spoke, I lost all sense of my individual self, even though I was trying to start over. Carl wrote, "I've started a new religion. Eating meat, wearing makeup, nudity, and smoking tobacco are forbidden. We have to be celibate."

This was so different, and I didn't like rules, but Carl had just told me how to move forward. I was ready. I clung to his new way of life. I was reborn. I went back south to visit the women in prison at Chino and tell them about the new religion. I was surprised they weren't interested. Kat told me, "You're not one of us."

That hurt, but she was part of the past. Back in Sacramento, I tried to find followers at the university. No one was interested.

Cindy and I made ourselves red robes with hoods. I felt like Little Red Riding Hood in a world of human wolves. I worried about pollution.

343

Richard Nixon resigned as President of the U.S., and his hand-picked puppet, Gerald Ford, became president. All I knew about Ford was he didn't stop the damage to nature.

The old blind man I took care of on the ranch died 23 September. I went down to Death Valley for Thanksgiving. I felt at peace in the desert. On my own, I objected to violence, but I was loyal to Carl. I felt divided, but my loyalty to Carl was stronger than my loyalty to myself. I held onto the idea of him, because I didn't want to feel abandoned again.

Katrina Pricewinkle
1975 – 1976

We got to plant flowers outside in the yard where
we took our walks. I planted blue cornflowers,
because I realized I was still a weed. A university
teacher came to the prison and taught us classes.
She helped me and Sheila understand we were
victims of the age-old lie that women were inferior
to men and had to obey them. We'd believed
everything Carl told us, because he was male, older,
and bossy. Since we'd been off drugs for years, we
could think clearly; and we questioned everything.

I was angry at Carl, because he used us.
When we were on trial, he manipulated us to take
his blame and demonstrate our loyalty to him. I
realized he was not only a coward, but a typical
man who thought women were property to be
owned. I very much regretted the lives I took for
him. He used drugs to manipulate us. Having us
chant over and over whatever he said was a form of
mind control. I was just one more of his victims. He
was totally self-serving and never cared what
happened to any of us. I enjoyed sex, but the men
never loved me; they just used me for their own
pleasure. On my own, I would never have stabbed
anyone.

I wrote to a judge, "Carl manipulated us. He
gave us all those drugs, so he could make us his
puppets. Now that I'm drug-free, I can see how he
used us. Does your honor think I might have been a
victim of mind control by Carl? I've never denied I
took part in the murders, but I want to know why." I
wanted to know if I could be legally recognized as a
victim. I needed to know if there was any hope for

me to ever become part of society—to be accepted as a true flower. But the judge never answered.

Like Sheila, I denounced Carl. He got us to kill for him, and then he set us up to take the blame for him. I felt I was brainwashed by him, and I was angry. Now I couldn't escape boundaries and rules.

Tommy kept visiting. She wanted us to stay loyal to Carl. I told her, "It's over." When she wrote, I returned the letters unopened. I admitted my guilt. I was under his influence and on drugs, but I stabbed people to death. I just questioned if I was really responsible, since I wasn't in my normal mind at the time. I didn't wish those people harm.

Sheila, Anna, and I were transferred from the isolation of what had been death row to the prison psychiatric unit. Apparently, the staff believed Sheila and I were now sane, because we were released into the main prison population. I wasn't surprised when they didn't release Anna with us. Maybe they could help her.

Then Sheila's lawyer got her a new trial. I was happy for her. She had a chance at life. She was transferred back to the L.A. area. I remembered how I had to show her how to stab that woman.

I made new friends. By the time Anna got out of the psych ward, she was in with the Jesus freaks. *That was the best they could do?* I laughed to myself. *But then they didn't have much to work with.* I steered clear of Anna and her friends. Anna had no conscience and no concept of right and wrong. If the Jesus freaks could teach her that, more power to them, but it was a little too obvious why she used them. She was never a good actress. Still, it was humorous. *She might actually come to believe she's saved; then the joke will be on her.*

I heard Lawson denounced Carl in favor of Jesus, but to me, he was more believable. Lawson said his place was in prison ministering to other inmates. He wouldn't try to use religion for parole. I could picture him as a minister. Maybe he'd been a religious martyr in another life. Anna, on the other hand, who never believed in anybody but herself, either thought she could use Jesus to get paroled, or she just exchanged one cult for another. Maybe she still believed Carl was Jesus and they were lovers. Maybe Carl believed it too. I laughed at both of them. I laughed at anyone who was sure they'd get their parole.

Sheila Von Lueten
1975—1976

The worst part of being in prison was the lack of
stars. I missed the stars. Otherwise, I managed to
cope. Kat, Anna, and I were visited by a woman
from a college who offered us a chance to continue
our education. We had nothing better to do. I found
the classes stimulating—especially as we learned
about the oppression of women by men throughout
history and the movements by women to free
themselves. Kat and I began to question our own
oppression. We became friends with the teacher.
     I realized Carl never took responsibility for
his part in the murders, even though they were all
his idea. I'd learned he'd ordered Billy to kill his
old friend Harry, and Anna and Ruby had been
there. I admitted my part in killing the middle-aged
woman, and Kat admitted she'd stabbed the woman,
her husband, and someone else the night before, but
Carl never admitted anything. The more Kat and I
talked about it with our teacher, the more we
realized we were brainwashed by Carl and the
drugs. We hadn't thought for ourselves.
     I publicly denounced Carl in 1974. Tommy
continued to write us. She wanted to keep us loyal,
but I refused her letters. I wanted to warn other
women and young girls not to make the same
mistake. I began to realize the enormity of what
we'd done by killing those people. I was
overwhelmed by guilt. I stopped eating. I felt I
didn't deserve food. The teacher told me I had
something called anorexia, and I needed to fight it.
If it wasn't for her, Kat, and my family visiting, I
wouldn't have bothered, but I didn't want to let

them down again. I worked hard to make myself swallow food.

One night I dreamt I was back in olden times somewhere in Europe. I was a queen and Carl was my king. I enjoyed the attention I got as queen, and it was an opportunity to reform life for the peasants, but Carl enjoyed and abused his power as king. He wasn't interested in reform, and he had no use for the ideas of women. He saw himself as superior, and I was mesmerized by position, jewels, and fine clothes. He hurt people, and I protested, but he had me imprisoned. I woke up in a cold sweat.

Why did I follow him? Why did I want to please him? The answer was obvious. I was taught by my parents to be subservient to men. The society I rejected was no different than Carl. If a woman served a man as a housewife or secretary, she was still imprisoned in his world and wants. I decided to be true only to myself. I vowed to not be violent. I would try to be kind and avoid anyone who was hostile or belligerent. It was the only choice left that I was free to make.

In the fall of 1975, we heard Tommy tried to assassinate President Gerald Ford. I never expected that. The last we'd heard she still followed Carl, but I never thought she was violent. Apparently, Carl hadn't either, which was why he didn't use her for any of the murders. Kat and I were both appalled and glad we were no longer in touch with her.

Tommy Feltener
1975—1977

In May 1975, I wrote to an L.A. judge, "My heart is
heavy with guilt. I wasn't able to get Carl acquitted.
I let my best friend down." Kat's words, "You're
not one of us," kept echoing in my head. I cried all
the time, but I didn't know what else to do.

In June, I called the judge I wrote to. "How
do you feel about all the death in Vietnam?" I asked
him. "How do you feel about killing nature and her
creatures? I'm going to do something desperate." I
hung up. It was just me and Cindy on the outside. I
felt hurt and abandoned. No one cared about me. No
one listened to me. I felt invisible, and I was angry.
Then I realized Carl used violence to get public
attention, because society understood violence.
He'd shown me how to turn people's attention to
my cause. I told Cindy, "We have to become
ecology terrorists."

I sent out a press release in Carl's name. It
threatened anyone who harmed animals or cut down
trees. No one would notice if I used my own name.
I needed to be heard. I wasn't at peace, and I cried a
lot. I put out a second press release in Carl's name,
which said Richard Nixon was responsible for
Carl's conviction, because Nixon made a statement
during the trial that Carl was guilty. I went on to say
Nixon ran the country through Ford, and if that
didn't change, there would be more murders. The
day after the press released my statement, President
Ford announced he would run for president in the
next election. I couldn't seem to make a difference.

At the end of July, I went to visit Adam.
"I'm scared," I told him. "I need a gun for
protection."

He showed me his antique .45 and how to use it. "You have to press with your thumb and pull the trigger with your finger at the same time to fire it." He also had ammo and showed me how to load it, but then he added, "It's not registered, so I shouldn't give it to you."

I took the gun and ammo and left. In August, I drove back to Berkeley to an industrial area, went into several businesses, and said, "If you don't stop pollution, your employees will die." Somebody called the police. I was told to leave town or be arrested. I left, but I'd told the truth. If pollution didn't stop, everyone would die. Why couldn't they get that through their heads?

Ivy moved in with us. She'd found a job in Sacramento, so she paid the rent and groceries.

I drove to L.A. I tried to visit people I'd known before I met Carl, but no one wanted to see me, so I went back to Sacramento. I cried as I drove. I worked so hard to save the earth and do what I thought Carl would want me to do—things that didn't come naturally—just to prove myself, but nothing worked. When I got home, I found the recent letters I'd sent to Kat, Sheila, and Anna. They'd all been returned unopened.

Wearing my hooded red robe, I went to see my lawyer friend. I told him about the letters being returned. "I'm still not allowed to visit Carl."

He listened. "So the family has fallen apart."

I nodded and cried.

"Tommy, the women in prison want a chance at parole. They won't have that if they stay in touch with you. Any connection to Carl would kill their chance of freedom in the future. Anna's become a born-again Christian. Kat and Sheila apologized for the murders. You need to move on. They have."

I nodded silently, continued to cry, and left. I felt rejected. The family was gone, and it was my fault. I hadn't kept them connected. I couldn't move on. I had nowhere left to go. I wasn't good enough. I just wasn't capable of the violence they needed from me. I felt I was splitting in two. I cried until I cried myself out and felt numb.

By 3 September, I had a head cold. I sent a three page letter of threats to the California Criminal Justice Committee. I signed Carl's name and prison address, because the threats just weren't me—they were what Carl would've done. I meant it as criticism of the justice system, but I knew no one would read it without Carl's name and threats. I didn't know what else to do.

The TV news reported that President Ford would visit. The coverage took precedence over clear cutting that endangered the giant redwood forest, the world's tallest trees. "People act like he's more important than the earth," I complained to Ivy and Cindy. "He's in charge of a country that destroys nature."

I watched his arrival on TV the next night. I was congested and didn't feel well. I worried about the giant redwoods. I couldn't think straight. I cried myself to sleep on the sofa, but I didn't sleep well.

The next day was Friday. I put on my red robe and strapped the holster for the .45 to my left leg. I'd never tried to fire it, and I didn't intend to. I loaded four rounds into the clip, but I made sure there was no bullet in the chamber. I reminded myself that even if I just pulled the trigger, nothing would happen. Even if there was a round in the chamber, it wouldn't fire unless I pressed my thumb down too. The gun was safe. I never liked guns. I put my long hair up so it wouldn't get in my way and went to meet President Ford. As he shook the hand of the woman next to me, I pulled out the gun and pointed it at him. Just as I did, I noticed his shirt button just above his waist was undone. I felt sorry for him with his shirt button undone in public. A Secret Service agent grabbed the gun with one hand and my arm with his other.

"It didn't go off," I yelled. "I don't have anything else." Once the Secret Service had my hands cuffed behind my back, I told them, "The country's a mess. If he were a public servant, he'd clean it up, but he's not serving the public."

I rode to the police station in the back of a squad car. Once there, I was taken upstairs and put in a small interview room. I told them my name, but I gave them a false address. Finally, a woman police officer came in, searched me, and found nothing. A lot of people with cameras took pictures of me from the doorway. After several hours, I was left alone with the woman officer. The door was closed. We talked—mostly I talked and she listened. She was very kind. I broke down and cried. She gave me some tissues.

I was taken to a larger room. On the way, we passed a room with an open door, and I saw Ivy and Cindy there. "They didn't know about this," I told the police and Secret Service. We went into the bigger room. They had equipment to record me. They read my rights and took off the handcuffs. I asked them, "Please, take the holster off my leg." They did.

As they questioned me, I only answered in the third person. I was exhausted and could only talk about what happened as if someone else had done it. In fact, I'd been watching Carl act through me. I always detested violence. Now I was scared, and I retreated into my true self, which I'd repressed for so long. I was taken to another room, where a doctor examined me and took some blood. Then the woman officer took me to the ladies' lavatory, and I urinated in a cup for her. They thought I was on drugs, but I wasn't. When I was introduced to a psychiatrist, I refused to talk to him. I felt spent and afraid.

I was driven to the federal courthouse, where I was turned over to a U.S. marshal. At my arraignment, I felt empty and said nothing. My bail was set at a million dollars. I was stunned. I hadn't even tried to hurt anyone. I was taken back to the county jail, where I was kept separate from other inmates and not allowed phone calls.

Monday, 8 September, I was visited by a private detective and a federal public defender. We talked about whales and trees. The detective knew a lot about whales, which cheered me up, but then they wanted me to see a psychiatrist. I refused. I was more afraid of an insane asylum than prison, because I knew I'd be found insane. I was sick, exhausted, depressed, and angry the morning I took the gun to see Ford. Now these guys, who were supposed to be on my side, talked about insanity and irrational behavior. I knew I'd let Carl work through me, but I never wanted violence, and Dad had threatened to put me away when I was just a kid.

I needed to alert people to the dangers to the environment. The only reason I had to live was to save the earth. I promised not to send any more threats, so they let me send post cards. I couldn't do that from an asylum. I felt better just being myself.

354

No one understood me. I was treated like a child, maybe because I was still innocent and in tune with nature. I knew I'd had some sort of a breakdown, and Carl had come through me while I was broken. But I couldn't let go of him, because being with him had been the only happy time in my life.

The judge issued a gag order on everyone involved in my case, but he said I could talk about anything except the case. He also lowered my bail and set my trial for 4 November. I returned to court for motions and hearings. I didn't understand the law, but insisted I represent myself. I didn't trust establishment lawyers, but at least I wouldn't lie. The judge ordered me to see a psychiatrist, so I had to, but I was very careful. I spoke to the doctor for less than two hours, and he found me mentally competent. I was relieved.

President Ford came back to California later that month. He stayed at the St. Francis Hotel in San Francisco. On 22 September, Amy Morgan, a woman from West Virginia, fired a .38 pistol at Ford outside the hotel. The bullet missed him but hit a cab driver. When I heard about it, I said, "I hope I didn't start something bad."

My trial began with jury selection. The judge had already decided against my wishes that they'd be sequestered. I wanted them to be able to go home to their families at night. Keeping families together was very important to me. I tried to plead no contest to stop the trial, but the judge said, "I don't believe you're guilty, so I can't accept your plea."

I was given a public defender. I asked to have Carl testify as a character witness to my nonviolence, so I could at least see him again. I wanted him to tell the court and the world why he didn't choose me to take part in his murders and explain the reason for the murders. But the judge said, "Mr. Hoessmann's testimony isn't relevant to this case."

"I want to change my plea to guilty."

"I can't accept your plea of guilty," he said.

When the prosecutor began his opening statement, I stood up and said, "If my family isn't allowed a fair trial, it's going to get bloody."

"Remove the defendant from the courtroom," the judge ordered.

As a marshal dragged me from the room, I yelled, "You can't have a trial without me. I want to plead guilty."

I was taken to another room for a short time and then brought back before the judge. The jury was no longer in the room. The judge lectured me about disrupting the court and making prejudicial statements in front of the jury. He said he was concerned about my future.

"Hoessmann is the only person who can speak for me," I told him.

"Will you sit down and be quiet in the courtroom?" he asked me.

"I'll be quiet in my cell."

"Then go to your cell."

A deputy marshal offered to escort me to a room where I could watch the trial on TV, but I refused. I couldn't grasp the reality of the situation, and I didn't want to deal with it. I knew I'd only pointed a gun at President Ford, because I'd had some sort of breakdown, and now I wanted to see Carl face to face. I needed to hear him say why I wasn't chosen to commit any of the murders in L.A., and I wanted to know why those murders happened. We weren't supposed to be violent.

On 9 November, when the deputies came to take me to court, I wore a bandana as a blindfold. "I don't want to go, but if I go, you'll have to carry me." So they did. When we got there, I removed my blindfold.

The judge asked, "Will you sit quietly in this courtroom?"

"No." I was sent back to my cell, and the trial went on without me. I didn't want to be in the courtroom. I was confused, stressed out, and felt more comfortable in a cell. Someone gave me an apple, because I wouldn't eat much. My nerves were so wound up I couldn't eat, so I played with the apple. I channeled my anxiety into it. I gently massaged it and mashed it with my fingers until, by the end of the trial, it still looked like a nice hard apple, but to the touch, it was soft and mushy.

I chose not to watch the trial on TV, but I listened to it. I was surprised that my lawyer told the jury about my concern for the earth in his closing statement. He told them the truth, and I was pleased.

Even though I was careful to not have a bullet in the gun's chamber, even though I never fired the gun even once, and even though I didn't even pull the trigger knowing there was no bullet in the chamber, the jury found me guilty of attempting to assassinate President Ford before Thanksgiving. At least they got to go home to their families.

I sent the judge a hundred handwritten pages for him to consider before sentencing me. The judge insisted I be present for my sentencing. I took the apple with me—it held all my frustrations. I intended to give it to the judge as a peace offering after he sentenced me. I wanted to show him that things and people aren't always as they appear. The judge saw the apple and asked, "Is that for me?"

"Yes, your honor," I smiled.

But then the prosecutor spoke and made me mad, because he didn't have a clue about me. He said I'd intended to kill President Ford, but I hadn't. I didn't think—I just reacted. I threw the apple at him and hit him in the side of the head. Because it was soft, it splattered all over his face, clothes, and hair, but he wasn't hurt. Of course, the judge assumed I'd intended to throw the apple at him, even though I hadn't. On 17 December, I was sentenced to life in prison.

Not long after, the deputy marshals woke me up in the middle of the night, put me in a prison van, and slowly drove me six-hundred miles to San Diego. I was transferred to federal corrections. I said good-bye to the deputies. "Thanks for being gentlemen."

Cindy and Ivy were arrested and charged with conspiracy to send threats through the mail. Cindy subpoenaed me to testify in 1976, and we shared a cell for a short time. I took the stand to testify dressed as a nun, but the judge had me removed from court. I screamed as I was carried out, and people laughed. Cindy was convicted and sentenced to ten years. Ivy was sentenced to five years.

In April, a TV movie aired based on a book by Carl's prosecutor. I thought it was ridiculous. It portrayed Carl as a mean moron.

In August, Ivy escaped from prison with another inmate after she hit a prison guard over the head. I used the prison phone to call the Associated Press to let her know what she did was wrong. She was caught two weeks later and sentenced to an extra ten years.

Carl was moved to the prison at Corcoran between Fresno and Bakersfield. Billy and Lawson were both doing their time in San Luis Obispo.

My lawyer appealed my conviction, but in September, I dropped the appeal. I didn't want to deal with the court system, nor did I want to apply for parole when the time came. I'd adapted to prison routine and was comfortable. I decided just to wait for my scheduled release date of 2005. I was at peace with myself again and able to reflect on my life. I had nothing to prove in prison and could just be myself. I still cared deeply about the earth, but I no longer felt I could save the world.

I had dreams of loss, dreams of things Carl said, and dreams of how unhappy I was in a society that didn't want me. One night I dreamt I was abandoned by Carl and my parents only to have Carl's baby in an alley. I had no way to take care of it, so I abandoned our child. When I woke up, I realized that, in a sense, everyone in my life had abandoned everyone else, and so had I. Another night I dreamt I was in labor trying to deliver Carl's baby, but it was too painful. I suffered greatly and died. When I was awake, I reflected that I'd tried desperately to deliver a message to the world, but had suffered terribly and failed.

In July 1977, I was transferred to a brand new federal women's prison in the Allegheny Mountains of West Virginia. Cindy arrived soon after. I liked it there. "Carl was originally from West Virginia," I reminded Cindy.

We were considered model prisoners, so when a newly remodeled women's prison opened back in Pleasanton, California, we applied for transfer. Our requests were granted. Once there, we were free to dress as we liked again, so we wore the robes we'd sewn for ourselves before we went to prison. Back in costume, we relapsed into our old characters. I found myself no longer well-adjusted and unable to cope. I tried to live as if there were no rules. My stress level started to build again.

Sheila Von Lueten
1976—1977

As far as prisons went, the one at Chino could have been a lot worse. When we were finally released from death row in 1976, we went into the psychiatric unit. Kat and I weren't there long, but Anna had to stay—little wonder. After that, Kat and I had nothing more to do with her.

My studies helped me to adjust to being with the other inmates. Women's studies—how other women had fought against gender oppression for the right to be treated as men's equals—and African American studies had helped me realize just how screwed up Carl and his nonsense teachings were.

Shortly after being transferred to the main prison population, another inmate gave me a small amount of marijuana. I accepted it as a gift. I didn't want to insult another inmate I'd only just met and make a potential enemy, since I had nowhere else to go. But I got caught. It was considered a minor infraction, because it was harmless.

My lawyer got my sentence overturned, because I'd been tried with the others for murders where I wasn't even present and didn't know about at the time. I was sent to back to L.A. to await a new trial in an isolation cell. Finally, I had hope. I only took part in one murder, which Kat had already seen to, and I was under the influence of LSD and Carl's cult. I'd been brainwashed. I'd since broken free of his influence and been a model prisoner, except for the one infraction. I'd studied college courses and demonstrated I was ready to rejoin society.

Shortly before my second trial began 27 January 1977, I was interviewed in jail for TV. I already wore bangs to cover the scar on my forehead. In response to questions, I said, "I slept with Carl a couple of times, but I never thought of him as a lover. I was just a pawn in the game he played, and I'm glad I'll never see him again." I wasn't allowed to answer any questions specifically related to my new trial.

This time, my behavior in court was normal and civilized. I was aware of my family and friends there to support me, none of whom was associated with Carl. The trial continued through the summer. Diana Bank testified again for the prosecution, "Carl programmed his followers to be virtual zombies."

Another former follower, a guy who'd left the group before the murders, testified on my behalf. "Carl claimed to be the reincarnation of Jesus Christ. He was obsessed with death. He said all the time, 'Death is an illusion.' I realized Hoessmann was obsessed with death and violence due to all his years in prison. I left, but he had a more mesmerizing affect on women. It was like he cast a spell on them."

A tape recording of Carl was also played. "Kat's color is yellow, and Shelia's color is green. I name her Gentle Tree. She can help fix the earth. She was planted for peace."

Many people testified about my good character and positive relationship with my parents. There was also testimony about my diminished capacity under the prolonged influence of LSD. It meant a lot to me that my mother testified. I told the jury, "I took part in the murder of a middle-aged couple I didn't know, because I wanted to show Carl I'd do anything for him."

My lawyers produced evidence of how people could be brainwashed into participating in violence they would not do otherwise. Meanwhile, in the jail, I was allowed to embroider doll faces for children in hospitals. I also crocheted a blanket for myself.

The trial ended 28 September with the jury deadlocked. I'd be tried yet again, but I had even more hope now. There were jurors who believed I was innocent or at least had reasonable doubt of my guilt.

I got to spend two hours an evening in the jail's dayroom. In October, I met some undocumented "aliens" from Mexico and Guatemala. We played charades and drew pictures that we named in English and Spanish. I enjoyed their company. In November, I was assigned to the sewing room to work on a cloth banner for the sheriff's office. It was a work of art. I also had to go to the dentist for eight cavities, but I gained eight pounds, which was a good start in my recovery from anorexia.

I was released on bail 27 December to await the next trial—fresh air with no fences and open sky again. I visited friends, went to the beach, watched the ocean, and breathed salt air. I got to hug my parents.

Anna Stukiss
1975—1977

I'd been told I was a good actress—maybe if I
joined the prison church group, the Christians
would help me convince the parole board I'd been
saved. It had worked for others. If they had a choir,
I could sing. Maybe I could get out on parole and
Carl and the other bitches would still be behind
bars. If I just kept my secret to myself and played
the parole board's game, I might outsmart them,
even though I didn't understand what the parole
board wanted. If I had another chance, I'd stay
away from the booze and drugs, because people and
society confused me enough, but I wouldn't let
another man take control of me. I could hunt down
that slut Diana and kill her.

      Jesus was different. He was kind and
forgave me. So, why were Christian women
submissive to Christian men? After all, Carl was
Jesus too, but he wasn't as kind. I could see God
and the devil were just men, and others would
always put me down, so I'd have to be careful. The
women on the parole board might be smarter than
me. Damn, there was still so much I didn't
understand. I had no more contact with any of
Carl's group, and I had plenty of time to think. For
some years now, I'd been a prison journalist doing
interviews for the prison newspaper.

      The Christians were very kind, loving
people. They welcomed me with open arms, even
though they said they knew I just came to them to
better my chance of parole. They made me feel
really stupid, but they accepted me anyway. They
said they'd help me, but they wouldn't lie for me. I
didn't understand. I'd been back in school for

several years. School wasn't easy for me, but it was part of the parole board game, so I worked on it. I took the most basic college courses to get my associates degree. There was no pressure if I couldn't pass a class the first time.

Finally the other Christian women wore me down. They said my life would be easier if I'd turn my burdens over to Jesus and let him forgive all my sins. I didn't understand, but whatever. Going to school was hard enough—so I confessed all my "sins"—even my plan to fool the parole board and kill Diana—to Jesus. Who knew Jesus was better than drugs? I no longer had to worry about what others thought of me, because Jesus would save me. He loved me. All I had to do was read his words and pray. Life was easy. Jesus would tell me what to do.

I heard Sheila was granted a new trial and freed from prison. If acquitted, she'd be free for good. I asked the group to pray for her. I daydreamed a lot while I pretended to pray.

I wrote my own religious songs, and I learned to make musical instruments. I loved the feel of the wood. I could make it into a body that could come alive with the vibration of music. It was like how God felt when he made a living body. It was the embodiment of an orgasm.

To make amends for my crimes in the eyes of the parole board, I wrote a book about my experiences—being a child of both Satan and God. I had no use for the royalties, so I donated them to help homeless women. How could I be denied parole if my book was a bestseller and the royalties helped homeless women? Now I was a published author, so no one could accuse me of being stupid. I wrote about the oppression of women by men and about degradation. Degradation was like dying a very slow death. It was part of bondage, oppression, and prison life. I had a man on the outside help me write it.

Jesus promised me I'd be famous for my prison ministry. He told me I'd save many, many people through my book, and the world would convert to Christianity because of me.

Sheila Von Lueten
1978

I was free to prepare for yet another trial. I enjoyed privacy, freedom to turn the lights on and off when I wanted, and the stars. I was liberated both from jail and as a woman. I talked on the phone as much as I wanted to whomever I wanted. I breathed fresh air and hoped for the future again. I had no grandiose desires or plans—I simply enjoyed a walk, the smell of clean clothes, and ironing. I got a job as a legal secretary. I no longer felt I was any better than anyone else. I was free from my own delusions.

Things had changed since I last lived in society. I had to adjust to shopping crowds, different noises, and freeway traffic. Nights were peaceful and quiet again, unlike prison. As much as my mother wanted to protect me, I couldn't hide at her place. A friend loaned me her apartment and car. I visited San Francisco and northern California. I saw sheep and horses grazing and eucalyptus. I worried about weight gain.

My third trial began in March 1978. I was surprised to learn in court a wallet had been stolen from the murdered couple. The charge against me was changed to murder committed in the act of a robbery. I remembered too late that Carl had gone into the house first. He must have stolen the wallet then. Legally, the new charge meant my state of mind wasn't relevant to my guilt. 5 July 1978, I was convicted on two counts of murder. One of the jurors said some of them understood I suffered from diminished capacity at the time of the crime, but they didn't believe it was enough to exonerate me. I went back to jail until I was sentenced. Seven years to life meant I had an actual chance at parole now, because I had already served almost nine years. The judge encouraged me to apply. I'd taken responsibility for my crimes. I'd been active in the main prison population and worked hard.

In August, I was sent back to the prison at Chino. It was good to see Kat again. She'd moved on from the past. She was happy for me. "If any of us stands a chance at parole," she said, "it's you. And once you get paroled, I should be next."

I had hope. I had life. I turned twenty-nine toward the end of August. I thought about the ages of the couple I was convicted of murdering and about how much I had experienced in my meager twenty-nine years. I realized they could have easily lived another twenty-nine years or more, but we'd taken it from them. Carl tried to make it look like Billy hadn't murdered Harry, but Billy was caught driving Harry's car, and the knife he'd used on him was in the trunk. Those innocent people were killed on a fool's errand, and I was the fool.

I settled back into the prison population. I had a college degree. I tried to comfort some of the inmates separated from their children. Those who were single parents with no relatives willing and able to help had lost their children to the system. I couldn't imagine how painful it must be to not know what had become of your own child or that the child might never know you were its mother. I was fortunate. I had family and friends from before I got involved with Carl who stayed in touch with me. I was keenly aware of how much I'd improved as a person as a result of not being executed. I was grateful for my life. I realized prison was a place to go to honestly see oneself. I had my own cell.

Sometimes it was lonely, but I was glad for the solitude and time for introspection.

Kat and I sewed together sometimes. There was a record room where we could listen to music. We also played volleyball and basketball. I was so bad at sports, games often ended in laughter. It helped relieve the stress.

AKA Diana Lisa Bank
1975—1979

In September 1975, Tommy Feltener was on
national news, because she tried to assassinate
President Gerald Ford. I didn't know her very well,
but I was glad I'd severed all connections. She was
convicted in December, and sent to federal prison in
San Diego. We lived in San Diego. Toby and I
discussed moving to the northern part of the state,
but we knew Tommy had friends up there too. We
tried to make the children feel safe.
         Then in 1976, Sheila Von Lueten's
conviction was overturned, and she was granted a
new trial. I had to testify for the prosecution again.
At first, I was even more nervous than at the first
trial, but the Sheila I saw across from me in the
courtroom was very different from the Sheila I'd
known before. She seemed more mature and not at
all crazy. Maybe being off drugs helped her. She
and Kat had denounced Carl, which reassured me. I
let out a deep breath and relaxed. I felt more at ease
on the stand. The trial ended in a hung jury. By
New Year's Eve, she was freed on bail pending
another trial. I had to testify in that one too. But her
freedom only lasted about six months. She was
convicted again just after the fourth of July 1977.
She went back to prison. I was both relieved for my
family and sad for Sheila. If three trials had been
stressful for me, I couldn't imagine how she kept
her composure. She'd denounced Carl, rehabilitated
herself, and had a brief taste of freedom, only to
have to return to prison.
         Toby and I looked for another state to live
in. We needed to move on. We found a new home
outside the town of Myrtle Creek, Oregon. I found

370

comfort in solitude. The children could grow up close to nature. The community was small enough we could get to know people with the added security that if strangers came around looking for me, our new friends and neighbors would let us know. They would also know the children.

I still remembered Tommy telling me pomegranates were related to crape myrtles. Once we settled into our new home, I planted pink, red, and white crape myrtle bushes all over the property. At thirty years old, I finally put down roots. When I planted, I noticed wild violets growing. They reminded me of Tommy—violets were her favorite flower. I felt sorry for her. She was intelligent, and her life could have been so different, but there was nothing I could do about that. After much contemplation, I planted a bed of lilies for Shelia. Kat had also denounced Carl, so I planted cornflowers on either side of the porch steps. In spite of all that happened, I could still forgive.

Tommy Feltener
1979

I lost my sense of inner peace. I was anxious,
stressed out, and out of control. One inmate really
grated on my nerves. She was in for her part in
hijacking an airplane, and I just didn't like her.
Cindy egged me on. I never wanted violence, but
Cindy and I fell into a pattern of intolerance and
hatred. We saw this one inmate as a snitch. She was
best friends with another prisoner who came from a
very wealthy family, and we didn't like her either,
because as soon as she went on trial, she too
became a snitch. She claimed she was a
brainwashed victim instead of taking responsibility
for her choices. Cindy and I saw those two as part
of society instead of fellow inmates. One day in
March, while I was working in a prison garden, the
hijacker snitch was there—as well as all sorts of
tools. I picked up a hammer and hit her with the
claw end. I let my rage loose on her.

　　　As a result, I was sent back to West
Virginia. Cindy rejoined me a short while later. I
was told my victim recovered, and I was glad to
hear it. I didn't like violence. In West Virginia, the
rules were stricter, and I tried to adapt as I had when
I was there before. I knew I had to find myself
again.

Sheila Von Lueten
1979—1983

Mom visited every Saturday. She was emotionally
strong, and I was proud to be her daughter. Dad
came to visit in the spring of 1979. It was great to
see him.

I started doing yoga. I was better at yoga
than sports, and it helped me stay centered while
trapped in the chaos of the increasing prison
population. I read books and tried to maintain my
weight at one-hundred twenty pounds. I kept losing.

I was denied parole in 1979. I was
devastated. I'd been locked up for so long, and then
had a brief taste of freedom followed by the
reduction in my sentence. The judge had sounded so
positive I'd be released soon, only to be denied—it
was like having all hope snatched away. Some days
I wished I'd been executed.

In January 1980, I was denied parole again. I
tried to concentrate on my studies to keep away the
blues. I tried to write poetry, but it wasn't my thing.
Over ten years had passed since the murders, and I
was a different person, but I was still here. I'd
honestly believed the judge when he'd encouraged
me to expect parole. I don't think he meant to be
cruel. I think he really believed it too. I tried to
console myself that things could be worse. I went to
work in the prison school as a clerk. I'd worked in
the clinic before that, but this was more relaxed. I'd
learned a lot of personal lessons since I'd been back
in prison.

A guy I knew, an ex-con, started to visit me
every week. We also wrote each other. I fell in love.
I needed love. He proposed to me in early
November, and I accepted. I was thirty-two,

mentally stable, and ready for marriage. After we married, we had a conjugal visit in February 1982. I was happy but anxious when he came for our three day visit in the prison's family apartment. He was tall and lean, and he loved me in spite of my past and my present incarceration. After making love, he said, "I've got a surprise for you. I've got a prison guard uniform, and I'm going to use it to break you out. We'll be free together."

I never saw that coming. I immediately filed to have the marriage annulled. I had nothing more to do with him. I felt I lived on a perpetual emotional roller coaster. Still, the experience was worth it. I'd needed an intimate relationship, and I learned a great deal about myself through it—especially a blind spot.

By June, the overcrowded prison was too much. Noise was stressful, even for one who liked loud music. Prison noise wasn't musical. So many of the women coming in were only convicted of drug possession. *Why weren't they simply treated and counseled? Possession of drugs wasn't violent. They shouldn't be in prison unless they were violent.* I thought back to my only infraction years ago, possession of marijuana. It was considered minor. *Why is society throwing so many women away?*

In June 1983, another bunk was moved into my cell and a roommate followed. I told this stranger, "We should try to give each other some time alone each day in the cell, so we don't stress out." Fortunately, she agreed. We felt even more like sardines in a can. I decided when I finally got paroled, I'd live in the country. I'd had enough of too many people and too much noise. I craved peace and quiet. I wanted a simple cottage with just enough garden space to grow lilies. I couldn't imagine anything as peaceful as a bed of fragrant lilies. I used the image of a lily bed in my head to stay calm.

AKA Diana Lisa Bank
1987—1988

Our youngest child had just finished first grade
when Toby and I separated. I guess Toby never
really settled down. When I found out he was
having an affair, I confronted him, and of course,
we argued. He packed his clothes and left. I was
thirty-eight. I didn't want to start over again, but he
did. I had no fear of independence. After all, I'd
stood up to Carl Hoessmann.

     Christmas Eve 1987 was marred by the
separation for both me and the kids. Then I heard on
TV that Tommy Feltener escaped from prison. The
news said the prison she broke out of was in West
Virginia, but it still gave me pause. I had bad
dreams of being stabbed in the throat. I'd had
dreams of being stabbed ever since the summer of
1969. My subconscious couldn't forget seeing that
pregnant lady stabbed when I was pregnant with my
second child. I was very relieved when Tommy's
recapture was announced. I knew it wasn't
rational—Tommy wasn't even there the night those
people were stabbed. She never killed anyone that I
knew of.

     By the time I turned thirty-nine, I was
divorced. The kids stayed with me. Toby knew I'd
never deny him visits with them, so it was a
relatively amicable divorce. I had a full time job,
and Dad set up accounts for each of the children, so
we were OK financially. I wasn't moving. I was
home. I had my children, my crape myrtles, friends,
and neighbors. Toby chose to leave us, but he'd
always be the father of my children.

Anna Stukiss
1981—1991

He wrote to me and said he was a multi-millionaire from Texas, who wanted to use his resources to help free me from prison. It seemed too good to be true, but that's the nature of faith and miracles. I believed he was a miracle sent by Jesus to help me. We were married 9 September 1981. He brought me a small bouquet of carnations and daisies for my bridal bouquet.

"I thought red roses were supposed to represent true love. I love roses, and you can afford them," I teased him.

He laughed. "You know I can't bring you anything sharp. Thorns could be a weapon." I laughed too. I was so happy. We'd have conjugal visits, and someday I'd be free.

After a few months, I found out through friends in the ministry my new husband lied to me. He wasn't a multi-millionaire, so I had the marriage annulled. At least, I had friends, and Jesus loved me.

Several years passed. I wondered when the world would convert to Christianity because of my book. I wondered why Jesus wanted to keep our cosmic affair secret by keeping me in prison.

In 1987, I fell in love with a student at Harvard Law School. He was only twenty-four years old and Christian. Obviously, I was still pretty at thirty-nine. We got married right away. I still had the moves when it came to our conjugal visits. He was young and hot, and I had so much to teach him from all my experience with men. He promised to represent me legally at my parole hearings once he graduated law school. I told the women in the ministry, "It's a miracle to be so blessed. Jesus has rewarded my patience."

Right around my forty-third birthday, in May 1991, I found myself in a very dark place. I was still in the same prison with the same friends, but I kept having bad dreams. Carl was a judge who sentenced me to die. Then he stabbed me in the throat. Then he told me he was Jesus and laughed at me. I was depressed. It just wasn't fair to be locked up for so long. I withdrew into myself and didn't talk about it. I was angry at everyone—the ministry, the parole board, and Jesus. He hadn't saved me—I was still incarcerated. Being saved, my associate's degree, my book and ministry work hadn't done a damn bit of good with the parole board.

My husband graduated from Harvard Law School and represented me at my parole hearings. At first, I was proud of him. He was a devoted Christian, and I was glad to have someone on my side at the hearings. But when I turned forty-three, I was angry and sad. He was only twenty-eight and free as a bird. I wondered if he had other women on the outside, but he insisted he didn't.

After a few weeks, I started to slowly slip back into my old routine. Bit by bit, I went back to work out of habit. Eventually, I got past the anger and depression. It was like my sentence and marriage started all over again. I wasn't happy, but I stayed busy.

Tommy Feltener
1984—1994

In 1984, I was interviewed by a correspondent from a popular magazine. He recommended me to his editors. He said, "When you eventually get out of prison, you'd make a great researcher."

Cindy and I were together in prison a lot until she was released in 1985. I was eligible to apply for parole that year, but I didn't bother. To be paroled, I'd have to renounce my friendship with Carl like Kat, Sheila, Lawson, and Anna. I couldn't deny we were friends. The other women said they blamed Carl for instigating the murders, orchestrating their joint trial, and as a result, their incarceration. Carl had nothing to do with my trial, conviction, or sentence.

I made friends with another inmate. Her name was Amy Morgan, and she'd actually shot at President Ford in San Francisco a couple of weeks after I was arrested. She was older than me, and she was from West Virginia. In fact, she'd been a childhood friend of Carl's. We found common ground.

Then 23 December 1987, a friend on the phone told me, "Carl's been diagnosed with testicular cancer."

My anxiety level skyrocketed. What if Carl died, and I never saw him again? I was desperate, and I just reacted. An hour and a half later, Amy and I escaped in the rain. We climbed an eight-foot barbed wire fence. I wore a crocheted hat, green overcoat, sweater, and two pairs of pants, because the nighttime temperatures went well below freezing. It was bitterly wet and cold in the mountains. We wanted to go straight to California, but we didn't have any money to get across the country. We realized we couldn't make it, so we turned around and headed back to the prison. The next day, about two miles south of the prison, we spotted a car on the road with a couple of prison employees. They pulled over, and we got in. I was soaked through my layers of clothes to my skin.

I pled no contest to escaping, but the prosecution wouldn't accept my plea. I just wanted to see a friend who might die soon. I was the only witness in my own defense. I testified, "You have to find me guilty, because I am." They did. An additional fifteen months was added to my sentence, and I was sent to a prison in Lexington, Kentucky. I felt completely numb and depleted.

I was in Kentucky a little over a year, and then I was transferred to a women's prison in Marianna, Florida, north of Panama City in the Florida panhandle. I arrived 3 March 1989.

Later that year, Dad died of a heart attack. Once Dad was gone, I actually had a nice relationship with Mom. I realized how much I was like Mom. Neither of us ever blamed Dad for the way he treated us. Maybe we didn't fit in with society, because we didn't blame others for what happened to us.

Adam, my former lover who gave me the gun I pointed at President Ford, died in 1990 at the age of eighty-one. Hearing about his death helped me put some things in perspective, as I turned forty-two that October. Carl, the old blind man at the ranch, and Adam were all older men—like my Dad. I realized I still had half my life yet to live.

Carl didn't die of cancer. I overreacted—emotionally reacted—when I escaped from prison. I reflected that I was very emotional. I was also very

380

intelligent, but my emotions often overtook my intelligence—like when I attacked another inmate with a hammer. But I always took responsibility for my choices, even if they were influenced by someone else. I was honest. I never labeled myself a victim, and I didn't run from consequences. I wasn't part of society, so I might as well be in prison.

One night I dreamt I was back in the courtroom with the mushy apple I wanted to give the judge. When I woke up, I remembered I intended to show him I may have looked hard on the outside but was really very tender inside. Instead, I threw it at the prosecutor, who appeared hard and rigid to me. I knew then that the message I intended for the judge was really for me—even the prosecutor wasn't as bad as he seemed.

In the summer of 1994, I watched the O.J. Simpson trial on TV. Of course, I could relate to the courtroom scenario, and of course, I didn't like the prosecutor, but I really admired the lead defense lawyer. My life had become so empty I lived vicariously through the TV, like so many other people inside and outside prison. I was no different from them. That was a revelation. I also noticed O.J. was quiet during the trial and let his lawyers talk for him. He appeared calm and collected. I could never be, but then he was acquitted, and I wasn't.

That same year, an old friend I'd known in high school but hadn't seen since 1967, wrote me. I was happy to get her letter and wrote back. We reestablished our friendship by mail and exchanged pictures. I felt like I discovered a sister I thought was dead had come back to life. I didn't mention Carl. Instead, I asked her for books, including one on politically correct phrases. It helped to reconnect

with someone from my own past. Between my old
friend and Mom, I discovered the difference
between the sweet, sensitive, creative side of myself
and the emotionally out-of-control side of myself. It
was a start.

AKA Diana Lisa Bank
1 November 1995—1999

The day after Halloween, 1995, I came down with a
sore throat. I was forty-six and generally healthy,
but this was different from anything I'd ever
experienced. I didn't want to spend money on a
doctor for just a sore throat. I was sure it would
clear up on its own. But by the following evening, I
thought I was dying. I ran a high fever and felt like
my throat had been slashed. I'd been trying to force
down fluids, but I reached the point where I could
no longer swallow. Somehow I made it through the
night and managed to get myself to the doctor the
next day. I was very sick the first few days on
antibiotics, but I survived.

To celebrate my fiftieth birthday, I drove
with a friend up to Portland for the fourth of July.
Vancouver, Washington, just across the Columbia
River from Portland, had the largest fireworks show
west of the Mississippi River. The kids were grown
and on their own, and I enjoyed myself. The
fireworks were spectacular. We spent the night in a
motel in Portland. The next day we treated
ourselves to a day of sightseeing. We visited the
Portland Japanese Garden, the Portland Rose
Garden, the Lan Su Chinese Garden, and of course
the gift shop with each garden. I bought lavender,
chrysanthemum, and jasmine teas. Then we ate and
had ale milkshakes at McMenamin's. I had a great
time. We got home after dark.

That night I dreamt I was in an olden castle.
It was damp, cold, and dreary. I lived in one room.
I'd been married, but my heart was broken, and I
wasn't allowed to see my daughter. A good friend

Sheila Von Lueten
1985—2009

I applied for parole many times, but nothing I
accomplished proved good enough. For a while I
edited the prison newspaper. Then I got a job as a
secretary for the prison staff. I joined a group of
inmates who sewed quilts for the homeless. I even
joined and participated in Alcoholics Anonymous at
the insistence of a prior parole board, even though
I'd never been an alcoholic. I was still taking
college courses to get another degree. My one
infraction was over twenty years ago. I hadn't
associated with Carl or any of his followers for a
quarter of a century, and yet he was still held
against me at parole hearings. That brief time in my
youth when I trusted the wrong people will never be
forgiven, but no one on the parole board has
succeeded in making me hate myself. They've
certainly tried.

I don't think the many parole boards I've
appeared before realized the preparation and
attendance of each hearing was torture. Being
denied a chance at freedom every time was extra
punishment. Many times I thought I should just give
up, but my family and friends in the free world
pushed me to keep trying. It seemed to me that once
I proved myself rehabilitated, the parole board
changed their standards. Seven years to life was a
very vague sentence. When I went before the parole
board in April 1996, I was told I needed to show
more outward expressions of remorse—I needed to
show that I suffered. Who could live like that? I've
always tried to carry myself with dignity and not
burden others with my pain. The parole board just

wanted to see me suffer more. Wasn't that just revenge? How much was enough?

The next year, I saw on TV how people in the United Kingdom criticized the Queen of England for not openly showing her feelings after the death of Princess Diana, even though Queen Elizabeth II was raised to do just the opposite. I wasn't going to mope, cry, and make everyone around me miserable. I'd never survive in prison that way. I needed to maintain a sense of inner peace. The parole board asked for more than was humanly possible. I felt they inflicted cruel and unusual punishment.

I spoke out against Carl and cults and tried to tell young people to let my life be an example of what happens when you fall in with the wrong crowd. I understood there were still lost souls that worshipped Carl, even though he'd become a babbling idiot. I understood he was responsible for many more murders than the ones I knew about in 1969. Carl didn't value life.

I tried my best to live a meaningful life in prison. I wasn't perfect, but I wasn't violent. I avoided angry and violent women, and I tried to be of what little comfort I could to those who obviously suffered. I also steered clear of the "born again" Christians who used religion like a drug and preached that belief in what someone else told you would resolve you of all responsibility for your own actions. Personally, I believed heaven and hell were only states of mind. If you created hell for someone else, once you realized what you'd done, you'd be the one in hell, but that was just my experience. When I tried to ease someone else's misery, at the very least, I took my mind off my own.

386

I looked back at my own immaturity and vanity of my youth. Everyone wanted to be special. I felt special when I was homecoming queen, but I was too selfish to realize I had to share the honor. I felt special when I was with Mac, because society taught me I needed a man, but he gave up his free will to become a Kriya priest. Then I trusted Billy, who seemed trustworthy and on the road to success in the material world, but because I was a woman and supposed to be submissive to men, I didn't see him for who he really was. He had no conscience.

I accepted that my parents would die before me, and I wouldn't be there for them. I didn't have freedom, but I had dignity, kindness, and compassion. I got a job working for the prison chaplain. He actually brought me a bouquet of white lilies. I'd always visualized the image of them when things around me became too stressful, and then I finally actually had some. They were lovely.

I'd always had a conscience. I had to live with my horrible actions that could never be changed—with causing a wound that would never heal. I had intelligence, many talents and skills—I could work in society as a legal secretary, a computer programmer, an editor, a researcher, or a counselor. I was capable of deciding right and wrong as long as I relied on my inner peace. I'd never give that up again at any cost.

Anna Stukiss
2002—24 September 2009

My husband filed suit on my behalf in federal court
in 2002. He said I was a political prisoner, because
by that time I'd been denied parole sixteen times.
He pointed out to the court I was well suited for
parole due to all my good work with the ministry,
but he lost the suit. The recent seventeenth parole
hearing held the lawsuit against me too. I had every
right for him to file that lawsuit on my behalf, but
they used it against me. They said nothing I'd done
was enough, but Jesus was with me at my hearing,
and he loved me. I still had a cosmic romance with
God, and my husband promised to keep trying. I
was angry at the parole board. My friends in the
ministry said I shouldn't count the grievances
against me, and I should forgive. I didn't
understand. Was Jesus jealous of my Christian
husband?

The prison infirmary told me I had cancer. I
knew it meant I was going to die the long, slow
death of my mother, except without privacy. There
wouldn't be any naïve teenager to tell me
everything would be alright. I was terrified. I had
brain cancer, which had already spread. It was
terminal, and the doctor had to amputate my leg. I
couldn't even get up and go to the toilet by
myself—and I still had a long way to go before I
died. I knew they'd slowly chop me up into pieces. I
was scared of the humiliation and the pain. I had to
live in the hospital, guarded and handcuffed to the
bed, for a very long time. I thought I already knew
all about degradation, but this was the worst. I was
afraid if I told my Christian friends and husband
about my fears, no one would be kind to me. My

husband promised to do everything possible to get
me a compassionate release. I didn't understand.
There was no compassion in a parole board.

*   *   *

Someone was saying something, but I
couldn't quite make it out. It sounded like
chanting—no, it was prayer. Someone was
praying—probably for themselves. That's what
prayer was all about. I was too tired to focus on
words. I didn't even know whose voice I heard. I
was confused—lost in a big fog.

The prayer stopped. Good. I liked the quiet.
I didn't want to deal with words, but my mind
searched desperately for one. Words confused me.
What word did I need?

"Amen," I said out loud. I hoped it was the
right word. All was quiet again. I must have found
the right word. I'm not stupid after all.

*   *   *

I saw my emaciated, one-legged body below me
ravaged by death. My God, I was diapered like my
mother. I saw a Christian woman actually cry for
me. So they really did care. It wasn't just an act.
Did I cry for my mother? I don't remember. I don't
remember what she looked like. I wouldn't
recognize her. I was still dazed and confused from
the cancer, but the fog started to lift. My thoughts
cleared. I understood a lot more people cried for
each of the people I killed than for me. I understood
my victims didn't want to die. They were terrified. I
understood death wasn't a game, but Jesus forgave
me for all of it. Where was he? Not here. Maybe I

389

was never a true believer, but I thought God and I had a cosmic romance. Oh, that again. God was just another man. He didn't even get me paroled before I died. Jesus was supposed to be merciful, but he didn't give me that one simple mercy. The parole board said I didn't show mercy to my victims, but they died quickly. Maybe, like with Carl, it was all just a game.

My husband used me to establish his name and career as a lawyer. He didn't really want to bring a sick old woman home. Many men still thought nursing was women's work. He put on as much of a show for me as I put on for him. I used him too, but I was never released. Well, so much for romance.

So I was dead—I was free from pain, prison, and cancer. I had to be born into another body and live again. Maybe, if I was lucky, I could go to a prom. Or maybe I could just be a dancer and not need a man. Yes, I'd like to be a dancer, but not a ballerina—more of a gypsy rose.

Tommy Feltener
1995—2009

In hindsight, I was stressed out after all the others'
convictions, and the stress only snowballed into
1975. I tried to cope through my obsession with
saving the planet. I tried to carry the weight of the
world on my shoulders, because those I trusted were
gone from my life. I thought I tried to save the
world, but I just didn't know how to save myself.

I didn't understand or like society, and it
didn't understand or trust me. I was so unhappy; I'd
been unhappy most of my life. I was obsessed with
Carl. He'd taken care of me, made decisions, and
told me what to do. Prison did that for me too. I
tried to go back to school in Sacramento, but I was
too unhappy. So instead, I found my own way to
follow Carl and the others to prison.

I'd only ever been happy in a world of drugs
and fantasies. Except for those few years, I'd been
depressed my entire life. And except for those few
years, I'd always been obsessed with something. I'd
always been depressed and obsessed. I thought there
was something wrong with society. Finally, I
understood what was wrong was inside me. I
needed drugs to be happy and carefree. I was more
afraid of a psychiatric hospital than prison, because
I didn't want to admit I was mentally ill.

Once I learned that being mentally ill was
really a physical, treatable illness and not just crazy
like Dad had told me, I read everything I could find
on the subject. I accepted I had a personality
disorder and was chronically depressed. It was OK
to be flawed.

Much of what I wrote between 1971 and
1975, including pages I gave my trial judge, was

391

full of frustration and anger that I didn't know how to express otherwise. Mom had never shown frustration or anger while I was growing up—at least not in front of me, so I didn't know how. I was never a violent person—just out of control. When I didn't write, I turned my rage inward on myself. I'd been doing that since I was a child. I'd spent my entire life being confused, angry at myself, and very unhappy. Maybe I brought it with me from a past life.

Carl said, "Sense makes no sense." It made sense to me, because life had never made sense to me. I was desperate when I followed him. We were children playing adult games to block out all the pain of the world. I was always sensitive to nature. Did I channel her pain into me, or did I project my pain onto her? Either way, the pain was too much to handle. Violence was all around me—the Vietnam War, the crimes, Dad, my neighbors who manufactured weapons, all the people imprisoned for just possession of marijuana. None of it made sense. I mistook obsession for loyalty.

I wondered what my life might have been like if I hadn't gone with Carl. I would have sought out abuse and drugs anyway, but I might have found something to live for. Or maybe I should have tried harder to kill myself as a teenager.

After more than thirty years in prison, I still didn't understand society, but I knew more about myself. I was intelligent, creative, talented, caring, emotionally immature, depressed, and obsessive. I didn't believe in Armageddon anymore. I was no longer racist or anti-Semitic. Pain was always everywhere.

I was released from prison at the Federal Medical Center in Carswell, Texas, 14 Aug 2009. I moved to the town of Marcy in Oneida County, central New York State. Marcy was small, on Interstate 90 and the Erie Canal, and near the Adirondack Mountains. It was also home to the Central New York Psychiatric Center. I started over again.

I had to focus on what wouldn't cause pain to me or others—to search for joy everyday. I talked to Mom and my friend on the phone. I took walks and breathed. I was near the forest, the river, and the sky. All I ever needed was to be with nature.

Carl had taken us into a barren desert. He was spiritually barren. Maybe that's why he got testicular cancer. I thought it broke my heart at the time, but my heart was broken before I was born. Carl used me and the others. The other men used me, and I used them. I let myself be trampled like a wild violet.

I grew African violets in my little apartment. I thought about going back to California to be near Mom and my high school friend, but I'd also be closer to Cindy and others from the group. I didn't want to go down that road again. I felt lucky just to know Mom loved me and I had a friend in this world.

I hoped, if I had to live another life, I could have a stable childhood with parents that really loved me unconditionally for myself. Maybe that was just a fantasy, but I didn't want to live again unless I was in an ecologically sustainable community that didn't harm the earth.

Katrina Pricewinkle
1980 – 2010

After I got my bachelor's degree in human services,
I taught illiterate prisoners to read. I was active in
Alcoholics Anonymous and Narcotics Anonymous,
and the people I met there helped me deal with my
feelings about my life. I learned to talk about my
feelings, and as a result of not being mocked, I
became more considerate of others. I taught dance,
wrote poetry and music, and played guitar. I helped
train service dogs, which was very rewarding. I'd
always loved animals, and animals didn't judge the
way people always did. I worked hard and had lots
of fun playing on the prison volley ball team. I lived
a full life without the Carl circus. I blossomed, even
though society considered me a weed.

I had a couple of rough patches. 1989 was
the twentieth anniversary of the murders. I couldn't
ignore what I did, how I let myself be brainwashed,
and how I just let my arm stab those people. I
wanted to die. Now that I thought about how others
felt and all the fear and pain my victims suffered, I
just wanted to die. I realized from a dream, when I
was stabbed in the throat in a past life, I had been
ready to die. My victims wanted to live. I felt dead
inside. My biggest regret was that I killed a young
woman, who was simply reading a book in bed. She
died in terror, and her parents knew that when they
buried her. Parents should never have to bury their
child. That her parents had to bury her was almost
more than I could bear, but somehow I pulled out of
it.

Then in 1995, I crashed. I hit bottom again. I
was depressed, cried a lot, talked to my sponsors in
AA and NA, and then felt numb for a while. I felt I

had to start my life over again, but eventually, as I went back to doing the activities I enjoyed, I got better.

I heard Anna died. With her gone, I'd been in prison longer than any other woman in California. There was no chance for parole, even though I was legally eligible to keep applying. Sheila hadn't been granted parole yet, and her convictions were a lot less than mine. I'd never had a single disciplinary violation in all those decades, but that didn't matter. Tommy was paroled, but she never killed anyone.

I read that some considered this particular prison to be nicer than others. I didn't see it that way. We could walk outdoors, which was nice, but it was still a prison—guards, barbed wire, boundaries, and rules. We were treated humanely, but it was prison. I would die here. I didn't know when or how, but it didn't matter. At first, I was supposed to be executed, and death would still be my release. I'd probably die in my bed, which wasn't so bad.

But I hadn't wasted my time. I'd accomplished a lot as a person. I learned from Sheila's example to not judge people, and I learned from the people in AA and NA. When I remembered how it felt to be bullied and laughed at as a child, I could stop myself from laughing at others. I probably learned to laugh at others in self-defense and in imitation of those who laughed at me. In my sixties, I could see everyone else as a child. I realized I had a very sarcastic sense of humor at the expense of others, so I could work to change that.

I hurt my family and the families of the murder victims. I hurt the other people who joined

Carl Hoessmann after me when I encouraged them to stay. I caused a lot a grief, and I learned that causing and accepting grief and responsibility were part of being human. I wanted to be better than I'd been.

Most wildflowers were considered weeds by civilized people. People had been around so much longer than civilization and nature so much longer than people. We were all part animal—part weed. Our downfall was through violence, but we were also connected to the gentle side of nature. We needed to be aware before we could consciously choose. Without awareness, we just reacted. On drugs and alcohol, we just reacted. We were only free when we were consciously aware of our true animal nature. The service dogs helped teach me that. I thought back to those little sky blue cornflowers that I'd always loved, and I thought about how some people judged them to be weeds, while others, like me, just accepted their natural beauty.

If I ever got a chance at another life, and I wanted to think I might, I'd simply like to be a nice person. I didn't want to be important or famous or even pretty. I just wanted to be kind.

AKA Diana Lisa Bank
2010

I took part in a documentary on the 1969 nightmare of my past on the condition that my current name and whereabouts be protected. I felt it was important to tell the story, so the next generation would understand the danger of cults and doing only what others said. I told my own kids what happened and the part I played in it before the oldest started high school. They had a right to know. Life was hard much of the time, but good.

I was glad Lawson, Sheila, Katrina, and even Anna renounced Carl and took responsibility for their own actions. I was never their judge—just a witness. I watched them on cable TV over the years at their parole hearings. Carl had descended even further into madness. Katrina seemed to have accepted her fate. Sheila got a little tearful at her last parole rejection. She wanted to be with her aging parents. Lawson and Anna got religion. Lawson was in charge at all seven murders, and I'd never forget the way Anna licked the blood off her fingers. But if Jesus could save them, there was hope for everyone.

On 14 August last year, the anniversary of the day I was cleared and released from jail, Tommy was released on parole. I had to trust she wouldn't have been paroled unless she also renounced Carl. I heard she'd refused to apply for parole at first, because she wasn't willing to abide by the board's rules. She was always smarter than Carl. I understood she moved to upstate New York somewhere, and that also bode well. I hoped she was able to make a fresh start in life. As far as I knew, she never actually killed anyone. If nothing else, she was honest.

Then I heard on TV that Anna had cancer, and her lawyers had made a special appeal to the court for mercy, because her cancer had spread to her brain. They said she should be released to die with dignity. Her request was denied, because she denied mercy to her victims and didn't let them die with dignity. *"What goes around comes around."* When I knew her she didn't live with dignity. I didn't know if the word was even in her vocabulary. She died in prison last September. I didn't feel any loss.

Lawson Tascher said his place was in prison. He started some sort of ministry, got married, and had children. The woman who married him must have really loved him to know she would have to raise their children alone.

Carl clearly had no chance for parole. He was just plain crazy and consumed by hate. I wondered if he'd be reborn as a snake after he died. Maybe it would be more appropriate for him to be a spider and be eaten by a female. I wondered if he could ever find redemption as a human being.

I hoped, if I came back again, and I believed we all would, that I'd broken whatever bound me to that group. I hoped at least Sheila was able to find peace.

I thought about all those people on that ranch back in 1969 when I was outside with my crape myrtles. The bright blooms all summer cheered me up, so I tried only to think about that time when I looked at my flowers. Since my birthday was the official start of summer, I always found it a good day to think about what I'd experienced and learned. I had a good life. I raised my children, and I was free.

I look back at my youth, and I did some crazy things, but I also learned the value of self-education. I have the schools and library in New Hampshire to thank for that. I did my best to share my love of learning with my children. I taught my kids that an education can be used to get a job and make money, but it can also be used to learn from the mistakes of all those who have lived before us. Any past mistake we can avoid repeating means less painful consequences. As long as I keep learning from my own mistakes and those of others, and as long as I listen to that wise, self-educated voice inside me, when I do something because it feels good—because I know it's right—others will benefit besides myself. It's a lofty goal, but I believe it's worth pursuing. Surely by now, I've learned this simple truth: what's truly good benefits others.

A seed germinates instinctively
Grows automatically toward the sun
Life plan programmed genetically
But anything can happen

One has faith but does not know
How long the life?
How far to go?
How strong the strife?

What joy will flow?
Will one survive to complete the show?
Will life be shared or lived alone?

A beautiful flower can only grow
From deep within the dirt below

traveled a long way to see me. I was happy to see her, but my heart gave out.

The next morning, about twenty minutes after breakfast, I doubled over in pain. The pain seemed to radiate throughout my chest and abdomen, and I wondered if I was having a heart attack. I couldn't get my breath and thought I was going to pass out. Maybe I did. By the time the episode passed, and I could think and speak, I called my friend to come get me. I was admitted to the hospital through the emergency room for a necrotic gall bladder. After surgically removing my gall bladder, the doctor told me, "If you hadn't made it to the hospital when you did, you could have died."

I was lucky to be alive. I laughed, but I was glad I'd celebrated my birthday when I did, just in case.

www.ingramcontent.com/pod-product-compliance
Lightning Source LLC
Chambersburg PA
CBHW070352260626
47161CB00001B/114